Dangerous Obsession

A novel by

Sloan Christopher

DANGEROUS OBSESSION
ISBN 978-0-6151-5108-3

Copyright © Sloan Christopher, 2007

Printed in U.S.A.

This novel is dedicated to
the law enforcement officers,
especially those in Burlington, North Carolina,
who risk their lives every day to keep us safe.

To my best 'buddy,' Garrett D'Eirinn,
for his unwavering support, encouragement,
and constant pushing to keep at it
even when I'd shut down my computer in frustration...
and of course, for all the time he spent proofreading
and making suggestions for improvement.

To Mark, a 'rare artist' who was a tremendous help
when I was writing the "scenes."

And finally, to the memory of Becky Scott,
my best friend from years back,
and my inspiration for Niki Shannon.
I'll never forget how she pushed me daily
to get this story down on paper.
And though she's been gone for some time,
she'll always live on in Niki.

July 26...

Elizabeth Johnson lay blindfolded across the custom-made spanking bench, her arms draped over a bar at the front. She wore nothing save the collar around her neck and a crisscrossing of leather straps, a cage harness the Master had ordered her to wear tonight. He stood behind her holding the suede flogger he'd fashioned especially for just such events. Holding the handle in his left hand and the tips in his right, he dragged the tails across her ass and up her back. She moaned, anticipating the harder blows she knew would come. It was their pattern. They had performed this ritual together several times. She knew she would have more bruises after the scene, but that was all right. The Master always took very good care of her.

He stepped back and swung harder. Liz arched and moaned. Again, he swung the flogger; this time the knotted ends of the tails brought forth whelps. Harder he swung, repeatedly until small, marble-sized bruises appeared. Finally, Liz did the unthinkable. She used their safe word, something she had never done before. What she didn't know was that the Master detested safe words. He became angry whenever a slave used them. The Master laid his flogger aside and wrapped his throbbing cock in a dry condom before smearing lubricant all over it and Liz's tightly clenched anus.

"Master, please don't. Red! Red!"

Liz hated anal intercourse, but the Master didn't care. He held her down and swiftly drove his cock into her unyielding orifice. She screamed in agony. Tears streamed down her face while the Master violated her. After several minutes, the Master had had enough. He let go of her shoulders, threaded the fingers of his left hand through the collar around her neck, pulled back, and twisted it. Liz couldn't breathe. She clawed at the collar to no avail. Her resistance was just what the Master needed to reassure himself of his control. Liz stopped struggling and went limp just as he grunted and filled the condom with his spunk.

The Master regarded Liz's lifeless body, pulled his spent member from her, and removed the condom. He left the dungeon long enough to shower and put on a change of clothes, all black. He removed the leather harness and tossed it to the floor, then carried Liz's body upstairs and bathed her, taking great care to scrub underneath her nails before redressing her in the suit and dress pumps she had worn over the harness, which he then retrieved and put away in his secret place. He'd use it to relive the event later. As a final touch, he dried and styled her freshly washed hair and applied make-up to her face, then studied her for a moment before carrying her to a black pick-up truck. He secured the seatbelt around her, got inside, and drove away.

Chapter 1

Ten days later...

"Oh great, what else is gonna go wrong today?"

"Good evening, Ma'am. May I see your driver's license and registration please?" Jess had to dig through her purse to locate the requested documents. "Mmm hmm, just as I thought. Miss Mitchell, I have a warrant for your arrest."

"What?! Arrest for what? I'm not a criminal!"

"Step out of the vehicle please. I'm placing you under arrest." Okay this was *not* funny anymore, but with much trepidation, she did as ordered. "Now turn and face your vehicle, spread your legs, and place your hands on the hood."

Expecting the standard body search, she was caught off guard by his technique. He traced the lines of her figure, sensuous and erotic, down her thighs and calves, then back up the inside of each leg to her bottom, where he molded his hands around the swell of each cheek. Standing so close she could feel his warm breath in her hair, he continued upwards to her breasts, his huge palms a perfect fit. Jess was a lot nervous and a little afraid, but in truth, she was becoming aroused by this unheralded arrest.

Reality slammed back into her when he slid his hands across her shoulders and down her arms to her wrists, which he forced behind her back and restrained with a set of handcuffs. The cold steel sent shivers of apprehension *and* desire down her spine. The man led her to the other side of the squad car, but refrained from putting her inside. She tried to see what he was doing when she felt her jeans being unfastened. He pulled out her shirt, reached underneath, and grabbed her breasts, pinching her nipples...hard.

"Ow, that hurt. What are..."

He reached around and put his finger to her lips, "Shhh."

Jess stiffened in alarm, then shook, half from fear, half from lust. Still behind her, he crouched low and slid her jeans down just below her knees. He rested his face against her backside. Was that a mustache? He slid one hand down the front of her panties, while the other still clutched a breast. She was moist and growing wetter. He found her secret button and massaged it, dipping his fingers inside her.

"Oohhh yes," she moaned.

As quick as he began, his hand was gone. Jess whimpered in protest. A second later, something hard traveled up her thigh, his nightstick. For a moment, arousal turned to terror when he pushed her, face first, over the trunk of the car.

"Spread your legs wider."

Fear melted into desire once again when he pushed the end of the billyclub into her and at a snail's pace slid it in and out. It was cold, like the handcuffs, but felt so good.

"Yes more, no, don't stop." He paused to bend his helpless prisoner further over until she was nearly doubled, then buried his stick to the hilt. Reaching beneath her, he prodded her pubic mound, driving her mindless with need. "Oh God, yes, right there."

He rubbed harder, the strokes more rapid, all the while feeding her lust with the club. At once, her entire body began to shiver and tighten. Spasms contracted every muscle, rolled through her, and centered deep inside her abdomen. She was exploding, muscles clenching around the stick. She rocked her hips faster, driving herself onto the stick as far as she could, yearning for more.

"Oh shit, oh Jesus, yes. Yes, oh God, fuck me!"

His fingers left her mound and went to his pants, hastily unzipping them. He quickly replaced the club with his cock. Holding onto the cuffs for balance, he pumped harder and more furiously, until he imparted a low growl and pulled out, spraying his hot, sticky load across her lower back.

Abruptly Jess woke up...with her hand nestled between her legs. Still groggy, but lucid enough not to let a good dream go to waste, she rubbed her pulsating flesh until she felt the familiar beginning of an orgasm. She arched up, grinding around her own fingers until the spasms subsided.

"God, where the hell did that come from? Niki's gonna love this," she said aloud, reaching for the phone. She glanced at the clock, 5:28. "Shit, I can't call her this early. She'd kill me. Oh well, might as well get up, since the alarm is gonna go off anyway."

She lazed around the apartment for a while before finally dressing for work in her usual garb...snug, faded Levis and a plain, white shirt with the sleeves rolled to her elbows. She checked the time again, 7:15. Niki would be up by now, so Jess dialed her number. While passing the time, she had concocted a plan, even though she knew Niki would want to strangle her for what she was about to do, but such a wicked idea couldn't be ignored.

"*Hello.*" A loud yawn followed the greeting.

"Good, you're up!"

"*Yeah, just barely, what's wrong? You never call this early.*"

"Nothing, we're going to breakfast."

"*What? Why?*"

"Why do I need a reason to take my best friend out to eat?"

"*Because you know I don't eat this early in the morning and neither do you half the time. I've known you too long, you're up to something. What's really going on?*"

"Just get dressed. I gotta tell you something big."

"*What is it? Did you get laid or something?*"

"Just..."

Jess was cut off by an excited scream. "*I knew it! Who was it? Do I know him? Was he hot? What am I thinking? Of course, he was hot. You wouldn't screw a toad.*"

Niki's comment received an amused chuckle. "Just be ready. I'll pick you up in twenty."

Jess checked her hair and makeup, then headed to her car. "Ugh, hello August." The heat wasn't so bad this early, but the Carolina humidity was stifling. She fired up the engine and popped in her current favorite CD. "Oh yeah, that's what I needed," she said aloud and cranked the volume. With a wave to the security guard, she drove through the gate and headed for Raleigh, singing to the music.

> *I need to feel you. You need to feel me. I can't control you. You're not the one for me no. I need to feel you. You need to feel me. I can't control you. So why's it even you and me?*

> *I love the way you look at me. I love the way you smack my ass. I love the dirty things you do when I have control of you.*

Niki was waiting outside when Jess rounded the curve. She hopped inside before the car came to a complete stop. "Damn, you got that loud enough? Some folks are still sleeping, you know."

"I like that song," Jess said, trying to justify the noise.

Niki switched off the radio and launched into attack mode. "Okay, spill it. Who was he? Do I know him?"

"Hold your horses. Let's get some food first. I'm famished."

"I'll just bet you are." Minutes later, seated and having ordered, Niki started again. "Okay, you're killing me with the suspense. If you're not gonna tell me who, how about when?"

"Last night."

"And?"

"And what?" Jess grinned at her friend.

"Damn, you're being cryptic! Who was it?"

"I dunno, never seen him before."

"Oh my God! Saint Jess slept with a perfect stranger?"

"Saint Jess...please!"

"Well, it's true. So tell me about him."

"All I know about him is he's a cop."

"I thought you swore off cops."

"I did, but God, he was hot."

"That should narrow the search down, what with your connections. I mean hell, how many cops can there be around here?"

"Who said I was looking for him?"

"You're gonna go out with him again. Aren't you?"

"I dunno. It depends on whether or not we meet up again."

"Jess, you don't do one-night stands."

"First time for everything."

"Yeah, for everybody *else* on the planet. Details, details, I need more information. Where'd you meet him?"

"I was driving home and he pulled me over."

"No shit? Why? What did you do fuck him to get out of a ticket? No, wait. You wouldn't have to do that. Cops don't give each other tickets."

"I'm not a cop."

"Close enough, but even if he did, all you gotta do is go to work and talk to the brass. He musta been some kind of hot for you to fuck him."

"This story is much better the way you tell it. Keep going," Jess said.

"Oh, bite me! What did he look like?"

"He had dark blonde hair and a nice tan, but other than that, I don't remember. I never really got a good look at him. I really only remember his eyes."

"What?" Niki gasped.

"Shhh, calm down. People are staring at us."

She lowered her voice before continuing her inquisition. "I cannot believe you! You only remember his eyes?"

"Yeah, they were intense and wild. Amber, kinda like, I dunno, a lion. I really don't know how to describe them."

"How the hell is it that you, of all people, fucked this cop and didn't get a good look at him? I mean, shit, I know the uniforms all start to look alike after awhile, but the bodies in 'em are another story, not-to-mention the fact that you're the most observant person I know. So why is it you can't remember a damn thing about him?"

"I remember his voice. It was deep, a nice baritone. He was soft-spoken, but there was authority in it. He meant business and I knew it." Niki's eyes were wide. She was truly stunned. "Oh, and he had a mustache."

"Were you drinking or maybe stoned or something? Why'd he pull you over in the first place?"

"Me, drunk and stoned? You're funny." Jess paused when an attractive waiter brought their order. "Your version really *is* better than mine. Why don't you finish it?"

Niki cut her eyes at Jess and studied the waiter. "God, I love this city," she stated while ogling the man. "Alright, get back to the story."

"I dunno why he pulled me. He never gave me a ticket."

"Hell, I guess not. No cop is gonna hand a ticket to a gorgeous chick, after she's given him a good ride. But I'm still confused. You got pulled over, but didn't get a ticket. Then you got laid, but can't remember what the guy looked like."

"He was behind me most of the time."

"Oh, he was kinky? Okay, I'll give you that one, can't see what's behind you. Finally, something makes sense. Now start from the beginning and don't leave anything out."

"Okay, yesterday evening I was on my way home from work when I saw blue lights, so I pulled over and waited. Then this cop comes up, looks at my license, and tells me he has a warrant for my arrest."

"Oh my God!"

"So then he tells me to get out of the car and assume the position. Then he frisks me...and not your run-of-the-mill body search either. He was feeling me up, big time, squeezing my tits and all." Niki gasped and covered her mouth. "Then he bent me over the trunk of his patrol car and handcuffed me,

4

then marched me around to the other side and pushed my jeans down around my ankles, so I was totally immobilized. I couldn't move. He started massaging me all over. Scared the shit outta me, but at the same time, it totally turned me on. You know what I mean?"

"Hell no, but what happened next?"

"I was so horny I was shaking and then he stopped. I stood there for a sec when I felt his nightstick sliding up my leg."

"Oh my God, did he hit you?"

"No, but for a second I was afraid he might. So anyway he made me bend over further and shoved it inside me and screwed the living daylights out of me with it."

"Holy shit! You're not serious!"

"As a heart attack, so he did that 'til I got off, and oh man, did I ever get off, surprised even myself. Then he threw it on the ground, and replaced it with his dick. He was your kind of man too, by the way, hung like a wild stallion." Niki's eyes were as big as saucers. "He only took a minute before he pulled out and came all over my back."

She sat there speechless for a moment, her mouth hanging open. "Honey, you didn't get a piece of action, you got assaulted. You need to call the police and report him. I don't give a damn how hard you got off, that was a clear-cut case of rape! Come on, we gotta get you to a doctor and get you examined."

"Chill out, I'm not going to the hospital and I'm not gonna report this to the police."

"Why the hell not? This creep can't go around doing shit like that! What if he tries that with somebody else?"

"I doubt that's going to happen."

"You never know. Did he threaten you or something?"

"No."

"Hell, what if he comes after you again."

"I wish he would."

"You're unbelievable! What happened next?"

"I woke up."

"You woke up," she repeated back before it hit her. Jess couldn't hold it in. She started laughing hysterically. "You woke up? Oh, you bitch! You bitch! You are evil! You really had me going! I can *not* fucking believe you did that to me."

Still laughing, "I'm sorry. You know I love you. I was gonna call you, but it was too early when I woke up and you know how creative I get when I have too much time on my hands."

"Damn! You really missed your calling. You shoulda been a writer instead of a shrink. Oh my God, I *still* can't believe you. Payback's a bitch."

Nodding her head, "Yeah, I got a big one coming, but you gotta admit it was hot."

"Hell yeah, *I* need a cigarette now." She lit up and offered the pack to her friend. "You wanna join me?"

"Nik, you know I don't smoke. One of these days those things are gonna kill you."

"You gotta die from something. It's gonna be these or men. Either way I'll have a smile on my face."

"So was that crazy or what?"

"Or what! Now that I know that guy was only a figment of your overactive imagination, I wouldn't mind being arrested by him myself." She took a bite and chewed for a moment. "No honestly, I think its official."

"What?"

"You are officially a textbook case of what happens to a person suffering from that dreaded affliction they call sexual frustration." Jess rolled her eyes. "The good news is that it's curable."

"How, pray tell?" Jess asked.

"You have to get laid, of course."

Jess laughed. "I guess Freud would have a field day with me, huh?"

"I think Freud would just tell you to get laid."

Both women broke into a chorus of giggles. "You're crazy, you know that?"

"Yeah, yeah, that's why you love me."

"Well that, and you're the only person I know who will let me call them at seven in the morning to tell them about a dream."

"Speaking of getting laid, I ran into your ex the other day."

"Who Billy? God, let's not even go there."

"How many exes do you have?"

"Good point. What'd you tell him?"

"I told him to fuck off. I can't believe you wasted so much time on that jerk. How long has it been since you broke up, like a year?"

"A little over, actually."

"Jesus Jess, no wonder you're having crazy dreams. You really need to get out more."

"Why? So another guy can screw me over?"

"No, so you can live a little, but since you insist on working so much, there must be some hot, eligible hunks over at the Bureau."

"Oh, good Lord, no way. I've sworn off cops. Remember? I'll never date another one."

"Never say never."

Jess glanced at a clock across the room. "Damn, it's almost nine already. I have to meet with the DA on a case at ten."

"Is he cute?" Niki asked as they were leaving.

"Who?"

"The DA."

"Josh? I suppose." She paused for a moment. "Actually, now that I think about it, he's got that GQ look."

"Really?"

"He's your proverbial tall, dark, and handsome; probably six foot with very dark, almost black, hair and gorgeous blue eyes, nice smile, straight teeth."

"So ask him out."

"No."

"Why not?"

"I dunno. He's just not my type."

"What exactly is your type, Jess? Wait! Lemme guess...tall, blonde cops with amber eyes and mustaches?"

"Hell no! How many times do I have to tell you that I've sworn off cops?"

"You're too damn picky. You need to broaden your horizons."

"I do not."

"Yes, you do. Put yourself out there and live a little."

"I'm living just fine, thanks."

"Yeah, all by yourself."

10:40 AM...

"Ground control to Agent Mitchell, come in."

"What? Oh, sorry Josh, guess I zoned out on you."

"No problem. Jess, you know it's your work that bagged this guy."

"I'm just glad the case is airtight and he'll be put away for a long time, Josh."

"So we're good on your testimony. No surprises, right?"

"None."

"Good, should be cut and dry, and you're one of my first witnesses, so hopefully your part in this will be over sooner rather than later. Maybe then you can take a well deserved vacation."

"Vacation? What's that?"

He chuckled. "That's where you take a few days off work and take in a change of scenery, go on a trip or something."

"You should explain that concept to Carl."

"How is the old slave driver?"

"Still a slave driver, don't see that changing anytime soon."

Josh smiled and nodded. "Listen, I'm gonna get out of your hair. I'll be in touch."

"Thanks, Josh."

Jess studied the man as he turned to leave. He really was quite handsome in the classical sense, from his aquiline nose and straight forehead to his angled cheekbones and square jaw. When he smiled, stark white teeth gleamed against olive skin, and bright blue eyes contrasted sharply with thick and wavy, almost black hair.

"Hey, maybe when this is all over, when there won't be a conflict of interest, you'll let me take you out to dinner."

"You wanna go out with me?"

"I'd love to take you out. You're beautiful, vibrant, and intelligent, and as far as I know, still single. I'd consider it an honor to have you on my arm."

"I dunno Josh, nothing personal, because you're sweet and attractive, but I try not to mix business with pleasure."

"I won't say I'm not disappointed, but I understand." He looked defeated for a second. "Any hope of changing your mind?"

"Never give up hope," she said with a smile.

"I'll remember that. You should think about changing your policy."

"Why's that, Josh?"

"You never know what you may be missing," he said as he opened the door. "Hey, if you *do* change your mind, lemme know."

"You'll be the first," Jess replied.

He had given her something to think about. After all, he was an attorney, not a cop, and a DA at that. And they didn't *really* work together.

CB⬥CB⬥

"Yo, Jess." She stopped in mid step, but didn't turn around.

"Yo, what?"

"Hold up, Sweetheart. We need to talk."

Jess sighed and looked towards the ceiling. "Oh man, so much for sneaking out of here early," she mumbled.

"I heard that. Come on back here. Let's have a chat." She turned around and went back to her office with her boss hot on her heels. He pulled up a chair and sat across from her. "I got a new case for you, effective immediately."

"Shit Carl, come on. Can't you find somebody else?"

"No can do, this one's yours, Darlin'."

"I don't want it. I haven't finished Warren yet."

"Sure you have. Trial starts next week. All you have left is a day on the stand."

"Why me?"

"Because you're my best shrink, that's why."

"I'm your *only* shrink, Carl."

"Details, details. I can't believe Quantico hasn't scooped you up. Besides what else have you got to do?"

"Uh jeez, I dunno, sleep maybe?"

"Don't roll your eyes at me. You'll get plenty of sleep when you're dead," he chastised.

"There's something to look forward to. Give it to Frank. He's not on anything big right now." Carl shook his head. "Why the hell not?"

"Because *your* assistance was specifically requested."

7

Her ears perked up with sudden interest. "Really? By who?"

"I thought that would get your attention, Burlington PD."

"Dean?"

"Yeah, he called me this morning."

"Well damn! Why didn't you say that in the first place?"

"Cuz I like to get you all riled up," he said, chuckling.

"Are we talking about the serials?"

"*Alleged* serials."

"Whatever."

"Yeah, 'at's the ones. They need some help with 'em and if anyone can figure it out, Jess, it's you."

"I'm glad you both have so much faith in me."

"Faith? Nah, we just know you can do it. You got some kind of weird psychic crap going on that I'm not gonna *try* to understand."

"Ya think?" she asked with a giggle.

"Yeah. Listen, I think it would be a good idea for you to relocate to Burlington. I realize we're less than an hour away, but this case is the biggest thing this state has seen since Blanche Moore or maybe that Petersen guy over in Durham. There's no sense wasting two or three hours a day commuting."

"You have a point there."

"Hey, come to think of it, wasn't Blanche from Burlington too?"

"Yeah, in fact, we both know the pair who worked that case. Scary huh?"

"Dean and Chuck Edwards, right?"

"Yep."

"I'm assuming you'll stay with Dean, but you know the Bureau will put you up in a place if you want."

"Yeah, I'm sure I'll stay at Dean's. Maybe I'll get to ride my bike a little more now."

"There's an idea, good time of year for it."

Jess looked at the clock behind Carl. "It's getting close to rush hour. I should go home and pack some clothes."

"You want me to let Dean know you're on the way?"

"Nah, I'll do it."

"Call this a vacation since you won't have me on your case all day for a while."

"I'm sure you'll find a way to crawl up my ass."

"Probably. Hey, when's the last time you were home?"

"July fourth, for the annual bar-b-cue."

"That was a month ago. Your pop misses you. You need to visit more often."

"I would if I didn't work for a slave driver."

"Hey, I resemble that remark. Dean has a uniform en route to your place with the files as we speak. So you'd have time to take a look in case you didn't get down before next week."

"Good thinking."

"Get outta here, Sugar."

"You don't have to tell me twice." He got up and walked out the door. "Oh, by the way, Carl?" She yelled.

He stopped. "Yes?"

"I'm not your Baby, or Darlin', or Sweetheart," She said in jest, knowing he would never stop calling her by his pet names.

"Yes, Dear," he guffawed as he walked away, then he stopped and turned back around. "Hey, Jess?"

"Yes, Carl?"

"Knock 'em dead, kid, and I want a report every day."

"Of course you do." She grabbed her briefcase and went home.

Chapter 2

Jess drove up just in time to meet the young officer who was delivering the case files. He checked her identification, then carried the bundle upstairs to her apartment. Mmm, shame she'd sworn off cops. He was cute. Eye candy aside, she could hardly wait to dive into the case, but knew if she opened those records, she'd never get to Burlington, so she dialed Dean's office instead.

"Good afternoon, Chief Johansen's office."

"Hey, Maggie, it's Jess."

"Jess Mitchell, now there's a voice I haven't heard in a long time. How have you been, Dear?"

"Very busy, Carl's working me to death."

"I'll bet. I've been reading about you in the paper. Warren, I believe, right?"

"That's the one. Listen, is Dean around?"

"He sure is, and he's been waiting to hear from you. Hold on. I'll put you through."

Jess waited for a moment before he picked up. "Jessie, I'm glad you called. How are you, Sweetheart?"

"Hey, Dean, I'm doing great. I hear you need my help."

"Do I ever. You know I've got bodies turning up left and right."

"Yep, and you know I think you have a serial, based on what you've told me off the record."

"Well, I'm finally ready to call in the cavalry. We just don't have murders in my city, so you can understand why I want this stopped."

"Yes, I know."

"Most of my newer boys have never even seen a corpse."

"This must be difficult for them. I just got the case files, but I haven't opened them yet. I was afraid I would get in too deep and not make it down there today."

"You're coming today? That's wonderful!"

"Yes, and you're gonna be stuck with me for a while. Carl has made this case my top priority as of today. He wants me to relocate to Burlington while I'm working on it so I won't waste time commuting every day, which suits the heck out of me."

"Wonderful, you're room's here anytime you want it."

"Are you sure? I don't want to impose. The Bureau will put me in my own place."

"Jessie, this will always be your home. You're welcome anytime for as long as you want to stay and it's no imposition. You still have your key?"

"Yeah. Listen, I'm gonna get on the road. Barring traffic, I should be there in about an hour."

"Splendid, I'm looking forward to it. Bye, Honey."

CB&>CB&>

The drive to Burlington seemed to take forever, much longer than she had anticipated due to a traffic accident right in the middle of RTP, and there were no convenient exits in the area. A half-hour later, traffic began moving again. Tired of her *Puddle of Mudd* CD, Jess played with the radio, searching for something different when a local country and western station caught her ear. Going home always seemed to bring out her inner redneck, so she turned it up a little louder and sang along.

> *He got the gold-tooth look from a stiff right hook he's proud he took for his right-wing stand on Vietnam. Says he lost his brother there.*

Exit 145 loomed straight ahead. "Hot damn, almost there. Okay Jess, snap out of it."

> *...and the band starts to play Ring of Fire as he walks up and stands there by the stage.*

She took the exit and drove up Maple Avenue to the police department, thinking she would stop in and say hello before heading to the house. She'd been back to Burlington many times in the last few years, but very seldom made it downtown, so she was surprised at how the city had changed. Businesses had come and gone and the main drag held nothing but restaurants and automobile dealerships. Even the old *Holly Hill Mall* had been renamed twice in recent years.

> *And he says hell yeah. Turn it up. Right on. Hell yeah, sounds good. Sing that song. A guitar man playing all night long, take me back to where the music hit me. Life was good. Love was easy.*

Minutes later, Jess stood in the lobby of the Burlington Police Department. "Hey there," she glanced at the officer's stripes and nametag, a corporal. He was a newer officer who'd come on board in the last couple of years. She didn't recognize him. "Corporal Bailey, I'm here to see Chief Johansen. He's expecting me."

"Yes Ma'am, just a moment." Finally looking up from his work, he stared for a moment. "Oh hello," he said, suddenly very interested. "Can I get your name please?" He asked as another officer joined him.

"Doctor Jess Mitchell."

"Just a second." He picked up the phone. "Yeah Maggie, Doctor Jess Mitchell is here to see the Chief...Okay, I'll send her up. Up the stairs and circle around, then turn left, and go to the end of the hallway."

"Thank you," she said, smiling at him. She caught a snippet of their conversation as she started up the stairs and laughed quietly to herself. Jess knew the effect she had on men, though she wasn't comfortable using it to her advantage, unlike her best friend, Niki, who would've milked the situation.

"Man, I'd love to have a swing like that in my back yard. Dude, who was that?"

"That, my friend, was Doctor Jess Mitchell...*the* Jessie Mitchell."

"No shit? The one that's gonna work the serials? I thought it'd be a guy." Their voices faded as she moved up the stairs out of earshot. A moment later, Jess stood by Maggie's desk.

"Yes, you boys have a nice day," she said before hanging up the telephone and looking up at Jess.

"Hello, Maggie."

"Jessie, come here," she said, rising. "Let me hug you and get a good look at you. You get prettier every time I see you."

"Thanks," she said with an abashed smile.

"You've already got a fan club. Those two downstairs called up here to ask about you as soon as you left the front desk."

"They didn't."

"They did. I told them you were single and looking."

"Oh Maggie, when are you gonna stop trying to marry me off?"

"Call me a hopeless romantic. Nice, pretty girls like you should have handsome husbands, homes, and children."

"You're as bad as Niki. Only she's just trying to get rid of her competition. And then there's Dean," Jess said with a laugh.

"Well, I've known you for a long time. You're like a daughter to me and you know how mother hens are. We want our girls to find nice husbands and give us lots of grandbabies."

"Maybe one of these days."

"I suspect the love bug will creep up on you when you least expect it, probably sooner than you think."

"Maybe, but I'm not looking right now."

"That's when it usually bites," she said with a wink.

Jess talked with the older woman for a few moments longer, pumping her for information on the detective she'd be working with. Maggie raved about his good looks without ever really giving her any insight into his personality. Jess finally gave up with a shake of her head and went into the Chief's office.

At that precise moment, Staff-Sergeant Kevin Slater crossed the reception area on his way out. "Hey, yo Sarge, your new partner is here."

He stopped and turned around. "Bailey, what the hell are you talking about? What new partner?"

"You know, the one the Chief called in to *consult* on your case. In fact, they're talking right now."

"Oh yeah, him. What's his name? Michaels or something."

"*Doctor* Jessie Mitchell," the officer said with a smirk.

"Yeah, that's it. Great! Just what I need to end the week," he grumbled.

"Sarge, I think you're really gonna like this one."

"Why's that?"

"Trust me."

"Famous last words."

CؒؒؒؒؒؒؒؒCؒؒؒؒؒؒؒؒؒؒ

"Jessie!" Dean got up and picked Jess up in a full bear hug. "I didn't think I'd see you until tonight."

"I thought I'd pop in and say hey."

"Well, I'm glad you did. You remember Mike Shelley."

She looked over at Mike, who stood up, "Of course, can't forget you, can I? What's this?" She asked, fingering the new stripes on his shoulder. "A promotion? So, do I have to call you Major now, or is Mike still okay?" She teased.

"You'd better call me Mike," he teased back while giving her a quick squeeze. "Dean tells me you're moving back to Burlington."

"I am while I'm on this case. Carl pretty much ordered me to, 'cause of all the publicity it's getting."

"Say, how's big city life? Is Raleigh treating you okay?"

"Raleigh's hardly a big city."

"It is when compared to Burlington," he said laughing. "You know we don't see nearly enough of your pretty face around here, gosh, since you left for college and then went to work with the SBI."

"I know, I know, and I've already gotten the settle-down-and-visit-more-often lecture from Maggie. She's trying to marry me off again."

"Is that a bad thing?" Dean teased.

"Of course not, I just haven't found the right man. Dean, you're the only one who can stand me for very long."

"Nonsense you're a gem," Dean scoffed.

"I happen to agree with him. But you're not the problem Jess; it's him," nodding towards Dean. "Nobody can live up to his expectations," Mike teased.

"Only the best will do for my Jess."

"You guys are a trip. One of you, answer a question for me real quick, 'cause I'm confused about something."

"Sure, Jess."

"How did your guys get to be in charge of the investigation into the campus murders?"

"Bill Davis bowed out of it. Most of those guys are fresh out of BLET and have no experience with murder investigations, nor do they have easy access to the forensic resources that are readily available to us," Mike stated. "Namely you."

"What about the Elon city police? Chuck's got great connections."

"True, but he only has twenty officers, total. We also believe the campus killings may be related to ours," Dean stated. "Mike and I met with Bill and Chuck on Monday. We agreed to pool resources rather than working separately on what could very well be parts of the same case."

"Then Dean and I put our heads together when they left and decided it would be a good idea to call in the big guns."

"Okay, I understand now. And the lead knows all of this? I don't want to ambush anybody."

"He knows. I won't lie to you and say he was pleased, but he knows," Mike added.

"Oh boy, time to go home and have a good, stiff drink."

"Jessie, you don't drink," Mike snorted.

"Which means it'll only take one. I'm gonna get out of here. Dean, I'll see you at home. Mike, it's been a pleasure."

"Hey, don't stay away so long next time."

"Be careful what you wish for. You may be stuck with me long enough that you'll wanna run me outta town."

"Ah, we'd never run you off."

"So you say...bye, guys."

"Hey Jess? I hope you'll let me take you out to dinner tonight."

"Only if you'll let me make you dinner in return very soon."

"Deal!"

"Dean, if we're finished, I'm going to run on too."

"Sure Mike, go ahead."

"Hey Jess, wait up, I'll walk ya out," Mike called from behind her.

CB€CR€

"Maggie, would you get Detective Slater on the phone for me?" Dean waited for a moment before he was connected.

"Yes Sir, Chief, what can I do for you?"

"Slater, the profiler just left my office and will need somewhere to work. I think it might be a good idea to set up base camp at the substation. Do you have an empty office or some extra room there?"

"Yes Sir, there's an office."

"How about getting it ready. I'm sure Jessie will want to dive right in first thing in the morning."

"Yes, Sir."

CB€CR€

"Goddamn it!" He grumbled, slamming the receiver.

"What's up, Kev?"

"Not only has my case been handed over to a subbie, but now I gotta give him a fucking office too. Come and help me straighten up in here. Chief wants it ready pronto, so he can move in first thing in the morning."

CB€CR€

"Would you like to view our dessert menu?"

"What do you think, Jessie?"

"I think I'd love to, but I can't possibly hold another bite. I am stuffed, maybe next time, but how about a glass of water."

"Certainly, Madam."

"Have you had a chance to immerse yourself in those case files yet?"

"No, but I was planning to when we get back to the house."

"You might wait until morning so you won't have to pack it all up again. I've got you an office."

"Great! Where?"

"Tucker Street substation...do you remember where it's at?"

"Sure, I passed right by it today."

"That's where Slater is based. He's the lead on this one."

"Slater? Yes, his name came up when I was talking with Maggie earlier. I don't remember him. Have we met?"

"Probably not, you don't spend as much time at the station as you used to. And well, even if you did, he tends to stay on Tucker Street, unless he's called to headquarters for a reason."

"Well, it looks like we're gonna meet now for sure. Tell me about him."

"Kevin Slater, he's one hell of a good cop."

"Personality?"

"Pig-headed, just like you, but I like him. I like him a lot. I think you'll get along famously," Dean laughed. "As soon as you both figure out who's in charge."

"Oh great, a control freak, that's just what I need."

"Well now, I wouldn't quite go that far, though he does keep his officers in line, and there has been a considerable drop in that area's crime rate. You want to have a little fun with him?"

"How?"

"Slater's boys have been teasing him quite a bit about having his case handed over to subbies."

"Subbies?"

"That's what they call you folks over at the SBI. They've got him all worked up over it."

"Interesting, so back to the fun part...how would you know about the licking Detective Slater has been taking? The *Chief* isn't supposed to listen to office gossip."

"Well, my secretary *is* one of the busiest busybodies in the department."

"True, but she means well."

"He is going to be mighty surprised when he learns that his new consultant is the prettiest and smartest, not-to-mention, the most headstrong lady, I know. Word has it Detective Slater is expecting a man."

"Uh oh, I'm picking up a vibe and I'm not sure I like it. You're not gonna start playing matchmaker, are you?"

"Well now, I hadn't thought of that, but I *do* like Slater an awful lot. He'd make a fine son-in-law."

"God help me. I don't stand a chance with you *and* Maggie tag-teaming me."

"We only want the best for you, Hun, but I think in this case, we'll let nature take its course. You and Slater *would* make a mighty fine-looking couple though."

11:14 PM

"Oh my God, Nik! Dean and Maggie are trying to set me up already."

"*Damn, that was even faster than normal. Who with?*"

"The lead detective on this investigation, Kevin Slater."

"*Is he hot?*"

"I dunno, haven't met him yet. Maggie seemed smitten with him though, says he is, and I quote, *a handsome devil.* But she and Dean dodged the question when I asked about his personality, so I'm not holding out high hopes. I gotta feeling we're gonna butt heads, hard and often."

"*Hard and often being the key words here.*"

"Damn, you're as bad as they are."

"*Oh come on, Jess, you're not gonna have any chemistry going into it with that attitude.*"

"Going into what? I'm not here to meet men. That's more your style, Girlfriend," Jess teased.

"*Well, get my room ready. I'm there,*" she laughed.

"Anyway, I'm gonna see if I can catch some Zs. I'll talk to you later."

"*Okay bye, and call me if that detective is hot and available, and if you don't want him.*"

Chapter 3

Jess tossed and turned for what seemed like hours before finally falling asleep. Her faceless cop plagued her dreams once again, waking her at 4:30, in the throes of another intense orgasm. The mysterious dream cop had her in a state of perpetual arousal. He was also her incentive for going against character and acquiescing to Dean's idea of having some fun with Detective Slater, so she jumped in the shower to prepare for her first day on the new case.

The forecast called for another hot and steamy day, so she decided on her usual form-fitting, faded blue jeans paired with a white, poet shirt that was just thin enough to cast a shadow of the lacy, black bra she wore beneath it. She pushed the sleeves up to her elbows and strapped on her holster. To complete the look, she added a touch of color to her cheeks and a coat of mascara to her lashes, then tousled her waist-length hair before grabbing her briefcase and heading out.

Dean was already up. "Good morning, Sunshine. You're up bright and early." He looked at his watch. "It's earlier than I thought, only six."

"Yeah, I woke up a while ago, couldn't go back to sleep. I figured somebody was trying to tell me to get my butt outta bed and get a jump start on the day."

"Well, you look absolutely ravishing, though I'm surprised you're wearing your hair down. I didn't realize it had grown so long."

"I'm sure I'll regret it in a couple hours, but I thought I'd do something a little out of the ordinary, you know, to keep you on your toes."

"Well you look beautiful. You should wear it down more often."

"Thank you."

He winked at her. "Wouldn't have anything to do with a certain detective would it?"

"Of course not," she scoffed. "I don't even know him. I gotta run."

"There's something else I'm not used to...seeing you on duty. You've got your gun."

"Yeah well, better to have it and not need it than to need it and not have it."

"Very true, you're still a crack shot?"

Jess smiled. "I do pretty good at qualifying each month."

"I'll bet you do."

"What can I say? You taught me well."

"Good, did you have breakfast yet?"

"I'll get something later."

"Nonsense, come join me for a bite."

"I really have to get into these files. You know they're burning a hole in my briefcase."

"They're not going anywhere. Come eat. Besides, I know you. You'll get into those files and be so busy saving the city that you won't eat all day."

"If you insist, but it'll have to be a quick."

"I insist. Sit." The pair sat for the next hour catching up over omelettes. "Listen, I know you're itching to get out of here. Can I give you a ride?"

"No, it's supposed to be a nice day out today. I'm gonna ride my bike. Besides, I need a refresher on the streets." Jess gave Dean a hug and opened the door. "Hey, thanks for breakfast."

"You're welcome and be careful. You know I get nervous every time you get on that motorcycle."

"Promise."

"Good luck, I'm gonna want a full report when you've gone through those files."

"Yeah sure, Carl," she joked. Jess twisted her hair into a loose knot, put on her sunglasses, and strapped on her helmet, then took off.

Fifteen minutes later...

The day shift would be starting by now, she thought as she parked the bike. Grabbing her things from the saddlebags, she strode inside. The tired-looking officer quickly woke up, surprised when a

14

beautiful woman emerged from under all the protective riding gear. He stood up and gave her an appreciative once-over, lingering for a time at the gun strapped to her side, before speaking.

"Can I help you, Ma'am?"

"Good morning, I'm Jess Mitchell. I believe you're expecting me." She showed the officer her badge and credentials.

His expression changed from male appreciation to one of astonishment. "Yes Ma'am." He stood there, staring as if entranced.

"Is everything okay?"

"Yes Ma'am, pardon me, Doctor Mitchell, you surprised me. You're not exactly who we had imagined."

"We?"

"Yeah, me and the other guys."

"You were expecting green skin and a wart?" She asked with a smile.

"Not exactly."

"Ah, you thought I'd be a man," She teased.

"Uh yes, something like that, I guess we all assumed *Jessie* Mitchell would be a guy," he replied, embarrassed. "We've got your office set up right over here," he said, pointing at a door to the right. "Let me help you with this." He picked up the briefcase and carried it inside.

"Thank you."

"You're welcome. By the way, I'm Brian, Brian McCaskell."

"A pleasure to meet you Brian, and please call me Jess."

"Yes Ma'am, um sorry, Jess."

"Are we it?"

"Beg your pardon?"

"I was under the impression it was a little busier here. Is it just you and me?"

"Oh, you'll meet the other guys later. There's usually three of us on duty at a time. Rafferty's out on a call, and Sarge has kinda been working 'round the clock with this case he's on. He'll be in later."

"Sarge?"

"Staff-Sergeant, actually. Kevin Slater, he runs this office. Sarge is sort of a nickname."

"I see. I'm going to go get set up." Jess walked towards her new office, then stopped and turned around. "Hey Brian, do you have any thumbtacks?"

"Yes Ma'am, I mean Jess. I'll bring them right in."

"Thanks."

CBEOCREO

"Did Kev get a new bike?"

"I don't think so. Why?"

"There's a killer bike outside, a little girlie, but still nice. He's the only one I know who rides. I thought maybe it was his." Rafferty asked.

"Oh that? You wouldn't believe me if I told you."

"Try me."

"It belongs to Doctor Mitchell."

"He's here?"

"Yep," Brian said, grinning.

"What the hell are you smiling at?"

"What? A guy can't smile?"

"Not when subbies are involved. You know Kev's is in a shitty mood and he ain't gonna be any easier to live with now that the guy's here."

"I think he will. I think you're *both* gonna be real surprised. I kinda like the guy."

"You're queer anyway, you would like him."

"Ooh Dean, you thought of everything," Jess said to herself as she looked at the huge wall map. "I can tag locations while I'm making notes."

She sat down cross-legged in the middle of the floor, spread out the case materials, and started the task of sorting through it all. Grabbing a legal pad, she started writing in her own brand of shorthand while she read aloud from the case files.

> *vic number one*
> *Susan Huffman, age 35*
> *divorced - 3 years*
> *secretary*
> *res. Ragland Terrace apartments, Glen Raven Road*
> *body found December 31, 2003 in North Park, by 6-year old boy and mom*

"Oh my God! How awful!"

> *5 days after rep. missing by mom, dump site 6 miles ENE of res., ten miles NE of job*

"Weird, she wouldn't be in the woods in a skirt, especially not in that part of town." Jess continued writing notes.

> *Brought to this location maybe?*

She paused to find the scene photos. "Hmm, pretty lady."

> *shoulder-length, curly blonde hair*
> *5'4"*
> *medium build, tan*
> *COD, ligature asphyxia*

Next, she studied the autopsy photos and kept writing.

> *ligature marks on throat, measure 1½ inches wide*

"What would he use to make those wide marks? A belt maybe?"

> *vic number two*
> *Diana Rigsbee, age 24*
> *Assistant Manager at CD Planet, Colonial Mall*
> *res. garage apartment at father's home, Highview Street*

"That's way across town; must be at least ten miles."

> *body discovered June 29, 2004 – 4 days after MPR filed*
> *store Manager filed MPR after 2 missed work days*

"So, six days altogether."

> *body discovered in wooded area, Fairchild Park, 8 miles east of home, 11 miles east of Colonial Mall*

"Where's the photos? Ugh, no accounting for taste. Okay Jess, that wasn't nice. She's probably quite pretty minus the vampire look. So, I have two victims with no obvious physical similarities. But the dumpsites are both parks. Coincidence?"

waist-length, straight, dyed black hair, very pale skin
5'8"; skinny
multiple piercings, two tattoos; a black bird-raven or crow, left shoulder; tribal band
type, w/3-sided yin yang symbol, right ankle
wearing black corset and black, leather miniskirt
COD, ligature asphyxia

"Hmm, cause of death is the same. She certainly doesn't look like a jogger or the athletic type, especially not in that outfit."

definitely posed. another dump?

"Not the best part of town again. And there are those marks again. Another link maybe?"

vic number three
Carrie Hamilton, age 20
Liberal Arts major, Elon University, 2.9 GPA
res. Loy Center-sorority house

"What? This one's different." Then she got to the crime scene photos. "In the bushes?"

found July 12, 2004 in bushes a few yards from Smith Hall
last seen previous evening with boyfriend
very popular, well liked on campus, active member of Zeta Tau Alpha sorority

"Pretty girl."

long, wavy blonde hair, 5'6", athletic build
COD, cerebral hemorrhage, blunt force trauma to base of skull

"This is weird, not at all like the first two." She set that file to the side and moved on to the next one.

CZEOCREO

Detective Kevin Slater stopped to eyeball the motorcycle. "Nice bike," he mumbled to himself before going inside.

"Hey Sarge, nice of you to grace us with your presence."

"Fuck off, Dave!"

"A jolly good mood we're in today. Who pissed in your Wheaties?" Slater glowered at David Rafferty. "You're just in time to meet your new partner."

"Suck my dick."

"In your dreams, Pal."

"Well, how is he?"

"I dunno. I haven't met the guy yet; door was closed when I got back from a call. Hey, I think McCaskell is queer."

"What would make you say that?"

"Never mentions a girlfriend or *any* girl, for that matter, then all-of-a-sudden he turns into a doe-

17

eyed sap when he starts talking about him," Dave said, pointing towards Jess' closed door.

"Don't start telling people that. You'll ruin the kid. He can't help it if he's easily impressed with flashy credentials. Give him a few years to get jaded. One of you start riding?"

"I thought it was yours until Brian told me it was his," he said, pointing again at the door. "It's kinda girlie if you ask me, all white and purple and with all that fringy stuff hanging off it."

"This should be interesting," Slater said derisively. "Where *is* Brian?"

"Out on his social rounds."

"Well, no time like the present. Might as well get this over with." Slater walked to the door and beat on it with the side of a closed fist.

CB∞CB∞

> *vic number four*
> *MaryAnn Hunter, age 40*
> *self-employed software designer*
> *lived at...*

"What the hell?" Jess looked up as someone pounded on the door so hard the hinges rattled.

"Mitchell, open up."

The voice sounded familiar but she couldn't quite place it. Assuming it was Detective Slater, she walked over and yanked it open, leaving the both of them noticeably shaken. The pair spoke almost at the same time.

"Good God!" Her hand instantly flew to her mouth as his eyes raked her in a quick assessment.

"Holy shit! 'Scuse me, I mean..."

He cut a formidable-looking figure...tall, broad-shouldered, and handsome, with a beautifully proportioned body that towered over her. Jess couldn't determine whether or not he was friendly. His jaw was visibly tense, suggesting someone who would not relinquish control without a fight, while his eyes held the hint of a smile, though without a thorough search, one would be hard-pressed to find it through the scowl he wore. Those extraordinary amber eyes burned with an inner fire. She may have read him wrong, but those eyes seemed to send the private message that he was not nearly as daunting as he would have the world believe. A head full of tawny, sun-streaked hair, which contrasted sharply with his deeply tanned skin, completed the package.

Jess was enthralled, though determined not to show it. Her heart hammered in her chest at the shock of seeing him. She thought for a moment that it might jump out of her chest. Continuing her perusal of him, she lingered much longer than she should have on his mouth. Wide and generous, his lips were firm and sensual, and topped by a well-groomed mustache that was a shade darker than the hair on his head. Before she could catch herself, she licked her lips.

She'd been called psychic before, though she had never believed in that sort of thing, but this was uncanny. A naysayer would call it impossible or even ridiculous. A believer would call it fate. In an instant, Jess shook off a mental flash of her dream cop. Was it possible? It couldn't be. Was her dream a premonition or merely wishful thinking? Granted, she couldn't remember her dream cop's face exactly, but the body, the voice, and the mustache made Kevin Slater a dead ringer...then there were those eyes.

"Don't worry about it," she interrupted.

Like his new partner, Kevin Slater regained his composure in an instant and stood there, boldly intimidating, with his arms folded across his chest. But Jess stood her ground and scowled back at him, willing herself to go cold. She was not about to let him intimidate her. She crossed her own arms, obviously mocking him, raised her chin, stared him fearlessly in the eye, and silently challenged him to a battle of wills.

"Detective Kevin Slater, I presume?"

"No, you were right the first time," he smirked. "It's God." Was that the hint of a sense of humor or just his way of telling her who was in charge? As much as she wished for the former, she decided on the latter. "Have we met before?"

"I don't think so," she snapped. "You just reminded me of someone."

"Anybody I know?"

"Trust me. You wouldn't believe me if I told you."

"Suit yourself," he said, shrugging matter-of-factly.

"Hey, I'm Jess Mitchell," she said and offered her hand.

"Slater," he said.

He ignored the outstretched hand, which she immediately pulled back. Fine, she decided. She could play his way. He was cocky, arrogant, and rude. Her earlier thought that she and Detective Slater would butt heads often seemed destined to become reality. Saved by the bell, Brian McCaskell picked that moment to return from his rounds.

"Morning Sarge, Dave. Hey Jess, I picked up another box of thumbtacks for you, in case you run out."

"Thank you Brian. That was very kind of you," Jess replied with a smile.

"Looks like you guys have met Jess."

"No, actually, we have not all been introduced. Hi, I'm Dave Rafferty," he said, tripping over himself to step around Slater. He smiled and gave her a long, appreciative look, and then offered his hand, which she accepted. "It is my pleasure to meet you, Jess Mitchell."

A wolf in sheep's clothing, she thought. "Charmed," she said, returning his smile, then turned back to Detective Slater, to whom she directed another recalcitrant glare. "And you as well, Detective. If you gentlemen will excuse me, I need to get back to work." Jess turned her back on them and closed the door.

Chapter 4

"Hot damn! *She* is a *babe*," Dave said, smacking Brian. "You shithead! Why didn't you tell me our new roommate was a gorgeous, blonde BTM?"

"BTM?" Brian questioned.

Dave and Kevin laughed. "Brian, you have a lot to learn, my friend," Kevin said with a chuckle, but then reverted to his fowl mood.

"It's a big titty mama," Dave added, still laughing.

"Oh..."

"Dude, are you still a virgin?"

"No!" He exclaimed in vindication.

"I mean, it's okay if you are," Rafferty continued.

"No! The looks on your faces were priceless, though. But hey man, in my own defense, I was as surprised as you two, maybe more. I thought I was hallucinating when she walked in."

"Yeah, I'll bet. Asshole!" Dave slapped Kevin on the back. "Hey Sarge, you gonna ask her out?"

"Why the hell would I do that? I don't even know her."

"Never stopped you before."

"Biker chicks aren't exactly my type."

"Yeah right, and that, Brian, comes from a man with a big, old hog parked in his garage. You better go for an eye exam because I got news for you, Buddy. That in there ain't your run-of-the-mill biker chick. But if you're not gonna ask her out, I'm gonna get me a little piece of that action."

"Leave her alone," Kevin growled.

"Damn, listen to him, Brian. Mighty possessive for somebody that ain't interested. I think he likes her," Dave teased.

"Dammit, I'm not interested and I don't like her."

"Whatever, but *she* likes *you*." He turned back to Brian. "Did you see the way she looked at him?"

"He's got a point, Sarge. It was nothing like when she first walked in here this morning. She was in a great mood and even teased me, but with *you*, she was different."

"Yeah, she got all flustered and her eyes glazed over. Dude, she was checking you out," Rafferty continued. "The jewels too."

"You've both lost your minds!"

"I'm telling you, she was!"

"Really?" Slater asked, cocking an eyebrow.

"Hell yeah! She wanted you. I know that look," he boasted. "I get it all the time."

"Give me a fucking break. If you got half the pussy you claimed to, you wouldn't have time to come to work."

"I get my share. And I'm gonna get a piece of her too if you ain't gonna move on her."

"Jess is off limits to you! That goes for both of you. Got it?"

"I see you got on a first-name basis with her real quick-like."

"I'm warning you, Rafferty."

"Seriously Sarge, she's all yours, and good luck. You're gonna need it."

"What the hell's that supposed to mean? You think I can't get her?"

"No, I don't think you'll have much trouble getting her, seeing as how she's already into you but..."

"Uh oh, here it comes."

"I think she's gonna get under your skin...maybe already has."

CS&CR&

Jess had no choice but to lean against the door. Her legs were shaking and she wasn't at all certain they would hold her up. She shook off another mental flash of her dream cop, one where he'd taken on a new face, that of Detective Kevin Slater.

"How in the hell am I supposed to get him out of my head when he's right in the next fucking room?" She stomped over, snatched up the phone, and dialed Niki's office.

"*Good afternoon, Chandler Trucking. This is Kelly. How may I direct your call?*"

"Niki Shannon, please."

"*She's in a meeting. May I take a message?*"

"This is Jess Mitchell. Have her call me when she has a minute. She has my cell," she said, looking down at the display. "Damn, it's nearly dead," she mumbled to herself. "Lemme give you another number."

"*Sure, what is it?*"

Jess frowned upon not finding it posted on the phone. "Haven't got a clue, I just moved in here. Can you hang on a sec?"

"*Sure, no problem.*"

"Shit, now I have to go back out there where *he's* at," she grumbled to herself. She walked out into the main room, taking the three men by surprise. They looked at her and clammed up. "I'm sorry to interrupt, but could one of you tell me the telephone number to this office? It's not marked on the phone."

"The offices have extensions," Brian said with a sappy grin.

"We're not that high tech around here, Miss Mitchell," Slater interjected derisively.

"What they mean is whoever's out here will transfer your calls to you," Rafferty said amiably while glaring at Slater.

"So what is it?"

"336-555-4687," Slater finally said coolly.

"Thank you, Detective."

"Sure."

"Asshole," she muttered under her breath before going back to her office and giving the door a hinge-rattling slam.

○§⑤○⑥§○

Dave broke out laughing. "Sarge, I could be wrong, but I'm sure I heard her call you an asshole right about the time she tried to shake the hinges loose."

"I must have missed that."

"Why'd you have to be such a schmuck? She only wanted the phone number. *We're not that high tech around here, Miss Mitchell,*" he aped.

"Go to hell, Rafferty," Slater said as the telephone rang. He jerked the receiver from the cradle and growled, "Burlington Police Department, Slater speaking."

"*Hi, this is Niki Shannon. I'm returning a call to Jess Mitchell.*"

"Hold on."

○§⑤○⑥§○

"God, I hope that's Niki. Jess Mitchell."

"*Hey, what's up?*"

"Oh God, I'm so glad it's you."

"*You sound upset. What's going on?*"

"You are not *fucking* going to believe this!"

"*Whoa, she used the F word. This is big. Try me.*"

"Remember my mysterious dream cop?"

"*How could I forget him?*"

"Well, he's real and he works right here in this office."

"*You're right. I don't believe it.*"

"Dammit, Niki, I'm serious."

"*You're pulling my leg again aren't you? Jess, have you got a fever?*"

"Hell no, I'm fucking serious!"

"Whoa, there she goes again!"

"Uh yeah."

"Well after that dirty trick you pulled on me yesterday, I had to be sure. Jess, I know you're clairvoyant and all, but what makes you think he's real? You said you never saw his face."

"No, I said I couldn't remember his face, but I do remember his eyes, his voice, the mustache, and God help me, that body."

"You really are serious, aren't you?"

"Fuckin'ay, hell yes, I'm serious. What am I gonna do now?"

"What kind of question is that? You're finally going to get laid...and regularly."

"I don't think so. He's arrogant and rude, and one seriously cocky son-of-a-bitch."

"Well yeah, just like Mr. Dream Cop. I mean hell, the guy pulls you over then fucks the living daylights out of you right there on the street, and you loved it. That sounds like a cocky son-of-a-bitch to me."

"Oh yeah, he was, wasn't he?" Jess answered, dejected.

"Uh yeah, so is he really hot? When do I get to meet him?"

"Oh my God, you wouldn't believe. I nearly passed out when I opened the door and found *him* standing there. But damn, why does he have to be an ass?"

"You probably surprised him as much he surprised you. You know it's always been my experience that when a man makes an ass of himself around a woman, it's because he's attracted to her."

"No way."

"Way! Have I ever steered you wrong? Don't answer that. A guy named Slater answered the phone. Was that him?"

"In the flesh."

"He sounded pissed, but he did have a nice voice. What's he look like?"

"He's a big guy, must be a foot taller than me, and probably has me by at least fifty or sixty pounds. Blond hair, mustache, oh, and the eyes were identical to my dream cop's. He's got a nice ass too."

"What about his package? Is he hung?"

"Well gee, Nik, I didn't exactly strip-search him."

"Well, Miss Observant, you looked at everything else. You can't tell me you didn't look at that too."

"I may have taken a small peek."

"And?"

"There's definitely some*t*hing there."

"If he's half as sexy as you say, I see great things in your future. Great, big things," she added with a laugh.

"You're no help."

"Hey, you asked what you should do. I think you should fuck him."

"Terrific! Those are sage words of wisdom if I ever heard them," Jess said, her tone disdainful.

"That's what I'm here for, Babe. Listen Sweetie, the boss is calling. I gotta run. I'll call you again later."

"Okay, I'll talk to ya then. I have to get back to these case files anyway. Bye." She sat back down in the floor. "Okay, now where was I? Oh yes, Carrie Hamilton. Completely different MO and everything. We'll set that one aside. Who's next?"

> *vic number four*
> *MaryAnn Hunter, age 40*
> *self-employed software designer*
> *reported missing November 30, 2004*
> *found December 3 in train tunnel, Burlington City Park*

Jess got up and went to check the location on the map. By day, the park was a haven for parents and children with its many amusement park rides. By night, the common areas were well lit, but the majority of the park was dark and deserted. It wasn't inconceivable that someone could dump a body there without being seen, especially not inside the train tunnel, as it was quite a ways back in an unlit, wooded area. She was a little surprised though that the perpetrator would select a dumpsite right in the middle of town, and so near the police department.

"If it's the same guy, he's either getting brave or he's incredibly stupid, and this is miles away from the others, but the same MO again and another park."

vic number five
Alana Lewis, age 19
biology major at Elon University

"Hmm, another student."

res. Brannock Hall
dumped behind retaining wall outside dorm, December 14, 2004
COD, massive cerebral hemorrhage from blow to base of skull

"Okay, I've got two student deaths that are most certainly connected to each other. Victim was raped post-mortem." She flipped back to Carrie Hamilton's autopsy report. "Post-mortem vaginal penetration...another one." She placed Alana Lewis's file with Carrie Hamilton's. "These two have to be related."

vic number six
Elizabeth Johnson, age 43
professor of Women's Studies, UNC-CH
res. Queen Street, Hillsborough, lived alone

"Uh oh, this may have just gotten complicated."

reported missing July 22, 2005
found July 29 in alley off Rosewald Street propped against back side of dumpster

"I need something bigger to write on." Jess walked out into the main office talking while looking down at her notes. "Hey Brian, is there a whiteboard around here?" Her three officemates were again startled from their huddle by her sudden presence. "Oh, I apologize for interrupting again. I'll come back," she said as the main door swung open.

"I don't think so. Want me to see if I can get one from headquarters?"

"Good afternoon, Princess."

Brian and Dave exchanged a puzzled look as Dave mouthed *Princess* to Brian.

"Dean! Where'd you come from? Are you checking up on me?"

"Of course not, I'm checking on my boys. I see you've all met my daughter, Jess?" He winked at her.

Brian and Dave's mouths fell open in shock while Kevin sputtered on his coffee. "Your daughter, Sir?" Dave asked.

"Sort of, Dean raised me after my parents passed away."

"Oh man, I'm sorry Jess."

"Did I hear someone mention a whiteboard?"

"Yes Sir, Jess was just asking if we had one."

"Well, not to worry. There's plenty of them at the office. Slater, you're driving that C.O.P.S. truck," Dean stated. "Drive over to my office and pick one up, and bring Jessie along too. She needs to get some air. If I know her, she's been slaving away all morning."

23

"Yes Sir."

"Well, I'm going to get out of your hair. Jessie, I'll see you back at home later tonight. Have a good day, boys."

"Goodbye, Dean."

"Yeah, take it easy, Chief," Kevin added.

The foursome stood there for a few moments before Kevin broke the awkward silence. "Doctor Mitchell, I need to make a couple calls and then we can go whenever you're ready."

"Sure Detective, I'll just go wait in my office." She left the door open this time, leaving Brian and Dave outside in their joint state of shock from Dean's disclosure.

Dave wandered in a minute later and planted himself on the sofa across from her. "What's it like growing up the Chief's kid? Must have been kinda weird."

Jess smiled at him. "Not really, he wasn't the Chief then."

He laughed, "Didn't think of that. He's been the Chief for as long as I've been on the force, hard to imagine him as a regular Joe."

"I've known him all my life. I guess I never noticed. When I was a kid, he and my father were partners, so he's always been just Dean to me."

"Hey Doc, you ready to go?"

"Sure Detective, see ya around Dave, Brian." Jess grabbed her half-charged cell phone and followed Kevin.

"Bye, Jess."

Detective Slater held the door for her. "After you, Madam."

"Thank you."

When he motioned Jess ahead of him, his hand brushed the small of her back. Unsure if the touch was accidental or not, she was almost certain she'd find a handprint if she stopped to check. The heat from his hand seared through her thin, cotton shirt and blazed through her. That heat was further compounded when Kevin's hand closed over hers as they each reached for the door handle on the truck to which Jess pulled back quickly. Kevin waited for her to climb inside, then shut the door behind her. Jess had made up her mind earlier to get along with him even if it killed them, but she couldn't resist the opportunity to needle the guy one last time. She waited for him to get his seatbelt on.

"Well, what do you know? Chivalry's not dead after all." Her voice dripped with sarcasm.

"No Ma'am, only wounded." They rode in silence for several minutes.

"Detective Slater, I'd be lying if I said I wasn't happy about this assignment because I was dying to get *officially* involved in this investigation."

"What do you mean officially involved?"

"Dean's bent my ear off the record a few times."

"Oh."

"It's the kind of case that can make or break a career, and I guarantee you, it won't break mine. So that leaves us kinda stuck with each other. Don't you think it would be nice if we could at least get along without all the hostility?"

"Listen, Miss Mitchell, I'll admit we got off on the wrong foot. My earlier rudeness was completely uncalled-for. I only hope you'll accept my apology."

He seemed sincere, but Jess remained guarded. "I will with a couple conditions."

"And what would those be?"

"First, don't be all nice to me just because I'm the Chief's kid. We'll either get along or we won't. I'm not into kissing up."

"Neither am I. It's just that I've been kicking myself for not catching this guy yet, and it's getting to me. And I've been getting a load of shit from the guys about the Chief calling in a profiler."

"I understand better than you know how that might happen. This isn't my first day on the job, and you're certainly not the first resentful lead detective I've met."

"Yeah, I'm sure. You probably get stuck with us all the time."

"More often than I'd like, but if it helps, I'm only here to help you. I'm not interested in taking the credit for your work."

"I believe you." He paused for a moment. "I'm the problem. I've never needed help with a case, so I guess I'm just a little pissed at myself and a little hardheaded. I'm genuinely sorry for taking it out on you. What's the other condition?"

"Stop calling me Doctor or Miss Mitchell. My name is Jess."

"Jess it is, but only if you'll call me *anything* besides *Detective*," he teased, mocking her earlier tone. "Do you have a preference?"

"God was kinda nice," he said, grinning mischievously. A hint of mirth crept into his voice.

So he *did* have a sense of humor, she thought. "Mmm hmm, Kevin it is then. You know you have a nice smile."

"Thanks," he said, this time beaming at her.

Jess was glad to know she hadn't read him wrong at their initial introduction, and now that they were off to a fresh start, her new partner became even more attractive. This assignment was going to be a challenge, though not because of the crimes. She found herself daydreaming about her sexy dream cop and sneaking an occasional glance at the well-defined bulge at Kevin's crotch as they drove up Maple Avenue. Though it took mere minutes, it seemed like hours before they made it to headquarters, where Kevin loaded the whiteboard. The early-August heat combined with the physical effort he put into disassembling and loading the contraption caused beads of sweat to break out across his forehead.

"Can I help?"

"No, I got it. Why don't you just wait in the truck? I'm almost done."

"You're sure?"

"Yes Ma'am."

She got inside and turned around in her seat to watch him. A cigarette dangled from his mouth while the muscles in his shoulders bunched as he picked up and slid each piece of the disassembled whiteboard into the back of the truck. She imagined for a moment what his bare chest would look like, but before her thoughts had time to get away from her, her near-dead cell phone rang, jolting her from the fantasy.

"Hello."

"*Jess, it's me. Sorry about cutting you short earlier. You know how they get around here.*"

"No problem, Nik, don't worry about it."

"*I called your office. Some guy named Brian said you were out. He sounded cute.*"

"He is, but he's not your type, way too sweet. You'd eat him alive, then leave him broken-hearted and ruined for any other woman."

"*Oh please.*"

"Okay, we're all set," Kevin said as he opened his door and sat down.

"*Who was that?*"

"Nik, I'm gonna have to call you back. I'm kinda in the middle of something."

"Oh sorry, didn't mean to disturb you. I'll give you a minute." Kevin started to get back out of the truck.

"No Kev, come on. It's just my girlfriend, Niki, calling to see if I'm settled in yet."

"*Kev? Is that him? Our sexy dream cop?*"

"Yes."

"*Oh my God! You're out with him now?*"

"Yes."

"*Alone?*"

"Yes."

"*Kev, that's a bit endearing don't ya think? I thought he was an arrogant jerk?*"

"That was true."

"*But not anymore? Damn girl, you didn't waste any time?*"

"Listen, I have to go. My phone is nearly dead. I'll call you later."

"*You'd better. I want details.*"

"Of course you do, goodbye Niki." Jess tucked the phone away, looked at Kevin, and smiled. Sweat trickled down his brow. "You're all sweaty now." Without thinking, she ran her palm across his forehead and wiped it on the leg of her jeans. He closed his eyes and stiffened slightly at her touch. "Now then, isn't that better?"

"Um yes, much, thank you," he said unevenly. He tossed his half-finished cigarette to the ground then cranked the truck and started to drive away. "It's damn hot in here. Do you mind if I put the windows up and turn on the air?"

"By all means..."

Chapter 5

They rode in silence for a few minutes before he finally broke it. "Hey, have you eaten lunch?"

"No."

"Can I take you out for a bite?"

"Is that a good idea considering our rough introduction?"

"Sure. We'll call it a peace offering and start over, so the speak."

"Um okay, in that case, it sounds like a great idea. But just so you know, I think I can take you if we ever come to blows."

"I'd probably let you," he returned with a chuckle. "Do you have a preference?"

"No, surprise me. I'll eat anything."

"All right, a real woman...how's Italian sound?"

"Delicious."

"Good, there's a great place called Paolo's over on Restaurant Row."

"Restaurant Row?"

He laughed. "Huffman Mill Road...the only thing there now besides the mall is restaurants and car dealerships."

"Makes perfect sense to me," Jess said, chortling.

ೞೞೞ

"Can you fucking believe the hot chick in our office is the Chief's daughter?"

"Kinda puts a little kink in your plan to get a piece of her action, eh Buddy?"

"No doubt! I like a nice piece of ass whenever I can get it. But Dude, I'm not stupid. I draw the line at nailing the boss' daughter."

"Wonder what Kev thinks?"

"He kept his cool, but it had to shock the shit out of him. Then the old guy tells him to get her that whiteboard and practically ordered him to take her with him. Man, I'd have freaked."

"Definitely puts a new spin on the situation."

"Hold that thought. I gotta make a call." Dave turned on the speakerphone. "Yeah Bailey, you son-of-a-bitch! Why didn't you tell me that our new consultant, Doctor Jessie Mitchell, was the fine and lovely Jess Mitchell?" Bailey's laughter echoed throughout the room. "I'm gonna kick your ass!"

"*Is she a dish or what?*"

"Yeah, or what! You know what else she is?"

"*No, what?*"

"She's Johansen's kid."

"*The hell you say?*"

"But you probably already knew that. Didn't you, ya bastard?"

"*Hell no, I didn't know the old guy had any kids.*"

"She's adopted or something."

"*Well shit, me and O'Reilly were just sitting here wishing we had her swing in our back yards, so much for that fantasy.*" He laughed again. "*Still, I'd love to have seen your faces.*"

"Yeah well, fuck you too!"

ೞೞೞ

"Burlington is really moving up in the world. This is nice," Jess said as they took their seats in a quiet corner. They perused the menus while waiting for their server.

"Is it? I don't know much about Italy, but they say everything is supposed to be authentic, including the staff." Jess was surprised to discover that her new partner was so cultured.

Just then, the waiter arrived and spoke in a thick Italian accent, "Hello, Signorina e Signore. My name is Antonio."

27

"Buon giorno, Antonio."

"May I tell you our specials for today?" He asked.

"Yes please, parlo Italiano se quello è più facile."

Kevin looked at Jess quizzically. "You speak Italian?"

"Si Signore," she replied with a wink.

"Wow."

"Molto buono, le odierne minestra è Minestrone Piemontese. L'insalata è verdi mescolati con il vinaigrette della casa.

"Okay, I'm feeling lucky," Kevin said, rubbing his hands together. "I'm gonna take a stab at it."

"This should be good," she teased.

"Minestrone." Jess nodded in agreement. "And then there was something about a green house." Kevin said, then looked at her and grinned. She laughed. "Or maybe not."

"I was impressed for a second there," she said, smiling then looked at Antonio. "Continui, per favore."

"Le odierne entrate sono bistecca cotta alla griglia di Nuovo York con la salsa di fungo e gambero scampi che Napoletana spaghettini eccessivo ha seguito da un dessert della crema di Amaretti con il biscotti della mandorla."

"*That* was a mouthful, something about New York and Napoleon, but I can't imagine what they have in common." Jess giggled again and translated the menu for her partner. Confirming her translation, Antonio left them to decide. "You're full of surprises. Anything else I should know?"

"Oh yeah, I meant to tell you earlier. I solved your case," she said in a serious tone.

"No shit? Oh sorry, jeez and just when I was starting to like the idea of having you around."

"No, not really." His choice of words suddenly dawned on her. "Really?"

"Yeah."

"It's a good thing this case is going to take a lot more work then, isn't it?"

"Yes Ma'am."

"I'll tell you this much. From what I've read so far, I believe you have two killers working independently of each other."

"Really? You got all that from half a day's studying notes?"

"'Fraid so." Antonio interrupted the conversation to take their order.

"See anything you like?" Kevin asked.

"I sure do," she said, looking directly at him. She paused for a moment, glancing back at the menu. Through the corner of her eye, she noticed him watching her intently. "I'd like il gambero scampi che Napolitano."

"An excellent choice Signorina," the waiter said. "And for Signore?"

"What she said."

"Si, I shall return shortly with bruschetta."

"Grazie."

"What's bruschetta?"

"That would be sliced and toasted Italian bread," she said, laughing. "You have been here before, right?"

"Yeah, but they always speak English. Why'd you learn Italian over something more useful like say, Spanish? Italian's not exactly common around here."

"I dunno. I took Latin in high school, so in college, Italian seemed like the logical leap...and I like the culture more."

Jess and Kevin lost track of the time as they talked and learned more about each other. They found that they had more in common than they had thought at first, especially their shared love of motorcycling.

CR80CR80

28

"Damn, they've been gone for nearly three hours. I wonder what's taking so long."

"Dude, you are entirely too nosy. You're like my mom. Don't you have something to do?" Brian asked.

"I can't help it. We've got this totally hot subbie profiler-chick working in our office who we thought was going to be a guy. Kev totally did not want SBI brought into his case, then the hot subbie turns out to be the Chief's kid and Kev's ordered to entertain her. Hell yeah, I wanna know what's going on!"

"It must be terrible having to amuse a pretty girl."

"Fuck off."

CKEOCKEO

"So how was it?"

"It was delicious. Thank you."

They arrived back at the substation at about four o'clock. Kevin held the door and followed behind Jess, again with his hand on the small of her back. An anxious David accosted them before the door was fully closed wanting to know what kept them. Kevin only threw his keys at the overly curious pair and sent them after the whiteboard while Jess retrieved her messages.

CKEOCKEO

"It's me. What are you gonna do, call me every hour? Come on, Nik," Jess teased.

"*I can't help it. Inquiring minds want to know. What the heck took ya so long to call me back?*"

"I just *got* back."

"*It took you three hours to go get a bulletin board?*"

"Whiteboard, and we went to lunch."

"*Whatever. His idea or yours?*"

"His."

"*Mmm hmm...is he still a jerk?*"

"Actually, he's quite pleasant."

"*Does he look as good up close as in the dream?*"

"Even better and you, you have the worst timing."

"*What are you talking about?*"

"He was getting all sweaty when you called me earlier today."

"*Oh? And what were you doing to cause that?*"

"Nothing, it's like a thousand degrees out today. I was just watching," Jess said, laughing.

"*Yeah? You got him all hot and bothered just from looking at him? I bet he'd spontaneously combust if you touched him.*"

"I *did* touch him, and he didn't explode."

"*No shit! And? Are you getting laid later or what?*"

"Oh please, it wasn't like that."

"*Well, that's not the way you made it sound.*"

"I was teasing. He *did* look good though, got my imagination going. Seriously, I rode with him to pick up a whiteboard for my office and I just watched him load it up."

"*And you didn't jump in there and help him?*"

"He wouldn't let me."

"*A gentleman...hmm...so get back to the touching, what happened?*"

"I wiped the sweat off his brow."

"*And?*"

"And what?"

"*How'd he react, you big dummy?*"

"He kinda shivered."

29

"*Nah, he's not interested,*" Niki said sarcastically.

"Please how do you get interest from a shiver?"

"*Damn, you're thick! Think about your reaction when Mr. Dream Cop frisked you.*"

"Oh yeah, but I wasn't trying to come onto him either."

"*That's even better. He'll think he's the one working you. Men like a good chase.*"

"I'm not working him."

"*Yeah, whatever, if you say so.*"

"Well look, I gotta go. I have lots of work to do, just didn't wanna leave ya hanging."

"*Mmm hmm, no doubt it's a tough assignment with so many distractions around there. Call me later.*"

"If I don't I'm sure I'll hear about it," she laughed.

"*You know it. Go save the world. Bye, Hun.*"

"Ciao."

☙❧◌ℭℜ℮ᴔ

As the first week came to a close, Jess and Kevin and had become more comfortable with each other. A loose sexual tension had developed and seemed to flow between them, though it had gone no further than a few brief, heated glances. They usually left the office by six each evening before the night shift reported for duty, but Friday was an exception. They were so deep into the case files, they paid no heed to the time. It was after midnight when Jess finally got home. The house was quiet and dimly lit. Dean had left dinner in the oven and a humorous note on the kitchen counter before going to bed.

> *Call Niki. She's maddening. I'm starting to think she may be related to Maggie. I told her last time that I was going to let the machine pick up if she called again. Someday soon, you must tell me what's going on in your life that's got her in such a tizzy. Sleep well. Love, Dean.*

"*Hello,*" a sleepy voice answered.

"Hey."

"*Hey, you hussy, I didn't think you were gonna call me.*"

"I just got home a few minutes ago. It's Friday night. What are you doing in bed so early? It's only 12:30. Are you sick?"

"*I was just tired. Burning the midnight oil are we?*"

"I do have a job, you know. We've been working."

"*We?*"

"Yes, me and Kevin."

"*Working huh? You and Kevin?*"

"Yeah, with the exception of lunch breaks."

"*You eat lunch together too?*"

"Every day."

"*When did that start?*"

"Um, last Friday...you knew we went out."

"*Yeah, but every day since?*"

"Yeah."

"*In or out?*"

"Out."

"*You move fast. Next thing you know it'll be dinner, dancing, and wild sex.*"

"It's not like that."

"*Please, he's a man isn't he? And you're a hot, unattached female. Where do you go?*"

"With the exception of last Friday, it's always a quickie."

"*Quickies are nice too. What was last Friday?*"

"We went to a nice Italian place."

"*Paolo's?!*"

"Yeah, you know the place?"

"*Yeah, that's a fancy joint. And you're just now telling me about this? I can't believe you!*"

"You didn't ask."

"*Well, how was it?*"

"It was great, a very nice restaurant."

"*Did you practice your French?*"

"I don't know French."

"*Yes Lord, she proves every single day that she's a natural blonde. I know you can't speak French, you dope.*"

"Oh that," Jess laughed. "No, I haven't kissed him. I hardly know him."

"*Oh no, Sweetie, you've known him for a while.*"

"Those were just dreams."

"*Just dreams. Yeah sure, I'll bet Kev wouldn't think they were just dreams.*"

"*Kev* isn't going to find out about my dreams, is he?"

"*So don't keep me in suspense. It's been a week. You should have an idea of what he's really like now?*"

"Well you already know that he started out a complete asshole, but I like him. He's quite pleasant to work with."

"*And to play with too?*"

"Not much playing goes on in a murder investigation."

"*Of course not, but you don't work all the time.*" Niki razzed her friend for several more minutes before Jess cut her off, though not before Niki made her promise to keep her updated.

Chapter 6

Early Saturday morning...

"Hello," Jess answered sleepily. It was 4:52 in the morning.

"Jess, it's Kevin. I know I probably woke you up and I apologize, but we've got another DB on campus." She sat up in bed, wide-awake in an instant. *"When can you be ready to go?"*

She shook off a yawn. "Um, fifteen minutes?"

"Perfect, I'll swing by and pick you up. See ya in a few."

"Okay bye. Hey, make sure nobody, including CSI, touches anything until I can have a look at the scene."

"Already got that covered."

"Okay great, see ya in a bit."

Jess got up and made a quick pass through the shower, dressed and piled her towel-dried hair into a plastic clip, then went downstairs to wait for Kevin. Dean was just rising. "You're up and ready to go awful early for a Saturday. Did I hear a telephone?"

"My cell, bad news. It was Detective Slater. Another body on campus. He's on his way to pick me up."

"This has got to stop!"

"I know." She looked out the window. "I think he's here. Gotta run," she called on her way out the front door. Kevin leaned over and opened the door for her to climb in. "Hey."

"Morning, wish I could say it was a good one, nothing like a corpse to drag you outta bed at five AM on a Saturday, eh."

"Yeah that," she said, fighting back a yawn and rubbing her eyes.

"I brought you some wake-up juice. Mountain Dew, right?"

"Thanks, an überjolt of caffeine is just what I need. So what do we know?"

"Not a hell of a lot, no ID yet." Kevin's cell phone interrupted them.

"Yeah, Slater."

"Sarge, it's Dave."

"What's up?"

"I had the luck of being first on the scene."

"I'm glad it was you. I know you'll keep everything secure until I get there. What's going on?"

"I knew this would piss you off, so I didn't use the radio. Sarge, the medical examiner is here, and the guy's being a real jerk. He's trying to bully me into letting him in." Rafferty's tone was curt and irritated. *"What should I tell him?"*

"Who is it?"

"Bob Morton."

A shadow of annoyance distorted Kevin's features. "I hate that son-of-a-bitch," he mumbled. "Tell him to go to hell," he shouted coldly. A muscle in his jaw twitched. "The girl is dead already so he can wait. Keep him and everybody else out of my scene. I'm less than five minutes away. Better yet, let me talk to him."

"Yeah, Slater, what do you want?"

"Morton, I'd better not find you contaminating my crime scene or I'll haul your ass to jail." His tone seethed with rancor.

"Yeah, yeah fine, just hurry up. I don't have all day."

"Hey Boss, it's me again."

"Yeah Dave, one more thing, keep the media out."

"Too late, they're already here."

"I don't give a rat's ass. Make sure they don't get anywhere near the body. The last thing I need is a pack of reporters trampling everything and putting her face all over the tube before *we* even know who she is."

"*Will do.*"

"I apologize. I don't usually speak French so fluently in front of ladies."

"Good thing he didn't radio you," Jess said with a muffled giggle. "So this Bob Morton is difficult? I don't believe I've had the pleasure of meeting him on a prior case."

"You haven't missed much," he replied sharply. "Sorry, I didn't mean to be an ass...again. I can't stand the guy. He thinks he's God."

"Heaven forbid, we can't have two of you, now can we?" She teased. The corners of his mouth and eyes crinkled slightly in a near smile, his annoyance at Bob Morton abating somewhat at her ribbing.

CR800380

"What do you think, Jess?"

"I think you'd better catch that one before he gets hurt." She nodded towards a rookie officer who had turned a sick shade of pale. Kevin caught him just before he hit the ground in a dead faint, then walked to the side to stand with Dave, who was chatting with several CSIs. Jess wrote some notes, made a quick sketch of the scene, and took some photos. "You can let forensics in now." Kevin motioned for the team to come in.

"Hey, what about me?" Bob Morton sauntered over and asked impatiently.

"What about you?" She asked crisply.

"I've got a job to do, lady," he ripped out impatiently. "Who the hell are you, anyway?"

Bob Morton was obviously perturbed that Jess had free reign while the police treated him like an intruder. Kevin and Dave, who were a dozen yards away, but still within earshot, took a couple steps towards them, then stopped and watched from the sidelines when it became apparent that their officemate was in control of the situation.

"I'm your worst fucking nightmare if you don't take a few steps back and wait until I let you in," she told him coolly, not trying to disguise her annoyance.

"You got a real mouth on you," he snapped mockingly.

"I'm a pretty good shot too, and I'm not going to let you or anybody else contaminate my crime scene. You wanna test me?"

"Since when did it become *your* crime scene?"

"I don't have to answer to you, Doctor Morton, but if you really *must* know, this became *my* crime scene when Chief Johansen contacted the SBI and specifically requested *my* assistance in this investigation."

"Lady..."

"Whoa, *Bob.* My name is *not* Lady. It's Jess Mitchell, *Doctor* Jess Mitchell, to be exact, and from this point on, you *will* refer to me as Doctor Mitchell. Got it?"

"Yeah whatever, *Doctor* Mitchell. I have to get a liver temp."

Damn, this guy was a nuisance! Kevin had not exaggerated a bit. Bob Morton had really started to piss Jess off. She walked towards him, backing the man up against the dormitory steps, and though she never touched him, he was clearly intimidated. He looked away as she glared at him.

"Listen, Buddy. I know how your job works. I may not be the ME, but I think can safely say that she is *not* gonna get up and run away. You can get your goddamn readings and determine TOD later. Now, get the hell out of my face before I move you myself." Jess turned on her heels without waiting for a response and returned to the body.

"Damn Sarge, did you see that?" Dave asked as he and Kevin joined her.

"Yeah, you handled that very well, Jess. I don't believe I've ever seen him slink away quite like that."

"Yeah Jess, that was awesome!" Dave added. "You're one tough cookie."

"God, I was such a shrew. I *really* don't like being nasty, but that guy was a jerk and about as pleasant as a swarm of mosquitoes." Both men cut loose with a round of hearty laughter as Jess looked beyond them. "The sun's coming up and we're getting more spectators."

"David, get Junior over there, now that he's awake again, and have him go with these campus cops to work crowd control." Kevin said. "Then I want to know all about her; who found her, who she is,

33

and who saw her last."

"Oh God, Debbie!"

"I think you just got the answer to at least one of those questions," Jess said, nodding towards the hysterical young man who had just exited the building.

"Whoa, hold up, amigo." Kevin grabbed the young man's arm. "Do you know her?" He asked.

"She's my girlfriend. I gotta go to her."

"You don't want to go see her right now. What's your name, Son?"

"Lance, Lance Ericson."

"I'm Detective Kevin Slater, and this is Doctor Jess Mitchell. Lance, what's your girlfriend's name?"

"Debbie err, Deborah Anderson. Is she gonna be okay?"

"No, Lance, I'm afraid not."

"She's dead. Isn't she?"

Kevin nodded. "I'm sorry."

"Oh God, oh no," he slumped down on the steps, covered his face with his hands, and sobbed. His misery was palpable. "I kept telling her not to go out by herself! Why the hell didn't she listen to me?"

Kevin questioned Lance about his and the girl's itineraries the day before to which the young man did his best at retracing their steps. He'd spent the night in Deborah's room so he'd be there to help her unpack when the movers came. That done, he went to football practice, after which the coach treated the team to dinner. It was late when he returned to his dorm room, so he called her and left a message when she didn't answer. He didn't know his girlfriend's plans, only that she was going out with some friends.

"Hey Sarge," Dave interrupted. "I got a girl over here who says she was with her last night."

"Okay Lance, thank you for your time. I'll be in touch."

"You're gonna catch this sick mutherfucker aren't you?"

"That's the plan, Lance. David, can you finish up with him?"

"Sure, Sarge."

"And see if he knows how I can contact her folks'."

"Will do, Sarge."

CR80CR80

Saturday afternoon...

"Damn!"

"What's wrong?"

"Look," Kevin said, pointing towards the television.

"We made the news?"

"I was hoping to keep our mugs off the tube."

CR80CR80

Ten more days went by. Kevin and Jess were still sorting through the mounds of reports and evidence from the string of homicides and relating better with each day. All the while, the sexual current that had been present between them from the start was growing. A day earlier, Mike Shelley had held a press conference, giving some details of the investigation, including their belief in two separate killers. The media wasted no time giving the pair nicknames, and very original ones at that.

"Headbanger, that one's right up your alley."

"A much different kind of head banging, I assure you. I'm surprised you noticed. I've been quite the redneck since I started this case."

"Jess, there's not a damn thing redneck about KISS," Kevin said, grinning.

"Well no, that's true. I'm surprised you know them."

"I have the CD you were listening to the other day."

"The MTV Unplugged album, it's my favorite. That's surprising. You don't seem like a big KISS

34

fan to me."

"My little sister, Samantha, is into that scene."

"I like her already."

"So tell me about these killers."

"Who do you want first?"

"Go with Mr. Clean. I got a feeling he's gonna be the tricky one."

"He's extremely smart. He covers his tracks well."

"I think I read somewhere, or maybe heard it in one of those seminars the Chief sends us to, that making the body presentable was a sign of remorse," Kevin stated.

"That's usually true, but that's not why Mr. Clean is doing it."

"I'm all ears."

"He's cleaning up behind himself. He doesn't feel an ounce of sorrow. He's thumbing his nose at us and saying, *Look what I did. Catch me if you can.*' If he were feeling regret, he'd leave obvious clues that would help us catch him quick."

"You think so?"

"Definitely. He may still do that, but it'll be after he escalates."

"Headbanger, well, you already know my opinion of him. He's just a serial rapist who goes a bit too far."

"Yeah."

"Hey Sarge, it's six o'clock, we're outta here," Dave called from the outer office.

"Yeah, okay guys, see you tomorrow."

"Bye Jess."

"Good night, Brian." That left Jess and Kevin completely alone in her office for some time.

"Do you know Gerald O'Reilly or Mark Jones?"

"I'm not sure. The names don't ring a bell."

"You haven't missed much. They're a lot like Brian and David."

"They sound like a handful."

"That's putting it mildly. We've been dodging them so far, but we may not be so lucky tonight. They'll be here shortly and then we get to replay the last two weeks.

"So, what's the problem?"

"The problem is that I've only just got Rafferty and McCaskell to settle down," Kevin said.

"Settle down from what?"

"Uh, they've just been hazing me is all, especially David."

"About the case again?"

"No."

"What about?"

"You don't wanna know."

"Sure I do. What are they hassling you about?"

He remained silent for a long moment before answering her. "You."

"Me? Why?"

"You...and all the hours we've been putting in together on this case. Think about it," he said. The innuendo behind his statement was impossible to miss.

"You're kidding."

"No, I'm not."

"They can't rag you if they can't see you." The tone of her reply was a bit more beguiling than she had intended, so she averted her gaze while she closed the door, then leaned against it and looked up at him demurely.

He gazed at her with a single raised eyebrow. "Are you sure that's a good idea?"

"Why wouldn't it be? You're not afraid of me, are you?" She teased, feeling a tad audacious.

"Jess, you scare the hell out of me."

"Oh." Missing the meaning of his words, she looked down, at once crestfallen, and twisted a strand of hair between her fingers, trying to swallow the lump that suddenly arose in her throat.

"Especially when you do that."

"Do what?"

She looked back up, expecting to be let down easily. Instead, he closed the distance between them and brushed her hair back from her face, and caressed her cheek with the back of his hand. Jess looked up into his eyes and smiled slightly.

"When you look at me like that...so tempting...God, I may be a fool, but I have the feeling that you've got no idea of the effect you're having on me, or any other man for that matter. You're so...It would be so easy for me to..." He trailed off and looked at her, unsure how to finish the thought.

"To what?"

"Forget I said that. I feel protective of you but at the same time I wanna just...God."

He crushed her body against his and wound his fingers through her hair, then leaned down and kissed her. It was a gentle, tender kiss. His tongue just did graze her bottom lip, just a taste. Though she battled the urge to wrap her arms around his neck, she didn't resist his advance, as common sense told her she should. The flirting was fun and sexual tension had left her with a more keen awareness of her femininity, but still Jess wasn't entirely sure she wanted to become involved with the sexy detective. Never mind that she'd had sworn off men, cops in particular. Her resolve was slipping fast, leaving her almost powerless to withstand Kevin's sensual assault. Neither trusted themselves to speak after he pulled back. Kevin's breathing was ragged and uneven, while Jess' heart did a flip-flop upon seeing the dark passion in his eyes.

After a moment of awkward silence he finally spoke. "I'm sorry, I shouldn't have done that."

"Why not?" She asked, perhaps a little too quickly.

"I don't want you to get the wrong idea."

"What idea would that be?"

"That I'm out to take advantage of you."

"Kevin, I don't think..."

"I was a creep and I'm sorry."

"There's really no need to apologize."

"Are you sure?" She nodded. "Look, it's getting late. I think maybe we should call it a night."

"Is that what you really want?"

"What I *really* want is to be off-duty and completely alone with you, but I'm afraid of what will happen."

"Really?"

"Oh yeah."

He caressed her cheek again then opened the door and escorted her into the main office where officers Gerald O'Reilly and Mark Jones were leaned back in their chairs. O'Reilly had his feet propped on the desk. Startled, the men jumped to their feet at once.

"Evening Sarge, I didn't know you were still here," Jones said.

"That much is obvious. Mark, Jerry how's it going, guys?"

"Hey Sarge, we had a couple calls at the beginning of the shift, but it's been pretty quiet since," O'Reilly stated.

"Usually is the middle of the week. You boys take it easy. We're outta here."

CSEOCREO

Mark looked at Gerald. "Who the heck was that? They looked mighty chummy."

"That, my friend, was Jess Mitchell."

"Jess Mitchell, name sounds familiar. Oh yeah, the hot subbie everybody's talking about!"

"Yeah, that's her. Is she a babe, or what?"

"Damn right! Must be nice, that asshole always gets the hot chicks."

"Trust me, Mark. He's got his hands full if he starts something with her."

"Why's that?"

36

"She's Johansen's kid."

"No shit?"

"I kid you not."

⋯⊗⋯⊗

"Oh my God, Niki, you're *not* going to believe it."

"*What?*"

"He kissed me."

"*He what?*"

"Did I stutter?"

"*Details, I need details.*"

"We were in the office late and he mentioned the guys coming in. I hadn't met them yet."

"*Yeah and?*"

"Apparently, David's been giving him a hard time about *me* since I started this assignment. Apparently, it's taken the last two weeks for Kevin to get him to stop the ribbing. Anyway, he said he dreaded going through all that again with these two guys...the ones I hadn't met yet."

"*So get to the kissing.*"

"So anyway, *I* started teasing him, told him they couldn't harass him if they couldn't see him. Then I shut the door."

"*Yeah and?*"

"And he asked me if that was a good idea. So I said something like *why not, unless you're scared of me.*"

"*What'd he say to that?*"

"He said I scared the hell out of him."

"*Whoa, that's heavy.*"

"Then he says '*especially when you do that.*'"

"*When you do what?*"

"Hell if I know. I was just leaning against the door."

"*You must have given him the look.*"

"What look?"

"*The one that got his juices going, all men have one.*"

"Evidently, he couldn't seem to complete a sentence, then he said I had no idea of the effect I was having on him. Then he walked over and took me in his arms, and kissed me."

"*Wow! So how was the kiss?*"

"Sweet, he has soft lips."

"*Sweet? He must be saving up the good stuff for later.*"

"If you say so."

"*What happened next?*"

"He suggested we call it a night and go home."

"*Bummer.*"

"But that's not all. I didn't exactly invite him for more, but I asked him if that's what he really wanted."

"*What'd he say?*"

"He said what he really wanted to do was be alone and off-duty with me, but he was afraid of what would happen if he were."

"*Oh cool! I bet he went straight home and whacked off. It's a shame you didn't stick around to give him a hand with that.*"

"Oh jeez Nik, you just *had* to go and make it all crude."

"*That's me all right, rude, crude, and debauched. No, seriously, he is into you.*"

"You think so?"

"*Hell yeah! If you'd stayed, somebody, meaning you, woulda got a little something-something.*"

Chapter 7

For two more weeks, the pair worked closely, *very* late on several evenings. Kevin didn't kiss Jess again, but his desire to was obvious. Their flirting was never-ending, and only served to prolong the inevitable, an accidental touch here, a steamy look there. He had begun driving her to the office every day unless she rode her bike. They lunched together every day and sometimes even had dinner before stopping for the day. Neither would admit it, but they used any excuse to be together just a little longer. Their mutual attraction was slowly overcoming them.

"Okay then, so now that we've thoroughly gone through these case files, do you have any theories on how to catch either of these crackpots?"

"Actually yes, I do have one, but I don't think you'll like it."

"Might as well let me have it." The phone in the outer office rang. "Hold that thought. Burlington Police Department, Slater speaking." He paused and listened for a moment. "Sure hold on. Coming in to you, Jess."

"Jess Mitchell."

"*Jess, Carl here. I thought you were gonna keep me updated.*"

She motioned for Kevin to come back inside. "Carl, great, I'm glad it's you. Actually, I was just getting ready to phone you so I could run a theory by you and Detective Slater. Do you mind if I put you on speaker so I only have to do this once?"

"*Nah, do it.*"

She hit the speaker button. "You there, Carl?"

"*Yeah, Sugar, go ahead.*" Kevin cocked an eyebrow at his partner.

"First of all, Carl, this is Detective Kevin Slater. Kevin, my boss, Carl Barnes."

"Good to meet you, Sir."

"*You too Detective. Okay Lulu, get with it.*"

Kevin flashed another curious smirk. "Tell ya later," she whispered. "Okay, with all the recent news coverage, everyone knows we have two perps. Carl, do you have my notes so you can follow?"

"*Yeah yeah, keep going, Sweetheart,*" he mimicked in a terrible Bogart impression. The trio spent several minutes going over the evidence before Carl grew impatient. "*Get with it, Doll. What's going on here?*" Carl asked.

"I want to make it clear that he's not into necrophilia. I believe he thinks that he's only knocked them unconscious."

"Why is that important?" Kevin asked.

"Because necrophilia is a very serious mental illness..."

"*...that would get him off on an insanity plea when he goes to trial.*"

"Exactly, Carl."

Jess took another twenty minutes to go over her assessment of the cases. She had to assure Carl that she would have the official profile ready in the next couple of days, before he was satisfied and ready to end the call.

"Seems like an interesting guy."

"He's an oddball. It's like having a second father constantly checking up on me."

"He's just looking out for you...Sugar," he teased.

Jess couldn't help but laugh. "You caught that?"

Nodding, he joined her in laughter. "It was hard to miss, along with Lulu, Doll, and Love."

"Let's not forget the God-awful Bogart impression."

"Oh no, of course not, Sweetheart, that guy's a trip."

"How well I know, but I can't fault him for caring, I guess."

"Nope, so back to our cases...what we need to concentrate on is finding connections between the other three victims."

"Assuming they exist, yes."

"So let's turn this board around and start over."

They worked tirelessly on the victimologies of Mr. Clean's casualties. Conversation flowed easily between them as they drew columns and pinned photographs, mostly about the case, but eventually their talk turned more personal when Kevin realized that he hadn't smoked a cigarette all day. Congratulating his strong will, Jess described her childhood and her long-time friendship with Niki. When prompted, she had no trouble revealing the loss of Dean's wife, JoAnna, from advanced ovarian cancer, and subsequently, her parents' tragic murders. Kevin understood, as nobody else did, her motivation for working in law enforcement, particularly her pursuit of the most deviant of criminals.

Jess had accomplished so many of her goals that Kevin was amazed to learn that she was only twenty-eight. He'd never heard of anyone starting college at the tender age of sixteen and then acing straight through graduate school. He admired her obvious intelligence and appreciated that her accomplishments hadn't made her arrogant. Jess found Kevin easy to talk to, but eventually, she grew uncomfortable in the spotlight and turned the topic back to him.

Kevin's youth was the opposite of hers. He grew up on a farm in a large, tight-knit family with both parents and grandparents. Like Jess, he'd been somewhat spoiled, but for different reasons. As the only son, he was beleaguered by three sisters. The youngest, and the one with whom Jess shared the most in common, worked as an assistant district attorney.

"All of my family is in Minnesota, except Sam. She lives in Wisconsin, just across the river from Minneapolis."

"Do you have children?"

"No and no ex-wives either, maybe one of these days..." Jess cocked a curious eyebrow at him. "Kids, I mean. I don't want an ex-wife. I hear too many bad things about 'em," he said with a chuckle.

"I hear that. Call me old-fashioned, but when I get married, I want it to last forever. Now tell me something I can't find out from a background check," she teased.

A peculiar expression came over him. "You ran a history on me?"

"I like to know a little something about a guy if I let him get close enough to kiss me. I hope you're not offended."

"It just proves, once again, how smart you are. Let's see...ah, how about this. I'm tri-lingual."

"Really? So does that mean you are fluent in three languages or that you'll try anything?" She joked, drawing a rowdy chuckle out of him.

"You're funny. Maybe a little of both," he teased in return. "Seriously, I learned some Spanish when I was in the army but really dove into it when I moved here, since it's pretty much required for police work these days. And I grew up in a bi-lingual household."

"You grew up so close to Canada, I'm thinking French."

"Nope, Norwegian."

"Norwegian? That's different."

"My Ma is Norwegian to the core. Most everybody from those parts has a little in them. She taught us all."

"I would have never guessed. You certainly don't resemble my mental image of a Scandinavian."

"What are we supposed to look like?"

"Well, I don't how accurate it is, but smaller, very fair, you know, with the light blonde hair and white skin, and blue eyes. I don't know where I got that from, Dean certainly doesn't look that way either."

"You're right, actually. My sisters and Ma all look the part. All I got was the light hair and even it's much darker than theirs. I took after my dad's family. You know, you could probably pass for a Viking wench."

"Wench, is it?" Jess tried to appear intimidating. "Looks can certainly be deceiving."

"Oohhh, I'm scared now. Honestly, just to look at you, I would have never thought you'd be intelligent and level-headed."

"Why's that?"

"Gorgeous women don't have to be, especially in the south. They can get whatever they want with their looks."

"Ouch! At least you didn't mention the bubble-headed-blonde syndrome, although to hear Niki tell it, I tend to go blonde without notice."

"Hey, I'm not knocking it. I've watched all three of my sisters use it to their advantage. Forgive me?"

"I dunno, maybe if you teach me some Norwegian."

"Sure, and maybe you'll hook me up with some Italian so I'll know what I'm ordering at Paolo's."

"Now who's being funny?" She tried to stifle a yawn. "Pardon me."

Kevin stared at her, then shook his head and let out an amused chuckle. "Yeah, I know I lead a dull life, nothing like catching serial killers for a living."

"Oh no, it's not that. Actually, I find you quite fascinating. It's that 4:30 wake-up call catching up to me."

"4:30? As in AM?" She nodded. "Why?"

"A rather interesting dream woke me up and I couldn't go back to sleep."

"Must have been some dream. What was it about?"

"I wish I could remember all the details. I just have a few flashes here and there," she fibbed. Jess was not about to tell Kevin that he was the leading man in that dream, and she certainly wasn't ready to give him the intimate details.

He looked at his watch. "Well it's late and you've only been up for eighteen hours. I should let you get home so you can get some rest, wouldn't want that fella, Carl, to come after me. Let's call it a day."

"If you insist."

"I could sit here all night, but *you* should get some sleep. Riding a motorcycle when you're tired is dangerous. Do you mind if I follow along to make sure you get home okay?"

"Not at all, thank you."

CB&ꝏCR&ꝏ

"*Hey Jess, what's up?*"

"Nothing, just figured I'd call you before you called me a dozen times."

"*Very funny, so how's our sexy dream cop?*"

"He's fine."

"*Just fine, have you fucked him yet?*"

"No!"

"*Has he kissed you again?*"

"No."

"*God Jess, you need to get off your ass and put a move on him before someone else does.*"

"We're getting to know each other slowly."

"*Too damn slow if you ask me. What do you know about him?*"

"Lots of stuff."

"*Like what?*"

"He's from Minnesota and he's been a cop for about fifteen years."

"*Holy shit! How old is he? You ain't getting a daddy complex, are you?*"

"Of course not, he's thirty-five, or will be in November."

"*You know his birthday too?*"

"I ran a background check on him."

"*No, you didn't!*"

"I did. I even told him so."

"*I bet that went over well!*"

"Actually, he said it was a sign of my superior intellect," Jess teased, using her most haughty tone of voice.

"*Oh please! Anyway that's perfect, makes him a Scorpio or Sagittarius. When's his birthday?*"

"November 11."

40

"*Ah, a Scorpio.*" Nikki seemed pleased with the information. "*Did you know Scorpio and Cancer are supposed to be soulmates?*"

"No, really?"

"*Yeah, what else?*"

"He has three sisters. His dad and granddad passed away several years ago, rest of the family is still in Minnesota."

"*That's a helluva lot of information for two people who aren't interested in each other. Anything else?*"

"Not really, wait, yeah there is. You'll like this part. He's tri-lingual."

"*Does that mean he'll try anything or that he speaks in tongues?*"

"That's exactly what I asked him," Jess said with a giggle. "He kidded around with me that it was a little of both, but seriously, he speaks in tongues."

"*I bet he'd speak to you with his tongue if you'd let him.*"

"Niki!"

"*What? Hey, Let's do lunch on Friday. I took the day off.*"

"You're gonna drive all the way from Raleigh just to eat lunch."

"*Yeah, and it's my treat.*"

"What are you gonna do?"

"*I'm gonna take my best friend out to lunch. Something wrong with that?*"

"No, but you're up to something."

"*Who me?*"

"What is it?"

"*Nothing, I swear, scout's honor.*"

"You were not a girl scout."

"*Okay fine, I can't stand it. The suspense is killing me. I wanna see Mr. Dream Cop for myself, you know, up close and personal.*"

"Oh no you don't."

"*Why not?*"

"'Cause you'll do something crazy."

"*I will not.*"

"Are you sure?"

"*Of course, I'm sure.*"

"You're not gonna embarrass me are you?"

"*Hell no,*" she scoffed. "*When have I ever embarrassed you?*"

"Um well, there was that time you..."

"*Don't answer that.*"

"So where do you wanna meet?"

"*At your office...where do you think?*"

"I dunno about that."

"*Tucker Street, right?*"

"You know where it is?"

"*Of course I do. Remember, I grew up just down the road.*"

"I meant the substation."

"*Yeah, it's in those apartments.*"

"You'd better be on your best behavior."

"*Cross my heart, hope to die.*"

"Let's hope not."

"*How's noon sound?*"

"Sounds fine, see you then."

"*Okay, I'll let you go to bed.*"

"Good night."

"*Lata Hun.*"

ଓଃ୫୦୦୪୫୦

The kiss, his fingertips burning at her lower back, those intense yellow eyes that seemed to look straight into her soul...all the time spent with her sexy dream cop was driving Jess mad. She was in a state of perpetual arousal. She knew she wouldn't be able to sleep, horny as she was, so she rifled through her nightstand until she located her vibrator. What a fine invention, she thought...Eight lifelike inches long, two inches thick, and with realistic-feeling skin. It even had balls and tiny vibrating beads across the top for added stimulation.

As she studied the toy, she finally admitted to herself that she had no intention of adhering to her '*no cops*' rule. Jess wanted Kevin Slater more than she had ever wanted any man. She had no idea how she'd go about it, but she intended to get him, one way or another.

"If the real Slater is half as good as you are, my little latex friend, you're looking at an early retirement."

Chapter 8

"Hey Jess, lemme know when you're ready to pick up again."

"What?" She looked up, jerked from her daydream. "Oh yeah, come on in anytime you're ready, Kevin."

He poured himself another cup of coffee, came in, and sat down. "Did I interrupt? I can come back later."

"No, you just busted me...daydreaming."

"Judging from your smile, it must have been a good one."

"Mmm yes, it was quite nice," she came back cryptically, leaving him to wonder. "So, where were we?"

"I've been thinking about the other night."

"Which part?"

"Something you said about getting into the victims' heads."

"Oh yes."

"How do you do that with a corpse?"

"Through the people they knew and by studying tangible objects. We have to analyze every aspect of their lives under a microscope starting with their family, then friends, way beyond what's in the reports."

"What do you mean *beyond what's in the reports*?"

"It's more than just marital, employment, or even criminal history. We're looking for what she did with the rest of her time. Where'd she go? What'd she do? Who'd she do it with? Inclinations and aversions. And if the next of kin permit, I like to dig through the victim's personal belongings."

"It sounds like we're putting the victim on trial."

"In a way we are, only *my* notes never become public record."

"That's going to get a little dicey. What if there's opposition?"

"Yes, it's dicey and very personal, more than you can possibly imagine, but if these folks want justice, they'll have to let us do our job."

"What do you mean *more personal than I can imagine*?"

"We could stumble upon something that won't paint the victims in a favorable light. Simply put, these aren't your average murders. They're sex crimes. I haven't figured out sexual element yet, but it's there. The COD plays a big part. Serial killers get off on killing...literally...the ultimate power trip, control over life and death, if you will. In some cases, they can't become aroused at all and if they do, they can't have an orgasm without killing or without at least mentally reliving a past event. I guess you could call it a paraphilia in its most extreme form."

"Paraphilia?"

"An obligatory fantasy or stimulus necessary for sexual arousal or activity."

"Now in English."

"Whatever it takes to get off, a fetish taken to the extreme." Kevin shuddered visibly. "Yeah, and there's a reason Mr. Clean selected these particular women, and since it's not something obvious like a physical trait, I think it must be something lifestyle related. But in order to find out, I need to dig into the victims' personal histories, especially their sexual practices."

"Won't be easy, especially if we find out something their families may not wanna hear. Tell you what, since these folks already know me, they may be more open to the idea if it comes from me."

"I agree."

"I'll start making calls and try to get this ball rolling. When do you want to start?"

"As soon as possible."

Later that same day...

"Hey Jess, Aggaline Phillips and Stan Rigsbee are ready for us right now. They're willing to do anything to help find this guy. You got time to go over and see them?"

"Let's go."

Susan Huffman's mother lived just a few miles away, so they arrived in minutes. They made the required small talk before following the woman to a small bedroom at the back of the residence. As soon as she left, Kevin and Jess went to work sifting through several boxes of items. After an hour with no luck, Jess quit with her clothes.

"Kevin have you seen a jewelry box or photo album, anything like that?"

"I think so." He looked around the room for a minute. "Here."

"Perfect, a woman's taste in jewelry says a lot about her personality."

"I never really thought about it beyond the diamond speech that's drilled into every boy after birth," he commented dryly.

"Hey, look at this."

"It's a necklace."

"Recognize it?"

"No, should I?"

"I've seen this before." She flipped through her notebook. "Aha, the little charm is the same symbol in one of Diana Rigsbee's tattoos."

"It is?" He studied it for a moment. "Looks like a yin yang."

"Close, but a yin yang has only two sections. This has three."

"What is it then?"

"I'm not sure, but you can bet I'm going to find out. With any luck, it'll lead to the connection we need. I wonder if Mrs. Phillips will let us take this."

"Only one way to find out, let's go ask." The walked back out into the living room. "Mrs. Phillips, Jess found a necklace and we're wondering where your daughter may have acquired it or if you know what the symbol means."

The woman studied the necklace, shaking her head. "I have no idea. Is it important?"

"We're not sure. But it's a very interesting piece, and we'd like to find out how your daughter came by it. Can we take this back to headquarters for a while? I promise, it'll be returned."

"Take it, and anything else that might help catch the monster that killed my girl."

"Mrs. Phillips, there's no mention of a boyfriend or significant other in our reports. Was your daughter seeing anybody?"

"I don't know. Susie was very secretive about her personal life. She probably wouldn't have told me about a man."

"Thank you, Mrs. Phillips. If you think of anything at all that might be helpful, please call me."

C3ED3OCR80

Next, they drove to Rigsbee house. Along the way, Jess took another look at the crime scene photos. "Hey Kev, what caused all the little bruises on these women?"

"Don't know. Bob said it looked like someone had shot marbles at them."

"This is the weirdest case."

"We're here, but don't get your hopes on a long conversation. He'll let you dig through her stuff for as long as you want, but I doubt he'll talk much."

Kevin escorted Jess up the walkway. Diana Rigsbee's father answered the door, and as Kevin had predicted, avoided talking, opting instead to give them the key to his daughter's place. Jess followed Kevin to an apartment over the detached garage.

"He's not dealing very well, is he?"

"No, it was just the two of them, kinda like you and the Chief."

"Poor man, he's lost his only connection in the world. Whoa, look at this place. This girl was a real

44

piece of work." She pulled out a camera and started snapping photos. "I kinda figured she was into the Goth scene from her appearance, but this is unreal."

"She was popular with the ravers too. She had a record, minor drug charges for X and pot. I think there was one on her juvie record for speed, but nothing real serious."

"Judging from her décor, I think the best thing about Diana Rigsbee was her taste in music."

Kevin picked up a CD, and upon doing so, learned another interesting tidbit about the woman who drew him as no other ever had. It seemed that Jess had a more eclectic taste in music than he'd realized. She raved over *Type O Negative* and *Marilyn Manson* while shooting down their contemporary, *Nine Inch Nails.* He set the discs aside and grinned, shaking his head when she offered, or rather threatened, to play them for him. While Kevin got a lesson in music culture, Jess looked through Diana's closet, medicine cabinet, and other personal items but didn't find anything out of the ordinary until she got to the woman's dresser.

"Hey, look at this."

"It's a dog collar."

"Did she have a dog?"

"No."

"Any history of a dog?"

"None that I know of."

"Hmmm, this along with her taste in clothing and music is making me uneasy, but I think I've seen enough. Let's lock this place up and go back to the office."

"Are you sure you want to keep working? It's seven o'clock."

"You can drop me back at the office and go on home if you want, but I'll never go to sleep if I don't at least *try* to figure out what that symbol is."

"No can do, remember, I brought you to work today, so you'll need a ride home. Besides, we're in this together, so I'm staying as long as it takes."

Kevin's large frame was stretched out on the tiny sofa across from Jess' desk in a position she imagined couldn't be very comfortable. He had drifted off into a light doze with his arms crossed over his massive chest with one long leg sprawled out to the side and the other hanging over the arm when Jess' outburst woke him.

"Hot damn!" Jess looked up at the clock, 11:37.

"What!" He sat up abruptly. "What is it?"

"I've found it."

"Found what?"

"The symbol from the tattoo and necklace."

"Great!" In seconds, he was by her side staring at the image on the monitor. "What is it?"

"It's the logo for the BDSM community."

"Excuse me? BDSM? What's that?"

She navigated back to the site homepage. "Bondage, domination, and sadomasochism, it's a lifestyle with quite a large following, judging from the wealth of information that's available here."

"That sounds scary. So tell me about the BDSM lifestyle and how does it apply to this investigation?"

"I can't believe I didn't think of this the other day when you mentioned Gacy."

"Okay, you just lost me."

"Gacy selected his victims based on *lifestyle*, not looks. This necklace represents a *lifestyle.* It's the common denominator, Love. Bondage is self-explanatory. Domination, you know what a dominatrix is?"

"Yeah, the whip-wielding, little hottie in the vinyl bikini and thigh-high boots."

Jess found his description humorous. "Yeah, that's the stereotypical model, and every man's fantasy," she added with a wink.

"Not *this* man's fantasy."

"And what would *this* man's fantasy be?"

"You first," he shot back with an impish twinkle in his eyes, leaving Jess momentarily stunned. Unsure how to respond, she changed the subject by broadening her assessment of BDSM.

"Her male counterpart is a Dom. Their roles are those of Master or Mistress; says here that they control the lives of their slaves or submissive partners to various degrees. They give orders, reward, and punishment as they see fit. In some cases, they plan their partner's entire life down to the minute. As for the SM part, you can figure that part out."

"I'm almost afraid to ask how you know so much about this."

"Sweetie, I get paid to know these things."

"Okay, now you're scaring me."

"Don't worry, Hun, I won't be cracking my whip at you anytime soon," she teased. "Seriously though, this is the first time I've ever seen this stuff. I thought folks into this kinda thing were just kinky." On that note, she closed her eyes and stretched.

"Whoa."

"What?"

"Nothing," he said quickly, almost too quickly, and there was an odd gleam in his eyes.

"And this dog collar, I don't think it was for a dog at all. I think she may have been *collared* by someone at some point or wanted to be."

"Collared?"

"By her Dom." Kevin looked at Jess inquisitively. "Did you ever give a girl your class ring when you were in high school?"

"Yeah."

"Same idea."

"That's interesting." He looked thoughtful again for a moment. "This is great! I think. Is this the break we've been looking for?"

"It could be. But before we go drawing conclusions, we need to really dig into the backgrounds of the other victims to see if they also had a similar interest in this sorta thing."

"You are brilliant."

Kevin became so caught up in the discovery that he swung Jess off her feet and kissed her full on the lips, not a romantic kiss, but still a kiss. He quickly set her back on the floor and pulled back, surprised at his own reaction almost as much as she was, but then he looked at her for a response. Jess touched her fingers to her mouth, then licked her lips. It was the only encouragement that Kevin needed.

Again, he pulled her against his hard body, cupped her face in his hands, and kissed her, this time in slow motion. Jess was frozen. She could only wait for his lips to meet hers in a burning kiss, and she wasn't disappointed. The tip of his tongue brushed her bottom lip then darted into her open mouth, grazing her teeth. His moist, firm mouth demanded a response. Jess hesitated only for a split-second, then wrapped her arms around his neck and returned his kiss with equal abandon, sucking his tongue, biting his lower lip.

"Mmm," she moaned.

Her knees grew weak when his lips left hers to nibble at her earlobe. A moment later, they seared a fiery trail down her neck and shoulder. His confidence bolstered, Kevin closed a hand over her breast and kneaded it while he opened the first few buttons of her shirt with the other. Then those same large hands began a lusty exploration of the soft lines of her back, waist, and hips, finally pulling her curves neatly against his own hard contours. Jess became consciously aware of the rigid hardness pressing against her belly, but when she reached to caress his back he pulled away, leaving her taken aback.

"Jess." They were both breathless. Their desire for each other was all consuming. "Jess, I can't do this."

"Kevin, why not? Did I do something wrong?"

"No, Jess...You're perfect, but Honey, you're too damn special for this to happen...like this, not here. I just don't know how much more of this I can take. I want you so bad."

"I want you too."

"Not like this, not with you."

"Kevin please..."

He put a finger to her lips. "Shhh, it has to be right." Shamed by her wanton behavior, Jess lowered her gaze to the open buttons of her shirt and watched Kevin refastened them. "Come on. We've done enough work tonight. Let's go get something to eat and I'll take you back home before I remember how much I hate taking cold showers and change my mind."

⊂ঙ৺⊂ঙ৺

Jess awoke once again to images of her dream cop taking her by the roadside. But this time, she saw his face in vivid detail. It was the face of Detective Kevin Slater, and he had her spread against a familiar C.O.P.S. truck rather than the squad car from previous dreams. She was wound so tight she reached between her legs and worked two fingers against her mound until she came.

"God, it's been weeks already. I gotta stop waking up like this."

She climbed out of bed, stretched like a cat and looked at the clock, 6:30...early, but better than 4:30. After selecting the day's attire, her usual snug-fitting jeans, and trademark white shirt, paired with a bra and matching panties of dark purple lace, Jess jumped in the shower. She towel-dried her thick hair and applied a trace of make-up before heading downstairs to begin the day. Dean was preparing breakfast in his usual fashion.

"Well, hello there. Sleeping in today?"

"I guess so," she said, stifling a yawn. "I got in bed kinda late last night."

"I really appreciate how hard you're working on this assignment, but you should take a break."

"I know, but I'm on a roll now and it's hard to stop. It was late when Kevin and I left the office, but we made a connection between at least two of Mr. Clean's victims."

"Splendid! What's the word?"

"It's very risqué and a long story, so let me finish interviewing the other families today before I get into it. I promise. We'll get together this afternoon and I'll fill you in, if you have time."

"Terrific, I'll have Maggie clear my calendar."

"I've also got a theory on Headbanger, and if it turns out to be what I think, we should be able to catch him fairly quickly. In the meantime, you should think about putting together a task force for a sting."

"I'll get together with Mike when I get to the office. So, you and Slater are getting along." She nodded. "I was a little concerned you might clash at first. I like Slater, but you both can be very headstrong individuals."

"No, he's fine. Though I admit, I didn't like him much when I first met him, but we get along great now that we've gotten to know each other a little better."

"That's great to hear, Honey."

"Don't you go getting ideas."

"What ideas?"

"Like playing Cupid, I know how you get, especially if you spend too much time with Maggie."

"I gave up on that. You'll settle down when you're good and ready, and not a moment sooner, but I can still hope. Can't I?"

"Thank you, and of course, you can hope," She replied with a grin. "Hey, guess what? We're having company today."

"Really? Who?"

"Niki's taking me to lunch, but I think she's up to something."

"I hope you'll stop in with her and say hello."

"I'm sure she'll want to see you too. Kevin's here. I gotta go. I've got a couple bad guys to help catch."

"Okay here, eat something," he called after her, tossing a muffin.

"Thanks, see you later. Bye!"

Chapter 9

"Morning, Jess."

"Good morning, Dave."

"I just made a fresh pot of coffee if you want some."

"No thanks, I take my caffeine in a different form," she said, holding up a half-finished Mountain Dew that Kevin had brought her.

"Whatever works." A half hour later, Dave hailed Kevin in his usual, juvenile style. "Well, would ya look what the cat dragged in so early in the morning."

"Suck me, Dave," he said, grabbing his crotch. He peeked into Jess' office upon hearing her giggle at their banter. "D'oh sorry Jess, you weren't supposed to hear that."

"Not a problem guys, I've certainly heard much worse. Dave, Kevin dropped me off and then took the truck to be serviced."

"Mmm hmm, but what about every other day he's been in here early. You know, Jess, it's funny. He never used to roll up in here until around nine or ten, and sometimes, he wasn't in here at all when he was working a big case."

"I'm trying to change my evil ways. Gimme a break."

"Evil ways, my ass, it's not even eight o'clock yet. Why are you *really* in here so early?"

"I dunno, change of scenery?"

"I'll bet, but I don't blame you. The scenery is, without a doubt, a lot nicer these days, and smells better too."

"Whatever, hey Jess, where are we going for lunch today? I'm starving. I shouldn't have skipped breakfast."

"I can't do lunch today. I have a date."

"You do? Oh, okay." He retreated to his office, disappointed but curious.

11:45 AM

"Can I help you, Ma'am?"

"Hey Handsome, what's your name?"

"Uh Brian, Ma'am, Brian McCaskell."

"I've talked to you before. I'm Niki Shannon. I'm meeting Jess for lunch today. Is she available?"

"Yes Ma'am."

"In here Nik, you're a little early. Give me a few minutes to wrap up."

"Sure Jess...You're packing heat."

"Uh yeah, I'm at work. You sound like Dean."

"We're just not used to seeing you in your official capacity." Niki followed Jess into her office and sat down. "So where's he at?"

"Where's who at?"

"Where's who at, sexy dream cop, of course. Who do you think?"

"Shhh," Jess said, nodding towards the open door as Kevin walked through it.

"Hey Jess, I've talked to all but..." He looked up and saw Niki. "Oh sorry, didn't mean to interrupt. I'll come back later."

"No Kevin, come on in. You've heard enough about her, so you may as well be introduced...my best friend, Niki Shannon. Niki, Detective Kevin Slater."

Niki gave him a thorough once-over. "Charmed, I'm sure," she said, holding out her hand.

"Ah, the famous Niki...your lunch date?" He inquired, suddenly in a very good mood when Jess nodded. "Good to meet you Niki, I've heard a lot about you."

"All bad, I'm sure."

"Nah."

"Kevin, may I call you Kevin?" He nodded. "We were just heading out to lunch. Care to join us?"

"As much as I'd love to be seen with a beautiful woman on each arm, I'm gonna have to turn down that offer. You ladies may have things to discuss that I have no business hearing," he said with a sly smile.

"I beg to differ. I think you'd find my recent conversations with Jess absolutely riveting," Niki said to him while casting a cunning coup d'oeil at her friend. "I know I have, and it takes a lot to rivet me. In fact, Jess has had some very provocative..."

Jess cleared her throat rather loudly. "Niki, we need to get out of here. I still have a lot of work to do." She rose and motioned towards the door.

"Oh yeah, okay."

"You ladies have a good lunch." Kevin flashed them a boyish grin and held the door open.

"Want us to bring you back something?"

"No, but thanks, I'm on my way out. I'll grab something before I come back."

"Okay."

Dave was on his way inside when the women walked out. "Well hello, Hot Stuff," Niki said to him.

"Hello yourself." He turned and watched them drive off.

"I'm gonna kill you, Niki."

She laughed. "No you're not. You love me too much."

૭৪৩৩৪৩

"Who was *that?*" Dave asked as he came inside and pushed past Kevin.

"That was Jess' friend, Niki," Brian replied.

"Oh yeah, the one who calls here all the time. Hello Mama! Kev, you can have Jess, just send the feisty redhead my way."

"Feisty, eh?"

"Yeah, didn't you hear? She called me *Hot Stuff.*"

"Poor woman, she's obviously blind. And what do you mean, I can have Jess?"

"Everybody knows you two got a thing for each other."

"Everybody who?"

"The whole PD, Bro."

"What are you talking about?"

"Come on man, you two have gotten *real* chummy. She's even got you coming in early."

"And your point is?"

"And you take her out to lunch every day and work late just about every night."

"Dave, you're making too much of this. Jess and I are working on a case together and we're friends."

"Just friends, huh?"

"Yeah, we decided the first day that it would be a lot easier to do our jobs if we got along. Don't you agree?"

"Well sure, but are pet names necessary? Hell, she calls you Kev all the time now instead of the icy *Detective.*"

"So do you and Brian, but nobody's accused me of having the hots for either of *you.*"

"Why would anybody do that? We don't have long, blonde hair, big hooters, and the best looking ass in the city." Brian sat back and watched their exchange with a silent smirk. "Lots of late hours too, *and* behind closed doors at that. What do you wanna bet, Brian, that more than police work is going on in there, maybe a *lot* more."

"Dude, I'm staying out of this one," Brian said.

"Knock it off, David. I never kiss and tell, *and* what I do or don't do with Jess is none of your damn business."

"Kiss and tell? I knew it."

"Knew what?"

"Hey, I ain't nothing but jealous. You banging her too?"

49

"David, this is getting old. No, I'm not *banging* her."

"Yet."

"And if I were, I'd sure as hell pick a lot nicer place to do it than here; especially with you two creeps hanging around. She's too classy for that."

"What time did y'all leave here last night?"

"What are you now, my mother?"

"Humor me."

"I dunno, around midnight, I think. We got a bite. I took her home, then went home myself."

"That's another thing, you bring her to work now and take her home damn near every day."

"Yeah, and I make sure she gets home okay when she rides the bike. So, what of it?"

"You follow her home too? Shit, this is more serious than I thought. When's the wedding?"

"Oh man, now you're *really* blowing this *way* out of proportion."

"Am I? A blind man could see it."

"See what? I'm just making sure she gets home safe. This ain't exactly the nicest part of town for a good-looking, white woman to be driving around after dark."

"Are you an official item yet?"

"What?"

"Is she free to go out with anybody else?"

"Jess is free to do whatever she wants. Why?"

"'Cause if you don't hurry up and decide whether or not you want her, I'm gonna ask her out. And there's a long line of guys waiting behind me."

"Well, you can tell that line of guys that she's not available, and that goes *double* for *you*, Rafferty. Now, what's it gonna take to get you off my ass?"

"You could put in a good word for me with that cute, little redhead that just walked outta here."

"I'll see what I can do."

CRITICAL

"You still dreaming about him?"

"I plead the fifth."

"Don't give me that cop talk." Jess only grinned at her friend. "I'll take that as a yes. Jess, he's babelicious! Your description didn't do him justice." Niki studied her for a moment. "What's that look about?"

"What look?"

"Something happened."

"What are you talking about?"

"I dunno exactly, then there's the way he looked at you when you introduced us. It was weird."

"How's that?"

"I dunno, like he got the lead in a Rolaids commercial. You know, how do you spell relief."

"Oh that? He wanted to take me out to lunch today. I think he was a little disappointed when I told him I already had a date."

"And you conveniently left out that it was with me?" Jess nodded. "I thought you weren't interested in him."

"I guess I wanted to see how he'd react."

"So when are you two gonna go out on a *real* date?"

"Who said anything about dating?"

"I did. So when?"

"I dunno."

"But you *do* like him too? What am I thinking? Of course, you do, else you wouldn't be dreaming about him every damn night."

"I didn't say that. And what do you mean, too?"

"It's obvious to anybody with eyes that he's got it bad for you. Shit, all three of them have it bad for you."

"Why do you say that?"

"Well, the one at the desk, Brian, went all moon-eyed when I said your name. He kinda reminded me of a cute puppy. The one we ran into at the door...what's his name by the way?"

"That's David Rafferty."

"David, he's a horndog. Nothing against you, but he'd probably chase anything in a skirt. My kinda man, no strings. Of course he's not bad himself."

"I don't even want to know how you know that."

"And your sexy dream cop? Well, if I were to describe in a word the looks he gave you, it'd be hungry."

"Well, it was lunchtime. He probably *was* hungry."

"You can be *so* fucking blonde sometimes. He looked like he could eat you alive, and I ain't talking about any bad kind of eating either."

"Hmm well, you're the expert."

"Of course, I am."

"How can you possibly eat *and* talk so much at the same time?"

"Oh yeah, you're a real comedian, aren't you?"

"I try."

"Don't give up your day job. Seriously though, there's something else going on. You're starry-eyed. You got laid, didn't you?"

"No!"

"Well, what's that gleam all about then?"

"I could have gotten laid."

"With Kevin?"

"Who else?"

"Well, why didn't you?"

"It wasn't for lack of an invitation on my part. I made it crystal clear that he could have me."

"Damn, why'd you stop?"

"I didn't, he did."

"No shit! That guy must be a masochist 'cause we know he's not married and he sure as hell ain't gay. What happened?"

"You know we've been working late most nights on this case."

"Right."

"Well, last night I made a connection we've been looking for and when I showed him, he picked me up slam off the floor and kissed me real quick."

"That's all? Boy, your version of almost laid and mine are completely different. Mine includes shedding some clothes."

"There's more. When he put me back down, he just looked at me."

"So what'd you do?"

"I licked my lips."

"Hallelujah!" She shouted skyward. "That *Cosmo* subscription is finally paying off. I bet that tore him up."

"He kissed me again. And, oh my God..."

"Really? So he's a good kisser?"

"Oh yes, he puts his whole body into it. It was a toe-curling, Clark Gable kind of kiss, like you see in the movies."

"I bet he puts his whole body into fucking too," Niki said with a wink.

"You're awful."

"I know. What else?"

"Well, I was so into it, I didn't realize that he'd unbuttoned my shirt."

Niki's eyes grew wide. "And?"

"And then he stopped."

"Damn!"

"Believe me, short of begging, I tried to get him to keep going, but he just refastened my shirt."

"What the hell was up with that?"

"He said he didn't want it to happen like that, not there in the office."

"Oh gee, how fucking noble," she said acerbically.

"I thought it was kinda sweet, especially when he said that I was, and I quote, *just too damn special for that.*"

"He told you that?"

"Yes!"

"Damn, he's got it bad. This is worse than I thought. Ya know, it may be a good thing you *didn't* jump his bones as soon as you met."

"Of course it's a good thing," Jess said. "That's your style," she added, laughing.

"No seriously, you're really building the sexual tension. And when you two finally get it on...mmm, and you think his kiss made your knees weak. Which brings me back to my original question, *when* are you two gonna get together outside of all this police business?"

"I dunno. He hasn't asked me."

"So get with the twenty-first century, Woman, and ask *him.*"

"You know I don't do that."

"Yeah, and you've spent a bunch of Saturday nights at home alone too, not to mention the two losers you *did* end up with."

"Jake wasn't a loser."

"Okay, I'll give you that one since I hardly knew Jake, but Billy sure as hell was and still *is* a loser. That's part of your problem. You're too damn picky and the ones you *do* pick suck."

"You *used* to like Billy...sorta, and you're the one who still talks to him."

"I never liked that motherfucker, especially after he started treating you like shit. I only put up with him because *you* loved him. Sure, he has a rockin' body, but he's got about as much personality as an earthworm. And I don't talk to him. *He* runs *me* down to ask about *you.* Remember, I told him to go take a flying leap. Sometimes I'm amazed you're not still a virgin."

"Gee, thanks." Jess pondered everything Niki had said, then changed the subject. "Hey, are you going home from here or are you staying for the weekend?"

"I haven't decided yet. You gonna make it worth my while if I stay?"

"How?"

"Set up a double-date."

"For who, or need I ask?"

"You and your sexy dream cop with me and David."

"You're not serious?"

"Do I look like I'm kidding?"

"Nik, I don't ask guys out."

"How about if I do it for you?"

"No!"

"Okay fine, I won't push it...for now. Give Horndog my number."

"You really wanna go out with him?"

"I'm not ready to settle down, so your dream man is out, and Moon-Eyes would have a heart attack if I put a move on him. That leaves David, who's hot *and* looks like he knows how to show a girl a good time."

"I'll see what I can do."

CRSOCRSO

Jess was working on the profile for Headbanger when David returned from lunch. "Hey Hor...Dave, come here when you get a minute."

"Sure, what's up, Jess?"

"What'd you think of my friend, Niki?"

"You need to bring her around more often. She's a real hot tamale. Why?"

"I'm glad you think so." Jess slipped a scrap of paper into his hand.

"What's this?" He opened it and read aloud. "*Call me?*"

"That's her cell."

"Cool! When should I call her?"

"What's wrong with right now?"

"Isn't that too soon?"

"With Niki, there's no such thing as too soon. In fact, I think she'd be disappointed if you *didn't* call right away."

"Woohoo, hot damn!" He started out the door, but then turned around. "Hey, Jess?"

"Yeah?"

"Thanks."

"Anytime." She winked at him as he left, then she picked up the receiver and dialed Niki. "*Hello?*"

"It's me. Looks like you have a date tonight, better dress real nice."

"*What are you talking about, Jess?*"

"I gave Dave your number just like you wanted. He was very excited."

"*Really? What'd he say?*"

"I think you made him hungry. He says you're a hot tamale, wink wink."

"*Well, hot damn!*"

"I believe those were his exact words too. I'm pretty sure he's gonna call you today, probably any minute."

"*Already?*"

"That's my fault. I told him you'd be disappointed if he didn't call you right away."

"*Oh shit, I have to go shopping. Thanks for the heads up. Hey, I got a call coming in. Maybe it's him. Talk to you later.*"

CRSOCRSO

"*I know you like her,*" Niki said.

"And what would give you that idea? Can you hold on a second, Mrs. Jones?"

"*Uh, yeah?*"

"Hey, Kev? Oh sorry, can you come see me when you're done?"

"Sure Jess, be right there. Lemme finish up here. I'm sorry for the interruption, please continue."

"*Mrs. Jones? That was original.*"

"I could tell her who I'm really talking to."

"*Hell no, she'd kill me! As I was saying, I know you're attracted to her and I guarantee the feeling is mutual.*"

"And you know this based on?"

"*Come on, Detective. We've been best friends for fifteen years. You think I wouldn't know if she's into somebody?*"

"I didn't think about that."

"*Of course not, you're a man so you're forgiven. But that's as far as it will ever go unless you make the first move. She's not the forward type.*"

"What type is she?"

"*She's wonderful, loving, and loyal to a fault once you earn her trust.*"

"Why are you telling me this?"

"*Don't interrupt, just listen.*"

"Yes Ma'am."

"*Let me tell you a few things about Jess. Most people don't know it, but Jess Mitchell is a hopeless romantic.*"

"I kinda had that figured out on my own."

"*Good, now let me finish. Unfortunately, that's left her wide open to predators in the past. She's got the biggest heart of anyone I know, but she's a little short on experience in the romance department.*"

"This line of work doesn't leave much room for relationships. But inexperienced?"

"*She let's very few people get that close.*"

"Come on. There must be a line of guys a mile long waiting for her to just smile at them."

"*Of course there is. Hell, you got at least two of them right there in your office, but she doesn't want any of them.*"

"What does she want?"

"*She wants you, Dammit, but you have to make the first move, assuming you like her as much as I think you do.*"

"Why?"

"*Because she's not going to.*"

"Why not?"

"*I already told you she not that type. She's bashful.*"

"Gimme a break! Bashful? I've seen her at work. She's far from a shrinking violet."

"*With everybody else, but not with someone she's attracted to. Maybe bashful wasn't the right word. How about selective?*" Niki didn't wait for his response. "*And she's skittish, especially with guys who are cops.*"

"What's wrong with cops?"

"*Nothing, if you ask me. I think cops are sexy, but she's only been in two relationships her entire adult life, both with cops.*"

"Oh."

"The first one was when she was in California. He was okay, one of the few good ones with the LAPD. I didn't really know him. The break-up was amicable. She was graduating and he wasn't interested in moving to North Carolina, but that next one. God, he was a real winner...sorry son-of-a-bitch. She hasn't gone out with anybody since they broke up, well over a year ago, and it's not that she hasn't had plenty of attractive, eligible men vying for her attention. But her ex really did a number on her. When he wasn't being a perfect asshole, he was out chasing other women and running with the boys, so there's her experience."

"You're handing out a lot of personal information to someone you don't even know. For all you know I could be a real asshole outside this office."

"*I highly doubt that. Besides, you might be surprised at how much I know about you.*"

"What's that supposed to mean, and why are you so sure she wants me?"

"*Come on, Detective. You're a smart guy. What I just told you should clue you in to the fact that she doesn't play kissyface with just anyone.*"

"She told you about that?"

"*Yeah...after I dragged it out of her.*"

"What else did she tell you?"

"*There hasn't been anything to tell yet. Has there?*"

"I don't kiss and tell."

"*Of course you don't, which means you're a gentleman, not an asshole.*"

"You still haven't told me why you're doing this."

"*Because I love her, Dammit! So are you gonna ask her out or not?*"

"I've been thinking about it."

"*So hurry up with it. You two aren't going to live forever. Do it while you're still young enough to enjoy it. I need to get ready for a date. You think about what I said. And one more thing, she doesn't do*

54

one-night stands. When she gets involved, she's in it for the long haul, good or bad. So if it's a quick lay you're after, forget we had this conversation."

"I'm not interested in having a fling with her."

"*Good, ciao.*"

"See ya, *Mrs. Jones.*"

Chapter 10

"Hey, can I ask you something?"

Jess looked up from her notes upon hearing Kevin's voice. "Ooh, I'm glad you're here. I think I've stumbled onto something else that's not good for this case."

"Uh oh, I didn't come in here for bad news, but you might as well go ahead and lay it on me."

"We're going to have *two* more bodies by New Year's if we don't catch at least one of these guys soon."

She relayed to him what she'd figured out and left him to come up with a plan of action. He paced around the room before pulling up a chair and sitting down beside her and propping his hand under chin. Lines of concentration creased his brow as he studied Jess' notes, but she knew he had an idea when he looked up with that peculiar gleam that she'd come to know in his eyes, and ran a finger along his mustache.

"What if we create our own publicity and set Headbanger up?"

"How do you mean?"

"We make up a fictitious murder and feed it to the press."

"To coerce him into attacking someone of our choosing *before* the real Mr. Clean hits again."

"Exactly."

"An interesting idea, I like it."

"Mike handles all PR, so I should probably give him a call."

"And I promised Dean an update today. Maybe we can get them both in here for an impromptu meeting. Can you schedule that while I put the final touches on the Headbanger profile?"

"Yeah, and we should include Bill Davis and Chuck Edwards too."

"Definitely, I forgot about them."

"I'll start making calls," Kevin said on his way out the door. "Oh yeah, while I'm thinking of it, I was going through some of the notes on the other vics again and found something on MaryAnn Hunter and Elizabeth Johnson. You might find it interesting."

"What's that?"

"An old boyfriend of Hunter's said she liked for him to tie her up. Says he thought it was a little weird, but she got off on it and he got laid more. Sorry, his words."

"Hmm, interesting, what about Johnson?"

"Ex-husband said her sudden interest in rough sex was part of the reason they split. Guess he wasn't the adventurous type."

"That leaves a lot open to speculation, depending on exactly what you consider rough, but still adds to the S&M angle."

"That it does."

"I think I'm going to do some more research in that area."

"Okay, I'll go make the calls, then I'll be back so we can work on a plan that'll fly with the Chief."

4:30 PM

"Hey Bill, I didn't expect to see you here."

"Good to see you, Mike. Dean, how are you?"

"Doing very well, Bill, and yourself?"

"Not bad, I got a call from one of your officers a couple hours ago, a Kevin Slater. He said it had to do with the crackpot that's working my campus and it was extremely important that I be here."

"Bill, Kevin and Jess wouldn't have dragged you all the way down here if weren't extremely important. Why don't we head inside? After you gentlemen," Mike said, holding the door.

"Good afternoon, McCaskell, Rafferty."

Both officers were at once alert. "Hello Chief, Major Shelley," Rafferty said.

Chief Edwards reached for Dean's hand. "Afternoon Dean, Mike."

"They must have something if they've got us all together," Dean commented.

"Bill," Chuck said as he shook hands with the Chief. "Dean, did I hear right? Is Jess working on this now?"

"She sure is."

"That girl of yours is a woman after my own heart. You know I have an extra soft spot for her, being an ex-subbie," he said with a laugh.

"I'll bet you do."

"Rafferty, Detective Slater and Doctor Mitchell are expecting us."

"Yes Sir, Major, they're in Jess' office."

CriodCriod

"Chief, Mike."

"Slater, long time, no see."

"Yes, Mike, it has been."

"Jessie, how are ya?"

"I'm great, Mike, on a personal level, that is."

"Jessie, I don't believe you know Bill Davis. He's Chief of the Elon University campus police. Bill, this is my daughter, Doctor Jess Mitchell. She's a forensic psychologist with the SBI. We borrowed her to consult on this case."

"I believe I've seen your name in the papers recently."

"It's possible. One of my cases is in the middle of closing arguments."

"Warren, the burglary ring, great job, Doctor Mitchell."

"Thank you, Chief Davis, but please call me Jess."

"Chuck, you know Jessie, of course."

"Come here, girl, and let me give you a hug. I was just telling your pop if I were twenty years younger and still single..."

"Still a big flirt, I see," she said as she hugged him. "And how's Mrs. Chuck?"

"She's great. You should stop by for supper sometime. She'd love to see you."

"Chuck, I just might do that."

"And Bill, this is Detective Kevin Slater. I believe you spoke with him earlier."

"Yes Detective, good to meet you."

"Chuck, have you met Slater?"

"I don't think so, but I hear you're the best."

"I dunno about that. The Chief *did* have to call in a *subbie*," he said, shooting Jess a grin.

"Never hurts to have a fresh pair of eyes go over a case."

"Yes Sir, and again, I apologize for calling you and Chief Davis on such short notice."

"Will you gentlemen excuse me for just a moment? I'd like to have Carl in on this too." Jess turned on the speakerphone and dialed his office.

"*Yeah, hello.*"

"Carl, Jess here."

"*Hey Doll, how's the investigation coming along?*"

"That's what I'm calling about. Kevin and I have called a meeting that you need to be in on. You got a few minutes to talk?"

"*Yeah, sure.*"

"You're on speaker, hope you don't mind."

"*Nah, course not.*"

"For those of you who don't know him, Carl Barnes heads up my division at the Bureau. Carl, you know Dean and Mike Shelley. Bill Davis from Elon University is also here, and you remember Detective Slater."

"*Yeah, how you fellas doin'?*"

"Very well, Carl."

57

"*Slater, you're looking out for my star shrink, I hope.*"

"Yes Sir, always."

"Got a surprise for you Carl, Chuck Edwards from Elon."

"*Chucky! What's going on? How's the Chief's hat fitting?*"

"Carl Barnes, it's fitting pretty darn good. I can't believe they haven't run you off already."

"*Nah, somebody had to be here to take Jess' abuse.*"

"Carl, I think you have that backwards."

"*Of course I do, Jess. You boys know how these women are...always right even when they're wrong,*" he added with a guffaw.

"Mmm hmm, you'd better be glad I like you, Carl, since I'm the one making *you* look good."

"*So what's the scoop?*"

"Kevin, you wanna start?"

"Sure Jess, you gentlemen are already aware that we have two suspects."

Jess and Kevin spent the next hour explaining the profile and going over Kevin's plan to catch Headbanger. Mike Shelley would handle the media while Kevin selected his undercover team. The three chiefs would provide criminal histories on a select group of male university employees, which Jess would go through to weed out any who didn't fit the profile.

CB∞CB∞

"God, he is beautiful!"

"Who?"

"Professor Yarboro."

"You're joking, right?"

"No, I'd do him in a flat second. I wonder if he's single."

"Lees, you need to stop thinking like that. Besides, he's old."

"No, he's not."

"Yeah, he is."

"How old do you think he is?"

"I dunno, mid-thirties."

"That's not old."

"Um, Earth to Leesa, you're eighteen. Biologically speaking, that makes him old enough to be your father. That's gross."

"Well, he can get gross with me any time."

"You do what you want, but he gives *me* the creeps."

Chapter 11

"Okay Carl, what's up?"

"*I got a lead for you from Hillsborough. They have an unsolved similar to the ones in Burlington.*"

"Really? Before or after?"

"*Before, was in, lemme see, May of 2003. I'll fax you the details. You should be able to look at the full file. Lieutenant Lacy Daniels was lead. Just tell her who you are and I think you'll be set.*"

"I'm not sure if this is good or bad, but thanks, Carl."

"*Anytime Toots, I'll talk to you again probably next week unless something new comes up.*"

"Okay bye, Carl. Hey Carl?"

"*Yeah?*"

"Have a nice weekend."

"*Thanks Darlin', you too. Hey Jess, before you hang up, I'm gonna say something and hope it doesn't piss you off.*"

"What's that, Carl?"

"*I think that detective likes you.*"

"I like him too. He's a nice guy."

"*That's not what I'm talking about and you know it. You two kids have been working your butts off. You should get outta there and have a little fun before this case heats up.*"

"Good Lord, I'm glad I was sitting down. I don't believe I just heard you say that."

"*Hey, even I take a break sometimes.*"

"I'll keep that in mind, bye."

"My thoughts exactly."

Jess' heart skipped a beat when she looked up at Kevin. He was lounging casually in the doorway with his hands in his pockets. She chewed nervously on her bottom lip and shifted in her seat.

"How long have you been standing there?"

"Long enough...*Darlin',*" Kevin said, grinning. "Let's take your boss' advice and get outta here. You know...go out and have some fun."

"I'd love to. What do ya wanna do?"

"I don't care as long as there's no shop talk...something that has absolutely nothing to do with murder cases or *any* kind of police work for that matter."

"Sounds good to me. Where are we going?"

"Normally, I wouldn't suggest a bar, but how about we go for a drink, then decide from there?"

"Works for me." Kevin placed his hand at the small of her back and ushered her to his truck. "Hey, I just remembered that you wanted to ask me something this morning. What was it?"

"Um, I sorta just did," he said as he turned out of the parking lot.

"Huh?"

"I was going to ask you out...on a real date."

"Oh," she said, smiling back at him. "You were?"

"Yeah, look Jess. I really like you...a lot, probably more than I should."

"I like you too, Kevin."

"There's something going on between us. I don't know what it is, but I'm tired of fighting it because it feels right." He turned onto Garden Road, pulled into a parking lot, then stopped and turned in his seat to look her in the eye. His brow wrinkled with a flicker of anxiety. "God, I feel like I'm getting ready for prom night." Jess smiled as he continued. "I dunno, maybe we'll decide otherwise, but if you're game, I'd really like to see where it takes us."

"Me too."

He relaxed and released the breath he'd been holding. "Thank you," he said, looking up at the headliner.

"You ready to go inside?"

"I just have to do one thing first."

"What's..."

Kevin leaned towards her, cupped her face in his big, warm hands, and brushed her lips with his own in a soft kiss, silencing her question before she could ask it. Jess parted her lips slightly, allowing him to further explore her mouth. Encouraged by her response, his kiss grew more demanding. He slipped his right hand behind her and pulled her as close as the gearshift would allow, while continuing to ravage her lips. Spirals of ecstasy coursed through her and settled in the pit of her stomach. Reluctantly, he drew away with a groan and gazed at her. His eyes were dark with desire.

"Come on, let's go inside."

He got out of the truck and walked around to open the door. Jess looked down at his hand as he closed it around hers. His mouth curved up into an irresistible grin when she looked back up at his face and smiled. Hand in hand, they walked into Buffaloes Grill.

"A karaoke club?" She asked while throwing him a quizzical look. "Do you sing?"

"Only in the shower."

"Aw nuts, and I was hoping you'd serenade me, Detective."

"You'd have to get me well beyond the legal limit first," he said with a laugh.

"You're not bashful, are you?"

"Who me? It's funny you should use the word bashful." Jess waited, curious but silent. "Someone used that very word to describe you, not long ago."

"Who?"

"Can't remember, exactly, it just came up during conversation."

"And what'd you tell them?"

"I told them they'd never seen you handle a medical examiner if they thought you were bashful," he said with a chuckle.

"Oh you! Do you come here often?"

"Not very, only been a few times, but it was a riot.

"Uh oh, we got company, look." Jess nodded towards the bar. Niki was hurrying towards them with Dave in tow.

"Aww man, of all the places in town, I had to go and pick the same one they were at."

"Hey y'all! What are you doing here?" Niki squealed. She looked down at their clasped hands and grinned.

"We're tailing you," Kevin joked.

"We decided to get out of the office and go have some fun," Jess told her.

"Yep, brought her here to get her drunk so I can take advantage of her later," Kevin added with a wink.

"You won't need to get her drunk for that, Kevin," Niki said. "But then it's not really taking advantage if all parties are willing participants. Is it?" She added with a hard wink. Jess blushed when Kevin looked at her, his gold-flecked orbs glowing with an excited light. "Hey, come join us. We have a table right up front," Niki said.

She grabbed Jess' free hand and tugged them behind her without waiting for an answer. A waiter came by for their drink order shortly after they sat down. Niki further embarrassed her friend when she offered that Jess held her liquor 'by his ears', and then compounded her discomfort by ordering a pair or Jess' favorite mixed drink, *Sex on the Beach*, heavy on the vodka. And always the extrovert, she signed up for the karaoke contest, then began reminiscing about college.

"You studied criminology too, Niki?"

"Hell no, no offense, but the last thing I *ever* wanted to be is a cop. I turned into a complete nerd. I studied computer engineering at City University in New York," Niki said.

"John Jay is part of CUNY," Jess added.

"Oh okay, I got it now."

Jess had just started to sip her second drink when she heard the announcement and froze. "*And up next we got us a couple hotties, Jess and Niki, singing one from a few years back. Let's give them a big round of applause.*"

She looked up from the glass, horrified that Niki had signed them up without telling her. She had never done that before. "I am going to *kill* you," she bit out through clenched teeth.

"Aw, come on, Jess. Lighten up...and be glad I didn't sign you up for a table dance instead."

"*Come on up, girls.*"

"Hey, when did they start doing those here?" Kevin asked, teasing Jess.

"Come on," Niki said, dragging her friend along. "This used to be one of our best songs."

"I'm gonna get you for this." Kevin and David stood and led the round of applause and catcalls that followed them to the stage.

હ્ડ§ৄৎ৪৩

There ain't no easy way to start this conversation so I'll just say what's on my mind. Once our hearts both shared a common destination...

Kevin's mouth dropped open in astonishment. "Whoa."

"Damn, she's good," Dave commented. They listened without talking further for a couple minutes.

If we can fix what's wrong and just go on in love forever, Baby, I'll be begging please.

"Hey guys, your girlfriends are amazing," a random waitress called as she passed the table.

"Yeah, thanks," Kevin replied. Halfway through the song, Jess' anxiety abated as more alcohol seeped into her bloodstream. She really got into the performance.

Boy, you know your love's my one true weakness. When it comes to you, I'm helpless.

"Dude, she's got a set of pipes on her."

"She damn sure does. Both of 'em do." By the final verse, the pair had forgotten about the teleprompter and barely noticed the audience.

I'll do anything if it'll bring out hearts together. I'll stand and fight or get down on my knees. If we can fix what's wrong and just go on in love forever, Baby, I'll be begging please...Please.

A standing ovation was in order, and shouts for an encore continued long after they had returned to their seats. "*Well folks, forget the voting tonight, I think it's safe to say these two just took home the prize,*" the MC shouted.

"Oh man, Jess, we, I mean *you* were magnificent. They loved us!" Niki exclaimed. "That was truly amazing," she continued as they rejoined Kevin and Dave. "Didn't I tell you guys she could sing her ass off?"

The two men sat back down speechless for a moment. "Wow!" They both said in chorus.

"Is that all you can say?" Niki asked.

"You could knock me over with a feather right now," Kevin said.

"That was fucking awesome," Dave said. "I need to start listening to more country music," he added with a chuckle. "Jess, you look like you could use a drink. How about a fresh round, on me?"

"No, thank you," Jess said quickly.

"She's afraid I'll *really* sign her up for that table dance," Niki teased.

"Believe me, if I'd had any inkling that you were gonna do that, I woulda watched you more carefully and you wouldn't have ordered the first two," Jess said after draining the glass.

"Dang girl, slow down. There's more where that came from."

"Niki, I'm not having another drink," she half-snapped. Her initial anxiety at having to sing in front of Kevin was gone, having been replaced by anger at her friend.

61

"Jess, you are extremely talented. You really should sing more often. It'd be a shame to waste that voice," Kevin said. "Makes me wonder what other abilities you're hiding."

"She's not half-bad in the kitchen. In fact, she's cooking tomorrow night."

"I am?"

"Of course, you are. Remember? I'm staying the weekend. You guys should come over."

"Yes, please join us for dinner tomorrow night. I may need someone to keep me from murdering her," Jess said with a saccharine smile, her tone syrupy.

"Smart guys never turn down a free meal, especially when it's offered by such fine company. I'm there," Dave said to Niki.

"Aww, what about you, Kevin?" Niki asked.

"Hmm depends, you gonna sing for us again, Jess?" Kevin teased. "No seriously, count me in. I would love to join you for dinner," he added when she scowled at him. He leaned over, and rubbed her shoulders before nuzzling the back of her neck.

"The Marriot's right around the corner," Dave teased and laughed.

"There must be a flaw in here somewhere," Kevin said, still kneading her shoulders.

Before Jess could answer, Niki piped in, "She's only ever had three, and one of those seems to have taken care of itself."

"What's that supposed to mean, Nik?" Jess asked.

"You used to have rotten taste in men."

"If you're talking about him, she still does," Dave added, taking a jab at Kevin.

"Fuck you," Kevin said, flipping Dave off. "And the others?"

"She's a work-a-holic. You think you can do something about that Kevin?"

"I got her in *here*, didn't I?"

"Good point."

"Of course, I might regret doing that since what *you* did to her is sorta my fault for bringing her here in the first place."

"I highly doubt it. Besides, she had this coming. Remember Jess, payback's a bitch, ain't it?" Jess rolled her eyes.

"I'm not sure I wanna know what that means," Kevin said. "What's the last one?"

"Last what?"

"Flaw."

"Oh yeah, she's got a hot temper and a mouth that would make a sailor blush."

"I do not!"

"She'll cuss a blue streak in a flat second."

"She will?" Dave asked, laughing. "Cool! I thought that scene with the Bob Morton was a one-time deal."

"I most certainly will not."

"And here I've been trying to watch it in front of her," Dave added.

"Hey, don't hold back on my account. Let it fly"

"Cool!"

"She's feisty too. I like that," Kevin said. Jess shot him a devilish grin.

"Who's Bob Morton?" Niki asked.

"He's the assistant medical examiner. He and Jess had a run-in and she scared the hell out of him," Kevin said.

"Really? Jess, you didn't tell me about that."

"There was really nothing to tell."

"She didn't just scare the hell out of him. She put the fear of God into him. What was it she said, Kev? '*I'm your worst fucking nightmare if you don't back off,*' or something like that," Dave imitated, laughing. "Then she threatened to shoot 'im."

"That's about right, and she had him cornered against those steps too."

"I didn't realize y'all heard so much of the conversation."

"Oh yeah, we heard it all and that wasn't just a conversation. You really did scare him," Kevin said.

"Dave and I were on our way to take care of him when you went off on him. It became obvious real quick that you had the situation under control so we just watched."

"Okay y'all, now that you've all had your fun, and at my expense, I might add, I think it's time for Kevin and I to get outta here."

"You know you loved it. You sure you don't wanna get up there for an encore? The crowd's clamoring for it."

"Hell no!"

"See, didn't I tell you?" Niki cackled. "You two have fun and don't do anything I wouldn't do!"

"I have a feeling that doesn't leave too much out," Kevin answered.

"I draw the line at swinging from chandeliers," Niki called out as they left.

Chapter 12

"I have one hell of a time controlling my instincts when I'm around you."

"What instincts would those be?"

"These," he said as he leaned closer and kissed her again, leaving her breathless.

"I wish you wouldn't," she answered quickly.

"Really?"

"If you only knew."

"Knew what?"

"How you've invaded every corner of my life."

"There's a hidden meaning there."

"I dreamed about you before we ever met."

He pondered the statement for a moment. "A good dream, I hope?"

"It was...yeah, it was a *very* good dream."

"Maybe you'll tell me about it sometime."

"I'd rather *show* you, but I want us to get out of this truck in one piece," Jess teased with a smile.

His eyebrows drew together as he watched her with uncertainty. "What are you suggesting?" He scrutinized her while she responded.

"I'm suggesting you feed me before I perish from starvation, then take me home."

He put his hand to his chest and frowned. "I'm crushed."

"I didn't say you had to leave," she added with a wicked grin.

CR&OGRO

"Dinner was wonderful. Thank you, Kevin."

"I aim to please. I couldn't let you *perish from starvation*."

"You wanna come inside?"

"Yeah, I do."

Kevin followed her into the house, then closed and locked the door behind them. They sank into the overstuffed sofa where Jess pulled him into a kiss. He quickly pushed her back into the deep, soft cushions and took control. Deepening the kiss, he drove his tongue into her open mouth, sucking her upper lip, then biting the lower almost painfully before breaking away to trail tiny kisses across her cheek and back to her ear. Jess shivered when he nibbled her unadorned lobe, dipping the tip of his tongue into her ear as if guided by instinct, and outlining the circle of her breast, squeezing it. The feather light touch of his thumb drew her nipple to a stiff peak. Carried away by her own response, Jess took no notice when he unbuttoned her shirt until she felt his nimble fingers tugging it from her jeans.

"Mmm, oh Kevin."

Jess' moans jolted him back to reality. His breath came in ragged gasps when he sat up. "Good God, Jess, what am I doing? I want you so bad."

"I want you too. I am *not* gonna be happy if you stop again."

"I don't want to, Jess, but is this a good idea? Honey, we're in your father's living room, on his couch."

"I promise you, Dean will have no problem with us or with this."

"You're sure about that?"

"Positive." Jess stood up and took his hand. "Come on."

She dragged him upstairs to her bedroom, swept the covers aside and pulled him down onto the bed. Sitting up, he divested her of her shirt before removing his own. His muscled chest was covered in soft, dark blonde hairs that trailed down his rippling abdomen to disappear into his jeans. Jess was eager to see more, but before she could think about it further, Kevin eased off the slip of lace making up her bra and pushed her onto her back then crawled atop her, kissing her to oblivion. His mustache tickled every inch of skin it skimmed across as he moved down her neck. He paused at the base and flattened his tongue to lick the hollow of her throat, causing her to shiver and gasp as gooseflesh broke out all over

64

her.

"You cold?" He asked in a hushed whisper.

"Mmm, no...I'm on fire."

He caressed her face with the back of his hand and trailed his fingers down her neck to her breasts, tracing circles around their pebble-like, pink tips. Leaning down, he suckled one stiff nub and swirled his tongue around it, nipping lightly. Jess gasped as he pinched the other stiff peak at the same time and traced a wet-hot path down her belly, dipping the tip of his tongue into her navel.

Finally, he stood up and looked down at her before pulling off her shoes and tossing them aside. Staring down at her again, he leaned over and unfastened her jeans, then stripped them off slowly, adding them to the pile of garments already on the floor. With his fingertip, he traced the delicate edge of her panties as he eased them down her hips, exposing the trimmed triangle of tight, golden curls underneath. Consumed with lust, his eyes glazed over with desire as they traveled the length of her nude body.

"God, you are beautiful. You're sure you want this? Because if I go any further, I may not be able to stop."

"Oh yes, God, I want this so much. Please, don't stop."

Without another word, he gently pushed her legs apart, revealing her glistening sex. "I've wanted you from the day we met."

He deftly parted the silky curls, exposing throbbing flesh, which he teased with his tongue, his slightest touch eliciting a gasp from her. Encouraged, he licked her tiny love button, circling his tongue around it, sucking lightly. Her body drew towards him mechanically.

Jess sucked in a breath, "Oh God."

He moved down and lapped at her outer lips, tasting her juices and probing her wetness with his tongue.

"Mmm."

Going back to the sensitive pebble, he laved at it, this time pushing a finger into hot velvet, moving in and out, slowly at first. Jess clenched the sheet in her fingertips, spurring Kevin to add a second finger and increase the speed of his probing. With the addition of a third finger, he began rotating his wrist as he pushed and pulled, teasing her unmercifully. His well-timed licks were light and fast, then hard and slow, until Jess was certain she would die. Her breathing quickened and her hips undulated wildly as her climax continued building. Kevin ceased all movement and looked up at her until she grabbed the back of his head and pushed him back down, arching towards his mouth.

"Oh God, please, don't stop," she begged.

At her pleading, he lapped at her folds with renewed vigor. At once, she was hit by a flood tide of energy. She tightened her hold on the back of his head and ground her hips into his mouth. Pelvic muscles squeezed his fingers tighter as wave after delicious wave of orgasmic bliss rocked her body. Removing his fingers, he held her hips with both hands, pulling her ever closer to his hot mouth.

"Oh Jesus yesss," she moaned, sucking her breath through her teeth. "Mmmmmm yes, yes...oh fuckkk!" Her body was shaking uncontrollably; he had to hold her legs open to prevent them from slamming shut. Panting, Jess pleaded, "Oh God, please, stop. I can't stand anymore."

He brought her down slowly. Starting at her throbbing pleasure-gem, he trailed tiny kisses across her belly and up to her breasts, taking the time to swirl his tongue around each nipple, and moving up her neck. He took a moment to brush a stray lock of hair from her face, then kissed her fully, exploring the inner recesses of her open mouth. Without breaking the kiss, he rolled onto his back and pulled her body across his. Feeling frisky, Jess straightened up, and ground her hungry mound against the massive erection straining against his zipper.

Kevin growled, "Woman..." He rolled her onto her back again, then stood up, kicked off his shoes and shed his jeans, leaving them in a heap at his feet. White boxer-briefs stretched to accommodate the immense power between his legs. "Last chance to change your mind, I won't like it in the morning, but I can still stop."

"No, Kevin, please, make love to me."

He groaned in relief and shed the briefs, watching her eyes grow wide at the site of him. In her limited experience, Jess had never seen anything quite like him, making her wonder if he would even fit. Climbing over her, he nudged her legs apart with his knee, then slowly guided his huge cock into her until his entire length was sheathed snugly inside her tight folds. Allowing her to become accustomed to his size, he didn't move at first.

"You feel so good," he groaned.

He slid in and out at an unhurried pace, steadily speeding up when she urged by digging her nails into his back. Another orgasm began building inside her as he ground his pelvis against hers. Her breath came in gasps as his thrusts came harder and faster. Jess locked her legs behind his knees when he slid his hands under her buttocks, pulling her further around him.

"Oh God, mmm please, harder." He pounded harder than ever, faster and faster while she rose slightly and met every thrust.

"Come on, Baby," he urged, feeling her tighten around his shaft as she came again. The spasms came from deeper within than the first.

"Oh yesss, yes...oh my God."

"Yeah, that's it," he groaned and with one final hard push, his seed gushed out in rapid spurts. His thrusting slowed as his own tremors washed through him. Still inside her, he rolled onto his back and took her with him, yet again.

Jess rested across his torso for a moment before finding her voice. "This isn't real. I'm dead, aren't I?"

"No way," Kevin said. "Unless we're both in Heaven," he added with a quiet chuckle.

"Oh good, I was sure I was dreaming again."

"You didn't tell me it was *that* kind of dream...or that it was recurring...musta been something else."

"It was, but let's save that story for another time," she purred.

"I'm holding you to that." He pulled the covers over them and they fell asleep snuggled together, his arm around her, her head on his chest.

CASCACAS

Dave looked at his watch. "Man, he's out late. It's after three."

"Who?"

"Kevin, that's his truck."

"That's very interesting."

"Yeah."

"David, I had a great time tonight."

"Me too, Nik."

"Come inside for a while."

Niki looked around when David followed her into the house. Knowing her friend wouldn't have gone motorcycling in the dead of night, she had Dave check for Jess' car. Upon confirming that it was, indeed, in the garage, Niki smiled as a knowing look crossed her face. She ran up the stairs and crept down the hallway, stopping at the last door. She rapped lightly.

"Jess?" Opening the door a crack, she peeked inside when there was no answer, and smiled at the sight before her. She quickly tiptoed back downstairs. "They're up there."

"Okay."

"No David, you don't understand. They're *up* there...in bed."

"That sly dog," Dave said, grinning. "I told him she was gonna get under his skin."

The next morning...

Catlike, Jess stretched long and lazy when she awoke, keeping her eyes closed against the bright, morning sun. Unaccustomed to waking up next to someone, she froze in place when her hand met human flesh. Quickly snatching her hand back, she sat up, but relaxed upon remembering the night before.

"Mmm, do that again." Jess opened her eyes slowly and looked over, then smiled when her eyes locked with Kevin's. "Good morning, Beautiful."

"Hey, Handsome."

"Sleep well?"

"That was the best night's sleep I've had in a long time."

"Me too." Realizing she was still completely naked, she timidly reached for the sheet and tugged it up, covering her bare breasts. "Aww, don't do that."

"Don't do what?"

"Cover up that perfect body."

"Oh." Her cheeks grew warm from embarrassment. "What time is it?" She asked, still clutching the sheet to her chest.

Kevin turned over to retrieve his watch from the bedside table. "It's about a quarter 'til ten."

"God, that was a better night's sleep than I thought."

"I'm gonna hate it when you stop calling me God," he teased.

Jess leaned over, gave him a good morning peck on the lips, and laughed at him. "You clown."

"I thought I was God. Sheesh, make up your mind." His countenance became somber.

"Uh oh, what's that look for?"

"I was just thinking it's been a hell of a long time since I had to sneak out of a girl's room. I'm just wondering how the hell I'm gonna climb out of your window without either breaking my neck or having my own co-workers called on me by the neighbors."

"Boy, would that be embarrassing, and even if you get away, you'll have to explain why you left your truck here all night."

"Damn, that's right."

"Oh, and watch out for the rose bushes."

"Oh crap, there's rose bushes out there too? I don't remember seeing those."

Jess burst into peels of laughter. "No silly, I'm playing with you. Why in the world would you need to sneak out?"

"Well gee, I dunno. I just spent the most incredible night of my life in my best girl's bed which, by the way, is in her *father's* house...let's talk about him for a moment. Not only is he well-trained in using the firearm he carries *legally* every day, *but* he's the Chief of Police."

"Oh please, you're being paranoid. I told you he'd be fine with this."

"I'm not done. Not *only* is my best girl's father the Chief of Police, *but* he's also *my* boss. Nah, I got no reason to worry, no reason at all."

Laughing again, she said, "Dean's a pussycat."

"An interesting choice of words."

Jess rolled her eyes and smiled. "In all seriousness, I'm twenty-eight years old. Dean has had no input as to *who* I spend my time with or *how* in a very long time."

"Maybe not, but this *is* his house."

"This is true, but I really don't think you have any reason for concern. In fact, I'll bet ya he'll be ecstatic when he learns you spent the night."

"What? Honey, I got three sisters, and I can tell you for a fact that fathers don't get happy about their little girls having sex, not even after they're married."

"Mine will. I'd put money on it, but if it'll make you feel better, come shower with me. At least you'll be clean and fresh when he shoots you," she teased.

Later...

"My goodness, it's after ten. Jessie is sleeping late this morning. I wonder if she's feeling okay."

"Dean, you know she's been working her butt off and we were all out pretty late last night. She's probably just catching up on her Zs."

"We all?"

"Yeah, I got her to introduce me to David Rafferty. The two of us went out and then next thing we knew, she showed up on that wicked-hot Detective's arm. I think they got a thing for each other, but you didn't hear that from me."

"Oh really? That's fascinating."

"They were pretty tight, holding hands when they came in, but again, you didn't hear that from me."

"Hear what?" Dean said with a wink. "You're probably right about her being exhausted, then. Jessie's been working so many long hours on this case."

"Did I hear my name?" Jess asked, standing in the doorway. Kevin was right behind her, though out of their sight.

"Well, good morning, Princess. Your ears must have been burning. Niki and I were just talking about you. You slept most of the morning away, almost right through breakfast. Come, sit down and eat." Jess' fingers remained laced with Kevin's as he stepped out from behind her. "Oh, good morning, Slater. I didn't hear you come in."

Kevin's stance was stiff and uncomfortable. "Good morning, Sir, Niki."

"That's because he was already here, Dean." Jess paused for a moment before continuing. Dean studied the couple curiously, taking note of their interlaced fingers. Niki took in the exchange with a smirk. "Kevin spent the night," Jess added.

"All night?" Dean asked in a serious tone. "Is that so, Detective?"

Kevin's nervous look turned apprehensive as he shifted his weight. "Yes Sir."

"Well, how about that?" Dean paused for a moment. "I'm glad to see that you two are playing nice." Niki let out a quiet snort. Jess knew Dean would approve, but she hadn't expected him to be *this* accepting, so even *she* was somewhat stunned by his reaction. Kevin was clearly shocked. "Slater?"

"Yes Sir?"

"I like you." Dean got up, walked before him, and gave him a stern look. Though Kevin was larger, the two men were of equal height, so Dean was able to look him directly in the eye. "Don't do anything to make me change my mind."

"Absolutely not, Sir."

Dean's expression lightened. He gave Kevin a friendly slap on the back and invited the man to join them for breakfast. Between bites, Jess and Kevin took turns replaying the previous evening for Dean and Niki, omitting everything after their dinner at Paolo's. An hour later, Dean excused himself to run errands.

"Chief?"

"Yes, Kevin?"

"I appreciate you being so cool about me seeing Jess."

"Why wouldn't I be? Jessie's a big girl. I trust her to make good decisions."

"Dean, he was afraid you might shoot him," Jess continued with a grin.

"Shoot you? Son, why on Earth would I do that?" He asked, winking at Niki on his way out the door.

"Do you two have plans today?" Niki asked.

"At the moment, only dinner tonight, assuming that's still on." Jess looked at Kevin.

"After last night, I wouldn't miss it for the world." Niki replied with a smirk. "What about you, Kevin?"

"Absolutely, but I have to go home for a little while first."

"Just like a man, love her and leave her," Niki teased.

"Not on your life, I've just spent so much time working lately that I've neglected a few boring household chores."

"Like?" Niki questioned.

"Like laundry, I need clean clothes to wear tonight," he laughed.

"Clothes? Who needs clothes? You're just gonna strip 'em all off anyway," Niki teased. Kevin sputtered and coughed, nearly strangling on his coffee. Niki laughed harder and patted him on the back. "Relax. You handled getting busted very well. Such superb technique, I'm impressed," she teased.

"Technique? What technique?" Kevin asked. He looked from Niki to Jess in a silent plea for help.

"I think even *I* could learn a trick or two from *you*, Kevin," Niki continued.

"Jeez Nik, give it a break."

The trio cleared the table before Kevin got ready to leave. Hand in hand, he and Jess walked to his truck, where she wrapped her arms around his waist and squeezed him affectionately, then stood on her tiptoes to give him a quick kiss. He enveloped her in his arms and deepened the kiss with all the passion of the previous night before breaking away.

"If I don't leave now, I'm not going to."

"Is that a promise?"

"It's a guarantee. Hold that thought. I'll see *you* tonight." He kissed her again before driving off. Jess stood in the street watching the truck disappear from sight.

CB80CB80

"Okay, spill it!"

"Spill what?"

"The details, what else?"

"What details?"

"Don't yank my chain, Jess. I *know* you didn't stay up half the night *just talking.*"

"What would give you that idea?"

"Well gee, I dunno, maybe the fact that I peeked in to see if you were home and found the two of you in *bed,* for one thing."

"You did what?"

"Relax! I didn't see anything. You were sleeping, but you looked *real* cozy though."

"Did you and David hit it off?"

"Oh no you don't, you're not changing the subject on me *that* easily. Is he good?" Jess looked at her friend and smiled, remaining silent. "Of course, he is, and judging from the look on your face, he ain't too shabby when he wakes up either."

"What's with the inquisition?"

"You know me, something *this* big happens with you and I wanna know all about it."

"You seem to know everything, so I don't see the need to elaborate."

"Oh yes you do, you hussy! You know your secret's safe with me, but I wouldn't advertise it so blatantly if you don't want it getting out."

"What?"

"Hey, I know the freshly-fucked look. You had it on your face when you strolled in here this morning. Hell, it's still there!"

"It is?" Jess asked, touching her face. "Oh my God! Did I really?"

"Aha, I knew it."

"Yeah, okay, you busted me."

"And Kevin looked like a kid who just got caught with his hand in the cookie jar. I thought he'd bolt when you told Dean he spent the night. Poor guy, I almost felt sorry for him." Niki sat staring at Jess as if waiting for something.

"What?"

"Well, tell me! How was it? Did he live up to the dream?"

"It was a hundred times better, a thousand times even. He is amazing."

"I ain't nothing but jealous."

"Didn't Dave put out for you last night?"

Niki poked out her bottom lip. "David was a perfect gentleman."

"Aww, poor Niki," Jess giggled. "All that hard work for nothing, and I thought *I* was the one living vicariously through *you.*"

"Well?"

"Well what?"

"Details."

"What details?"

"What details she asks. Is he hung?"

"Must be at least nine inches and thick, don't think my hand would fit around it."

"Really? How can you be sure? It's been ages since you've seen a real, live penis. Even a little one must seem gigantic."

"Well, he's a damn site bigger than my vibrator and it's eight by two," Jess said matter-of-factly.

"Oh my God! You have a vibrator?"

"Yeah, so what, a lot of women have them."

"Not Saint Jess! You need to go adjust your halo. I think it's crooked, in danger of falling off even."

"Oh, good God!"

"How's the mustache?"

"Huh?"

"Don't go blonde on me, Jess. When a woman describes a man as amazing in bed, it ain't just because he can fuck all night."

"Oh that, it tickles, but in a good way," Jess said, grinning.

"I always did love getting munched by a guy with mustache."

"Good grief," she said, rolling her eyes.

Chapter 13

Jess was standing in the closet in her underwear trying to figure out what to wear when Niki burst in. "Holy shit! Damn, Niki! That's a good way to get shot."

"Oh damn, sorry, I forgot you were packing heat."

"You scared the hell out of me! How'd you get in?"

"Dean let me in, said he was off to pick up his date and he won't be here for dinner."

"Really? I didn't know he was seeing anyone. I wonder who she is."

"You got me, but he was looking pretty spiffy."

"Well, since you're here, help me. I don't know what to wear."

Niki stepped into the closet and looked through Jess' minimal wardrobe, making snide comments about the lack of variety. She finally handed out a pair of skin-tight Levis and a low-cut, peasant-style blouse. Jess balked at wearing such tight jeans, but Niki only laughed and pointed out the possible increased need for mouth-to-mouth resuscitation should Jess pass out. Keeping with the peasant look, Jess pulled two thin locks of hair from her temples and plaited them together in a thin braid that hung down her back, then applied a minimal amount of make-up and waited for Niki's approval. Niki fiddled with the shirtsleeves and untied the lace on the top to reveal more cleavage.

"Here, wear these boots and you'll be set. You look gorgeous. Hell, I almost wanna fuck you."

"Niki, sometimes I worry about you, but I'll take that as a good sign."

7:34 PM

"You're here early," Dave told Kevin when they got out of their cars.

"Yeah, so are you."

"So much for that threesome I had planned," Dave teased.

"Threesome? Oh yeah, you're fucking hilarious," Kevin snorted.

"You're looking sharp, Bro, and you brought out the Beast."

"Gotta drive *something* when I'm off-duty."

"You coulda rode your bike."

"I suppose."

"Wine? Looks like I'm not the only one with plans. Gonna get the little honey schnockered and take advantage of her again, eh?"

"Unlike you, Rafferty, I don't need to get a lady drunk to have a good time."

"How well I know." David looked Kevin up and down. "And looks like you lived to tell about it. The Chief must really like you if he's letting you come back for seconds."

"Huh?"

"Never mind, come on. I got me a hot, little redhead inside and I don't want to keep her waiting."

CB&CR&

Kevin's eyes locked with Jess' as soon as she strolled into the foyer. "Salve, bellissimo Signorina."

"Gratzie," she returned with a smile. "Hey, that was Italian. Come on in, David."

"Yeah, I learned that just for you."

"You did?" She asked in surprise. "You brought wine. Let's get a corkscrew and you can open it up to breathe. I was just going outside to fire up the grill. It won't be long."

"I'll do it. I know it's going to sound cliché, but you look wonderful."

"Thank you. You're not so bad yourself, Detective."

"Thank *you*." Kevin followed her into the kitchen and as soon as all eyes were off them, drew her into a smoldering kiss that left her in a near swoon. "Mmm, you smell good, too."

"Good evening to you too!"

"I've been waiting all day to do that. So what did you and Niki do today?"

"Oh, just your average interrogation and by the way, we got *so* busted."

"I knew that this morning."

"No, I mean we had an audience...*last night.*"

"Come again?"

Jess replayed most of the Niki's inquiry, all but the kiss-and-tell-all. Kevin laughed with a headshake and went to light the grill. A moment later, he was back. His mustache tickled her nose when he spun her around, pulled her against him, and kissed her again. Jess' already shaky knees grew weaker when he probed her open mouth, grazing her teeth, and sucked her lips, already swollen from his first kiss. With Jess firmly encircled and supported in his arms, he trailed kisses down her neck and into the valley between her breasts. Distracted by a sound, he stopped abruptly to look over Jess' shoulder at Niki and Dave, who were standing in the doorway.

"Man, you two could fuck up a wet dream," Kevin said, irritated at the interruption. "Sorry, Baby."

"That was wet alright. You two will have plenty of time for playing later. Jess, I'm starving, so the sooner you feed me, the sooner I'll leave," Niki teased.

"Best idea I've heard all day," Kevin mumbled.

9:00 PM

The dinner party went well, with fabulous food and drink, but as is typical of new lovers, Kevin and Jess were anxious to be alone. He followed her into the kitchen, intending to uncork a fresh bottle of wine while she prepared the dessert, but his plan was quickly forgotten, when the sight of Jess' denim-clad rear offered a temptation he couldn't resist. Dropping the bottle back into the ice bucket, he walked around to her side of the island and took her into his arms, groaning as their lips met in a bruising kiss, his mouth ravaging hers. A jolt of electricity zipped through Jess' body and nestled between her legs when his kisses trailed down her neck, his tongue tracing a wet-hot path into the hollow of her throat. With one hand on her back and the other cupping her behind, he pulled her closer, crushing her against his large frame.

"Mmm, ohh God," she moaned as his stiff cock throbbed between them.

"There you go, calling me God again. Do you have any idea how bad I want you right now?"

Jess glanced at his crotch, then looked into his eyes. "Yes, I think I have some idea."

"When will the Chief be back?"

"I don't know. Why?"

"Because the last thing I want is for him to stroll in and find me making love to his daughter right here on his kitchen counter. I guarantee you that will happen if we don't get out of here soon. And just because he didn't shoot me this morning, doesn't mean he won't tonight."

"That wouldn't do, would it?" They took the wine and gelato back into the dining room. "Oh jeez, forgot the spoons."

This time, Niki followed her friend back to the kitchen. "Jesus Jess, mighty distracted tonight, aren't we?"

"This is a new experience for me. I've never been with such a distracting man before."

"I'll say. That big-ass schlong distracted me too," she said, laughing. "He's been walking around with a stiffie all night.

"You looked?"

"How the hell could I miss it!? Let's finish this show up so you and Kevin can stop torturing each other and go fuck."

"Jeez Niki, could you get any more crude?" Jess was asking as they came through the door back into the dining room.

"Crude is good. What are we talking about?" Dave asked.

"Never mind, just pretend you didn't hear that."

"If you say so, Nik," Dave said.

"So Jess, you had anymore of those wild dreams lately?" Niki asked.

"What dreams?" Jess asked, feigning ignorance. Kevin winked at her, then squeezed her hand under the table.

"You know what I'm talking about. I think Kevin would find them fascinating."

"Okay, now's the time in the script when I go upstairs and get my gun, so I can shoot Niki."

"Ouch, them's fighting words. You know Jess, that's the third time you've threatened my life since yesterday. I could get a complex. Kevin, I think you need to slap some cuffs on her."

"I'm lost."

"Me too, Dave, but I am really enjoying this."

"When are we dragging out the mud pit and bikinis?"

"There's an idea!" Kevin said animatedly.

"I don't think so," Jess snarled.

"Whoa! That sounds like our cue. Niki, you wanna go for a drive or something?"

"David, I thought you'd never ask. Do you mind, Jess?"

"Absolutely not, you kids have fun, and David, make sure you give her something to chew on, so she won't talk so much when you bring her back."

"Oooohh, there's a visual. Jess, dinner was awesome. Thanks for the invitation. Niki, you ready?"

"Yes, ta-ta, you two."

Kevin and Jess walked onto the front porch and watched them drive away. "Mind if I smoke?"

"Of course not, you really don't need to ask every time."

"Chalk it up to my wounded chivalry." Jess laughed at him and rubbed her arms. She leaned against his chest when he stepped behind her and enfolded her in his warm embrace. "Are you cold?"

"Not anymore."

He nuzzled her hair. "Dave had a good idea."

"What's that?"

"Leaving, let's get out of here."

"Still afraid Dean may change his mind and shoot you?" Jess teased.

"I'm not taking any chances."

CΒΕΟΟΒΕΟ

"So where are we going?"

"Lake Macintosh, I wanna show you something." He passed her a CD wallet once they were settled in the car. "Pick something. Sorry, I don't have a wide selection of hair bands."

"I like all sorts of music." Jess flipped through several pages, stopping to pop in a *Keith Urban* disc.

"Niki seems determined that you're gonna tell me about those dreams."

"Ooh, oh boy, you're gonna make me blush."

"I sure hope so."

"You really like watching me squirm."

"I like *feeling* you squirm even more."

"Okay, I'll tell you, but I have to start at the very beginning, the day we met."

"I've been trying to forget it. I was a complete ass."

"Yes, you were, but I won't hold it against you," Jess noted.

"You didn't have to agree with me so fast," he remarked with a low laugh.

"I'm teasing. Anyway, I dreamed of you a couple nights before and I was startled to find the man from my dreams right in front of me when I opened the door."

"The man of your dreams? I hope I did more than just stand there, especially with *you* as my leading lady."

"Oh, it got pretty steamy."

"So you said and you've got my full attention, but you just caught a break. We're here." Jess caught her breath at the sight before her and waited while Kevin came to open her door. "Have you ever been up in here?" Jess mumbled a quick 'no' and shook her head. "I found this place when I first moved here. Kinda reminds me of the fishing spot I had on my grandfather's farm. In five years, you're the only person I've ever brought up here."

"I feel honored. Thank you for sharing it with me. So you're a fisherman?"

"They throw you outta Minnesota if you don't fish." Kevin chuckled at the look of disbelief that came over Jess. "No, seriously, I like to fish. It's a good way to blow off steam and if I happen to catch dinner in the process...well, that's even better. Shhh...stop."

He drew up short and pointed to the woods ahead of them. A young fawn scampered by the tree line while its mother kept watch. Standing perfectly still, they watched the animals until they walked undisturbed back into the woods. The lovers ambled to the water's edge where Kevin picked up a stone and told Jess to make a wish before skipping it across the water.

"What'd you wish for?"

"If I tell you, it won't come true," Jess asserted, smiling up at him.

"In that case, I don't wanna know." They slowly made their way back to the car where Kevin helped her inside. "Would it be too presumptuous of me to take you back to my place?"

"Now why else do you think I brought that bag?" Jess asked teasingly. "I love this car by the way. Mach I, 4-speed...this is what, a seventy model?"

"Yeah."

"You look surprised."

"I probably shouldn't be, but I never imagined I'd find myself a great girl who knows cars, rides a bike like she was born on one, and just happens to be the sexiest woman I've ever laid eyes on." Jess looked away and chewed her bottom lip. "I'll admit to telling a few in my lifetime, but I wouldn't lie to *you* about *that*," he declared.

"I guess I'm not your typical girl."

"*That* is for *damn* sure."

"One of these days, I'm gonna trade my 'Vette in for one a little older. I want a '63 fastback."

"You think big."

She sized him up and down. "Yes, I do."

"Crazy woman! You do that and you just might convert me...won't be easy, though. This Beast is the only car I've ever owned," he added with a laugh.

Kevin's house was close to Dean's, though about thirty minutes from Lake Macintosh. Holding her hand, Kevin led Jess up the steps and inside. "Welcome to my humble abode. Kinda chilly in here, I'm gonna start a fire. Make yourself at home."

"Nice place."

"It serves its purpose. Gives me somewhere to keep all my stuff." He worked a moment longer until a roaring fire blazed. "Want something to drink? Another glass of wine, maybe?"

"I don't think so. Any more than my two-drink limit, and I might be down for the count."

"That's no way to hold your licker," he teased while Jess' cheeks reddened.

"What can I say? I'm a cheap drunk," she laughed and sat on the floor by the fireplace.

"Sweetheart, you're a lot of things, but cheap ain't one of them. I have beer, water, and Mountain Dew. Any of those sound good?"

"You have Mountain Dew?"

"I bring you one every day, don't I?"

"I thought you just picked it up on the way. Aren't you sweet?"

"Good Lord, don't let that get out. You'll ruin my reputation."

"I won't tell a soul."

Kevin sat in the floor beside her and handed her a glass. "So, where were we in that dream? I believe you were just getting to the good part when we stopped. What did I, or rather we, do?"

Jess began relaying the details of her dream as she'd told it to Niki, except that she adopted her dream cop's role and mimicked his actions on Kevin. She was blushing furiously by the time she came to the part with the nightstick.

"You didn't bother to pull down my panties. You just kinda yanked them aside then buried that thing inside me all the way to the handle..."

"Whoa, I did what?"

"Yeah, I told you it was disconcerting, and with this hand, you reached around and started stroking me."

74

Assuming his role in the dream, Kevin crawled behind Jess, stood on his knees, and rested his cheek against her shoulder. "Like this?" He asked, reaching around to massage her pubic mound through tight, warm denim.

"Mmm, mmm hmm, just like that. You keep doing that and I'll never get through this." His touch became softer, though he didn't stop altogether.

"Please continue. This is getting good."

"You stroked me with your fingers and pounded me with your nightstick until I..." Jess couldn't say the words.

"Until what?" His touch grew firmer as he began to stroke her denim-clad pubis faster.

"Ohh, and then I was begging you to...mmm, that feels so good."

"Say it," he whispered in her ear, nipping the back of her neck. "What were you begging for?"

"I was begging you to..." She sucked in a quick breath and told him in a breathy whisper. "Fuck me."

Kevin gently pushed Jess onto her back and removed her clothes; first the boots and jeans, then the shirt, and finally her bra and panties. His pupils dilated with lust. Drowning in those dark pools of desire, Jess could almost feel his gaze physically raking her body. The embers of desire they had been stoking all evening suddenly burst into flames. Straddling her, Kevin pinned her to the floor, holding her arms over her head, and just as quickly, he leaned over and caught one pebble-hard nipple between his teeth biting and sucking it alternately, turning it blood red, hovering on a fine line between pleasure and pain.

"Ohh, oh."

"You like that, Baby?"

"Ohh, ow yesss, please."

"Please what? Tell me what you want," he said as he let go of her wrists.

"I want this," Jess cried, reaching to unfasten his pants. "I want you."

"How?"

"Inside of me."

"Say it!" He commanded.

"I can't."

"Yes, you can. Say it," he ordered again.

"Fuck me! I want you to fuck me."

"Mmm, my pleasure."

Kevin stood to remove his confining clothing before rejoining Jess on the floor. Quickly, he parted her legs and drove into her with an unexpected, though not unpleasant, ferocity before rolling onto his back. At once bashful, Jess straddled him for a moment before instinct took over and led her to rock back and forth, slowly at first, then faster at his urging, grinding her hypersensitive flesh against the hard contours of his pelvis, muscles squeezing harder with every stroke.

"Mmmm ohh...oh yes."

"Sit up. I wanna see your face when you come." Jess leaned back, giving him a perfect view of her heavy breasts as she rocked on him. Taking her right hand, he pushed it towards her core, positioning her fingers where he knew they would bring her the most pleasure. "Touch yourself," he commanded. Timorous, she leaned forward slightly, trying to hide from him. "Don't be bashful. Let me see."

He repositioned her body and fingers where he could see every touch, every stroke, every delighted grimace that contorted her features, until her passion culminated in explosive ecstasy. Her breathing quickened. Her moans became louder. "Oh God! Jesusss, I can't stop."

"That's it, Sweetheart. Talk to me."

"Ohh God yess, yesss...mmm, ohhhhhhh," she moaned.

Her passion out of control, Jess leaned forward, held onto his shoulders, and pressed on. Holding her hips, Kevin slammed into her from beneath, faster, harder, and deeper until his control fragmented.

"Jesus, Jess! Yeah, that's it, Baby, fuck me."

In one final stroke, he fired his love into her satin warmth. Jess collapsed over him, his iron flesh still throbbing inside her. They rested on the floor for some time, each lost in their own thoughts before finally succumbing to exhaustion. During the night, she awoke to find her lover gazing at her. The fire had died down to glowing coals.

"Let's go to bed." Jess stood up and stretched. Kevin followed and grasped her hand. "Man, I love it when you do that."

"When I do what?"

His lone response was a wolfish grin before he led her into the bedroom. The couple passed the next week in much the same way, working days on their case and loving each other every night.

Chapter 14

Unknown to Kevin, Jess had awakened early, deliciously sore from the evening's lovemaking but rejuvenated from the night's slumber. Not wanting to wake her sleeping lover, she slipped quietly out of bed, leaving him to awaken alone some time later. Noting the fresh smell in the air, he knew in an instant that she was cleaning. Preferring to pamper his newfound love, he put on his shorts and made to reprimand her for going at it alone, but stopped short at the vision that greeted him.

Unobserved, he took in the sight of her, beautiful and free from the inhibitions that restrained her most of the time. The white-blonde ends of her damp hair stopped just above the swell of her buttocks and swayed as she busied herself with the laundry, humming quietly to the tune of the spin cycle. Jess had clothed herself in one of his shirts, much too large, as revealed by the sleeves she'd rolled to her elbows and the shirttail that fell to her knees.

A bolt of instant desire slammed into his loins. He could not remember ever being so affected by a woman, so the quick intensity of his reaction took him by surprise. But choosing to follow the lead of his body rather than his head, Kevin padded behind her, intending to show her exactly what she did to his control. Oblivious to all but her task, Jess jumped when Kevin's hard body wedged her against the dryer.

"Sorry, I didn't mean to scare you. Mmm, you look good in my shirt."

"Thank you. I ran out of clean clothes, so I borrowed this and threw a load in the washer. I hope you don't mind."

"Sweetheart, I prefer your clothes in a pile on the floor, but you can throw them anywhere you want," he said, nuzzling the back of her neck then he looked up thoughtfully. "Does that mean there's nothing but you under here?" He asked, hugging her closer, caressing her body through the thin material.

Jess turned around and kissed him. "You keep that up and I'll show you what's under here..." She said throatily. He raised an eyebrow and grinned in anticipation. "...after breakfast," she added, smiling impishly. "Go jump in the shower and get ready for work. I'll have us some breakfast ready when you get out."

Disappointed that she wouldn't be stripping right away, but imagining what he knew would come later, Kevin ground his swollen crotch against her midsection one last time before following her orders.

Later...

"Delicious! What do you call this?"

"Um, eggs?"

"Oh my God, you're kidding!" Jess could not hold in a round of giggles. "Smartass. What's in it, Woman?"

"Eggs, cheese, and meat...I usually put in some fresh veggies too, but you seem to be sadly lacking in those..." she trailed off. "Its official name is frittata, but technically it's just an omelet. It's just all mixed up and baked instead of flipped."

"Well, it's great." Kevin contemplated his next words for a moment before saying them aloud. "Jess, I have a confession. I've really enjoyed having you here all week. I could get used to it."

Jess was stunned almost to the point of silence. While she didn't want to wear out her welcome, she never expected Kevin to practically invite her to stay. She pondered her words carefully before responding.

"You've certainly made me feel at home."

"I wouldn't have it any other way."

"Thank you...I have a small confession too. I've been snooping in more than just your kitchen cupboards."

"I noticed, but I have nothing to hide. Snoop to your heart's content. Find anything interesting?"

"Yeah, a couple of things...your train collection for one, it's impressive."

"Most of it came from my grandfather. He used to take me to the train yard when I was little. I loved trains, still think they're cool. Guess I'm still a big kid."

"I think it says a lot about you, the fact that you haven't lost your inner child. It's easy to get jaded by what we see every day."

"Especially in your case, I do get to see the good in people on occasion."

"Niki says I'm a master at compartmentalizing."

He cocked an eyebrow. "What's that?"

"An art form, according to her, the ability to turn emotions on or off at will. Certain people develop the skill as a way to avoid dealing with unpleasantness until it's convenient."

"Which keeps you from losing it every time you have to work a bad case."

"I guess so. I'm not sure I could do it if kids were involved." She quickly changed the subject. "I love the picture frames in the living room. They look like rail ties."

Kevin didn't push, knowing she'd just revealed something deep and personal that very few would ever know. "They are. I have to admit, the idea wasn't mine. I saw it on the tube one day, home and garden channel, I think."

"Gasp! What would all the guys say?" Jess teased playfully and giggled. "But I won't tell if you won't."

Kevin volunteered to do the dishes while Jess dressed for work. She was standing in front of the mirror when he joined her. Having noticed her reluctance to trade his shirt for her own, and relishing in it, he encouraged her to wear it, putting his arms around her and leaning to kiss the nape of her neck.

"God, you turn me on," he murmured into her ear. He moved to cup her breasts, pinching her nipples when they grew hard at his touch. "So soft, feel what you do to me," he growled, pressing his groin into her lower back.

Jess turned her head to look back at him. Leaning down, Kevin kissed her, his tongue sweeping a heated, wet path across her lower lip and down her neck. He yanked down the jeans that she had not yet buttoned along with her panties, and bent her over the bare countertop between the two sinks, then unzipped his own jeans. In a hair's breath, he freed his enormous cock and pushed into her ready heat.

"Oh God! Mmm," Jess moaned.

She gripped the edge of the counter for balance as he thrust with a wildness she'd never imagined, and reached to find the tiny ball of nerves that fed her desire. He caressed it in small tight circles, but only for a moment, until Jess looked down at his hand and brazenly replaced it with her own. Grasping her hips in both hands, Kevin pulled her body into his, pounding her harder and deeper...faster...while she met every stroke with an urgency of her own. Her increasingly louder moans and uncontrollable shaking alerted him when she was at her peak.

"Look into the mirror, Jess. I wanna see your face." She looked up to find his image gazing back at her. "That's it, Baby. You're so beautiful."

Unthinking, she closed her eyes when her climax began to roll through her. "Oh God, yesss," she screamed.

"Open your eyes and look at me," he demanded. On command, her eyes flew open. She stared at his reflection, panting as her body convulsed and her tunnel contracted around his thick shaft. "Yeah, come on, Jess. Let it out." She clenched him tighter, eliciting a grunt from him as his tight restraint unraveled, unleashing his thick seed to gush into her. "Fuck, yesss," he growled. Jess remained stiff while she caught her breath, the countertop edge still in a white-knuckled grip, and stared silently into the sink after Kevin slid out of her and zipped his pants.

"I don't know what came over me. I seem to turn into some kind of sex-crazed lunatic with you. I'm sorry," he said as he pulled up and fastened her jeans.

Jess fixed her eyes on his reflection. "Sorry for what?"

"You're so sweet, so innocent...and I damn-near rape you every time I wanna make love to you."

"Have you heard me complaining?"

"No."

"Enough said, now shut up and kiss me, you sexy beast," she said, turning and pulling him down to her level.

"Mmm," he groaned, picked her up, carried her into the living room, and placed her back on her feet. "We have an undercover team to brief, which means we'd better get going, else I'll be too tempted to skip it and carry you back to bed."

12:00 PM

"Ladies and gentlemen, you already know why you're here today and most of you know or have heard of Staff Sergeant Kevin Slater. He's lead in the case you'll be working on, and with the grapevine as it is, all of you have probably heard that we have a profiler on the case, as well. Doctor Jess Mitchell is a renowned forensic psychologist from the State Bureau of Investigation. So without further ado, I'm going to turn this over to them. Detective Slater," Mike said.

"Thanks Major. Folks, since you have an idea of what you'll be doing, I'm just going to touch on the specifics before turning it over to Doctor Mitchell. As you know, Burlington has a couple wack jobs running loose. The press is calling them Mr. Clean and Headbanger, respectively. Between the two of them, they've killed seven local women, three of whom were Elon students. We're concentrating on these three women and Headbanger, for now. Any questions so far?"

A roomful of curious stares spurred him on.

"Your task will be to pose as students at the university," Kevin said with a grin. "We're pretty sure our guy won't make a move until the end of the month, but to keep you from looking out of place, we're moving you onto campus as the semester begins. You'll be living there, two males, and one female per dorm, with the exception of Carolina Hall, where we'll have four loaned SBI agents posing as married graduate students. You are to eat, sleep, and breathe the life of a student...books, term papers, and all."

Anguished groans arose from the crowd.

"For you Burlington cops, you're *undergrads*, you have to look like *real* students, so don't skip all your classes. You might even rotate attending events with other real students. But above all, you're there to do a job. You'll work in shifts watching the staff, especially grounds and housekeeping. Ladies, I want you to become extra-friendly with them. You're intelligent enough to figure out what that means without going too far. Guys, your primary job will be to cover them, so don't turn your libidos loose on every cute sorority sister you meet. Any questions?"

"How do we watch the staff if we're in class?"

"You won't all be in classes at the same time. That's also why five of you will be *employees* rather than students, and also why we have the agents from the SBI. Those of you on the ground crew will be in and around the buildings when my *students* are not. You ladies and gentlemen from the Bureau, how about standing up so my team knows who you are."

"Interesting classes, I hope," someone yelled from the back of the room.

Kevin chuckled. "I'm sure they'll be fascinating, Larry. Doctor Mitchell made up your schedules. The details are in your packets. Anything else?" He was greeted with silent stares. "Okay well, I'm gonna turn this over to Jess."

"Thank you, Detective Slater. Here's what we're looking for. Headbanger is a white male, aged 28 to 35. He's not the smartest guy in the world, but he will know that something's amiss if your performance isn't flawless. Probably a high school graduate at best, he has no college experience and limited social skills. Any questions so far?"

Silence.

"From the angle of the blows, we've determined that he hits the victims from overhead and behind, but they don't appear to have been attempting an escape, telling us they know him. In fact, they probably shared some sort of social interaction on a regular basis because they're not alarmed at his presence, so the attack comes as a complete surprise. Questions or comments?"

More silence.

"I'm gonna go out on a limb and say that he's physically attractive. I wouldn't go as far as a bodybuilder or gym rat, but he has no trouble drawing the eyes of young co-eds. I'll even venture a bit further by estimating his height at around six feet."

"Whoa, hold up there, Doctor Mitchell. I was following until you started describing him. Nobody's seen the guy, so now you're sounding more like a sideshow act. What gives?"

"Simple deduction, Larry. It takes a fair amount of strength to hit a person hard enough to crush the back of their skull, which points to his build. The shortest of these ladies was five eight, so a little guy couldn't pick up a big rock or whatever and heft it high enough to hit her with enough force to do that. This tells us he's tall."

"What makes you think he's attractive?"

"Chris, this is where you have to read the victims. Human beings *are* typical animals, no matter what social class they come from. I think it's safe to say that we're all drawn to attractive partners. All of these women are from prosperous families, so they're not after his wallet. They're probably more well off than he is. That leaves the physical. Anything else?"

"I suppose you're gonna tell us his hair and eye color too?"

"Well no, I hadn't planned on that, but since you asked, his natural hair color is very dark. CSI collected several undyed pubic hairs from the scenes. However, he may color his head and facial hair, though my gut says probably not. But please don't go looking only for dark-haired men. He could be anybody. Eye color is as versatile as hair color so I won't go there."

"But why him? What would make these chicks go for him instead of some jock?"

"We're not all attracted to jocks. Some women like a man with brains," Jess stated with a smile. "But I digress. These girls are not going *for him*, per se. To them he's just a cute guy they can practice their flirting skills on. Headbanger is the one reading more into it than is really there."

"How does this profiling thing work?"

"It's not an exact science because nothing is ever a hundred percent where the human mind is concerned. The only constants are the very distinct behavior patterns we develop throughout our lives. Most of us prefer familiarity and keep certain habits we may not even realize. Behavior's based on basic intelligence, life experience, and current life circumstances. You may remember Mazlo's hierarchy from your academy days. Mazlo said all animals, including humans, have three basic needs...food, shelter, and sex. Beyond that, it's all cream. In profiling, we read the physical crime scene, the clues, evidence, and the victims themselves. Every little part tells a little bit about the perpetrator, how he selects a victim, and maybe even why he commits certain acts. You following me?"

Everyone nodded.

"In this case, we've got two things going on. Let's start with his MO, which can change from crime to crime. It's what the perp does to achieve a goal, or for Headbanger, sexual release. Here, the MO is a crack on the head with a heavy object found on the scene, in this case landscaping rocks, to immobilize the victim. It's messy, but it works, so I doubt he'll change this. The method speaks of cowardice and belies self-confidence. Next, he performs coitus with what he believes to be an unconscious woman when in truth, he's raping a corpse."

A chorus of disgusted murmurings rang out across the room. Jess waited for the crowd to become placid again.

"He didn't get this way overnight. He's been living with this his whole life. He's had at least one abusive authority figure, probably his mother, and a father who was absent emotionally, if not also physically. Questions?"

"Why not just ask her out?"

"That's easy for you, Steve, but he's not like you. He's socially inadequate, making personal interaction extremely difficult. It's likely he'd be a hit on dating scene *if* he had confidence and the required social skills.

"Why rich, pretty co-eds? Why not somebody off the street?"

"An excellent question, his choice of victims is both intentional, though I doubt *he* realizes it, and a matter of convenience. He was likely abused his mother as a child. I believe she was once just like the girls our perp is killing; a pretty, well-to-do co-ed."

"Explain that please."

"Certainly, but keep in mind that I may be slightly off on the minor details. I think she got herself in trouble by playing with fire and it basically ruined her life because she ended up with a baby she didn't want. The boy either abandoned them or couldn't provide the lifestyle she was accustomed to, leaving her to raise her child alone. She would have been cold and aloof to him, giving him only what was necessary for survival...no hugs and kisses, or doctoring of skinned knees...causing him to grow up a loner and social outcast, unloved, frustrated, and lacking self-confidence. Are we clear so far?"

Everyone nodded or mumbled in agreement.

"What's the second part?"

"Now the second reason for our choice in victims is convenience. Our perp has a readily available supply of pretty girls to choose from on campus. To that, we add the signature element of the crime. That is what he feels compelled to do and won't change, no matter what. That would be his disposal method. Are we cool?" Again, everyone nodded. "He leaves them in plain sight because he's immediately guilt-stricken and wants the girl to be found as soon as possible.

"This all makes sense, but I'm still not getting what it all has to do with his mother."

"Easy enough, figuratively speaking he's trying to kill the one woman he hates above all others, or his mother, the woman who treated him so badly growing up. Other questions?"

"Yeah, why the staff? What makes you so sure Headbanger isn't another student or jealous boyfriend?"

"It's unlikely that a string of identical domestic incidents would occur on a large campus. Elon is small, so it's even less likely to happen there. Also, it's common knowledge that spouses, friends, and lovers don't kill like this. They're more heated, more passionate. They use a more personal means of disposal, the main methods being manual strangulation, shooting or stabbing, and they usually do it face to face, not from behind."

"That makes sense."

"Moreover in this case, when you look at the people involved, not to be callous, but statistically speaking, wealthy people don't commit their own murders."

"Right...they hire contract killers."

"Exactly Jimmy, but I want to reiterate that this isn't an exact science. I could be wrong about *all* of this. So far, the clues point towards a blue-collar type person. I believe he works at the university in a job where he and the students come into regular contact, probably grounds, housekeeping, or something along those lines. Questions?"

"I thought serial killers tortured their victims for days, then hid the bodies."

"Most serial offenders are classified in one of two ways, organized and disorganized. Headbanger is of the *dis*organized variety. This type of killer prefers a blitz attack. His choice in victims is usually not random and he'll stay within his comfort zone, probably because he lacks reliable transportation."

"So he lives close by?"

"I believe so. Not only that, but it's small and dirty, and we'll find clippings of both his own and Mr. Clean's crimes. He'll also have a sizeable collection of pornography, his main source of sexual release. Any other questions?"

"I'm obviously missing something. If he's raping the victims, wouldn't that count as sexual release?"

"Actually no, rape is about power, not sex. He's getting the release he seeks, but in order to do so, he needs to be in complete control, and the rape does that. In addition, the medical examiner found signs of forced penetration, but no DNA, which tells us that one of two things occurred. One, he's not ejaculating at the scene. It's possible that he can't or maybe he's just saving it for a better time and setting. Or two, he's wearing a condom. Anything else?"

"Which one do you think it is?"

"My gut tells me that he's not a walking condom shop, so I'm going with the former. But this doesn't make him any less dangerous, so ladies please keep your guard up, and all of you remember we're all animals with animal instincts. If the hair on the back of your neck stands up, there's a reason. Other questions?" Jess waited for a moment, but there were none. "In that case, I'm going to turn this back over to Detective Slater."

"When you came in, you were given photographs of every male employee in or around the target areas. Each photo is labeled with the name, position, and current building assignment. They're also numbered from most to least likely suspect, but don't assume this means we know who Headbanger is. Doing so could compromise the case or worse, get you seriously injured or possibly killed. Our perp may not even be one of these men. Mike?"

Kevin stepped aside and motioned for Mike to take over.

"Folks, you're all on a reserved frequency. Kevin, Jess and I, along with our borrowed agents, Chief Johansen, Chief Davis, and Chief Edwards will also be monitoring radio traffic. I don't want to hear any unless one of our suspects makes a move. You've got your photos, classes, and dorm keys in your packets along with the basics of this profile. The first thing you'll need to do is report to Chief Davis at the campus police department for your university IDs. I don't think I need to tell you that it is extremely important for you to keep this under wraps. Study the profile and make whatever notes you need, but do not share this information with *any*body. Any questions?" He waited for a moment before dismissing everyone. "Get out of here!"

Jess joined Kevin and Mike at the door and waited for everyone to leave. "That was weird. I felt so scattered."

"Well, they didn't help you any. I think you did great, considering they were all over the place with their questions."

"Thanks, Kevin."

"Me too, but I have to ask. Is this going to work? Jess, I don't doubt *you* for a second. I know that *you* know your stuff, but I noticed some skeptical faces out there, even among your *own* co-workers."

"That happens every time profiling is used, Mike. Remember, Larry referred to it as a sideshow act because that's exactly what it is to most folks."

"For what it's worth, I have complete confidence in you two."

"We're certainly glad to hear that Mike," Kevin said.

"Listen, I have some paperwork to shuffle, so I'll see you later."

"Okay, ciao, Mike."

"Cya, Mike. That was thorough. You put on one hell of a presentation."

"I just hope it works."

Chapter 15

Two weeks later...
8:30 AM

"That's fucking hard up," Kevin commented to himself.

"What?" Jess asked.

"Did you know that some people are *so* into pain, they go to tattoo parlors for dry hits?"

"What's a dry hit?"

"Amazing, I know something you don't," he chuckled. "It's like getting tattooed without ink."

"No! *What* are you *reading*?"

"Believe it or not, an article in *Time* magazine," he said, chuckling.

"What a trip, I can't imagine that."

"When you learn something new, you get to take the rest of the day off."

"Is that right?"

"Well not really, but it should be a rule. You wanna play with me for a couple hours, instead?"

"Ohh, that sounds fun."

"We'll get to *that* kind of playing later, my beauty," he returned, arching an eyebrow. "I was thinking of something a little more applicable to the job."

"Oh? What'd you have in mind?"

"Come to the range with me."

"Okay...When?"

"Right now, before we go to work."

"If it'll make you feel better."

Twenty minutes later...

"What do you use? I'll admit to not paying much attention to your piece. I can't seem to get beyond the hips it's strapped to," he said guiltily.

"You're so bad." Jess handed her sidearm to Kevin for inspection. "Glock 23, 40 cal."

He passed it back with a set of earplugs, then set the targets while Jess prepared to shoot first. One, two, three...six, ten shots. Kevin retrieved the target for inspection. All ten shots made their mark carving out a small two-inch circle, dead-center in the chest area. He looked at the target, then at Jess, and cocked an eyebrow.

"Holy shit! Why'd we come here again?"

"I think you were concerned that desk work may have weakened my skill and wanted to be sure I could protect myself." He shook his head and expelled an amused snort. "We have to qualify once a month, same as you guys."

"Honey, that's beyond qualifying. You could easily be on SRT if you weren't so damn sexy."

"What's that got to do with it?"

"You'd distract the other snipers and cause them to miss their marks."

"Oh, good God," she retorted, rolling her eyes and laughing.

"There you go calling me God again. I've missed that these last few days."

"You are too funny. I *was* raised by practically the whole police department. Remember? I was an ace shot before I learned to drive."

"How are you with moving targets?"

10:45 AM

"Well, look what the cat dragged in," Dave declared when the couple walked in. "Might have known his bad habits would wear off on you sooner or later," he directed at Jess.

"Bite me, David," she shot back.

"Really?"

"Not if you wanna keep your teeth," Kevin said.

"Settle down, boys. That's enough. Kevin...Darling, I think I can take David if he gets too frisky."

"I think you're right," he agreed, then looked at Dave. "We've been up for hours, just got back from the range. You should see this one shoot."

"Yeah? You any good?" He asked Jess.

Kevin fished her target from his pocket and unfolded it for viewing. "Let's just say, you'd better not get on her bad side," he said.

"How many shots is that?" Dave asked.

"Ten," Kevin answered.

"Daaamn! You shot that?" Jess nodded. "I'll remember that. Oh yeah, Sarge, Major Shelley sent this over...said it was extremely important."

"Thanks, Dave." Kevin followed Jess into her office and closed the door, then enveloped her in his arms and kissed her. "Had to do that before we opened this."

"Feel free to do it again. What's in there?"

"It's the press release. Check it out."

> *Late last night, Burlington police were dispatched to the scene of what appears to be the latest in a grisly string of murders reportedly committed by the serial killer, Mr. Clean, who has yet to be identified.*
>
> *Information is sketchy, and the identity of the victim was not releases, as her family had not been notified of her demise by press time. The police are warning all women to remain guarded and not travel alone, especially after dark.*

"Not bad," Jess commented.

Kevin gave her a serious look. "I guess this is it. Ready to play school?"

"I dunno. Are you gonna be my teacher?"

"As long as you want me. Do you have a vest?"

"Not with me."

"That's tops on our to-do list. We'll stop at the supply room at headquarters later and get you one. What about a back-up?"

"Never carried one."

"You do now." He removed a .38 snub-nosed revolver from his ankle and handed it to her. "Can I assume you've used one of these?"

"That would be a safe assumption," she replied with a sly smile as the phone rang. "Jess Mitchell."

CB&DC8&D

Later while online, Jess stumbled into a chat room where the BDSM lifestyle was the main topic, *and* where she was befriended by another helpful member, SubMarine. SubMarine kindly took Jess, or SubDoer, as she'd taken to calling herself online, under wing and left her with a long list of helpful sources, many of which were online, that she then used to research the bondage theory.

That afternoon, the pair picked up a Kevlar vest for Jess and then at her suggestion, drove to her abandoned apartment in Raleigh to rotate her drab wardrobe, and then on to check in with her office. During the ride, she relayed all the information she'd found to support her hunch. When Kevin wondered when she'd had time to do so much research, she divulged that she'd had help from her new contact, SubMarine.

"Jeez woman, what'd you pack in here?"

"Just my collection of bondage gear; whips, chains, some rope...oh, and my own special set of handcuffs," she teased.

Kevin carried her bag down to the car. "Here's your keys," he said upon returning and tossed them to her.

"Thanks. Hey, speaking of whips and chains, I forgot to mention that when I was surfing earlier, I ran across a list of tools favored by Doms and subs alike. I have an idea what may have caused the little bruises on the vics."

"I'm all ears."

"Have you heard of a flogger? It's commonly mistaken for a cat-o-nine-tails."

"Sounds like a medieval torture device."

"Close, they're sort of like mini whips, but softer and with several strands. They can be made of almost anything, from a shredded pillowcase to horsehair, but there's a lot more information on deerskin, so my guess is that's the most popular kind. And, if the user isn't trained in the proper use of a flogger, especially those made from sturdier materials like leather, the tails could mar or even break the skin. There was also a blurb about adding beads or knots for added sensation."

"Sounds painful, I'm sure your new buddy, Bob, would be interested in hearing about it. Anything else worth sharing?"

"Oh gosh, all sorts of clips, clamps, and restraints, but enough about that. Come here you. I seem to remember having plans for us."

Jess walked backwards towards the bedroom pulling Kevin along by his shirt. When the backs of her knees touched the bed frame, they kicked off their shoes and hastily shed their clothing. She then spun Kevin around, pushed him down onto her bed, and climbed atop of him, impaling herself on his hard length. She couldn't resist touching herself as she rocked her hips back and forth, slow at times, then faster, while Kevin cupped her heavy breasts in his hands and rose slightly to catch a hard nipple between his teeth. Jess hissed in pleasure-pain, and in her excitement, rocked harder on his mighty staff.

After some time, she laid over him and rested her head on his shoulder, close enough that he turned his head and caught her lips in a fiery kiss before rolling her underneath him and assuming control. Withdrawing from her velvet heat, Kevin glided down her body until his face was nestled in the honey-colored thatch between her legs. After exposing her swollen nub, with his thumbs, he leaned down to flick the tip of his tongue across it, causing Jess to come unglued. Of its own volition, her body arched up against him, nearly bucking him off, as the first intense shockwave of her climax rocked her. She sucked in a long breath, and clenched the comforter while Kevin held her thighs and probed all the way to the epicenter of her passion.

"Oh God, oh God, oh God," she panted.

Reaching down, she pushed him away just far enough that she could slip out from underneath his prodding tongue. He speedily crawled back over her, plunged into her, hammering her harder than ever, and with only a few quick thrusts, he groaned and stiffened, filling her with a steaming river, then collapsed on top of her, leaving their bodies moist and sticky from exertion. Kevin rolled onto his side, leaned up on his elbow and looked down at her with a wide grin.

Winded, Jess could barely speak. "That was amazing!"

"Yes, you are," he replied and swept a wisp of hair back from her face. "You know, as much as I don't want to move, we need to get outta here and get over to your office, unless you want to be stuck in the I-40 parking lot for a while."

"Oh, I dunno. If we wait long enough, I'll miss Carl. Besides, I can think of all sorts of ways to pass the time while we wait."

She giggled when he flashed her his signature look, a single raised eyebrow. "You are something else. You know that?" Kevin observed as he zipped his pants.

"So you keep saying."

SBI Headquarters...
4:30 PM

"Afternoon, Agent Mitchell."

"Hey, James."

"Long time no see, must be one hot case they've got you on these days."

"Yes, it is. Carl made me relocate, so I haven't been in the office much. This is Detective Kevin Slater from the Burlington Police Department. He'll be joining me in my office."

"Evening Detective, I need to check your weapon and identification, please, Sir." Kevin handed over the requested items. James wrote in a logbook, then returned the items. "Thank you, Sir. This is your visitor pass. Please keep it visible and remain with your host at all times."

"I will. Thank you."

Jess had hoped Carl would be gone for the day, but there was no such luck. She hustled Kevin up the six flights of stairs to her floor and made a beeline for her office, hoping to check her messages and sneak back out again before her boss saw her. Again, no such luck. Carl emerged from his office a few doors down just as they exited hers.

"Hey Sugarpie, come in here and talk to me. What's going on?"

"Just checking in."

"Well good, we miss ya around here. The place just ain't the same without your screechin' music." Kevin laughed with Carl. "Who's this?"

"Carl, this is Detective Kevin Slater. Kevin, this is my boss, Carl Barnes."

"A pleasure to finally meet you, Sir."

"Ah, the famous Detective. Come on in, have a seat."

"How's the case going?"

"The team moved onto campus a couple weeks ago and we've been debriefing twice a day."

"Anybody jumping out at you yet?"

"Not yet, but I don't think it's been long enough. Make sure you pick up the Burlington paper tomorrow, if you can find it this far east. The bogus write-up is supposed to be on the front page. We've also leaked it to the *Herald-Sun* and the *News and Observer*, the difference being the *Times-News* editor is the only one who knows it's bogus."

"Cool! Right on schedule. You realize it'll probably go nationwide if the *Associated Press* gets wind of it."

"Yep, but that's not a bad thing. Listen, we gotta go. I don't want to be stuck in rush hour traffic any longer than necessary. Oh, and one more thing." She handed her boss a card. "Happy Boss' Day."

"Aw Jess, you shouldn't have."

"You're probably right, but I kinda like you, even if you *are* a slave driver."

"You're a good girl, Jess. Thank you. And Slater, you better take real good care of this one," he added, shaking Kevin's hand.

"Absolutely, Sir."

"Good, you kids get outta here."

Chapter 16

Kevin and Jess debriefed the team twice a day for the next ten days of the undercover operation, and they were getting bored, until day twenty-five, when the suspect list narrowed considerably during the morning session.

"First things first, anybody creeped out, yet?" Kevin asked.

"Yeah," a female officer answered.

Christine Parezi was an exceptional beauty. Exotic, she was the opposite of Jess, petite with golden skin and dark, almost black, curls stretching midway down her back. She drew more than her share of attention, so it wasn't difficult to believe that she would also attract Headbanger.

"What's going on, Chris?"

"There's a man working in my building who, in Jess' words, makes the hair on the back of my neck stand up. Something about him weirds me out."

"Who is he?"

"His name is Mark Thompson."

"That name's not on our list," Jess noted.

"I know. He's on the maintenance crew."

"Why haven't you mentioned him before?" Kevin asked.

"Because he just started working in the building a few days ago, so I just met him."

"Doing what?"

"He's working on the plumbing."

"What happened?"

"Nothing really, he's really nice to me, but I get the willies when he looks at me."

"Tell us about him. Mike?"

"Say no more, Jess. I'm on it," Mike said as he turned and left the room.

"He's about five eleven, I guess, a hundred seventy pounds, maybe. If I weren't creeped out, I'd be looking back, dark hair, clean-shaven. It's his eyes. They're cold and piercing. He talks to me a lot. I think he's lonely."

"Lonely or not, you can't let your guard down. What else?" Kevin continued.

"I can't pinpoint anything. He just makes me nervous."

"What do you talk about?" Jess asked.

"Nothing really, I don't know anything about him, except that he lives alone and doesn't have a girlfriend. I don't think he has many friends either."

"Chris, you're about to start dating," Jess added.

"Say again?"

"You pick your man."

"Why?"

"I want you to have more backup close by, in case he's our guy."

"How 'bout the Sarge?" She asked.

"I'm afraid he's not available for the job."

"Yeah, that's what I heard, but it was worth a try." Kevin glanced at Jess and shrugged his shoulders.

"Volunteers?" Every man on the team raised his hand. "Oh boy, this isn't gonna be easy. We'll draw for it." Jess scowled. "*Married* guys and *employees*, put your hands down. That's better." She retrieved a small wastebasket from the corner and a stack of paper. "Boys, write your names, ball it up, and toss it in the can." Jess walked around collecting the *trash*, then stopped before Chris. "Okay, you pick. That way I won't get blamed if you're not happy with your choice." Raucous laughter filled the room. Chris drew out a wad of paper then handed it to Kevin. He read it and looked around the room before settling on an attractive officer towards the back. "Steve, looks like you're Chris' um, boyfriend. Congratulations."

"Hot damn!" Steve strutted to Chris then performed a suggestive dance around her. "Yeah, Baby!"

"Oh please," Chris said, rolling her eyes.

"Paul and Jim, where are you? How popular is Chris?"

"She's a big hit. Nearly every guy in the dorm has asked her out," Jim yelled.

"A couple chicks too," Paul added. Again, laughter along with many whistles in Chris' direction filled the room.

"That's great. It'll reinforce our suspect's low self-esteem when Chris starts giving him the cold shoulder in favor of Steve."

Just then, Mike reentered the conference room. "Hey Jess, Bill emailed me this information and photo. What do you think?"

"Hold up folks. You're not leaving yet," she called. "Chris is right. He's attractive, but his eyes...I can see why a girl might be weirded out by him. Where is Lebanon Avenue in relation to campus?"

"It runs parallel to the railroad tracks, adjacent to campus," someone called.

"Ed, John, where are you?"

"Right here, Jess."

"I don't want you two to get bored."

"Too late for that."

"Since we're not concentrating on Smith, I want you to keep an eye on this guy when he's not at work."

"No problem."

"You guys will also run backup at Hook, since Steve will be spending more time at Barney. Chris, where, in your building, is Mark Thompson working?"

"The laundry room."

"When's he in there?"

"Different hours, he mentioned it'd take several days because he was waiting for parts, I think."

"Nights too?"

"Yeah."

"Okay, you've got laundry to do. Do it when he's there and wait as late as possible. That way you're more likely to be alone, and if he's our man, he'll be more tempted to make a move. Don't carry a basket. It could get in the way and get you hurt if you have to hightail it outta there. Do small armloads daily that you can carry and discard quickly, if necessary. I don't care if you have to wash the same clothes every day."

"Hey, I got some laundry she can do," another officer teased.

"Screw you, Dixon. You can do your own damn laundry."

"Children, knock it off," Kevin chided.

"How's the room set up?" Jess asked.

"Like a dungeon, dark and creepy, the washers are between the far wall and the door, and it's downstairs away from everything."

"Perfect!" Jess was excited. "What's close by?"

"There's a lounge with TV and a pool table one floor up and just down the hall."

"Jim, you any good at billiards?"

"Fair, I guess."

"What about you, Paul?"

"A little rusty, but not bad."

"Paul, you're on stairwell duty in case Chris needs help in a hurry. Stay within earshot, but blend in. Jim you're gonna start playing a lot of pool. Hang out as often as you can without drawing too much attention. Kevin?"

"Paul, if anything happens, radio Jim, pronto," Kevin said.

"Yes Sir."

"For the rest of you folks, if Paul calls, get your butts over there ASAP," he continued.

"That's it. Please take a good look at this photo. I'll have copies and information on the new suspect ready for our next meeting. And above all, keep your guard up." Kevin, Mike, and Jess waited for the team to vacate the conference room. "Mike, can you get me a background and juvie records?"

"The background, yes. Juvie will take longer."

"Thanks, we need to be ready for a warrant too."

"Absolutely."

Jess' cell phone rang as Mike was leaving. It took only a moment for her to recognize the voice on the other end...her old boyfriend, Billy...and for Kevin to sense her distress. He remained quiet, but watched with a curious, but worried expression.

"Why don't you go die? And lose my number, you jerk!"

"Gimme that." He said with sudden clarity, snatching the phone from her. "Who the hell is this?"

"*Bill Atkins, who the hell wants to know?*"

"Someone you're gonna have a major fucking problem with if you bother the lady again." He ended the call and returned the phone.

"What the hell'd you do that for?" Jess snapped.

"You looked like you needed help."

"Well, I coulda handled it," she snarled.

"Was that the old boyfriend Niki told me about?"

"She told you about him?"

"Yes, but she didn't tell me his name. You mad at me?"

"Yes, I can deal with him."

"Jess...Baby, I just wanted to help. I'm sorry."

Jess turned her back to Kevin and fumed inwardly for several minutes, but seeing his sincerity, she turned back to him and placed her arms around his waist. "No, I'm the one who's sorry," she acquiesced. "I shouldn't have snapped at you. It *was* kinda nice to have a white knight come riding to my rescue."

"I dunno about that white knight bit...jealous fool, maybe." Kevin chose his next words carefully. "So, this is off topic and probably not the best time since I just showed my ass, but how much convincing would it take to get you to move in with me?"

"For how long?"

"What do you mean how long?" She hesitated and cocked an eyebrow at him. "You've been practically living there for a month, anyway, and I'll rest easier knowing you're safe where I can protect you."

"I've been taking pretty good care of myself for years."

"Well, I'm here now, so let me do it." He studied her for a moment. "You never know when we might need to jump outta bed at a moment's notice and run off to school. Sure would be easier if we were both in the *same* bed."

Jess had very strong feelings for Kevin, but she'd heard of so many instances where living together became the death knell of a relationship rather than the glue that bound a couple closer. She didn't want that to happen to her and Kevin, but from experience, she knew a break-up would hurt less if it happened sooner rather than later. She considered Kevin's proposition for a bit before giving her consent, though she added a condition designed to test Kevin's commitment to her. *He* would break the news to her dad.

CRESORCRESO

Two days later...

It was after eight, and Chris was folding the last piece of the same load of laundry she'd been washing each day. Lost in her quiet solitude, she didn't realize that Mark Thompson was even in the room, though he'd been leering at her from a dark corner for over an hour. Picking up her load, she made for the stairs just as Mark materialized and startled her with a crude comment, forcing her to turn and question whether she'd heard him correctly.

CRESORCRESO

"Jim, get down here. Something's happening," Paul said quietly.
"On my way, Buddy."

CBEOCRBO

Kevin was outside having a cigarette while Jess cleared away their dinner dishes when he heard Paul's call. He quickly crushed it and yelled for Jess, and within seconds, they were en route to Elon University.

8:22 PM

"You're all worthless whores."
"I don't have to take that. I'm outta here, and I'm gonna report you too."
Chris turned her back on Mark and started up the stairs. He picked up a pipe wrench in one hand and snatched her ankle with the other.
"I don't think so, bitch!"
Mark raised the wrench, but Chris turned suddenly, threw her laundry at him, and kicked the tool from his hand. He lunged for her and they struggled on the stairs before tumbling to the hard, concrete floor with Mark landing on top of her. Chris' scream echoed in the stairwell as he ripped at her shirt.
"Paul, Jim, where the hell are you guys?" Chris called.
"Right here, partner," Paul yelled on his way down the steps, his gun trained on Mark Thompson, and with Jim on his heels. "Hold it right there, Pal."
"You okay, Chris?" He asked.
Jim extended a hand to help her off the floor and took a good look at her, checking for injuries. Chris' shirt was torn and her bra was hanging open where the front hook had snapped during the scuffle, but she was otherwise uninjured. Jim removed the flannel shirt he'd worn over his t-shirt, put it on her, and pulled it closed.
"Thanks, Jimmy. I'm fine; just do something with this asshole."
"Hey, I got here as fast as I could," Steve said, breathless as he took the stairs three at a time. "How's my girl?" He eyeballed Chris and pulled her close.
"We got him, and Chris is fine. One of you guys check him," Paul said.
Minutes later, Kevin and Jess arrived on the scene. Jim had restrained Mark Thompson while Paul read the man his Miranda rights. Still shaken, but calmed by Steve, Chris was being attended by a paramedic. Seeing that she wasn't seriously injured in the scuffle, Kevin found a quieter corner to call Mike and divert him to Judge Hastings for the search warrant, while Jess and the remainder of the team kept onlookers at bay.

9:23 PM

"Oh God, look at this place. It's filthy and it reeks."
"Don't touch anything!" Jess called to the officers.
She walked through every room, ending her self-guided tour in Mark Thompson's bedroom where she yelled for Kevin to join her. He found her examining a large mishmash of news articles and clippings that were taped on the wall.
"Holy shit! This guy must have stuff from every newspaper in the state."
"He's got one of us. It's a good thing we didn't hang out on campus. And look, AP got wind of it too, just like Carl thought they would."
Time rushed by after the suspect was taken into custody. Jess was unable to scrutinize the home's contents, as she would have liked, due to time constraints. Kevin wanted to interview Mark Thompson before he had the chance to invoke his right to council. On their way out, Jess heard her name being called. She and Kevin followed the voice into the living room, where a CSI pointed to a framed photograph of an attractive woman. Her eyes appeared to have been used as targets.

"Who wants to bet me that's his mother?" Jess asked.

"Not me."

"No way, I'm not into losing my hard-earned cash."

10:01 PM

After dodging a throng of journalists in the parking lot, they wound their way downstairs and through a maze of hallways to a cramped interrogation room. It was a small, white-walled room of about ten feet square. Its meager furnishings consisted of three uncomfortable, folding, metal chairs, and a small table in the center that was bolted to the floor. The room's only remarkable feature a large, framed painting hanging on the wall to the right. A beautiful seascape, it masked a two-way window to an observation room where interviews were monitored and recorded as they progressed.

Kevin had the suspect brought in as he lit another cigarette. Several minutes later, the shackled prisoner sat before him, refusing to do more than look up at the sound of his name. Frustrated, Kevin motioned for Jess to leave when Mark announced that he'd talk to her...and only her. Concerned for her safety, Kevin initially refused the request, but grudgingly changed his mind at her urging.

Mark turned his piercing stare on Jess and asked for a cigarette, which she obtained and lit for him. Taking a long drag, he exhaled, blowing the smoke straight into her face. Her eyes watered at the unexpected irritant, but she intentionally refrained from waiving it away, not wanting to give him the impression that she was the least bit intimidated or afraid. With a blasé expression, she waited for him to initiate an exchange, though he didn't at first.

"You're the pretty lady from the newspaper, Jess Mitchell. You're not like them."

"What do you mean, I'm not like them?"

"You're not a whore and you're nice. They threw themselves at me and just when I was ready to take what they were giving, they'd snatch it away again. I was never good enough...just like her."

"Just like who, Mark?"

"Vikki."

"Who's Vikki?"

The man went on to tell Jess about his mother. Her mistreatment of him, which usually included the boy being locked in the dark basement while she went out or entertained friends, had fostered hatred in her son so deep that Jess feared it would never be breached. As a teen, Mark had even planned his mother's murder. Jess let him ramble on until he started sobbing. Resting his forehead on the table, he confessed to the murders of Carrie Hamilton, Alana Lewis, and Deborah Anderson.

The man became more distressed when he realized that Jess would leave now that she'd obtained what she came for. He stood and took a step towards her. Anticipating his movements, she remained seated, though she released the strap on her holster and rested her hand against the butt of her pistol, ready to defend herself should the need arise. She worked to keep any trace of nervousness out of her voice as she asked him to remain seated and directed an almost imperceptible glance to the two-way window, a signal for backup. The last thing Jess wanted to do was to give Mark Thompson the impression that she feared him. A moment later, Kevin and two more officers entered the interrogation chamber.

"Come on, Thompson. Time to go back to lock-up," one of them said and took his arm.

"That had to be the quickest, easiest confession I've ever seen, just like a movie," Kevin said.

"Sometimes it works that way."

"That guy gave *me* the creeps. I'm glad we have him inside and you out here. He seemed taken with you."

"That happens sometimes too."

"They're starting to bring in the evidence from his house. And you'll be interested to know this guy matches your profile to a tee. Other than his job, you were only off on one thing."

"Oh?"

"He had a car," Kevin said with a big grin.

"Really?"

"It's a rust bucket with a blown engine," he added, laughing.

"I never said he didn't *have* a car, only that he didn't have reliable transportation."

"Gotcha! You had him down with the porn and the news articles too. You saw the place. It was a complete mess, and that talk you had with him about his mother blew me away. I kinda felt sorry for him for a second there when he started talking about the basement. I almost hated it when you signaled for us to come get him."

"He was getting agitated. It was time."

"Yeah, I know."

"He stood up and took a step towards me right after I signaled you."

"He did? Musta been when I was on my way out the door."

"Yeah, made me kinda nervous there for a second."

"I'm sure. You did great. Less than three months and you've caught a guy that we've been after now for over a year."

"I didn't do it alone. I was but a small part of a great team."

Jess took his hand and followed him back through the station to his truck. Undeterred, the press was still waiting when they exited the building.

"Detective Slater, can we get a statement?"

"Yes Detective, please."

"No comment, talk to Mike Shelley."

11:58 PM

"Mmm, come here, woman," he growled, hugging Jess tight against him. "Let's go inside. I wanna make love to the sexiest, most brilliant shrink on the planet."

Kevin led her to the bedroom. They just did make it inside before they were all over each other with Jess meeting him, kiss for blazing kiss. He dropped his jacket where they stood and pulled her closer still, one hand on her back, the other caressing her behind, and ravaged her lips like a man starved, breaking away only long enough to tear away her clothes.

Undressed to her undergarments, Jess stood on display for her lover, forcing him to step back to admire her. He drew a ragged breath as his gaze slowly and seductively raked her body, lingering for a moment on the crimson bra and panties. Reaching out, he touched her cheek with the back of his hand, trailing it down her jaw and neck. When she turned her head slightly, he planted a kiss in the hollow of her throat as he traced the contours of her shoulder with his fingers, hooking them through a lace-trimmed bra strap and caressing the skin below, though he didn't remove it.

His voice simmered with barely checked lust. "God, this is...you are so beautiful."

Sweeping her into his arms, he carried her to the bed and put her down before ripping off his shirt and tossing it aside. Uncovered were the big, strong arms she never tired of, the broad, furred chest, and rippling abs. Jess rose slowly, raking her short nails up his abdomen and torso until her hands rested on his shoulders, then turned him around and pushed him down onto the edge of the bed then straddled him, turning her attention to his nipples. They hardened instantly. She gave one taut nub a tongue-bath, biting it, and rolling the other between her fingertips, moving downward to lick the skin of his taut stomach. She pulled off his shoes and socks, unbuckled his belt, and went to work easing off his pants, revealing black boxer-briefs, simple, yet always so sexy on him, not to mention, quick to remove.

He was long and hard from head to toe; like a rock. She could barely contain her need. She wanted nothing more than to fuck him hard and fast, but she wasn't eager for their lovemaking to end soon, so she took her time. Dropping to her knees before him, she kissed and licked her way down one sinewy leg, nipping here and there before arriving at his feet, where she massaged the pads before beginning the journey back up, at last, finding her way to his briefs. He rose slightly, allowing her to remove them, and then lay back against the pillows when she rested between his legs.

Grabbing his distended cock in her hands, she stroked it up and down, forcing a groan from him, and then wrapped her lips around the smooth head to lick a drop of moisture from its tip. He shuddered with a sharp intake of breath, scarcely able to control himself when she sucked his thick shaft deep into the back of her mouth, winding his hands through her long hair and moving his hips while she bobbed up and down. Mmm, she started to hum.

He gasped. "God, Sweetheart, you can't keep that up."

Jess pulled back and peered at him through hooded eyes. Pent up longing caused his stiff rod to quiver and twitch every few seconds. Once again, she leaned down and kissed the taut head, then licked the velvety skin along the sides before taking his entire length into her throat. Holding back her hair, he pumped vigorously for a moment then pulled his organ from her lips.

"Sweet Jesus! I can't take anymore," he groaned. "Come up here," he said raggedly, pulling her up across his chest.

Lying back on the bed, Kevin closed his eyes for a second, not to sleep, but to regain his composure, while Jess traced random patterns through the silky hairs on his chest. He rolled her over, sucked one pebble-hard nipple between his teeth, and nibbled it lightly, sending a multitude of fiery sensations straight to her core. He was methodical as he worked his way down her body with his lips and tongue, removing her bra and panties when they got in his way.

The whiskers of his mustache tickled every inch of skin they touched. The sensations were maddening. Bypassing the aching flesh between her legs, he opted to go lower, stopping at her feet. One by one, he sucked each toe, working his way back up the other leg to stop where Jess wanted him most. She could have died the moment his tongue flitted across the magic button guarding her woman's heat, his flickering tongue and neatly trimmed whiskers inducing a tingling in her nether lips as they skimmed across. Without realizing it, she held the sides of his head, not only to better guide him, but to keep him there.

"That feels so good. Make love to me now, please!" She begged.

"No, Darlin'," he drawled. "I'm not done."

Finally, drawing one hand from his hair, Jess inserted her own fingers into her slick tunnel. The visual was more than Kevin could endure. Removing her fingers, he raised them to his lips, and sucked the juices off.

"Mmm...finger-lickin' good. Tell me what you want, my beauty," he requested.

"I want you to..." Jess trailed off when his teeth and tongue grazed the swollen sentry and pushed her over the edge into orgasmic bliss.

"You want me to what?" He asked.

"Oh God," she screamed, arching against his lips. "Fuckkk me, please," she pleaded.

He rolled her onto her belly, wrapped his arms around her and spread her legs, then speared her from behind. Unable to move, she could only feel him sliding in and out, ballocks slapping against her cheeks. She turned her head to the side, giving him access to the tender flesh of her neck, a blatant invitation for him to sink his teeth in. Leaving his mark, he stiffened. Jess felt the drawing of his testes when he came.

"Goddamn, you feel so good."

He rolled to his side when he was completely spent and cradled her in his arms. They slept spooned, his rod making its home inside her, until dawn, when its early morning stirring awakened her. At first, Jess thought she was dreaming until he shifted and rested a hand on her thigh.

She moaned and tightened her muscles around him, arched, and pushed her derriere and shoulders against him, waking him. He kissed her shoulder and moved up her neck, dipping his tongue into her ear, sending a shiver of lust rippling down her spine. Jess slipped her hand between her legs and worked a finger against her throbbing mound, riding the climactic waves to their crest.

Chapter 17

8:13 AM

"Hey Honey, check it out. We made the front page. *Local detectives catch Headbanger,*" Kevin said, walking through the front door with the newspaper. The barrage of telephone calls started almost before he got the door closed. "I think this would be a good day to turn off the ringer and let the machine have 'em all."

"You'll get no argument from me."

"Hello, big brother. Congratulations, you made the news all the way back home. Obviously, you're not available or I wouldn't be talking to this damn machine."

"But I should probably get that one." He grabbed the telephone before Samantha hung up.

"Anyway, I just wanted to call to say hi and give you a long-distance pat on the back. So gimme a ring, would ya?"

"Wait Sammy, I'm here. Sorry, I was a little busy and couldn't get to the phone," he said, flashing Jess his arresting smile. "So we made the news all the way in Minnesota, eh...Yeah we, I couldn't have done it without her." He sent Jess another brilliant smile. "You keep watching. We'll be there again, soon...I hope," he said as he laughed. "Among other things...Who? Jess? She's the best...Yeah, I do, a lot...Yeah, she's here...Early for you, maybe...Yes, it's official...I dunno...You know I couldn't take off right now even if I wanted to. I mean, I love you and all, but..." he held the phone out to Jess. "It's my little sister. She wants to talk to you." Jess hesitated. "Go ahead, you'll like her."

"Hello?"

"Hi Jess, this is Samantha. How are you?"

"I'm great, and you?"

"Wonderful, and even better now that my brother's decided to settle down."

"Is that what he told you?"

"Of course not, I figured it out on my own. It's obvious he's crazy about you. You're all he talks about, and that's a big deal. He's not easily impressed."

"Is that so?" A gleam of comprehension came to Jess's eyes and left a secret smile in its wake.

"Yeah it is. I hate that you two are so busy right now. I'd love to meet you."

"Apparently, we have quite a bit in common. Kevin's told me so much about you that I feel like I already know you. Hey, the holidays will be here soon. We'd love for you to spend them with us."

"Really?"

"Oh sure, it'll be fun."

"I'll definitely keep that in mind. Jess, it was great to meet you finally, sort of. If you don't mind, lemme talk to Kev again."

"Sure." Jess returned the receiver to him.

"Sure, you're welcome any time...Okay Runt, love you too. Bye."

"She seems real sweet."

"Sweet and sour maybe, nah, she's great, a good mix."

"The youngest, right?"

"Yeah, twenty-nine. You'd like her, and it was thoughtful of you to invite her down for the holidays."

"The more the merrier, besides I'd love to meet her. So, is she coming down?"

"She said she'd see what she could work out with her boss."

"Oh, I just realized that I invited her down without asking first. I hope I didn't put you in a bind."

"Jess, my house is your house. You don't need permission to invite anyone over." Kevin paused before continuing with an admission that Jess had longed to hear. "I never thought I'd ever say that to anyone, but I never expected to feel for anyone what I do for you."

"Really?"

"Yes."

"Oh, Kevin..." Jess wound her arms around his neck and kissed him. Though she wasn't ready to admit she was falling for him, his disclosure made her more comfortable with her feelings. "So what's that article say?"

"Oh yeah," he said, then started reading aloud while Jess skimmed over his shoulder. "*The nightmare is finally over.*"

"If only that were true."

"Yeah, really."

> *An undercover sting operation lead by local detective, Kevin Slater, ended quickly and without grievous injury late yesterday evening when Mark Thompson, the alleged campus killer, also known as Headbanger, was nabbed in the act. Using a profile constructed by famed forensic psychologist, Jess Mitchell, police officials from the city of Burlington, with assistance from the Elon Police Department, the Elon University campus police, and the State Bureau of Investigation, put together an ingenious undercover operation tailored to coerce the perpetrator into attacking an undercover police officer.*

"Famed forensic psychologist?" Jess questioned with a nervous laugh and continued reading. "That's scary."

> *Several weeks ago local police officer, Christine Parezi, posing as a co-ed, moved into Brannock Hall with fellow officers, James Reynolds and Paul Sanders, along with more than a dozen other undercover officers and SBI agents in surrounding dorms. Several undercover female officers served as bait to draw out the killer. Police were unable to anticipate which, if any, officer would become a target until the alleged killer became alarmingly friendly with Officer Parezi. The quick response of Officers Reynolds and Sanders saved Officer Parezi from serious harm after the alleged killer attacked her as she was leaving the dormitory laundry room.*

"That's some article."

"I can think of at least three cops who won't have any trouble with the promotions board."

"I know a certain detective too, who shouldn't have any trouble making Lieutenant when the time comes."

> *The profile used in this case was nearly perfect. Doctor Mitchell said the perpetrator would be a white male between the ages of 28 and 32. Mark Thompson is 29-year-old white male. She predicted he would be a university employee working in a service-type position. Mark Thompson worked as a maintenance technician. Doctor Mitchell also stated the perpetrator would live nearby and lack reliable transportation. Mark Thompson resides on Lebanon Avenue just two blocks from Brannock Hall. A car was located at the residence. However, it had four flat tires and a blown engine. Perhaps her most uncanny prediction was that the perpetrator would be a physically attractive man at six feet tall and one hundred seventy pounds.*

Kevin stopped reading and looked at her. "They're right about that part, for sure. How the hell did you figure that out?"

"Simple deduction, my dear Watson," she shot back with a giggle.

> *Sources say Mark Thompson is an attractive man at five foot eleven and one hundred sixty-seven pounds with movie star looks. Due to their ongoing involvement in yet another high-profile investigation, neither Detective Slater nor*

Doctor Mitchell was available for comment at this time.

"Not bad. Jeez!" Jess exclaimed, flipping through the pages. "Half the paper is devoted to this case, or to profiling in general."

"Well, you should know from growing up here that Burlington's pretty quiet, with the exception of the occasional serial killer. This is big news around here."

"True, I think the biggest thing to hit this area was the Blanche Taylor Moore case until now."

CRSORROR

Jess combed through the evidence again, in hopes of finding an overlooked clue, now that she had a better idea of the monster they were seeking. The dig proved that MaryAnn Hunter was a card-carrying member of a social group called KLAASP when a fresh look through the crime scene photos revealed a candid shot of the woman's membership card lying in plain sight on her desk. A quick Google search turned up a nationwide network of these groups, and their purpose excited Jess to the point she could hardly wait to tell Kevin.

Encouraged, Jess went deeper. She compared a series of vague appointments from Elizabeth Johnson's PDA to the upcoming KLAASP calendar. Nearly every one matched. Armed with this telling new information, and more certain than ever that S&M was the factor tying the victims together, she signed herself and Kevin up as members, positive they'd somehow be able to use it to their advantage.

"So what exactly is KLAASP?" Kevin asked.

"Kinky Lovers and Alternative Sexual Proclivities."

"That's...different."

"I signed us up. We're official card-carrying members, or will be when we pick them up."

"You did what?"

"Mr. Clean could be a member. He has to meet likeminded people somewhere."

"Could we get so lucky?" He paused a moment then continued, laughing as he spoke. "Woman, you scare me. So when do we go?"

"After the newbie munch."

"What is that?"

"It's basically a luncheon for new members or others interested in the lifestyle, no fetish wear required. They'll go over the basics and give us our membership cards, the upcoming lecture schedule, and calendar of events while we're there."

"That sounds easy enough. When and where?"

"Next Friday night, 7:30 at the Java Hut. I think we should come up with aliases. These folks are secretive and our names are all over the news from the Headbanger case. We don't want to blow our cover."

"Good idea."

They put their heads together and decided on variations of their own names. Kevin would use Reese, his middle name, while Jess went by a childhood nickname, C.J. While they were brainstorming, they also thought of simple disguises to help with the illusion. With the Chief's approval, Kevin would override department policy and allow his beard to grow, while Jess planned to borrow a wig and club clothes from Niki.

11:30 AM

"Morning Bailey. O'Reilly"

"Morning Sarge, Doctor Mitchell."

"Hi boys," Jess said as she and Kevin walked past the front desk.

CRSORROR

"Damn, look at her. That woman is fucking hot."

"Damn straight."

"Lucky bastard."

"Who?"

"Slater, who do you think?"

"Why's that?"

"You mean you don't know?"

"Know what?"

"He's hitting the sheets with her."

"No shit? Where'd you hear that?"

"A very reliable source."

"Come on, who?"

"Rafferty."

"How the hell would he know? They doing threesomes or something?"

"Yeah, in Rafferty's dreams. Does she look like the threesome type to you?"

"A man can dream. Can't he?"

"Evidently, he's got a thing going with a friend of hers. If that ain't a reliable source, I don't know what is."

"True. Damn, must be nice."

☙℘ℭℛ℘

"Hey, Maggie."

"Jessie, Detective Slater, how are you?"

"Great, Maggie, and you?" Kevin asked.

"Oh, I am just terrific. A little birdie tells me you two have become fast friends," she said.

"You could say that. Are they ready?"

"They're waiting inside for you."

"Thanks, Maggie."

They strolled into Dean's office confident, their heads held high, and closed the door. "Good morning, you two."

"Hi Chief, Mike."

"Dean tells me you have some thoughts on catching Mr. Clean."

"Yes, Mike," Jess confirmed.

"So, lay it on us."

"We've found the connection between the victims. It's very controversial and well, you won't like it, but the fact remains that it's our best lead, so far."

"You're right, I don't like the sound of that."

"You both know that in my business, we classify serial murder as a sex crime," Jess continued.

"Yes."

"Well, Kevin and I have found the sexual element."

"And it's a doozie," Kevin added.

"What do either of you know about BDSM?" She asked.

"Never heard of it. Dean?"

"BDSM? What's that?"

Glossing over nothing, Jess explained the inner workings of the lifestyle, and as expected, the men were not happy with the new information. It would automatically put the victims and their families on defense, which would make closing the case that much more difficult. Because average people had little to no understanding of BDSM, they would assume the women asked for what happened...to be tortured to death and left on display. Public support for the case would diminish once it became common knowledge that the women weren't nearly as average as first thought. In the public's eye, the women would suddenly be no better than common prostitutes.

"Here, take a look at this." Jess passed out copies of a story she'd found online and waited for the three men to read it.

"God, where do you come up with this stuff? This guy sounds like a walking nightmare. Is this true?" Mike asked.

"I dunno. I imagine a lot of this kind of stuff is urban myth, but this particular tale kinda got me to thinking that something like this really *could* happen. My guess is our victims probably used their safewords or protested at some point, but our guy doesn't care about safewords or the BDSM creed because like the Lord Grey in this story, he's not a true Dominant. He's a psychopath with a sadistic streak. He's not interested in the lifestyle. He's probably always had fantasies where absolute control is the key element and at some point that control fanned out to include control over life and death. He gets off on killing and he'll keep at it until he's either dead or institutionalized."

"Okay, so lemme get this straight," Mike said. "You think Mr. Clean is a sadist with a penchant for murder who discovered a ready supply of women in this KLAASP group who were willing to let him torture them to death."

"Well, sort of, except they had no idea he planed to torture them to death."

"But that's what the public will assume," Mike answered.

"And you want me to agree to a plan for you and Slater to look into this group to see what you can find out."

"Yes, Dean, that's exactly what I want."

"This is a bad dream come true. This guy sounds like Ted Bundy."

"You got it, Mike."

"How in the hell are we supposed to catch a monster like that?" He asked.

"We won't catch him, not in the act, that is. We'll catch him through his own carelessness or through some unrelated event, just like they caught Bundy."

"There goes my happy retirement," Dean said.

"And my happy ascent to the throne," Mike joked.

"Dean, you'll get your happy retirement. I just hope you weren't planning it within the next few months, and Mike, I have no doubt that you'll make a terrific Chief someday. We'll catch him and this will end up being a great career move for all of us."

"This plan of yours sounds dangerous. You're setting yourself up as bait," Dean said.

"I guess, in a way, I am."

"I don't like this idea, at all. Who'll be looking out for you?" Mike asked.

"My Dom."

"And that would be?"

"Kevin, of course. Who else?"

"Who else, indeed?" Dean wondered aloud, amused. "I'll agree to this on a provisional basis. If there's *any* sign that you're in any danger, I'll pull the plug."

"Dean, I understand exactly where you're coming from, but you're letting personal feelings get in the way of your job. You're thinking like a father and not like a cop," Mike said.

"I realize that, but I don't care. I don't want my Jessie or Kevin put in any more danger than necessary. This killer has taken too many lives already, and I won't have my daughter or my best cop added his list."

"We'll be extremely careful. I promise," Jess said.

"Chief, I'd lay my life down for her," Kevin added.

"Yes, Kevin, I believe you would, which is why I'm agreeing to this for now, but I want to be apprised of every new detail that comes up as *soon* as it comes up."

ଓଃରଠଓଃରଠ

"That was a hell of a lot easier than I thought it would be," Kevin said.

"I was kinda surprised by that, myself. He really thinks a lot of you."

"Who?"

"Dean."

"I think a lot of him too. He's a good man." He put his hand on her back and they walked back out to his truck. "So, back to the meetings..."

"Oh yes, SubMarine...did I tell you that he or she was a member?" Kevin shook his head. "I mentioned the group when we were chatting and he admitted to being a member. I'm sorry. I've learned so much in so little time, I must've forgotten. Anyway, he told me this month's topic. I think you may find it fascinating."

"Okay, I'll bite. What is it?"

"Safe flogging."

"You think our victims were flogged."

"Yup."

3:45 PM

"I just got the strangest phone call."

"Yeah, from who?"

"Niki. She wants us to go get malled on Saturday."

"Mauled? You're gonna have to explain that one."

Jess giggled. "She wants to go shopping, at the mall."

What jess didn't know was that Kevin had arranged the surprise shopping trip. He had big plans for his ladylove on Saturday evening, but he needed help setting his plan in place, and Niki was just the person to do it, though he told her as little as possible. He wanted his plans to remain secret.

"Oh okay, I get it, malled. Well, since I'm in here, I thought I'd check out KLAASP for myself. Interesting group, by the way. I got the rules for the munch and meetings. It seems pretty relaxed, and you weren't kidding about them being secretive. We have to wear street clothes and we're to tell whoever's at the door we came for *the meeting in the back room.*"

Chapter 18

Friday evening...

"Check *you* out. I didn't think I liked redheads."

"Well, I should hope not," Jess sassed. "And you weren't kidding. You really do grow a beard quick," she added, rubbing her hand along his jaw. "It's sexy, too."

"It itches like hell, but if you like it, that's all that matters."

Later at the Java Hut...

"Hi, we're here for the meeting in the back."

"I don't recall seeing you before. What are your names?"

"Reese and CJ."

"Ah yes, our newest members. Welcome, I'm Meryl. This is Natalie. You've been to the newbie munch?"

"We just left."

"Natalie will show you to the conference room. I assume you know tonight's topic. Please remain seated quietly until the lecture is over. Afterwards, there will be time for mingling with the other attendees," she said. "Or more, if you're interested."

"Thank you." They followed Natalie into a large room near the back of the coffee house and took out-of-the-way seats where they could observe everyone. "She was checking you out," Kevin whispered as they sat down.

"Who?"

"Meryl."

"Ewww not!" Jess' received a grin and quiet snicker from Kevin.

"I can't say I blame her. I'm a diehard lesbian, myself."

9:37 PM

The couple remained seated while Lady Elaine answered questions from the audience, and became particularly interested when an audience member asked about constructing his own flogger. The variations seemed limitless. Lady Elaine's favorite flogger, which she had used during her demonstration, was handmade from suede, but one could use deerskin, elk hide, leather, horsehair, or most any other material. The experienced Domina was as thorough in her answer as she was with her demonstration, recommending a shredded pillowcase for beginners before upgrading to something firmer as the user gained experience.

"That was enlightening and even a bit interesting."

"I'll say, makes me want to take you home and flog you."

"Is that so, Mister?"

"Yes, heads up, we got company."

"Good evening, I don't believe we've met. You must be new."

"This is our first time here. I'm Reese and this is CJ."

"A pleasure to make your acquaintance, I am Elaine." She did not introduce her male companion. "Are you new to the area or just to the lifestyle?"

"Both sorta, CJ is originally from Raleigh, but hasn't lived in the area for several years. We moved down from Minnesota."

"What brings you to KLAASP?"

"CJ came across a book called *The Sensual Submissive*. I skimmed it when she finished reading and found it interesting, so we decided to learn more."

"You've come to the right place. Most everyone is very helpful."

"*Most* everyone?"

"You'll find an occasional Dom who doesn't follow the creed as closely as he should or a brat, which don't get me wrong, can be desirable at times."

"A brat?"

"Rebellious sub."

"Ah."

"They're easy to spot once you know the signs."

"What are the signs?"

"Unwelcome touching and harassment after being spurned are the big ones."

"That's just common courtesy."

"True, unfortunately a lot of people don't use good manners anymore, but respect for personal boundaries is even more important here. Abusive Doms and brats tend to use groups like KLAASP in much the same way that vanillas use singles bars. Fortunately, they are few and far between."

"That's good to know. Thank you."

"You'll probably want to find a mentor if you decide the lifestyle is right for you."

"What sort of mentor?"

"As the dominant partner, you'll need to learn the art of topping. While you're learning, your sub can help in this by communicating her needs to you. We call it topping from the bottom."

"I read something about that."

"Even while you're both learning, remember that CJ must always know her place. She must learn exactly how to fulfill *your* every desire. She can do this only if you make it clear to her when she has pleased or displeased you. When she pleases you, you will reward her. The opposite is also true."

"You mean punishment?"

"I prefer to call it discipline. In order for her to learn what pleases you, *you* must handle the majority of her training. When you're comfortable as her Master, you'll take over and she will fully assume her role. Come, let's talk."

Elaine snapped her fingers at her companion as she sat down and he immediately left them. Upon his return, he knelt before her and offered her a drink. Kevin gave the man only a cursory glance.

"Very good my pet. Sit, Armand," Elaine said as she caressed the top of his head and turned back to Kevin. "Discipline CJ in much the same way you would a child. Removal of privileges works well for many Dominants, myself included. It's common to choose a method other than corporal punishment, since that is often part of scening and more reward than punishment. But if you do choose it, never use it in anger. To do so goes against the creed and is tantamount to abuse, and is never acceptable."

"How do you determine a reward when *he* has pleased you?" Kevin asked, nodding towards Armand.

"That depends on the task and how well he does it. Armand loves a good spanking so when he's been exceptionally good, I may treat him with a leather paddle until his backside glows bright red and he begs to come."

"Really? This is fascinating," Kevin said. "There's so much to learn."

"And it never stops. It encompasses many areas...discipline and reward, limitations, scening and aftercare, and of course such things as flogging, which you saw demonstrated tonight, paddling, whipping, or anything else that turns you on."

"So if I'm into bondage, for example, I'd look for a mentor who knows the art."

"There are many forms of bondage...restrictive, suspension, mummification, and so on...so you'd look for an experienced teacher in the form you're most interested in."

"How do I find a mentor?"

"You simply ask. However, I would guard against asking anyone to mentor you until you have attended several play parties."

"Why is that?"

"At play parties, you have the opportunity to observe many Doms with diverse styles. This will help you determine what you like or dislike and also select a seasoned Dom with the right experience to help with your training."

"I've never been to a party. Tell me about them."

"A play party is a mixer where the more, shall we say, risqué activities take place. As far as I know, they are by invitation only. You will see many activities that are viewed as immoral by vanillas or even illegal by the authorities."

"I see."

"Are you in a twenty-four seven relationship?"

"We live together, but we've experimented only with occasional fantasies."

"That's not surprising. Many successful partnerships begin this way. You still have so much to learn. I'm hosting a small mixer in a couple of weeks. Would you be interested in attending?"

"I might be."

"Take my card and visit my website. You'll find my rules of attendance along with the dress code. You'll also find that I am quite strict, but if you're still interested, email me and I'll send you the specifics. Until then, study everything you can find on D/s. And since you're already into scening, pay specific attention to aftercare. It's crucial to your sub's emotional well-being." The woman stood up and snapped her fingers at Armand again, prompting him to rise behind her. "It was a pleasure meeting you, but we must be going now."

"Yes, and thank you very much for the information and invitation."

"Come on, CJ, let's go home." Jess dutifully followed Kevin to the car.

"Oh my God, that was a trip!" She exclaimed as soon as they were out of earshot.

"Wasn't it? I nearly cracked up when Elaine called that guy her pet."

"Yes, that *was* funny until it sunk in that she was serious, but even worse was the way that guy, whose name is Armand, by the way, blindly followed her. I don't quite get what makes a person *that* dependant on someone else."

"Does this mean you're going to turn into a brat and rebel on me?"

"I just might! I mean, I recognize some submissive qualities in myself. I think probably everybody has both dominant and submissive aspects to their personalities, but that's just taking it to the extreme."

"Now you've got my attention. I've seen your dominant side. Tell me about your submissive qualities."

"I live to please *you*...Master. Is there *any*thing I can do for you now?" She asked brazenly.

Kevin laughed. "Hmm, I'll have to think about that and get back to you. Did you happen to notice next month's topic?"

"No, I didn't."

"I can hardly wait."

"Uh oh, now I'm afraid to find out."

"Orgasm on command," he said with a devilish gleam in his eyes.

"Oh, good Lord!"

"I think technically it was called controlled orgasm, but..."

"Yeah, yeah, I get the idea."

Saturday afternoon...

Niki made good on her plans for she and Jess to get malled, arriving shortly before three o'clock. She rushed Jess to the car and then made a covert call to Kevin to let him know they were leaving, though she let Jess believe it was David. Like Kevin and Jess, Niki and David had become inseparable over the past few weeks. As usual, Niki was a veritable chatterbox. She wasted no time is telling her friend about her own 'energizer bunny'.

They had ridden only a few miles when Niki glanced into the rear-view mirror. "What the hell?"

"What?"

"I got blue lights on my ass!"

Jess turned to look. "Well, pull over, for God's sake! Obviously, it's a mistake. You weren't speeding were you?"

"No, but this is a real inconvenience. I'm not riding away from here with a damn ticket. I got way too many connections between the two of us."

She pulled over into the abandoned parking lot of what was once K-Mart, but instead of asking for her license and registration, the officer walked straight to the passenger side.

"Jessica Mitchell?" He inquired in a very serious tone.

"Yes."

"Please, step out of the car and place your hands on the hood in front of you. I have a warrant for you arrest." Niki's eyes grew wide as she listened.

In an instant, Jess knew what was happening as déjà vu settled in. She did as told, smiling while the officer recited her rights. An unknown police officer could not have known that she answered to Jessica rather than Caroline, and only a few people knew she was out shopping with Niki that day. Jess knew that voice. The patrolman followed his announcement with a very intimate frisk, stopping to capture her breasts. She knew those hands *very* well.

"Ma'am, I'm afraid these are contraband. I'm gonna to have to run you in."

"But Officer, why am I being arrested? I haven't done anything wrong," Jess stated, feigning innocence.

"Oh, but you will," he replied.

She turned to look at him. Lo and behold, it was Kevin, and he'd even worn a real uniform. "Oh my! Are you going to give me a ticket?"

"No Ma'am, I have something else in mind for you. Turn back around please."

She faced the car again while he pulled her hands behind her. Click! Cold, steel handcuffs snapped shut around her wrists. She peered into the car and found Niki laughing hysterically.

"You knew about this, didn't you?"

"I had no clue he was going to do this. I was only supposed to take you shopping. By the way, love the goatee, Kevin. You look hot."

"Thank you. Let's go."

"But what about Niki?"

He looked inside the car. "She can entertain herself," he said with a mischievous grin. He pushed Jess into the back seat of a patrol car.

"Where's the truck?"

"Maintenance, this one's a loaner."

Arriving back at their house, Kevin helped Jess from the squad car and motioned for her to walk ahead of him. In seconds, it became apparent that the entire scenario had been carefully orchestrated. He prodded her towards the bedroom, then removed the handcuffs. Numerous candles cast a warm glow as they flickered around the room.

"Come on, I have a few things to show you," he said as he meticulously stripped Jess of most of her clothing before shedding his uniform. "Assume the position."

"Oh my, Officer, what a big gun you have!" She drawled as she turned her back to him, flashing a coy look over her shoulder.

"Brat!"

Kevin grabbed her around the waist and flipped her onto her back, and suddenly, she was impaled with his marvelous tool. He did all the work. She had only to enjoy the ride, not that she was given a choice, being restrained as she was. He had thrown her legs over his shoulders and pinned her arms over her head at the wrists, which allowed him better access to both her wet-hot folds and nipples, but he rolled away before he lost control and spilled his seed, then handcuffed her, yet again.

"You have the right to remain silent. However, I wouldn't advise it. You have the right to talk dirty. Anything you say can and will be used to your advantage. You have the right to come...over and over again. If you cooperate, I'll see to it that you're treated *very* well. Do you understand these rights?"

"Yes, Sir."

He spread her legs, lifted her to his lips, and began licking her with that fabulous tongue.

"Ohh yeah, keep doing that, feels so good. Please, fuck me now!"

"No, my Dear, not yet, your third right has not been exercised to best of my abilities. I promised to treat you *very* well while in my custody." He rolled her onto her stomach, then pulled her to her knees and slid just the head of his cock into her moist opening. "You know what I want. Say it," he commanded.

"Oh God, please fuck me," she begged.

"Again, I love it when you talk dirty," he whispered in her ear.

"Fuck me!" She screamed.

He plunged all the way into her sleek tunnel and pounded her like never before. "You like that, Baby?" He asked.

"Ohhh," Jess moaned. "Come on, give it to me!"

She groaned when he reached around with one hand to tickle her pleasure bud while using another slippery finger to caress the rim of her kazoo. A bolt of lightening wouldn't have shocked her more. After mere seconds, Jess' muscles clenched firmly around Kevin's rod in the most intense orgasm she'd ever experienced. With that, he let go with a stream of liquid fire that gushed so hard, it elicited more waves of pleasure from her. They rested for a moment, then Jess rolled to her back, her cuffed wrists remaining over her head as Kevin leaned up on an elbow and looked down at her.

"So...did I live up to your fantasy?" He asked.

"Honey, you went above and beyond any fantasy I could ever cook up."

"I don't know about that. I've seen your mind at work."

"Hmm, maybe. So um, you think you could loosen the bracelets now?"

"Oh yeah, sorry about that," he said, laughing as he removed the restraints.

He ran his fingers across her abdomen and crawled over her, tangling a hand in her hair, then kissed her. His mustache tickled her nose while the beard abraded her chin when he plunged his tongue into her mouth. As he delved deeper, Jess suckled his bottom lip, tasting herself on him.

Tuesday...

"Hey Kev, come in here. I'm in chat and I think you'll find the conversation real interesting."

He came and read over her shoulder. "Your friend, SubMarine."

"Not just any friend, take a look." Jess scrolled back, allowing him to read from the beginning.

He cocked an eyebrow and laughed. "SubDoer? Interesting screen name."

"Yeah, you like that?"

"It's cute."

"Cute wasn't exactly what I was going for, but it'll work," she said, grinning.

> *SubDoer: we went to our first KLAASP meeting last week*
> *SubMarine: Really?*
> *SubDoer: yes, it was quite fascinating*
> *SubMarine: I was there with my mistress. I wonder if we met.*
> *SubDoer: it's possible though we spoke to very few people*
> *SubDoer: since we're so new to the L/s my Master was more interested in finding a mentor*

"What's L/s?" Kevin asked.

"Cyberlingo for lifestyle."

> *SubMarine: i hope he's careful who he approaches*
> *SubDoer: we were invited to a play party next month*
> *SubMarine: my Mistress is hosting a party soon*
> *SubDoer: armand?*
> *SubMarine: who is this?*
> *SubDoer: this is CJ, looks like we meet again*

SubMarine: yes, i remember

"So SubMarine is Armand. This could be a big break, having someone on the inside. Baby, you're brilliant."

"Thank you."

"Let's see how long he'll talk."

SubMarine: will you be attending the party?
SubDoer: i think so
SubMarine: be sure to follow the rules, my Mistress is very firm
SubDoer: Armand what did you mean when you said my Master should be careful when choosing a mentor?

"Keep him talking. This is the kind of stuff we're looking for."

SubMarine: Oh, I must go. The mistress is home. I'm not supposed to be online this week.
SubMarine is offline.

"Shit, he's gone!" Jess exclaimed. Kevin looked at her in surprise. "What?"

"Such fowl language, I'm shocked," he said, laughing as she knotted her brow at him. "Relax, I'm teasing. I'm just not used to hearing you cuss."

She smiled, shamefaced. "One slips out every now and then when I'm upset."

"Or horny," he added as he kissed the back of her neck. "I like that," he said as he rubbed her shoulders.

"Well anyway, I've added Armand to my buddy list, so we'll know when he sneaks online again. Maybe I'll get to talk to him again before the party."

"Speaking of that, I checked Elaine's web site to see what we're in for and emailed her for the particulars."

"Yeah? Find anything interesting?"

"Your friend wasn't kidding about her being strict."

"Explain, please."

"Well, first, there's a dress code for the party."

"And what might that be?"

"Fetish wear, whatever that is," he said

"I know that one, loose interpretation for leather, latex, sexy clothes, goth...that sort of thing."

"You mean like that *nice* meter maid uniform you put on the other night?" Jess blushed hot, all the way to her ears. "You're not gonna wear *that* out in public, are you?"

"Hell no!"

"There you go again," he said with a chuckle. "Where are we supposed to find that stuff?"

"Mine's easy, I'll just raid Niki's closet again. You, on the other hand, we may need to go shopping for," she said, grinning while she sized him up and down before continuing. "Oooohh, you would be so hot in a pair of tight leather pants."

"You think so?"

"Uh huh, we should be able to get those over at Davis Harley, but accessories will have to come from a sex shop." He cocked an eyebrow at her remark. "What else?" She asked.

"Just one last thing, and I'm not sure you're gonna be comfortable with it. Hell, I'm not sure if *I'm* comfortable with it. There's probably gonna be a lot of kinky shit going on that we, as cops, are gonna have to overlook. Not to mention all the live scening we'll probably witness firsthand."

"I can feel myself blushing at the mere thought of it."

Chapter 19

Friday night...

"Wow! Holy..."

"I don't think this was such a great idea," Jess fretted, tugging at the hem of her borrowed micro-mini.

"Why not? I like the hell out of it." Kevin studied the outfit. "On second thought, maybe you shouldn't go out looking like that."

"Why?"

"It's bad enough that I have every cop on the force checking you out on a daily basis. I'm not sure I can take a room full of leather-clad fruitcakes putting the moves on my woman."

"I don't think you'll have a problem with that, but we should probably get going before I lose my nerve and decide not to go out in this."

Kevin wore a black, mock turtleneck with black, leather jeans. Jess had Niki's knee-length, leather trench coat to cover her party clothes. Elaine's instructions were specific. Attendees were to hide their fetish wear beneath street clothes.

"We *do* need to go, and it has nothing to do with your nerve. It's taking every ounce of my self-control not to throw you over my shoulder, take you into the bedroom, and strip that outfit right back off. Does Niki really go out in public wearing this?"

"She wears these boots and skirt together with a sweater, but she pairs the bustier with jeans. This would be overkill even for her," Jess explained as Kevin pulled from the driveway.

Thirty minutes later...

Jess reached into the back seat for the trench coat. "You look uncomfortable."

"I feel more like Jessica Rabbit than Jess Mitchell."

"I'll play Roger to your Jessica Rabbit any day. You look...damn hot!" Kevin ran his fingers along the edge of the bustier and pulled it up, covering a little more of Jess' overexposed, ample bosom, then pulled a long lock of hair from her auburn wig across her shoulder, covering a bit more. "There, is that better?"

"A little."

"This outfit may be enough to get you arrested again," he teased, winking at her. "Are you ready for this?"

"As ready as I'm gonna get." She looked down and tugged one last time at the skirt.

"Shall we?" Kevin asked after opening the car door and grasping her hand.

Elaine met them at the door. "Good evening, Reese, CJ. I'm pleased you could make it."

"Yes, good to see you again Elaine, and thank you again for inviting us. We brought some refreshments."

"You're quite welcome, and thank you. Please come inside. Armand will take your coat."

"Thanks, but I'd rather hold onto mine, for now."

Elaine's look was disapproving, though she refrained from further comment on Jess' attire. "Come, I'll introduce you to some of the others."

The couple trailed her down to a spacious, remodeled basement. The antechamber was flanked by several smaller rooms where couples and smaller subgroups had separated from the main gathering to start their scenes or try out various pieces of specialized equipment. In one room, they glanced several people using a spanking bench for what appeared to be a gangbang orgy. Two men had penetrated a woman, both orally and anally, while another woman used a strap-on dildo elsewhere.

"Oh my!" Jess gasped quietly.

"That's Max and Neesa. They've been experimenting with rape scenes. With her consent, he invited another couple to help them act it out."

The next room housed a massive Saint Andrew's cross. It was difficult to view the action due to the number of spectators, but it appeared to be quite the flogging scene. A tall, dark, and very handsome gentleman stood before a dazzling, auburn-haired woman.

Where she was almost nude, save for the studded, leather collar around her neck and the clamps strung between her nipples, he wore a non-fastening, leather vest over a most intriguing pair of leather pants. Styled in a similar fashion to Kevin's, these were different in that the crotch consisted of a separate, snap-on codpiece, which did little to hide his vociferous arousal as he struck the woman repeatedly with a long-tailed flogger, a treatment she seemed to relish.

"Nick and Sandy, flogging is his specialty. This is their first public scene together. The waiting list of those who want him as a mentor is phenomenal, not to mention the number of unattached slaves who would do anything to serve him."

"I can see why. He wields that flogger like an extension of his arm. He's a good-looking guy, too," Kevin observed aloud.

CʒﾛＯCʒﾛＯ

The following Monday, Jess drove to Raleigh to return Niki's freshly dry-cleaned party clothes. She had planned to stay a while to catch up, since the two friends had rarely seen each other since Jess' move back to Alamance County. She took a seat in a comfortable bar chair while Niki went into the small kitchen for drinks. Niki opened a Pepsi and handed her friend a Mountain Dew, and then sat down and lit a cigarette, wasting no time grilling Jess about borrowing *her* clothes, as they were far from Jess' style.

Although it was against protocol to talk about the case with civilians, Jess explained, without giving away critical information, about the investigation. Niki was dumbfounded when Jess hinted at her and Kevin's involvement in KLAASP and alluded to their membership in the group. In her usual fashion, Niki dug deeper, determined to learn more about this new and previously unknown facet of Jess' personality, forcing Jess to go against all of her professional training and reveal more sensitive details.

She told her friend all about the meetings and the play party that she and Kevin had attended. Floggings held little appeal for the wild redhead, but her attention was sparked at the mention of orgasm control. That led to her expressing an interest in joining the group to discover more, but Jess would have no part of it. She demanded that Niki stay clear of KLAASP and the danger it harbored.

"We were just playing. The hardcore folks are into whippings, torture, and stuff like that. And even worse, the guy we're trying to catch is into bloodletting. If that's not a good enough reason to stay away from these people, I don't know what is."

Niki laughed and accused her friend of being more interested in the lifestyle that she would admit, but agreed to Jess' terms...for the time being.

CʒﾛＯCʒﾛＯ

The following week brought with it Kevin's birthday. He'd all but forgotten it himself until Jess ran out of the office in a driving storm to help Stefano Damiano, from Paolo's, bring in a veritable feast for two. The man then set up two chairs and a small fold-up table, on which he laid out stylish linens and candles in the waiting area of the main office. Finally, he ushered the couple to their seats, served them food and drink, and then wished Kevin a happy birthday in his thick Italian accent, before parting and leaving them alone, once again.

"You know, we've got the entire place to ourselves for a while," Kevin observed.

"How'd that happen?" Jess flirted in coquettish manner.

"Hmm well, remember, Brian caught himself a bug, leaving only me and Rafferty to fill in for him, and right now, it's Dave's turn."

"Lucky us."

Kevin locked the main office door and closed the blinds, then whisked everything from the front desk, most of it falling to the floor. He lifted Jess onto the desktop, removed her gun from its holster and set it out of the way, then began unbuttoning her blouse. Underneath, she'd worn a front-hook bra that

107

he was able to unfasten quickly without removing her shirt. Leaning down, he caught a nipple between his lips while his hands fumbled with her skirt, finally raising it around her waist. Jess knew he'd discovered her other birthday surprise when he looked up with a wide grin.

"Crotchless? Yum! I knew there was a reason behind you wearing a skirt."

He slid his hands underneath her, raised her minge towards his mouth, and with his unbelievable tongue, lapped at her throbbing folds, occasionally dipping into the slick tunnel below. He knew exactly how to get her juices flowing. His oral ministrations continued until Jess bucked up off the desk, grinding against his prickly chin. As the final shudders of her climax subsided, Kevin removed his own firearm, unfastened his pants, and dropped them around his ankles. His rock-hard cock stood at attention. Jess leaned backwards, supporting the majority of their combined weight on her forearms, while he very easily glided into her. In and out, rapid strokes led to his entire body growing stiff as he fired his seed deep inside her.

They had taken a big chance making love in the substation, because just moments later, Dave pounded at the door. Jess jumped off the desk and pulled her skirt back down, then hurried to the bathroom to make herself more presentable. Kevin took no hurry fastening his pants and holstering his gun, humorously leaving his underling in the pounding rain. He unlocked the door and allowed a sopping Dave entry just as Jess reclaimed her seat at the table. Right away, Rafferty took in her disheveled appearance and flushed skin, and he failed to miss the mess left of the front desk. He immediately started firing off questions.

"What the hell is going on here, Bro? Did you not know it was fucking pouring out? And what the hell happened to my desk? You get attacked or something?"

"Yeah man, attacked by hunger pangs when I smelled all this great food Jess ordered from Paolo's. You have a key. You coulda let yourself in."

"I figured the door was locked for a reason. Thought I'd walk in on something I shouldn't."

"You know, you need some serious organizational development," Kevin said, ignoring Dave's innuendo. "I dropped half that shit on the floor trying to clear a spot for dinner," Kevin said, throwing a sly look Jess' way.

"What's the occasion?"

"My birthday."

"Oh yeah? Happy birthday, you old fart. What are you, like forty-something?" *Thirty-five* was Kevin's retort. "Something sure *smells* good," David continued.

"Those guys at Paolo's cook almost as good as Jess, and I've worked up quite an appetite, can't wait to dig in," Kevin said.

As with the desk, Dave hadn't missed the look that had passed between his co-workers. "Yeah right! When did Paolo's switch to Chinese, Bro?"

"They didn't."

"That's funny, because it smells a lot like cat in here... *pussy*cat."

Busted! "Aw man, no way Dave! That's just office air." Kevin looked at Jess again, grinning.

"David, you really need to crack open a law book. It's illegal to sell pussycat for human consumption." Jess relayed, holding back a giggle.

Dave was not buying their story. "Yeah well, it's not illegal to *give* it away."

"It looks like plenty here. Want some?" Kevin asked with a wicked gleam in his eyes.

"Thanks for the invitation, but I'll run down the street to the diner. I'll be back in a little while."

"Suit yourself."

"You guys need anything while I'm out?"

"No thanks." On his way out the door, Dave couldn't resist one last jab. "So, you planning on sharing a slice of the birthday cake?"

With a devilish gleam in his eyes, Kevin came right back with a quick rebuttal, "Sorry Pal, I dove into that first, before you came in. Damn good too, I gobbled up every crumb."

"Yeah, I'll just bet you did. You probably licked the plate clean too."

"As a matter of fact..."

"I hope you get heartburn," David interrupted. "Musta been one hell of a birthday cake."

"Why do ya say that?" Jess asked.

"You, uh, got sloppy and smeared the frosting on my desk. Exactly what kind of frosting was it, anyway?" He asked, still hazing them.

"I plead the fifth," Kevin replied.

"Musta been some of that good Chinese frosting. Mmm, my favorite," David stated with a grin on his way out the door.

"Oh my God, *that* was embarrassing!"

"Are you kidding? That was fun. I told you that you had a kinky streak just waiting to get out," he said as he winked at her.

"Yes, you did."

"So what are we having...in English."

Chapter 20

November 26...

"Hey, big brother!" A petite, blonde woman called from across the terminal before running to him. Kevin lifted her, hugging her tight. "Hey Runt, look at you. You're all grown up."

"Oh please, I was all grown up the last time you saw me, you big oaf."

"Yeah, but now you actually look it." He looked her up and down. "What is this, a suit?"

"That's what you get for going three years without visiting your family. Besides, I'm hardly a kid...and stop calling me Runt."

"Why? You are a runt!" The diminutive woman slugged him in the ribs. "Hey, it's not my fault you're short."

"Maybe not, but I can still kick *your* butt."

"You think so?"

She punched him again. "Hell yeah, now stand still and let me check *you* out. I like the goatee. Nice touch, but I thought beards were against regulation."

"I'm undercover, sort of. You should see Jess when she gets decked out."

"Why?"

"Talk about hot...she wears these itty-bitty, little..."

"Oh, God!" Samantha interrupted, rolling her eyes.

"...and a wig."

"Really? She's got gorgeous hair. It's a shame she has to cover it up. Not that the rest of her isn't gorgeous too."

"She's pretty damn hot with red hair too."

"Red?"

"Flaming."

"So, where is she? I was looking forward to meeting her. Your pictures are nice, but they're so one-dimensional and don't exactly tell you a lot about a person."

"She's at home baking." The pair walked towards the baggage area.

"Baking? Oh my God! My brother went and found himself a domesticated woman? Unbelievable! What would the folks back home say?"

"I don't know that I'd call her domesticated, but she *is* one hell of a cook."

"I can see that. You're not skinny anymore. You look great," she said, patting his tummy. "Mom would be proud. You need to work on maintaining this manlier figure."

"Sammy, if I get any more exercise, I'll have a damn heart attack," Kevin said, winking at her.

Samantha's brow furrowed in disgust. "Ewww, not that kind, you big jerk. What would Jess say if she knew you were advertising your sex life?"

"Probably nothing, but she'd turn the prettiest six shades of red you've ever seen," he replied, laughing.

"No shit! I wonder why, so tell me about her."

"She's the best. You'll love her."

"As much as you do?"

"Yeah...wait a minute. You're putting words in my mouth."

"I didn't put anything there you weren't already thinking."

"Oh jeez, another woman who knows everything."

"Another one?"

"Jess' best friend, Niki," he said, laughing. "She'll be over tomorrow and she *is* a trip. So did you bring that recipe I asked for?"

"For my favorite big brother..."

"What do mean, your favorite big brother? I'm your only brother, you goof. Come on. Let's find your bags."

"What makes you think I have more than one bag?"

"Because you never did believe in traveling light, and they're probably heavier than hell, if I know you. I can't wait for you to meet Jess."

"She must be something else."

"She is. She's beautiful and smart and sexy. She's the sweetest person I know...except for you, of course."

"Good save," Sam said with a wink.

"She's tough as nails when it suits her, though. You shoulda seen her handle the ME a while back. The guy's always been a real asshole, but she scared the living shit out of him," he said, laughing. "And did I mention that she's gorgeous?"

"I believe you might have, and I agree. You two look really good together."

"Thanks, I think so too."

"God, I never thought I'd see the day."

"What day?"

"The day my brother fell in love."

"Oh hell, here we go again," he said, rolling his eyes.

"Don't worry. I won't rag you for long. I just think it's sweet. And if she's half as wonderful as you say, you'd better keep her, hint hint."

"Count on it."

Thanksgiving Day...

The holiday dinner was a huge success with everyone contributing his or her own special dishes. The smorgasbord of international treats revealed a lot about the many different heritages represented by the crowd. Niki's mother brought several Irish dishes that paired surprisingly well with Jess' traditional southern fare. Samantha and Kevin shared their Norwegian background with Sam's lefse, bringing back fond, childhood memories for Dean. The group celebrated until nearly midnight, when filled with holiday cheer, they left, one by one, leaving only the hosts and Samantha, who retired, looking forward to the following day's planned shopping trip with Jess and Niki.

After settling Samantha in, Jess padded down the hallway to the room she shared with Kevin. He was sitting on the edge of the bed removing his shirt. "Sam says to tell you good night."

"Yes, it is. Come here, you."

He studied her openly as she approached him, then pulled her onto his lap and kissed her, drawing her ever closer when she laced her arms around his neck. Rolling her underneath him, Kevin brushed the hair back from Jess' face, then continued kissing down her neck and unbuttoning her shirt, raining kisses into the hollow of her shoulder while he unfastened her bra and slid the straps from her shoulders, freeing her breasts. A moment later, he lowered his head, took a nipple between his teeth, and nipped it before sucking it into his mouth and swirling his tongue around it. The other pink nub, he rolled gently between his fingertips.

Standing with Jess cradled against his chest, he laid her in the center of the bed and continued downward, brushing his fingertips across the sensitive skin of her abdomen. She moaned and sucked in a quick breath when goose bumps appeared on her flesh as nimble fingers unfastened her jeans and slid them, along with her panties, down her creamy thighs and finally, off. Kevin threw the cumbersome material to the floor and leaned over her, taking one leg into his powerful hands. He kneaded the tired muscles of her calf, working his way up her thigh and then repeated his ministrations on the other leg.

"Turn over, Baby."

He straddled her waist and turned his attention to her neck, using small concentric circles to massage away all traces of stiffness, working his way across her shoulders and down her arms. When he reached her hands, he worked her palms in the same circular pattern. He moved to her back, working out the soreness from it, as well, again in a circular pattern, and using the pads of his thumbs to knead down the edges of her spine.

"Mmm God, this feels so good. I had no idea I was so tense." The massage ended when he ran his fingertips back up her spine, prompting Jess to arch catlike towards his hand. "Oh, God."

She turned onto her back when he stood up long enough to shed his clothes before rejoining her. With his knee, he nudged her legs apart and very slowly slid into her satin warmth, leisurely moving in and out for some time before rolling onto his back with Jess astride him, watching her through passion-glazed eyes. She lay forward, hugging against him, and rocked back and forth, grinding her crotch against his, engorged and throbbing with unfulfilled longing. Straightening her spine, Jess threw her head back, dragged the ends of her long hair across her beloved's thighs. He reached out to cup her breasts, kneading them in his hands for a moment before grabbing her hips and grinding his cock up into her at a fierce pace. The increased speed and the friction pushed her over the edge. Jess leaned over, balanced herself by holding onto Kevin's shoulders, and bounced on him, squeezing as tight as she could while a floodtide of orgasmic pleasure swept through her.

"Oh, my God, yes, oh yes."

"Baby, look at me." Jess opened her eyes and looked into his golden depths. At that moment, he stiffened then drove his throbbing member into her, gifting her with a stream of thick, liquid fire. "Sweet Jesus...Baby."

Kevin pulled Jess down on top of him where she lay for a while. Eventually, they rolled to their sides and lay facing each other, so close their faces nearly touched. Jess snuggled closer and laid her head on his shoulder. Feeling safe and warm, she lay silent for several minutes when it hit her, the realization that she no longer wanted to deny her feelings for this man. She suddenly felt compelled to tell him how she really felt and take the chance that it wouldn't frighten him away.

"I love you, Kevin." She peered at him through half-closed lids. He was sleeping peacefully, oblivious to the gigantic leap of faith the wary woman in his arms had just taken.

The following morning...
7:28 AM

When Jess woke up, Kevin was not in bed. Looking around and finding no trace, she listened for a moment and heard humming in the bathroom, so she got up and walked to the door to peek inside. Kevin was trimming his beard. He set his razor on the sink, stopped humming, and turned around when he saw her reflection in the mirror.

"Morning, Baby."

"Good morning, yourself," she said, smiling. "Don't stop."

"Don't stop what?"

"Humming, it was nice."

"You think so?"

"I do. Did you already shower?"

"Yeah, I've been up for a while now." Kittenish, she poked out her bottom lip. "You were sleeping like a baby. I didn't have it in me to wake you, but jump in if you want while I finish shaving." Jess stepped into the steamy water and started bathing herself. The clear glass shower door left little to Kevin's imagination. "With a view like this, I could easily be talked into scrubbing your back," he said as he watched her reflection in the mirror.

"Oh really?"

"Yeah, really." Finished, she turned off the water and grabbed a towel for her hair. Kevin turned, pulled her wet, naked body against his bare chest, and kissed her. "Mmm, I've been waiting all morning for that."

"Don't wait so long next time. Look at that," Jess pointed out and lapped up the beads of water running down his chest. "I've gotten you all wet." Just then, there was a knock at the bedroom door.

"Hey Jess, rise and shine," Niki called.

"Damn," Kevin exclaimed quietly. "How'd she get in?" His vexation was evident.

"Sam must be up. You're sorta dressed," Jess said, eyeing his hard body up and down. "You wanna go tell her we'll be out in a minute?"

"Do I have to?"

"Persistence is her forté. She won't go away."

Kevin left a naked Jess in the bathroom and opened the bedroom door. "Yes, can I help you?" Niki was taken unawares when Kevin answered the door half-naked and dripping-wet.

"Daaamn!" Jess peeked around the bathroom door and almost laughed aloud when she caught Niki ogling her man. "What's a girl gotta do to get a greeting like this *every* day?"

"Depends on the girl," he teased.

"Well, you're no fun. Where's Jess? Is she up yet?" Niki asked as she stood on her tiptoes, trying to peer over Kevin's shoulder.

"Yeah, she's getting dressed now that you're here."

"Aww, poor baby. Twice a day not enough for you?"

"No, I prefer at least three...breakfast, lunch, and dinner...and on a *really* good day I like to add a snack or two in between, thanks, and might I add that your timing sucks. I had her wet and naked, and ready for breakfast."

"I live for threesomes! Seriously, I'm thrilled Jess is getting laid regularly. Want me to go out make your excuses?"

"You're lucky you're her best friend. And no, I don't think any excuses will be necessary. My sister still likes me and I'd like to keep it that way. The last thing I need is for you to announce to the world that we're in here...getting laid."

"Oh now, I don't think I'd put it quite that way."

"Oh, I think you would."

"As if the world doesn't know already."

"Yeah, well I wasn't planning to buy a billboard."

"I'll just tell Sam that we won't be going today, after all."

"Going where?"

"Jess forgot to tell you that it's tradition for us to hit the day-after-Thanksgiving sales. Didn't she?"

"She might have mentioned it, but we were kinda busy."

"I can see that. Go put some clothes on, you big lug. Jess, come on, Girlfriend," she yelled past Kevin before turning back to him. "I think Sam would kick your butt if we had to cancel on account of *you* distracting Jess."

"You two are a trip," Jess interrupted as she entered the bedroom, fully dressed. "You're lucky I love you both, else I'd throw the two of you outta here on your asses," she scolded lightheartedly.

"Did you hear that? She cussed!" Kevin exclaimed. "That's what, four times since we met?" Niki just laughed.

"I had to get your attention somehow."

He aimed a sly smile at her. "Make that four times when you weren't climbing the head..."

"Don't you dare!" Jess walked between them, leaned against Kevin, and faced Niki. He put his arms around her and rested his chin on her shoulder.

"...board."

"Come on, let's get out of here...and wipe your chin. You're drooling," she said to Niki. "And *you*...go put a shirt on, then join us for breakfast," she said, looking back up at Kevin.

"Yes Ma'am," he said with a formal salute. "Eating breakfast was exactly what I had in mind before we were so rudely interrupted," he grumbled on his way to the closet.

Moments later...

"He didn't even flinch when you said you loved him a few minutes ago."

"Huh?"

"Upstairs, you said you'd throw us out on our asses if you didn't love us. Remember?"

"Oh yeah, I guess I did. Maybe he didn't hear that part."

"He did too."

"How do you know?"

"Because he did that eyebrow thing and got a big shit-eating grin on his face."

"I already told him once, anyway."

"This is news. When?"

"Last night."

"What'd he say?"

"Nothing."

"What? What do you mean, nothing? No 'I love you too' or anything in return?" She turned to walk out. "I gotta talk to him."

"No, stop! He was asleep." Niki rolled her eyes and shot Jess a disgusted look. "I didn't know he was asleep. We were all snuggled up and it just came out. Hand me the olive oil." Niki just looked at her. "What?"

"You're being mighty flippant about it."

"No, I'm not! It took me forever to work up the nerve to say it, but then he was asleep, so what was I supposed to do? Wake him up?"

"Tell him again."

"I just did, as you so eloquently pointed out."

"Tell him what?" Kevin asked.

"Oh, not you again! You need to switch to one hundreds."

"I'm trying to quit. Please continue. This sounds intriguing. What are we telling him?"

"Not him, Dumbass, you! And she's supposed to be telling you that she's positively crazy about you. There Jess! I said it for you."

"I know, and I'm crazy about her too."

"I give up. I'm outta here."

Niki left the kitchen in a huff, opting instead, to get better acquainted with Samantha. Jess apologized to Kevin for her best friend's audacity. His response was to walk to Jess, wrap his arms around her, and rest his chin on top of her head, stroking her hair with his hand. They were startled when Niki burst through the doorway a bit later.

"Listen up, you two. Jess, you know I love you. You're the closest thing to a sister I've ever had or ever will have, and I want you to be happy, so naturally when I see the incredible effect this big galoot has had on you, I wanted to rush it along. And Kevin, I haven't known you long, nor do I know you that well, but it's obvious you care a great deal for my best friend and that makes me happy. Anyway, I just want say I'm sorry for being such a meddling pain in the ass."

"Don't sweat it, Niki," Kevin replied. "You're Jess's best friend and I appreciate how you're always looking out for her. Everyone should have such a good friend."

"You guys aren't pissed off at me?"

"No way," Kevin said.

"Definitely not," Jess added.

"You're positive?"

"Yes!" The couple shouted in unison.

"Okay then! How's breakfast coming? You ready for me to set the table?"

"Knock yourself out."

"Good, I'm starving and we gotta jet. All the good stuff will be gone by the time we get to the stores."

The foursome ate quickly with the women anticipating the deals they were sure to find. In haste, Kevin ushered them to Niki's car, promising to take care of the mess. He didn't mention that he had a surprise of his own in store for when they returned.

9:00 PM

"Oh wow, look at that!" Sam squealed.

"Am I at the right house?" Niki asked.

"Oh gosh, look what he did. It's beautiful. Look at all the lights," Jess said.

She and Sam retrieved their parcels from the trunk and Niki helped carry everything inside. The house was completely dark save for the gigantic Christmas tree lighting the front window. *Blame it on the Mistletoe* was playing on the stereo and a roaring fire burned in the fireplace as the sweet and spicy aroma of cinnamon permeated every room.

"Wow!"

"Somebody is working hard to impress you, Jess," Sam said.

"What do you mean?"

"My brother hasn't bothered with a Christmas tree since he left home to go play soldier."

"Are you serious?" Niki asked.

"As a heart attack," Sam replied.

"He must have worked all day on this. There's lights on the house, and the bushes outside, and everything," Jess gushed.

"Does that mean you like it?" Surprised, the women looked towards the sound of his voice. They hadn't noticed Kevin standing by the stereo when they came inside.

"I love it! It looks beautiful."

"Hey Sam, it's Saturday night and I'm on my own since David's on-duty tonight. Let's go out and give them some alone time?" Niki whispered to Kevin's sister.

"That's a terrific idea. Let's do it." Sam and Niki quietly set their loads by the front door and started back out.

Kevin looked up when the door creaked. "You got more? Stay inside, I'll go get it."

"No, that's everything," Samantha said. "We're gonna go out and give you two some privacy."

"Sam, you're our guest. Please don't feel like you need to leave," Jess said. "God, I'm a terrible hostess."

"Baloney, I feel completely welcome and I know I don't have to, but I'm going out anyway. It's not like I get to do this often. I'll be back later."

Kevin grabbed his keys, quickly pulled one from the ring, and tossed it to her. "Here Sis, you'll need this."

"Thanks, Bro."

"Sam, keep Niki outta trouble."

"Bite me, Kevin!" Niki shouted on her way out the door.

"The house looks beautiful."

"I'm glad you like it." With the back of his hand, he caressed her cheek, brought it around to cup her chin, and drew her into a warm, wet kiss. Grabbing the remote off the mantle, he restarted the song and pulled her into his arms. "May I have this dance, Milady?"

"You may." Jess lay her head against his chest as they swayed in front of the Christmas tree. On the ending note, he twirled her around, and tilted her into a full dip. "Oooh!"

"What? You didn't expect a barbarian like me to be so suave and debonair?"

"Actually, I thought barbarians were more s'wave and de-boner," she said, giggling.

"Oh really? You think you're funny, eh?" He asked, laughing. "I got de-boner right here, lady," he growled. He laughed and threw her over his shoulder, smacked her rump, and carried her to the bedroom.

Chapter 21

December 6...

"On your knees, slave!" He growled.

"Yes, Master." Sandy Vandenberg fell to her knees before him and bowed her head.

"Now, suck my cock!"

She took his huge cock between her lips and sucked it down her throat as far as she could manage. He was too large. She pulled back, but he forced her head down again, nearly choking her. Gagging through several attempts, she finally developed a rhythm.

"Yes, that's right, just like that." Sandy bobbed back and forth faster. "Not so fast," he said. "Mmm yes, you're a good slave. Get up!" Sandy spit out his cock and stood up. "Put your hands out." He revealed a set of handcuffs, which he used to restrain her wrists. "Now raise your arms over your head."

They took several steps backward before he growled at her to stop where a sturdy chain with a hook at the end hung from the ceiling. He secured the hook through a link in the handcuff chain and left Sandy hanging by her arms while he retrieved a whip from a nearby cabinet. Her eyes grew wide with fear as she realized what he had planned for her. He steadied himself, drew the whip back over his head, and snapped it quickly. The loud crack startled Sandy, causing her to jump, though the tip never touched her skin. Four more times he drew back the whip and cracked it just inches from her. Her fear diminished somewhat when he failed to strike her on the fifth lick.

"Turn, so I can see your lovely, white ass."

"No, please, Master."

"I said turn around, bitch!" Reluctantly, she turned halfway, giving him her profile. "All the way around. Now!"

"Yellow, Master."

Against her better judgment, she turned fully, exposing the pale, unmarred skin. He raised the whip and brought it back down again, this time striking the tender surface of her fleshy buttocks and raising a long, red stripe. She whimpered. Again and again, he struck her with the whip, raising several red whelps. Tears streamed down the woman's face as she begged him to stop. He ceased whipping her only long enough to eyeball her and estimate the distance between them, then took two steps towards her. Again, he raised the whip and brought it down, striking her. This time he drew blood. He watched a lone, red rivulet run down her creamy skin, bloodlust causing him to go crazed like a rabid wolf, then struck her repeatedly, opening several wounds and smearing the blood across her backside.

"Red, red," she screamed. "Master, please stop," Sandy sobbed. "Please, stop this torture."

"Stop this torture?"

"Yes, you're hurting me. Please, I'm begging you, stop."

He put away the whip and unhooked her from the chain, leaving the handcuffs in place. "Go to the slab and get on your knees." Sandy climbed onto the cold marble slab and sank down into a modified fetal position, using her forearms to support her weight. "Put your ass in the air." The blood had started to congeal around the edges of the wounds raised by his flaying. He raised his hand and brought it down, smacking the ragged wounds hard, raising a handprint, and reopening her scabbed lacerations. Blood oozed from them for a second time, which only served to excite him further.

"Owww," she whimpered.

He slapped her again, harder this time, before donning a condom and shoving his thick rod between her shaved lips. He pumped furiously for a few minutes before pulling out and ramming his cock in her ass. Sandy froze and cried out in pain at the sudden stretching of her anus. He sodomized her wildly and grabbed the studded collar she wore around her neck. He pulled back on it and twisted it, effectively bending her backwards and choking her at the same time. Struggling to breathe and free herself from his grasp, she clawed at his hands, but her efforts were to no avail. He growled and came just as she went limp. At once, he pulled free of her and let her lifeless, bloody body fall, then ripped off the used prophylactic.

He paced around the room for some time before finally checking the time, and then set about cleaning the corpse to remove all traces of evidence. He carefully bathed her body, taking great care to cleanse away every of trace dried blood from her wounds, and then rinsed her genitals. Last, but not least, he washed her face and applied fresh makeup to her livid complexion before dressing her. Disappearing upstairs, he showered, and changed into a pair of black jeans, a black t-shirt, and a plain, black, leather jacket before retrieving Sandra Vandenberg's motionless body and carrying it to a small, black pick-up truck. He gently placed her in the passenger seat and buckled her seatbelt, as if they were a normal couple going for a drive, then he got into the vehicle and drove away, vanishing into the night.

CB&DCR&D

In the days after Thanksgiving, Samantha had done nothing short of singing Jess' praises since returning home, leaving Kevin's family excited about the couple and ready to meet the woman who had brought such change to his life. Barring any scheduling conflicts, Sam planned to visit again for Christmas, leaving the couple eagerly anticipating the coming holiday season. Jess even suggested a short visit to Minnesota when she learned that Kevin's mother was deathly afraid of flying, as long as Kevin agreed to spend part of the holiday with Dean.

"Hot damn!" Kevin patted the cushion beside him. "Why don't you come over here and slip me some of that sweet Italian tongue?"

Jess kicked off her shoes, then sidled over and sat down next to him. Raising herself to one knee, she leaned on him, effectively laying him back on the overstuffed leather sofa, then wrapped her arms around his neck and kissed him. He opened his eyes and glanced at her when she stabbed her tongue through his lips and into the warm, wet cavern of his mouth, nipping his lips one last time before breaking the kiss and rising to her hands to look down and smile at him.

"Mmm, Baby, after that kiss, we can spend Christmas on the moon if you want."

Her smile grew wider. "Thank you."

Jess went on to describe the traditions she'd shared with Dean over the years, from trimming the tree on Christmas Eve over hot apple cider, to singing holiday carols and drinking eggnog around the piano with their guests. Kevin was surprised to learn that Niki and her father played guitars to Dean's piano, although he didn't dwell on the information for long, because he was more impressed with how Dean and Jess celebrated every holiday.

In addition to their close friends, they drew in every straggling police officer with no kinfolk or a place to go, and made them part of their own tiny family. He knew, from his years in the army, stationed far away from his large family, the isolation of a holiday spent alone. He couldn't imagine how just two people could bring such happiness to a large crowd of otherwise lonely people during such a special time, and he loved her even more for her generous heart.

The realization that he loved her was intrusive, but not unwelcome. It made Kevin want to begin his own holiday customs with Jess, but having her warm, pliant body across his was distracting. He tried to concentrate on their holiday discussion, but in true male fashion, Kevin's serious thoughts of family, love, and tradition detoured down the sexual path when he thought aloud of stuffing Jess' stocking.

He peered at her intently, the double meaning of his statement not lost on her. The air became charged as a spark of desire flared between them. Reaching up with trembling fingers, he unfastened the first few buttons on her shirt. Her nipples hardened instantly, though he had yet to touch them. Jess pushed herself to sitting in his lap, allowing him room to pull her shirt from her jeans, still fumbling with the buttons. Expelling an impatient growl, he ripped the offending fabric open and sent buttons flying across the room. Jess stared at him in wide-eyed astonishment.

"We'll get you another one...without buttons."

Sliding her from his lap, he took her hands and pulled them both to standing. Jess shrugged out of the tattered remains of her shirt as he shed his own. With nimble fingers, he unbuttoned her jeans and slid them down her hips. Caressing her bare back, he unhooked her bra with one hand, using incredible dexterity before pulling away. Kevin stepped back and sloughed his pants, then gently pushed Jess back down to the sofa, where she lay back, beckoning with a single finger, for him to join her. He eased his

117

hard body over her much softer one, flesh against flesh, man against woman. Jess gasped when he leaned down and touched his lips to one hard nipple, sucking it with tantalizing possessiveness.

She writhed beneath him, eager for his love. One hand trailed down her side to explore her belly and hip as he continued on a path toward her knees. Gently, but forcefully, pushing them apart, he plunged his rigid cock between velvety nether lips, holding the sofa arm to support his greater weight. As if by their own accord, his hips moved in a circular motion, his pelvis grinding against her, his scrotum slapping against the upper portion of her buttocks, while a gradual increase in speed caused her jiggling breasts to bounce harder. Out of character, Jess caught her nipples, and rolled them between her fingertips, moaning at the delicious sensation. Kevin leaned down, nudged her hand aside, and caught an erect, pink bud between his lips. He devoured it, suckling in much the same way as a starved babe might.

"Mmm, God," Jess cried, aching for release.

"Come on, Baby."

Her entire body tingled and burned. She began to quake and shiver while Kevin hammered her. Pleasure radiated from her core, out through every limb, half fire, and half ice. At once, she gasped in sweet agony and stiffened, arching against him, squeezing him. He held on for a minute longer before reaching his own peak and with one final thrust and a tortured groan, a torrential deluge gushed from him. The urgent need to collapse in an exhausted heap was upon him, but knowing he'd crush his love, Kevin rolled behind her, cradling her in his arms, and they dozed on the sofa, their bodies intertwined, their skin damp with the sweat from lovemaking.

Later when she opened her eyes, Jess turned slightly to look around the room. The house was dark. Realizing they must have fallen asleep, she snuggled closer to Kevin, inadvertently waking him. He reached around and cupped a breast while he buried his nose in her hair and kissed the back of her neck, causing her to shiver as goose flesh arose all over her.

"Cold?"

"A little, on the outside," she purred seductively.

"I can fix that."

"But that means I have to move."

"Only for a minute, I'll warm you up again."

Jess sat up and watched him as he stoked the fire, the strong muscles of his thighs and backside flexing with his every move. Jess studied him as he slowly ambled back towards her. He was a striking specimen of manhood, tall, tan, and muscular, but not overly so. His small nipples hardened in the cool, night air. Continuing her perusal of his body, she moved down his hirsute chest, following a treasure trail to the juncture of his thighs. Even flaccid, he was well equipped. Slowly, her gaze traveled back up his body to his face, where she caught his eye. He smiled.

"See something you like?"

"Yes, I like it very, very much," she purred.

"Damn!" The phone rang, startling them both.

"What time is it?"

"Half past two...AM. This better be good," Kevin said, grabbing the receiver. "Yeah, what? Oh, this is a cruel joke. Right?" He ran his fingers through his hair. "Does the Chief know, yet? Okay, Mike, I'll tell her and we'll be there as soon as we can get dressed."

"What was that about?"

"DB in Fairchild Park...looks like Mr. Clean's work."

"It coulda been worse."

"How?"

"That call could have come in a few hours ago."

He chuckled. "Yeah, well, not to make light of the situation, but the machine woulda caught it."

3:02 AM

"Morning, Bob." Jess greeted the Assistant Medical Examiner with a sweet smile.

Bob Morton whirled around when she and Kevin approached. "Doctor Mitchell," he said. His anxiety was obvious. "Detective," he added curtly, before turning to walk away. "I'll just wait over here until you're ready for me."

Kevin chuckled and shook his head. "He's still terrified of you. I've been trying to scare him for three years, but he's just an asshole to me. Wish I knew how you did it." Jess shrugged her shoulders in innocence.

"Hey, you two."

"Mike," Kevin acknowledged.

Had it been three in the afternoon instead of three in the morning, the scene would have looked perfectly normal. A woman appeared to be passing the time, soaking up the scenery from a park bench. She wore a navy blue, double-breasted suit with a white, silk shirt, nude pantyhose, and matching pumps. Her auburn hair was pulled into a neat French twist and her make-up was flawless, as if just applied. Her ankles were neatly crossed and there was a newspaper in her hand. A navy purse lay unopened on the bench beside her.

"Oh, he's good," Jess said as she observed the body's positioning. "Kev, she looks familiar. I swear, I think I've seen her before."

"Who called this in?"

"That's the best part, Kevin. See that tall, black guy over there?" Jess followed Mike's hand with her eyes. "That's..."

"Darius McAdoo," Kevin interrupted.

"You know him?"

"We've had a few run-ins, local gang banger."

The trio of investigators joined Darius and the officer detaining him. "Detective Slatuh, whadup dawg?" He asked, then looked Jess up and down. "Boo-ya! Who's the honey?"

Kevin curled his fingers into a fist and touched it gang-style to Darius'. "The *honey* is a special agent with the SBI. You don't wanna fuck with her."

"Hey Boo, Boneylove can show you what it's all about," he said as he strutted around Jess, giving her a once-over meant to intimidate.

"Bones, lemme put it another way. She *my* boo. You feel me?"

"My bad, I feel ya. This brotha smart enough not to play with the police man's boo."

"Kevin, I'll be over there with her," Jess said, nodding at the bench.

"Bones, I understand you found the lady," Kevin continued.

"Yeah."

"When?"

"'bout two, I reckon."

"Bones, what the hell were you doing out here at two in the fuckin' morning? I thought you were going straight."

"Ay, yo trip, I am straight. I was kickin' it wit some of my homies."

"Don't blow smoke up my ass. You saw a white woman sitting here alone and thought she'd be an easy mark. Didn't you?"

"Naw, my man."

"Gimme a break, you were gonna jack her up and take her money, then when you saw she was dead, you took off and called us 'cause you were afraid you'd get fingered for killing her, too."

"Naw, dat ain't how it went down."

"Relax, Darius. I'm not hauling you in for anything...yet. This ain't your style, but I need to know if I'm gonna find your prints on her stuff."

"What you talking 'bout, Slatuh?"

"Dammit, Darius, do us both a favor and tell me the truth, just this once, for a change."

"A'ight fine, you's right. I was gone jack her for some dough. But when I walked up she didn't move or say nothing, so I reached out and touched her like this." He poked his fingertips at Kevin's shoulder. "She still didn't move or nothing, so I figured she's dead. So I boned out and called you guys. I swear I didn't touch nothing else."

"All right, Bones, get the hell outta here. And don't pull any more stunts like this. Straighten up and get yourself a real job."

"Yeah, yeah...peace out, Slatuh."

Kevin joined Jess a moment later. "He swears he didn't touch a thing. For once, I believe him."

"Well, that's good."

Jess called over one of the CSIs and obtained a pair of gloves, then opened the purse. Inside were the typical items one would expect to find: lipstick, gum, a tampon for emergencies, and a condom for unexpected events. She handed each item to the tech for bagging as she removed it. Finally, she found the woman's wallet and opened it. Again, it contained the usual items, cash, credit cards, and an address book.

"Sandra Vandenberg," Jess continued, examining the rest of the contents. "Hey look," she said, smiling and holding up a KLAASP membership card. "I knew she looked familiar."

"I'll be damned."

"Only one thing missing."

"What's that?"

"Her keys."

"What makes you think they're missing?"

"Do you go anywhere without yours?"

"No."

"Exactly, let's see if we can find a friend or relative and get a positive ID on her."

"Mike's already gone. He's checking missing persons as we speak."

"If her driver's license is current, she lives on Mebane Street. I want to go over there with CSI when they're ready to process. Good thing we went to sleep so early, huh?"

"Looks like."

"Bob, you have our numbers. Give us a call as soon as you have anything."

"Will do, Doctor Mitchell."

Chapter 22

The following morning, Jess and Kevin learned that Sandra Vandenberg had not been reported missing, leading them to believe she was killed within hours of her abduction. Kevin obtained a search warrant for the woman's apartment and located her roommate, while Jess, with next to no effort, persuaded Bob Morton to allow them to view the autopsy.

LabCorp, downtown Burlington...
8:46 AM

"Julie there's a cop and an FBI agent waiting to see you," the receptionist said, nodding to the pair.
"What do they want?"
"I dunno. They wouldn't tell me."
Julie Cates led Jess and Kevin to an empty conference room, where they confirmed the identity of Mr. Clean's latest target using a photograph from the dead woman's wallet. Clearly distraught that her roommate and friend had been murdered, Julie tearfully agreed to accompany them to make the official identification. She feared Sandy's father wouldn't be able to handle such a shock to his already weak heart.
A scant while later, the trio followed Bob Morton through the maze of hallways leading to the morgue, where he pulled a slab from the refrigeration unit. With a surprising show of empathy towards Julie, Bob unzipped the body bag, uncovering only Sandra Vandenberg's face. Julie gasped and turned away, confirming what they'd already known. In a rare moment of agreement, both Bob and Kevin stepped forward to catch a suddenly pale Julie, both concerned she would faint. Instead, she became hysterical, hyperventilating as she ran towards the door. Jess jogged behind the woman back to a waiting patrol car and stood silent while an officer helped her inside and secured her seatbelt.
"I think I should tell her folks."
"Julie, I really don't think that's a good idea. You should have Detective Slater and me with you."
"If that's what you feel is best."
"Do you have somewhere else you can stay? We can't let you back into your apartment until we can rule it out as the crime scene."
"I'll figure something out. Can I at least go for some clothes?"
"I'm sure that'll be fine. Officer Jackson will take you, and Detective Slater and I will need to talk to you while this is still fresh."
"Just call me when you're ready."
"Are you going back to work?"
"Yes."
"Donnie, take Julie to her apartment and then back to LabCorp. Be sure and clear the apartment first. The victim's keys are missing."
"Sure thing, Doctor Mitchell."

Back in the morgue...

"Come here, Jess, look at these."
"Holy cow! She's been whipped."
"How'd you know that?"
"Profiling is only part of what they teach us, Bob. But these wounds aren't the cause of death."
"No, ligature strangulation." He pulled back her eyelids. "Note the scleral hemorrhaging and this wide band of bruising around her neck. She also has deep scratches on her throat across to her clavicles, defensive wounds, I'm sure," Bob Morton said.
"That's exactly like the others," Jess commented while Kevin nodded in agreement.
"I'm pretty sure I'll find a fractured or broken hyoid."
"Was she scrubbed?"

"You might get something from her clothing and shoes. I have them bagged up for you, but the body's immaculate. I've found no trace, though I did find a partial print on her left thumb nail," Bob said.

"Really? That's great. Did you pull it yet?"

"Not yet, thought I'd save it for you."

"Awesome Bob! Thanks," Jess exclaimed. "Kev, I haven't pulled a print in a long time. You wanna do it?" Kevin pilfered a set of latex gloves from Bob, then carefully dusted the fingernail and pulled the print for evidence. "What about a rape kit? You do one yet?" Jess continued as she stood back and watched.

"I did. Your victim engaged in some extremely rough sexual activity shortly before her death, but there's no seminal fluid. However, I got swabs of what may be a lubricant. There's a lot of vaginal tearing and evidence that she was violently sodomized. Her rectal cavity is hamburger."

"My, what an appetizing description," Kevin quipped. "Can't wait for lunch."

"I call 'em like I see 'em. I retrieved two pubic hairs that do not match the victim's."

"Can you identify race?"

"That's the hundred thousand dollar question, Doctor Mitchell...they're course and dark, Caucasoid or maybe Mongoloid."

"Any other donor DNA?" Kevin asked.

"No."

"Thanks, Bob."

"Sure, Doctor Mitchell."

"Bob, we're gonna leave you to your work. Kev, let's get this to the lab right away."

CBEOCBEO

The pair entered the small, though not completely cramped, sanitary room where evidence was processed and stored for the police department. A lone, female technician sat at a desk studying something under a microscope. She turned and waved them in.

"Detective Slater."

"Stephanie, how's it going?"

"Pretty quiet until this morning, I hear."

"Yeah, another DB in the park. Here's her garments and some trace that Bob Morton collected during the prelim."

"Is he still as big a jerk as I remember?"

"To everybody except Jess."

"Oh yeah? How'd you manage that?" She asked, looking at Jess.

Stephanie chuckled merrily when Kevin retold the infamous story of Jess' confrontation with the medical examiner. Laughter aside, Stephanie was concerned at the time it would take to process the evidence, as her lab wasn't equipped for certain procedures. She suggested farming the items out to LabCorp, but Kevin immediately put the kibosh on the idea out of concern about a conflict of interest. Always on her toes, Jess immediately dialed her boss, and held on, listening to the music while he pulled strings with the state crime lab.

"*Okay, I'm back.*"

"Hey, put me back on hold," she teased. "JJ was getting ready to spin *Soundgarden.*"

"*What are you talking about?*"

"When did the Bureau can the muzak and start playing 96 Rock?"

"*Can't say I've noticed. You know I don't listen to that crap you have blasting all the time. Listen Jess, I got a tech on hold for you. Everyone down there is itching to work on this case. When can you get the specimens here?*"

Steph added fifteen minutes to Jess' estimated forty-five minute drive to account for Jess' lead foot (according to Kevin), and quickly made arrangements to have techs meet them at the victim's apartment after a quick lunch.

They met a pair of CSIs at three o'clock, as planned, and waited while the men processed Sandy's bedroom. Among the collected items was a personal computer, a shoebox full of sex toys, and several pieces of exotic lingerie. No longer worried about contaminating possible evidence, Jess began her own silent perusal of the apartment while Kevin kept out of the way and watched her dissect Sandra Vandenberg's personality through her belongings.

"Wonder who this is," Jess observed as she studied a framed photo of a man.

"Looks kinda familiar, but I dunno."

"Maybe he's from KLAASP. You don't happen to have any gloves on you do you?"

"As a matter of fact..."

Jess slipped on the gloves and removed the photo, then read an inscription from the back. "Nick, September 2006. This is recent."

"We should take that."

"I agree."

Kevin glanced at his watch. "Jess, we gotta go or we're gonna be late for our meeting with the roommate."

A half-hour later, they sat talking with Julie Cates. She mentioned Sandy's boyfriend, Nick, but knew nothing of him, as they'd never met one another. The interview was tedious and seemed an effort in futility until Julie remembered that Sandy and Nick had met online and frequented the party circuit...exclusive parties that were by invitation only. Jess and Kevin looked at one another as identical thoughts ran through their heads. Were those invitation-only parties play parties?

Intrigued, Kevin steered the interview in that direction. Keeping all the pertinent details of the investigation to himself, he alluded that Sandy's murder was sex-related and let Julie know that he and Jess were very interested in speaking to Nick. Nick, whoever he was, didn't know it, but he had just rocketed to the top of their list of suspects. They could hardly wait to have a chat with him.

6:22 PM

The shrill ringing of the telephone jolted Jess awake. She bolted upright, at once aware that she had fallen asleep with her head on Kevin's shoulder. He smiled and caressed her cheek. They learned that Stephanie had cracked the passwords on the computer and was scanning the history. Knowing it would be a while yet, Jess had her jump to the address book and scan it for anyone named Nick. Moment's later, armed with a name, address, and telephone number, Kevin proclaimed it a day and ushered Jess to his truck. Neither of them looked forward to the morning, which would begin with Sandra Vandenberg's official autopsy.

The following morning...

"Have you been to an autopsy before?" Kevin asked.

"Several when I was in college and two case-related since I've been at the bureau. One of my graduate professors was a sadist, I think. Autopsy viewings were regular assignments. We profiled the victims to come up with suspect profiles. Dr. Hauser said we'd either decide against this line of work, or it would toughen us up and keep us from puking at a scene," Jess revealed, laughing.

"Gee, that was nice of him. Was the drop-out rate high?"

"Not really, but several of my classmates took jobs with the courts and social agencies instead of doing this. I still hate autopsies, though."

"Yeah, they're pretty gross. Let's show up late."

"Works for me, I could go the rest of my life without watching them run the gut again."

"Same here."

"I think I'll forgo breakfast too. Haven't had a problem before, but why tempt fate."

"Me too, but I did turn green a few times as a rookie."

9:32 AM

"Good morning, you missed the dissection," Bob said.

"That was intentional, Bob," Jess answered.

"Squeamish?"

"No, I just fail to see how subjecting my senses to the gut wash would help the investigation. We already know how she was killed," she added.

"Oh well, come and take a look. Along with the ligature marks, your victim's trachea is fractured, causing this swelling you see in her neck. Her larynx is severely damaged, cornu is fractured. Note the contusions, and as I suspected would be the case, the hyoid bone is also broken. For obvious reasons, I'm declaring the death a homicide. The official COD will be ligature asphyxia," Bob told them.

"We expected that much," Kevin said.

"She has perimortem lesions on her buttocks, as well. The good news is that he didn't sanitize the body as well as we thought. Inside several lesions, I found microscopic, dark fibers."

"Any idea what it is?"

"I can't tell."

"What about leather or suede?" Jess suggested, puzzling Kevin. "Think about it...suede flogger, bullwhip."

"Yeah, that makes sense," he returned in sudden clarity.

"Slater, help me turn her over. There's something here now that appeared overnight."

"Goddamn, he really beat the hell out of her," Kevin exclaimed. "He's big too. Look at the size of that handprint."

Jess' cell phone rang. "You guys finish up. I'm gonna walk outside and take this. Yeah, this is Jess."

"*Jess Mitchell?*"

"Yes, who is this?"

"*This is Dwayne Eddy from the state crime lab. Carl Barnes told me I was supposed to call you with any results from some evidence that was brought in yesterday as soon as they were available.*"

"Great Dwayne, what do you have?"

☯☯☯☯

Kevin exited the morgue as Jess was ending her call. "What's the scoop?"

"Let's walk and I'll fill you in." They walked slowly back to the truck while Jess relayed the lab results received so far. "That was Dwayne with the crime lab. The lubricant is a common brand called Slick, spelled S L I K, and he's working on DNA from the hairs now, but says under the scope, they're closer to Mongoloid than Caucasoid."

"That just narrowed down our suspect list."

"Yeah, only one problem."

"What's that?"

"I realize that outward appearances can be deceiving, but our guy, Nick, sure looks Caucasian to me."

"Damn, you're right." They continued on to the truck in silence. "You just got that look again," Kevin said as opened her door.

"What look?"

"The one that happens when that brain of yours starts running at warp speed. What are you thinking?"

"I'm thinking about the handprint."

"What about it?"

"Sandy knew her killer."

"How do you get that from just a handprint?"

"If the act were random, he would have hit her with an object. Skin-to-skin contact individualizes the crime, makes it personal. It's one of the factors used in rape profiles too," Jess continued.

"What else?"

"It was huge. Mongoloids typically aren't big and so wouldn't have such large hands."

"So doesn't that narrow it down even more if we know we're looking for a big Asian dude? Maybe he's mixed and got his size from another fork in the family tree."

"I guess."

"Hey, it happened to me," Kevin pointed out.

"True. Every time I think we're getting there, we end up on a new detour."

Chapter 23

One week later...

"Hey Kev, I have something."
"What is it?"
"Looks like Nick's familiar with KLAASP, but I can't tell if he's a member. Check it out."

> *SandWitch: hey cyberluvr*
> *DOMiNICK: hi there wicked lady*
> *SandWitch: are you coming tonight?*
> *DOMiNICK: cumming where? lol*
> *SandWitch: to the KLAASP meeting silly*
> *DOMiNICK: will you be there?*
> *SandWitch: of course*
> *DOMiNICK: i want to see you up close and personal*
> *SandWitch: maybe we've already met*
> *DOMiNICK: true*

"When was this?"
"May 28."
"So the roommate was right. She did know him a while. Talk about planning ahead."
"Maybe he keeps a harem and picks from it at random when he gets the itch."
Jess pulled Nick Yarboro's DMV photo from the case file and studied it while Kevin skimmed the chat logs. She gave an unexpected shout when recognition hit home. She knew why both he and Sandra Vandenberg seemed so familiar.
"Remember that first play party that we went to?"
"Yeah."
"They were there, on the Saint Andrew's Cross. Remember? Elaine said it was their first public scene and raved about Nick's popularity."
"Right!"

C3 EO CR ED

> *SubMarine is available.*
> *SubDoer: hello Armand*
> *SubMarine: CJ, how have you been?*
> *SubDoer: i'm wonderful and you?*
> *SubMarine: doing very well, thanks. how's the training going?*
> *SubDoer: Reese is still screening mentors*
> *SubMarine: it's good that he's taking his time in deciding*
> *SubDoer: we met another local Dom the other day who seemed to really know his stuff, we saw him at a party too, i wonder if you know him*
> *SubMarine: What's his name?*
> *SubDoer: i'm not sure i should say since we aren't supposed to talk about people or mention names without their permission*
> *SubMarine: I promise, I won't breathe a word. I like you, but you're new to the scene. I would hate to see you get mixed up with the wrong person.*
> *SubDoer: okay, if you're sure...his name is Nick*
> *SubMarine: GASP! :-0 Be careful of him.*
> *SubDoer: why? he seemed quite pleasant*
> *SubMarine: Looks can be deceiving. I've known several of his former slaves. He's,*

shall we say, more dominant than most. He's frightened a few off.
SubDoer: does he attend KLAASP meetings, i don't recall seeing him
SubMarine: Sometimes, he comes and goes depending on whether he has a slave.
SubDoer: thank you for the information, Reese is home so i have to go
SubMarine: You're welcome and good luck. I look forward to seeing you again.
SubDoer: yes, same here...bye
Your status is set to appear offline. All conversation windows will be closed.

"What do you make of that?" Jess asked Kevin.
"I think our best lead in this case is weak one minute then solid again the next," he said.

David interrupted them with a monstrous fax that turned out to be the expected background check on Nick Yarboro. The first thing Jess did was confirm his current residence. Nick Yarboro was a surprise. Not only was he young and attractive, but he was also highly intelligent, with degrees from UCLA and Stanford. He was locally employed as an Assistant Professor of English literature at Elon University. His list of prior appointments included positions at distinguished universities from San Francisco to Memphis. She read on and made notes until she came upon information dating from Nick's childhood...in St. Paul, Minnesota. Wasting no time, Kevin left Jess to her notes and phoned a convenient connection in that city, his younger sister and ADA, Samantha Slater.

Nicholas Alexander Yarboro, age 38
current address 1436 Eric Lane, Burlington
employment history
   San Francisco State University, Associate Professor, non-tenure
   Memphis State University, Associate Professor, non-tenure
   Elon University, Assistant Professor of English Lit, tenure-track
previous addresses, St. Paul, LA, Stanford, Frisco, Memphis
criminal record
   underage drinking, 1987, LA, 90 days community service;
   assault and battery, 1989, LA, case dismissed;
   domestic assault, Stanford, 1994, charges dropped;
   assault, 1998, Frisco, charges dropped;
   battery, 2000, Memphis, no charges filed.
family status – never married, no children

That afternoon...

"Hey Sammy, thanks for getting back to me."
"*Kev, to what do I owe the pleasure of your call?*"
"Official business, actually."
"*Really? That's interesting. What kind of official business could you possibly have with me?*"
"I'm in need of some information, if you can get it for me."
"*You know I'll try. What's going on?*"
"Remember that other big case that Jess and I are working on?"
"*Mr. Clean.*"
"Exactly, we finally got our first solid lead and possible suspect, and it just so happens he was born and raised in St. Paul."
"*Let me guess. You want to know if the DA's office has anything on him.*"
"You got it."
"*Sure Bro, that should be easy enough.*"
"You think you can crack juvie records for me too?"
"*Depends...Official or unofficial?*"

"Unofficial, we're just trying to get a feel for the guy for now, don't wanna be barking up the wrong tree."

"You know those records are sealed. Can I mention to my boss why I want a peek? You know how they are during election years. If they think something will help them..."

"Yeah, that's true. I guess that would be okay. Just keep it hush-hush. I don't want the papers getting wind of it."

"I can handle that. Gimme a few days though. You know how it is this time of year."

"All too well, I'm afraid. Thanks, Sam."

"You're welcome. Hey, am I still invited for Christmas?"

"You'd better come. I have something big planned and you'll be madder than hell if you miss it."

"Do I get a hint?"

"Hell no!"

"You're no fun."

"I know somebody who would disagree with that."

"I'm sure you do. Look Bro, I have to run. We'll talk in a few days."

"Okay, bye Sammy, and thanks again."

Two days later, progress was being hampered by slow returns in both the local police lab and the state crime lab. Jess was infuriated at the time they'd spent waiting for a hit to come back on the fingerprints. Kevin cocked an eyebrow and watched in amusement while she ranted. She finally dialed Stephanie Andrews and told the tech to narrow the search parameters to Los Angeles, San Francisco, St. Paul, and Memphis, and to concentrate specifically on Nicholas Yarboro. Kevin, knowing they had to attend another KLAASP meeting later, didn't want Jess distracted. Distractions were dangerous, so he calmed his love with a soothing shoulder rub and suggested they go home early.

7:15 PM

Their legs were entangled and the sheet lay almost entirely in the floor, where it had fallen unbeknownst to them when they made love after their shower. Their bodies were still flushed and moist. Kevin kissed Jess tenderly and brushed a loose strand of damp hair from her eyes, then caressed her back as he cradled her in the crook of his arm. As luck would have it, the telephone rang just as he was about to make love to her once more before they left for their meeting. At first, he made no move to answer it until Samantha's voice rang out from the answering machine.

"Kev, it's Sam. If you're there, pick up. This is important. I have that info you wanted."

"Damn, that always happens."

"What?"

"It's never a telemarketer when you want it to be." Jess giggled. "Always important calls when we're in the middle of something important, lemme get that. Hey, Sam, I'm here. What did you find out?" He paused, then looked at Jess with a surprised and interested expression. "No shit? I can't say I'm surprised, but then at the same time, I didn't expect to find out anything this big so soon." He looked at Jess and gave her a thumbs up. "I don't suppose you could send me a copy of the file? Really? Cool! Yeah, FedEx it to the office. Sam, you're the best...Thanks again...Yeah, yeah, love you too," he said, grinning at Jess.

"What was that?"

"We got a hit on Nick Yarboro."

As a youth, Nick Yarboro had a penchant for fire starting. His juvenile record served as further support for the case as Jess was well-aware of pyromania being part of the homicidal triad, a near-universal trait among serial offenders. She didn't know if he'd also been a bed-wetter, but she was willing to bet he'd had a cruel streak towards animals and other children.

8:00 PM

News of Sandy Vandenberg's murder had made the rounds through the BDSM community, especially in the local KLAASP chapter. Rumors had begun to circulate, and though they weren't speaking freely, KLAASP members were still talking. A Domina that Kevin and Jess had met at their first meeting, Meryl, made a quiet speculation that someone in the community, maybe even a KLAASP member, was the killer.

Without alluding to his professional interest in the case, Kevin prodded her for more information while she was being chatty. He went so far as to suggest Nick's involvement, though Meryl seemed certain that he was not the killer. Not wanting to blow their cover, Kevin didn't push for more. Instead, he steered Jess to an unoccupied corner when his cell phone began to vibrate, displaying the lab's number. He listened intently, speaking very little, for several minutes before ending the call with a self-satisfied smirk.

"Come outside with me," he said as he changed directions and pulled Jess along.

He lit a cigarette and checked the area for eavesdroppers before speaking. Stephanie had matched the print from Sandy's corpse to one she had found on the photo from the woman's bedroom. In addition, she'd received a near-immediate hit on IAFIS after narrowing the search parameters as Jess had suggested. The print belonged to none other than Nicholas Alexander Yarboro.

The news was positive, but it wasn't enough for a warrant. Kevin and Jess knew their suspect would slip away on a technicality if the case wasn't airtight. Though the prints matched and put him with the victim on the day of her disappearance, the hairs would blow gigantic holes in their case if they weren't his. Knowing they planned to meet with Lieutenant Lacy Daniels in Hillsborough to compare cases, they decided to sit on the information until they could also check for similar unsolved cases in Los Angeles, San Francisco, and Memphis. They were determined to apprehend this sadistic murderer, even if it meant prosecuting him from another jurisdiction.

Chapter 24

December 23...

"Your dad and Niki will be over tonight, right?"

"Yes, and David too. That's okay, right?"

"Sure, he keeps Niki too busy to harass *me*," Kevin said. His voice rang with mirth.

"Our first official soirée together here at home."

"The first of many. The Chief doesn't seem to mind us living in sin."

"He's thrilled that we're *playing nice*."

"Playing nice, cracks me up every time he says that," he said, chuckling.

"That and the fact that I'm living closer to home now, even if it's not in his house."

"Good point. I gotta hunt for something in the attic. Then I need to get out of here 'cause I have a couple errands to run before I pick Sam up at the airport, so I'm gonna leave you to that great smelling whatever-it-is you've got cooking in there.

Kevin climbed into the attic and searched for several minutes before he spotted it. He opened up the worn, old case and took out the guitar. "Haven't played you in months, I wonder if you're still in tune," he said to himself as he strummed the instrument. "Beautiful, you sound as good as the day I put you up here. I only hope I can keep up with everybody." He placed the guitar back into its case and began searching again. "Where the hell is that suit?" Finally, he spied a box in a dark corner. He opened it and pulled out a huge, red-velvet bag containing an old suit of the same material. "You don't look any worse for wear." He wrinkled his nose. "You smell like hell, though." He checked the time. "Cool! I still have time to run you through the cleaners before I pick up Sammy." He stuffed the guitar case into the velvet bag with the suit and emerged from the attic, leaving everything out of sight, and went to stand just outside of the archway leading into the kitchen.

"Did you find what you were looking for?" Jess asked.

"Sure did."

"How about a little peek."

"Um, no."

"You're being very mysterious."

"It's a surprise, but I'll trade you a peek for a taste of whatever smells so good."

"Not a chance, come here and kiss me."

He pulled her into his arms and kissed her senseless, taking a moment to cup her buttocks and pull her body against his. He was hard and ready. "Mmm, see what you do to me?"

"Mmm hmm," she purred before pulling away. "You'd better get outta here so Samantha won't be left waiting. We'll have plenty of time for *that* later."

"Mmm," he groaned. "I sure hope so." Kevin walked back to the living room to retrieve his parcels and peeked around the corner before sneaking out the front door.

Twenty minutes later...

An aging black man looked up from behind the counter when the door opened. "Well, Detective Slater, how are you?"

"I'm great. Abe, I need a huge favor."

"Sure, whatever you need."

"This has been in my attic for a long time, about five years. You think you could get the funky odor out?"

"What a nice suit."

"It was my grandfather's, then my father's, and now mine."

"It's just a little musty. I can get that out. When do you need it?"

"Tomorrow night, can you do it?"

"Anybody else would be SOL, since I'm officially closed," he chuckled. "But you're one of my favorite customers. How's forty-five minutes sound?"

"Great! Buddy, I need to run a quick errand a few doors down. Is it okay if I come back?"

"Sure, go ahead."

Ten minutes later...

Kevin waited before the glass showcase while a clerk retrieved a small, velvet-wrapped box from the store's vault. Moments later, he slipped the case into his coat pocket and hurried back down the walk.

Back at Abe's Dry Cleaning...

"Ah, there you are, all finished."

"*You* are a lifesaver, Abe. How much do I owe you?"

"It's on the house."

"Are you sure? You should be at home with your family, but here you're doing a last-minute, rush job for me instead."

"And happy to do it. Merry Christmas, I hope Santa makes someone real happy this year."

"Me too, Abe, me too. Merry Christmas, Buddy."

3:38 PM

Terese and Samantha Slater disembarked from the airplane and started down the walkway into the terminal. "Are you sure they won't mind me being here?"

"Jesus Ma, of course they won't mind. Kev hasn't seen you in forever and Jess is great. Hell, they were disappointed you didn't come for Thanksgiving."

"Samantha Kirsten Slater, watch your mouth, young lady!"

"Sorry, Mamma."

Terese fretted for another moment over the surprise trip before Samantha gently pushed her out of sight. She wanted to surprise her brother. Bursting through the doorway, she ran to Kevin, who grabbed her around the waist and hugged her.

"Hey, Runt!"

"No more beard? I kinda liked it."

"I shaved it off a few days ago, itches like a bitch."

"So does that mean you're not undercover anymore?"

"I wish. KLAASP held the December meeting last week because of the holidays, so I have plenty of time to grow it back before the next one."

"Oh well, hey, I brought you a *big* surprise. Actually, it's on the small side, but I think you're *really* gonna like it, and if you don't...well, it's too late for me to do anything about it now, so fake it."

"What is it?"

"Come on." She grabbed his hand and walked back towards the tarmac.

Kevin's eyes grew wide with shocked, but happy, surprise when he saw their mother's beaming smile. "Mamma!" He swung the petite woman off the floor in a bear hug and kissed her cheek before turning back to his sister. "How did you convince her to get on a plane? Did you slip her something?"

"No, but I wish I woulda though. She's done nothing but yap since we got on the plane."

"That's not true, Samantha! You know exactly why I came with you." Terese turned to Kevin. "I wanted to meet Jess, and I did *not* talk the whole time. Now put me down."

"Oh yeah, sorry Ma. I can't believe you're here. Come on. I can't wait for you to meet Jess." He put an arm around each woman and escorted them to the baggage claim area.

Kevin stepped in front of his mother to hide her from sight, intent on surprising Jess with their unexpected guest. "Honey, hope you don't mind. I picked up a bum off the street!" He gave Samantha a gentle shove inside.

"Oh you!" She exclaimed.

Jess laughed at their playful banter. "You two are so funny."

"Did ya miss me?" Kevin asked when she got to the door.

"Of course," she responded with a long kiss. "Hey Samantha," Jess said, hugging her.

"Are you sure it's no trouble us being here? We can go to a hotel."

"We who?"

"Damn Sammy, you never could keep a secret. Ouch!" He cried out as his mother gave him a sharp poke to the ribs. "Baby, look who else is here. Come on in, Ma."

"Oh wow!" Jess exclaimed. "Your mother! I see the family resemblance."

"Jess, this is my Ma, Terese Slater. Ma, this is my Baby, Jess Mitchell."

"Kevin Reese, Jess is a grown woman, not a baby. De viser damen noe respect." Jess had no idea what Terese said, but the woman's body language proclaimed that she was chastising Kevin for something, as only a mother could.

"Ja Mamma," he said sheepishly. "She's *my* Baby," he baited quietly.

Terese knitted her brow at her son and smiled, then stepped forward to embrace Jess while she chattered on. Jess returned the hug and drew the women into the cozy warmth of the house while Kevin brought in their luggage. Once settled, the foursome chitchatted a while longer before Jess excused herself to finish dinner. Kevin gave his mother a tour of the house and prepared her for their other guests, Dean, Dave, and especially Niki.

"Knock, knock. The life of the party has arrived," Niki announced as she barreled through the door with David on her heels.

"Y'all come on in," Jess called from the kitchen.

"Whassup, Sarge?"

"Just taking it easy for the next few days, come on in."

"Dean's right behind us. Hey, you shaved the goatee!"

"Yeah, I'm taking a break from it."

"You should keep it all the time. It looked good."

"Thanks, but cultivating a beard is much harder than shaving every day, not to mention the itch. Then there are department protocols."

"This, my dear Kevin, is why women wax. Mmm Jess, smells great in here! I'm glad I wore my loose jeans. Hey, Sam. How are you?" Niki asked as she hugged Samantha.

"I'm great, glad to see you again."

"You too, Hun."

"Evening, Chief."

"Hello there, David."

"Chief, Niki, Dave...Sam brought me an early Christmas present. I'd like you all to meet my mother, Terese Slater."

"Good Lord! You have a mother?" Dave pretended to be shocked. "I thought you were raised by wolves."

"Bite me, David."

"No seriously, it's very nice to meet you, Ma'am," Dave schmoozed.

"Welcome, Mrs. Slater, I'm glad you were able to come down," Niki said.

"Thank you, both of you."

"Ma, this is Jess' best friend, Niki Shannon, and her boyfriend, David Rafferty. Dave is also one of my guys at the substation."

"My goodness, another lovely lady, I'm not sure my old heart can stand it," Dean said as he took Terese's hand. "Welcome." She blushed and looked down.

"And finally, Jess' dad, Dean Johansen."

"Thank you. You're all so gracious."

"Jess, did you make sangria too?" Niki shouted.

"Of course," she called from the kitchen.

"Sangria? At Christmas?" Kevin queried.

Jess brought out a loaded tray and poured a round for everyone. "Kevin, you're south of the border now. We do things different here," Niki joked.

"No kidding. You still haven't told me, Jess. What are we having?" Kevin asked.

"Chili, with all the fixins."

"Feliz Navidad," Niki joked.

9:00 PM

At Dave and Niki's departure, Dean insisted on cleaning, so Jess retired to the living room with Terese and Sam while Kevin smoked a cigarette on the front porch. Teresa looked through the photos Jess had taken during Thanksgiving, remarking how much more Kevin resembled his late father with the beard. She shared her own family pictures, naming everyone, which helped Jess become more familiar with Kevin's family.

"Kate's son, James, came home for Christmas. He's in school at Boston College. Kinsey has her brood out of elementary school for the holidays. She didn't want to overwhelm you with four children and no notice, but they send their regards," Terese said.

"That's too bad. I think we could have worked everybody in," Dean said. "That's a lot of grandchildren. How old are they?"

"They range from six to twenty."

"That's some spread," Jess said.

"Yes, but we haven't had a baby in the family in so long. I'm looking forward to these two giving me many more grandchildren," she said as she looked lovingly towards her youngest children.

"I know the feeling," Dean added.

"Jess, what was that you said earlier about feeling pressured?" Sam tittered.

"Well, I hate to eat and run, but I need to get home. We've got an early day tomorrow."

Jess walked Dean to the door and hugged him. "Drive safe. I love you."

"Love you too, Sweetheart. Terese, it was a pleasure meeting you, and Samantha, a delight seeing you again."

"He is so sweet," Sam said.

A short while later, Sam followed Terese to bed and Kevin went outside for one last cigarette. Jess grabbed a windbreaker and followed him onto the front porch. Kevin lit up, sat down in the swing, and put his arm around her.

"Back in Littlefork, there's at least a foot of snow on the ground at Christmastime, but here, it's like springtime." He drew long on his cigarette.

"Yes, but this is odd even for here. You've been here long enough to know this is usually when the ice and freezing rain start," Jess replied.

"True."

"I've never seen a white Christmas."

"Not even in New York?"

"I came home as soon as the semester ended in early December, so I was here for the holidays. Sometimes it was snowing when I left and there was snow when I went back, of course, but I never saw it during Christmas." She snuggled closer to him and took in the quiet calm of the night. He gently pushed the swing back and forth with one foot while he finished his cigarette. "You've been a little edgy this evening. Is everything okay?"

"I'm sorry. I guess I haven't gotten over the shock of seeing my Ma."

"That must be it. I didn't think of that."

Out of the blue, she shivered as his raw virility...his cologne, the leather of his jacket, even the lingering scent of his cigarette...suddenly assaulted her senses. She turned to face him and pulled him closer by his shirt. Caressing the nape of his neck, she drew him into a searing kiss. He growled and held her tighter. Jess sucked his lips, then stabbed her tongue assertively into his mouth. It didn't matter that his mustache tickled her nose or that the day's growth on his chin abraded the soft skin of her face. She withdrew abruptly to catch her breath.

"What was that for?"

"I dunno. Something just came over me. You're like a drug that I can't get enough of," she confessed. "I want you all the time."

"Honey, that makes two of us. Let's go inside before the neighbors get a show they won't forget." Kevin opened the door and followed Jess inside in time to glimpse Sam going into her room.

"Come with me." Jess said, dragging him behind her. "I have a surprise for you."

She walked backwards through their bedroom door, loosening her clothes as she went. Nearly naked when she reached the bed, she lay back and beckoned to him. Without a sound, he stripped and climbed over her, reaching out to caress her cheek, and kissed her tenderly. Leaning up on one elbow, Kevin unfastened the hooks of her bra with his free hand, allowing her breasts spill out. He sucked one rock-hard nipple at a time, rotating his tongue around it from time to time, and kneaded the other, tweaking the rosy tip until Jess could endure no more. Slowly he inched his way down, dipping his wet tongue into every hollow, licking around every curve, and pausing to plunge his tongue into her navel. He left a trail of goose bumps as he snaked his way towards her wet cleft, discovering the crotchless panties she'd worn again to entice him.

"Mmm, Daddy likes..."

He leaned down and spread her thighs, then hooked her knees over his shoulders. Jess instinctively arched towards his lips. His feather-light touch was restrained, as he just barely grazed her tender flesh, but still enough to elicit a soft gasp from her lips. Gradually, he became more forceful; his tongue darting in and out of her hot opening and sucking her swollen diamond until she was certain it would explode. Without warning, he stopped.

"Don't stop, please."

"Oh no, min kjærlighet, you're not coming yet," he teased.

"You beast!" He half-laughed, half-growled, and nibbled at the tender flesh of her inner thighs. Jess was on fire. "Get up here and make love to me," she commanded.

"Patience, my sweet."

"You are evil," she groaned.

Though it was only seconds, it seem liked hours before he pushed two fingers into her and flicked his tongue over her sensitive spot. It was her undoing. Grabbing the back of his head, she ground her crotch into his mouth as she was overtaken by wave after wave of powerful tremors. Kevin held on tightly until her body no longer quaked, then laid his head on her belly and rested. After a time, he crawled up and hovered over her, cupped her breast, and slithered his scorching tongue across the still semi-rigid nipple.

There was no mistaking his arousal. His erection protruded straight up and rested against her sex when he stood and lifted her long enough to shove a fat pillow underneath her. With a mind of its own, his cock pushed against her sleek opening, as if trying to get inside on its own. Gathering her tightly against him, Kevin ground his pelvis against hers, though he did not enter her at first. Rather, he kissed her fully, deeply, bruising her tender lips.

The scent of her desire clung to his mustache. Jess tasted her lust in his kiss. The delicious musky aroma of sex and perspiration emanated from him. He tasted good. Sweat had left the acute tang of salt on his skin. She leaned closer and sucked an earlobe before trailing kisses down her lover's neck. His breathing quickened and a low groan escaped him.

He raised her slightly, and then pulled her against his hard body, impaling her on his massive organ. It was almost painful when he entered her, his immense size filling her so completely, so much more than either of her two previous lovers. His long, deep strokes were slow at first, becoming more hurried with every moan that escaped her lips. It seemed like hours rather than minutes before she felt the beginnings of another peak.

"Faster, oh God, fuck me...harder."

His thrusts became harder and deeper.

"Oh God, oh yes, yes!"

Jess dug her nails into Kevin's shoulders and contracted tighter around his rod when her body convulsed in an explosion of fiery ecstasy. He gradually slowed his pace while she recovered until there was no movement at all, save for the steadfast pulsing of his unspent yearning. A moment later, they disengaged briefly while Kevin removed the pillow from under her, and then knelt before her to carefully remove her forgotten panties while she looked on, admiring his form, hardly believing she had really ridden the enormous tool that was even now jutting from between his legs.

"Come here," Jess called.

As he stood before her, she took his enormous shaft between her lips and sucked it down her throat. He tasted and smelled of her juices. The flavor and aroma of their love turned her on all the more and made her more determined than ever to please him. Holding his muscled backside, she moved back and forth, her tongue teasing him with every stroke, and catching the occasional drop of moisture that wouldn't be held back. After a time, he pulled himself away from her lips and pushed her back onto the bed then climbed on top of her.

"I can't take anymore of that."

Positioning himself between his ladylove's thighs, Kevin drove into her, penetrating her over and over until his restraint was nil before collapsing on top of her with a violent shudder. After a few minutes, he rolled away and leaned up on an elbow.

"What was the surprise?"

"I was going to drag you in here and take advantage of you, but you kinda turned the tables on me."

"Really? Are we feeling a touch bratty tonight?" Kevin teased.

"I was," Jess said, flashing him a coy look. "Until my Master took charge and put me back in my place," she added with a giggle. She lay her head on his chest and fell asleep in his arms.

Chapter 25

Christmas Eve morning...

Kevin was sleeping soundly when Jess woke up. Were it not for the mustache, he would have appeared almost boyish. A lock of hair hung across his forehead while the rest lay tousled around his neck and ears. She resisted the urge to reach out and brush it back from his face, choosing instead to lay motionless, satisfied with merely resting in his arms. At last, he opened his eyes, looked at her and smiled.

"Morning, Handsome."

"Morning, Beauty."

"Did you sleep well?"

"Extremely, I love waking up like this. Last night was...incredible."

"It was for me too." Jess paused for several minutes. "I've been wondering about something."

"What's that?" Even before she said the words, she could feel heat creeping up her neck. "Uh oh, you're blushing. This is going to be good."

Heat continued to move up into her cheeks. "Why do you keep making me stop?"

"Make you stop what?" She averted her eyes in chagrin. "I wish you could see how stunning you are when you look like that," he joshed.

"Oh, this is impossible!"

"I'm sorry for teasing. You're just so beautiful when you're flustered. I can't help it."

"Oh forget it. This is too hard."

"Out with it, Woman. I promise I won't be offended and I won't laugh."

"I'm horrified that I even have to ask."

"Ask what, Baby?"

"Am I doing it wrong?"

"Doing what wrong?"

"At the risk of sounding crass, blowjobs."

"Good Lord, no, my beauty. I'm amazed you *need* to ask."

"But you make me stop every time."

"Sweetheart, your mouth feels so good, I'm afraid I'll blow any second. The last thing I want to do is turn you off." Jess sighed in relief. "How does a nice girl like you get to be so good at that? No, wait. Forget I asked. I don't want to..."

"*Cosmo,*" she interrupted. She giggled at Kevin's stunned silence and snuggled closer to him when he brushed a strand of hair aside and kissed her forehead.

"Jess, you are such a breath of fresh air."

She paused and studied him for a moment. "You're holding back. I know I'm not a worldly sex goddess, but I'm pretty good at reading people. What is it?"

"Worldly no, sex goddess, yes. Can I plead the fifth?" Jess shook her head. Kevin gathered his thoughts before continuing. "I um, was well-informed of your lack of experience before we got serious, which would have made it so easy for me to take advantage of you. But once I got to know the real you, there's no way I coulda done that."

Kevin told Jess the entire story of that fateful day when they'd first succumbed to their passion for each other. He admitted to talking with Niki and then keeping Jess unaware of her friend's duplicity. However, he didn't do so until he was certain she wouldn't lash out at Niki for meddling.

"So we're straight and you're not gonna give another thought to your...um, technique?"

Jess smiled at him. "Not a one, I just had to be sure. I want to satisfy you as much as you do me."

"Honey, everything you do pleases me."

11:30 AM...

Well-fed, the group split up to make their own preparations for the evening's festivities. Terese excused herself to the kitchen and Sam went outside to wait with Dean, who was whistling a merry tune. He was nearly giddy after Terese promised him a batch of her delicious lingonberry preserves upon her return to Littlefork. Kevin got up from his chair, walked up behind Jess as she was clearing the table, and wrapped his arms around her.

"Mmm, breakfast really was delicious," he said, kissing her neck.

"You got enough?"

"Nuh uh, I'm still ravenous." He held her hips and rubbed his swollen crotch against her denim-clad backside. "But not for more food," he added with a wicked laugh.

"My goodness, after last night and you still haven't had enough," Jess teased.

"There's something about you, woman. You're addictive, but it's a habit I don't want to break," he said with a chuckle.

"Mmm, maybe we'll be able to slip away later."

"I'm gonna hold you to that." They finished loading the dishwasher. "Looks like that's it and it's nearly noon. Something tells me you don't usually do this tree thing so late. You ready to go?"

"As ready as I'm gonna get."

Kevin led Jess to the Tahoe where Dean waited behind the wheel. Sam had claimed the front seat, so the couple slid into the back. A twenty-five minute ride took them to a dirt road that led to the patch of woods on the old Daniels farm where Dean and Jess had cut their Christmas tree for years. He drove slowly down the rutted pathway while Kevin interrogated Sam. He wanted to know the real reason why his mother didn't come along.

She steadfastly refused to admit anything, but Kevin was tenacious. He turned his tactics on Jess since she'd spent the better part of the morning in the kitchen with the women. Unlike Samantha, Jess caved. Terese had stayed behind to bake a special treat for her son, but Jess couldn't pronounce its Norwegian name.

"Fyrstkake," Kevin guessed, his eyes lighting up.

Jess looked at him and rolled her eyes. "Man, he's good," Sam said. "I know now why he's never had trouble solving cases. He just beats away at the suspects until they admit everything. Kevin, you woulda made a great attorney."

"Not! Cloud cream, too?"

Again, Jess looked at him crossly and pursed her lips. "You'd better act surprised," she said. "Or I'm gonna hurt you," she added, giving him an elfish look.

"Ooh, I'm scared."

"You'd better be. What exactly is first cake?"

"Prince Cake. Right, Brat?"

"I still have a hard time choking it down even though it's delicious. When I was little he used make me cry every time Ma made it."

Samantha relayed her childhood torment at her brother's hands to an astonished Jess. Kevin, like many older brothers, had gotten a thrill out of leaving his baby sister in tears. As a youth, he'd tell Samantha that Terese baked *fyrstkake* in honor of her only son, and favorite child, and how she didn't want another girl since she'd already had two daughters before Sam came along. Before Jess could properly berate Kevin for his youthful indiscretions, Dean announced their arrival at their destination.

The foursome fell out of the truck and trudged deeper into the woods. They bypassed several trees that would have done nicely, but kept wandering until Kevin pointed to a lone Blue Spruce. The beautiful tree caused Jess to forget that she'd planned to throttle him for his decades-old teasing. Dean cut it down and Kevin hefted it over his shoulder to prevent damaging the top. After tromping back to the truck, the men tied it to the roof while Sam and Jess sat inside, and then Dean drove them back to the house.

"Hey, Jess, why don't you take Ma and head on over to Dean's." Jess knitted her brow trying to guess what Kevin was up to. "I'll grab our stuff and be over in a bit."

"Okay," she gave in without argument, but remained puzzled by Kevin's latest display of odd behavior.

"And Chief, leave that tree. I'll unload it when I get there."

"Certainly, Kevin."

2:10 PM

Jess wasn't alone in noticing Kevin's strange behavior. He scowled at Samantha while she questioned his unusual attitude over the past days. He even snapped at her when she pointed out that he'd even acted nervous while Dean was there and demanded he come clean with her. In true alpha male fashion, he growled that he was fine and stomped through the front door to load gifts into his car. Moments later, he was apologizing for his meanness.

"Don't sweat it, and don't forget how well I know you, big brother. What's bothering you?"

"Nothing's *bothering* me, but I'm a ball of nerves, and have been for weeks now, even more since yesterday. Jess noticed it too, but I blew it off. She thinks it's 'cause you and Ma are here."

"What's the big deal? You and Jess aren't having problems, are you?"

"No, nothing like that. Walk outside with me." Samantha followed him onto the porch and waited while he lit his cigarette. "This is why." He pulled a tiny box out of his pocket. "I picked it up yesterday on my way to get you."

"Holy shit! Well, this explains a lot," Samantha exclaimed.

"I know how bad you are at keeping secrets, but don't you dare breathe a word!"

"Oh my God, I can't believe you'd show me something like that and then expect me to be quiet about it. I can't even tell Ma?"

"No! I mean it, Sammy."

"Okay, I promise. But when are you gonna ask her?"

"Don't know yet. She's kinda old-fashioned, so I'm gonna ask Dean's permission first."

"Aww, no wonder you were nervous around him. You're so sweet."

"Yeah, I know."

"Pompous ass and all."

"Hey, watch it! I resemble that remark. You're not gonna slip are you?"

"No, I won't spoil this for you. I promise."

"Good, let's get outta here."

3:00 PM

Jess didn't try to hide her curiosity as she watched Kevin unload everything from *the Beast*. But much to her chagrin, he refused to give her even the smallest hint as to what the gigantic, velvet bag hid from view. She scrutinized it a moment longer before giving up for the time being and opted, instead, to help unload the car. Picking up their overnight bag, she climbed the porch steps and sat in the swing. Kevin propped his red sack against the door, sat beside her, and put his arm around her shoulder before lighting a cigarette. Persistent, Jess continued her visual examination of the bag, trying to determine its contents.

"No peeking."

"Or what?"

"I might have to practice my spanking technique."

"Is that so, Mister?"

"Yeah, and I'm thinking leather paddle too. I bet Elaine could tell me where to get one," he teased. "Hey, I told Dean I'd help him with that tree, so you go on inside while I do that. I'll see you in a bit," he added with a wink. He took another long drag from his cigarette before jabbing it out in an ashtray.

Moments later...

Kevin hauled the tree into the garage. Lost in his thoughts, he was startled when Dean spoke up.

"What? Oh, afternoon Chief, I didn't realize you were out here. Yeah...yeah, I guess I zoned out. I was just thinking."

"About anything in particular?"

"Just life in general, but especially the last few months. Chief..."

"Kevin, I think we're beyond such formalities. Call me Chief when we're on-duty if you want, but please, call me Dean when we're not."

"Okay, Dean...can I talk to you about something?"

"Of course, Kevin, you can come to me with anything."

"Thank you, Sir."

"Grab that pair of shears and let's work on this tree."

Kevin picked up the trimmers and pulled out his cigarettes. "Do you mind, Sir?"

"Go right ahead. What did you want to talk about?"

"Your daughter, Sir, I'm in love with her." Dean looked up from his work without comment. "But it's more than that," Kevin continued. "I want to do this right."

"Do what right, Son?"

"Sir, I'd like your permission to ask for her hand."

"You want to marry my Jessie?"

"Yes, Sir."

"You know you don't need my consent, but I appreciate that you're going the old-fashioned route. Did you get her a ring?"

"Yes, Sir, right here." Kevin opened the tiny box.

Dean took the box and looked at the ring inside. "It's exquisite. I'm sure she'll love it...almost as much as you." He walked around the tree and pulled Kevin into a strong, manly embrace, then slapped him on the back. "Welcome to the family, Son. When were you planning to propose?"

"I was hoping to get your advice on that. Jess is real big on including family in everything, so I've been wrestling with whether or not to do it when everybody's here or privately, just the two of us." Kevin shoved the box back into his pocket and the two men went back to trimming the tree.

"Kevin, I can only tell you to go with your gut and do what feels right."

CK8O)CR8O

Jess led Sam into the kitchen where Terese was preparing yet another scrumptious family recipe that she couldn't pronounce. Leaving the sweets to Terese and Samantha, Jess put the goose into the oven and started prepping the rest of her holiday feast.

"That's it for the bird. I'm going to take the guys a drink."

"Okay Jess, I'm gonna help Ma in here for a bit, then I'll come out," Samantha said.

When Jess entered the den, she didn't see Dean anywhere. Kevin had strung the tree with hundreds of tiny flickering lights and was arranging gifts beneath it, Dean's and several from their house. Jess stopped behind him and reached around to hand him a glass.

"Thank you, Darlin'," he said, taking a long swallow of the sweet, iced tea.

"Where's Dean?"

"He said he was going to the attic to search for ornaments."

"I have your Ma and Sam occupied in the kitchen." She sat the other glass on the mantle. "Could be a good time to slip away," she suggested. Her hand wandered down to massage his cock through his faded blue jeans.

"Mmm, good idea. Glad I thought of it," he said with a husky laugh and turned around. Jess grabbed his hand and dragged him towards the stairs. "Hold on." He went back for the still full-looking red sack. Jess looked at him curiously. "I need to stash this upstairs," he said, his eyes twinkling in lusty amusement as he ascended the stairs behind her.

"You're up to something," she said, closing her bedroom door behind them.

"I'm up all right," he growled, tugging at her shirt.

139

Disrobing quickly, they left their clothing in a heap at the foot of the bed. Kevin pushed Jess forcefully onto the coverlet and hooked her ankles over his shoulders. She gasped in surprised wonder when he plunged his stiff rod into her, awed that she could be so wet and ready for him in an instant. From his vantage point, he watched her ample breasts bounce about from the intense pounding he gave her while he manually frigged her pleasure button. Leaning down, he caught a nipple between his teeth and twirled his tongue around it before nipping it, causing a jolt of both pleasure and pain to rocket through her.

"Oh God," she uttered through gritted teeth, squeezing her other nipple between her thumb and forefinger.

Kevin stopped thrusting long enough to switch his fingers for hers. "Show me how you do it."

Jess licked her middle finger and rubbed with great vigor, increasing speed until a familiar tightening started deep within her belly. Her channel contracted as the climax rippled through her.

"Oh fuck, harder please."

Her body undulated and her hips bucked underneath him. He pounded her harder when her muscles flexed and contracted around his cock. Reaching around, she grabbed his muscular cheeks in both hands, then pulled him deeper into her as her orgasm peaked, causing his control to slip as he came with a mighty stream. His rod pulsed as the last drops of thick, warm semen were expelled. They remained locked together for a moment before he unhooked her legs and raised himself up on his elbows over her.

"Good God, Woman," he said as a droplet of sweat from his forehead fell onto her chest.

"What?"

His breathing was still labored. "You're gonna be the death of me," he said with a grin. "But I'll die one happy man."

"What makes you think I do it?"

"Well nobody else could kill me with loving," he answered, misinterpreting her question.

"Not that, you told me to show you how I do it."

"Oh that. Doesn't everybody?" Naturally, Jess turned five shades of red while he chuckled at her embarrassment, then he looked up and sniffed the air. "Mmm, something smells good."

Jess pushed at him and jumped to her feet. "Oh my God, the goose! I have to go turn down the heat." Kevin laughed as she rushed around, trying to put on enough clothes to go downstairs. "Oh sure, go ahead and laugh. It won't be so funny when I have to feed your family a scorched bird."

"Sweetheart, as long as I get dessert later, I don't care what happens to the damn bird," he said with a wink.

"And I left Samantha and your poor mother down there by themselves. Oh my God, what they must think of me."

The comment brought forth a new round of rich laughter from him. "I'm sure they've found ways to amuse themselves. They probably haven't had time to miss you yet. I'll meet you downstairs."

Jess ran down to the kitchen, turned down the heat on the oven, and basted the bird. "I just checked it for you, Jess."

"Oh, thank you, Sam."

"You're welcome."

"I apologize. I'm such a terrible hostess. I kinda got distracted."

"He's good for that," she teased as Kevin strolled into the room adjusting his shirttail.

"He's good for what?" He asked.

"Distractions," Sam said. "Do you ever let this poor woman rest, big brother?" She teased.

"Of course I do, Runt...when she's tired." He grinned at Jess. "Is your goose cooked?"

"Very funny, no it's fine. See?" She opened the oven door a crack.

"Mmm, smells great. Where's Ma?"

"She's taking a walk in the back yard."

"How long has she been outside?"

"She went out right after Jess took your tea out."

"See Jess, she doesn't even know you abandoned her, so her opinion of you won't change a bit,"

Kevin teased. Jess' relief was evident.

"But she'll box *your* ears if you don't control your libido, Bro," Sam teased. "You know how she feels about premarital sex."

At once, Jess was embarrassed all over again at being caught in the act. "Um Honey, you failed to mention that."

"Please, she knew we were living together. It doesn't take a great stretch of the imagination to figure out that we're a little more than just roommates."

"I know that, but now I feel weird about it."

"Don't give it another thought, Jess," Sam said. "If premarital sex is the worst of your sins, I think you'll be fine, although I'd caution against making any babies before the wedding."

Jess was blushing furiously. "Baby, Sam's teasing you," Kevin said in an irritated tone. "Relax."

"He's right. Jess, I apologize, but actually, I was teasing *him*."

Kevin looked at his watch and announced that it was almost five. With everything under control, Jess dashed back upstairs to shower and change before everyone else arrived, leaving explicit instructions for Kevin and Sam to play nice, and to let Niki and her folks in when they arrived.

Outside on the porch...

"What the hell was that all about?" Kevin blasted. "You nearly slipped in there with that pre-marital, baby bullshit!"

"I did not! I knew exactly what I was saying. And you know it's the truth. Ma would shit a gold brick if you got her pregnant outside the sanctity of marriage, and at the rate you two go at it, it wouldn't take much for that to happen."

"Relax, she's on the pill."

"Yeah, well, so am I, but it's not exactly a hundred percent reliable."

Their sibling banter continued until Niki's father drove up. The pair walked down to the curb to offer a hand after which Kevin pulled Niki aside and sent his sister inside with her folks.

"Yeah, Kevin. What's up?"

"How good are you at keeping secrets?"

"Pretty good. Why?"

"I want your opinion on something I had made for Jess."

"Why mine?"

"Because you know her better than anybody."

"True."

"But you can't let the cat out of the bag."

"I won't tell a soul."

"You're sure?"

"Wild horses couldn't drag it outta me."

"What do you think of this?" Kevin pulled the velvet box from his pocket and flipped open the lid for Niki to view the contents.

"Oh my God, no, you didn't!"

"Yeah, I did."

"Well, hot damn! A man of class and distinction, you impress me more and more every day."

"I take it, you approve?"

"Of course."

"How do you think she'll react?"

"Oh God, she'll be thunderstruck. Hell, I'm in shock."

"Does that mean I need to put it away for a while, or give it to her now?"

"Well now, of course. You gonna propose tonight?"

"I dunno. I want it to be perfect." Kevin closed the box and tucked it back into his pocket.

"Well, if you want my *honest* opinion, perfect woulda been the minute you picked it up, but since you obviously didn't. It is Christmas and this would make an awfully nice present."

"That's what I was thinking. Not a word, I'm serious."

Back in the house...

"Here we are," Niki announced as she and Kevin came inside.

"Jess should be down in a bit," Sam announced.

"Where is she?" Niki asked.

"Upstairs, changing out of her chef's garb."

"Kevin, you remember my folks, George and Betty."

"I do, glad to see you again."

"Better practice those two words so you get it right," Niki whispered to Kevin and nudging him with her elbow.

Dean trotted downstairs to greet everyone, then politely excused himself to fetch his date. Betty Shannon turned back towards Kevin as Dean left and caught Jess coming down the stairs. "Speak of the devil."

Kevin turned fully to look at her as she descended. "Wow." He got up, walked to the bottom of the steps, and took her hand when she reached the landing. "You look stunning."

"Thank you."

"Jess, you look fabulous. You really should wear colors more often, especially this one. It's you, beyond a doubt." Niki made a big scene over Jess' outfit, a silk blouse, red, not her usual white, and an ankle-length, black, leather skirt, which she especially loved. Black, knee-high boots and a leopard-skin Santa hat completed Jess' festive outfit. "Sweetie, the only leather I've seen you wear in years is that beat-up, old bomber jacket you love so much."

"She doesn't know about that kinky streak of yours. Does she?" Kevin whispered in Jess' ear. She laughed quietly at his comment.

"What was that?"

"Oh nothing," Jess replied.

"Anyway, as I was saying before I was so rudely interrupted, this outfit is très cool. And the hat, nice touch. And look Kevin, she's even got mistletoe pinned to it."

"Yes, Niki, I noticed that."

He leaned down and kissed her. The tip of his tongue just did graze her lips. It was quick, but still full of passion that hinted of more to come. Jess reached up and whisked a trace of lipstick from his mouth with her thumb. Kevin jumped at the opportunity to lick her fingertip. The others didn't notice, but he wasn't quick enough for Niki to miss it.

Jess took Niki's arm and pulled her into the kitchen. "I saw that," Niki uttered when she passed Kevin as he reclaimed his seat on the other end of the couch.

Jess didn't speak until she'd removed the goose from the oven and transferred it to a large platter. "Your name came up during a conversation Kevin and I had this morning."

"Dare I ask what the tête-à-tête was about?"

Jess was attacked by a fit of giggling. "Blowjobs," she said, laughing harder at her friend's shocked expression.

"Whoa! How did *my* name get dragged in the middle of *that*?"

"I've been practicing."

"Practicing what? Blowjobs? You? Miss Prim-and-proper-no-penis-will-ever-pass-my-lips? I thought you weren't into that."

"People change."

"Other people change, not you. Damn, he must be something else."

"Oh, he is."

"That's all well and good, but I still fail to see why I have *any*thing to do with you giving your man a hummer."

"What exactly did you tell Kevin about me?"

"I rarely talk to Kevin."

"No, I mean months ago, when I introduced you. You called him that afternoon after we had lunch."

"He told you about that?"

"I sorta forced him to after he stopped me from going all the way again."

"And what did he tell you?"

"To make a long story short, he said he knew I was inexperienced and he didn't want to blindside me with the final product unless he was positive it was what I wanted."

"How noble of him, most men don't give a shit. They just come and tell you to spit if you don't like it."

"You are so crude," Jess said. At this point, Niki had joined her friend in hysterical laughter.

"Shit Jess, you know tact is not my strong suit. Are you sure you *want* to finish it? Especially if he's not pushing for it."

"Why would you ask that?"

"Because some guys are just gross."

"What do you mean?"

Niki considered Jess' query in disbelief. "You've really never sucked a guy all the way off have you?"

"I never gave a blowjob at *all* until Kevin, so tell me!"

"The flavor, the smell, and then some of them try to choke you to death when they get off, ramming their dicks down your throat like you're trying out for the sequel to *Deep Throat* or something. Then some of them get off really hard and cause your gag reflex to kick in."

"You're losing me, Nik."

"Girl, you need to go watch a few flicks."

"I've seen a few and wasn't impressed. They're too scripted."

"You have got a *lot* to learn."

"That's exactly why I asked you."

"So get Kevin to teach you all this shit. Men love being in control like that."

"Are you crazy?! It took all the nerve I had to ask him why he kept stopping me. And I was beet-red the whole time...took me forever to get it out."

"You always did blush at the drop of a dime," Niki said, laughing. "Well anyway, once you get past the act itself, there's the byproduct and let me tell you, not all jizz is created equal. It doesn't all taste very good. Hell, none of it tastes very good if you ask me; some just isn't as bad as most. And the consistency is kinda nasty too."

Niki finished her clinical analysis of felatio with a word of advice. If Jess chose to complete the act, she shouldn't expect Kevin to kiss her afterwards. To hear Niki tell it, a straight man won't let jizz within a mile of his lips for fear of being labeled gay.

"Niki, you make something beautiful sound so gross."

"Well, it is. Would you go down on another girl? That's sorta the same"

"Hell, no! So you never said. What did you tell him?"

"What are you talking about?"

"When you called him."

"Oh yeah that...I only told him that you'd only had two lovers and limited experience, and if he really liked you, he should ask you out because you were kinda bashful and wouldn't hit on a man no matter how much you liked him."

"Is that all?"

"Yeah, and I resent being interrogated, so let's get back out there before Loverboy calls in a search party."

Dean walked in just as Niki and Jess were taking their seats. Jess was flabbergasted at the identity of his date. She'd figured out long ago that she must know the woman because Dean would have no other reason to be so secretive of her identity, but she never thought she'd turn out to be...Maggie? Dean introduced Maggie to Kevin's mother and sister and ladled them each a cup of Jess' famous eggnog while

Maggie worked her way around the room, finally stopping at Kevin, who she greeted with a matronly kiss to the cheek. Jess still had not found her voice.

"Good evening, Maggie. You okay, Baby?" Kevin directed at Jess.

"Dean, I can't believe you didn't tell me you were seeing Maggie. And Maggie? After I practically begged you to tell me who she was…"

"Well, Sweetheart, given our positions, we had to be discreet," Dean stated.

"Oh please, like *I'm* gonna tell on you," Jess teased. "After all, Kevin and I have been *the* subject of water-cooler gossip for so long that no one would ever notice you and Maggie. Besides, what's a little romantic scandal at the office?"

Jess didn't get to finish her interrogation of Dean and Maggie. Her train of thought was diverted when David Rafferty materialized in the front doorway. "Hey, Sexy!" He called out to Niki.

"You're looking mighty slick in your uniform. I didn't think I'd see you until late since you got called in to work on your day off. You still on-duty?"

"Not anymore, thought I'd surprise you, but I had to wait until my shift was over. By the way, thanks for the invite, Jess."

"You're quite welcome, David."

"Guess we can add Kevin to that list of slave drivers," Niki joked. Kevin put up a mild protest at Niki's accusation, but Jess made a valiant rescue by announcing dinner.

8:00 PM

"God, I can't eat another bite," Niki said.

"Time to go take a nap," Kevin teased.

"Nuh uh, Buddy. You've been taunting me with that red sack for two days. It's about time you opened it." He leaned over and whispered something to Niki.

"Yeah, go ahead, Kevin. I'll help Jess clean up while the rest of you head to the den."

"Jessie, can I help with anything?"

"No, you're a guest tonight, Maggie. Now shoo, go play. We'll be done in a jiffy."

"If you're sure," Samantha said.

"Absolutely, we'll see you in a few minutes."

Puzzled by Kevin's sudden disappearance and suspecting Niki's involvement, Jess turned on her friend when everyone was gone. Like a pro, Niki deflected the attack with a dismissive wave of her hand, claiming he only wanted to know if the festivities were about to begin. She finished piling plates and silverware into the dishwasher and took off into the den with a load of mugs, not waiting for Jess.

"Grab that carafe. Coming through with hot buttered rum for everybody, or more eggnog if you fancy that, instead."

Jess was about to look for Kevin when she turned around just in time to see…Santa? And what a handsome St. Nick he was, though somewhat unconventional. Quite striking, his suit was form-fitting and fashioned from dark, red velvet. He completed the outfit with a matching hat and knee-high, black boots. He lacked only a long, white beard and hair, and a big belly.

"Ho ho ho, Merry Christmas, everybody."

"Look at you!" Jess exclaimed as he walked towards her, red sack in hand, and reclaimed his seat beside her on the couch.

He patted his knee as a devilish gleam appeared in his eyes. "Come sit on Santa's knee, little girl, and tell me how *good* you've been this year."

"I'm not sure if that's such a great idea," Niki ragged. "You should save that for later."

"Cool! Is that Da's old suit?" Sam asked. "I thought that red bag looked familiar."

"I wondered what happened to that old thing," Terese said.

Kevin looked at Niki. "And you, lady, have been a very bad girl this year. Nothing but coal and switches for you."

"Ooh, I can't wait," she shot back. "Can I have a whip too?"

"I just can't get one over on you, Niki," Kevin acceded. "Where's an elf when I need one?"

"Did somebody call for an elf?" Dave piped in.

"Give her a candy cane or something. Would ya?"

"You kids are crazy. What's in the bag, Santa?" George asked.

Kevin stood up and pretended to dig through the bag for a few seconds before pulling out a guitar case. "Now who put that in there?"

Jess' eyes grew wide. "Oh!" She gasped with joy. "You play?"

"Only if you're still singing. I haven't touched it in months, so it might take me a minute warm up."

"You two have been together for how long, and you haven't played for her, Kevin? God, Da would take a strap to you."

"Pesky little sisters, can't live with 'em, can't shoot 'em either," Kevin said as he rolled his eyes and chuckled.

Niki wasted no time retrieving her own guitar and argued briefly with her father over who had better taste in music. While Jess flipped through Dean's sheet music.

"Play this one, Dean. They'll catch up," Jess said, handing him the pages.

"An excellent choice, my dear."

> By now in New York City, there's snow on the ground.
> And out in California, the sunshine's falling down.

"Woohoo go, Jess!" Niki shouted.

> Christmas in Dixie. It's snowing in the pines. Merry Christmas from Dixie to everyone tonight.

"Sarge, you're pretty good with that thing," Dave said.

"Thanks, Dave."

> In Littlefork, Minnesota to Burlington, Caroline and all across the Nation, it's a peaceful Christmas time.

"Way to change the lyrics, Jess," Niki called.

Jess sang the final chorus and passed out fresh mugs of hot, buttered rum and eggnog. Several carols and a lot of rum later, a good time was being had by all. Everybody was tipsy, but it was getting late, and Niki was chomping at the bit to open presents, so Jess sat down beside Kevin and sang one final carol.

> Maybe it's early in the game. I thought I'd ask you just the same. What are you doing New Year's, New Year's Eve? Wonder whose arms will hold you tight when it's exactly twelve that night, welcoming in the New Year, New Year's Eve.

"She has a beautiful voice," Terese commented to Sam.

> Maybe I'm crazy to suppose I'd ever be the one you chose, out of the invitations you received. In case I stand one little chance, here comes the question in advance. What are you doing New Year's, New Year's Eve?

A round of applause filled the room. "Well, answer the lady, Sarge."

"Unless she's tired of me by then, I'm spending it with this beautiful lady," he answered with a smile.

"Good answer. Jess, you look parched. Who else needs a refill?" Jess shook her head.

"Okay, well I'm gonna go have a cigarette. Care to join me, *Santa?*"

Chapter 26

"That's some get-up you got there, Santa."

"This was my grandfather's and then my dad's. He used to wear it when my sisters and me were kids. We believed in Santa for years even after all of our friends had stopped because of this suit."

"It was definitely a hit tonight. I think everybody was impressed."

"There's only one person I want to impress."

"It worked."

"You think?"

"Without a doubt. The look on her Jess' face when you came down those stairs was priceless." They remained quiet for a moment. "Have you decided when you're gonna ask her?"

"Yeah."

"Care to share?"

"No."

"Oh well, I tried. Let's go open some presents."

CRSOCRSO

Niki playfully pointed out *Santa's* flaws. The most obvious, he had no beard, which he consistently defended as itchy, but that didn't stop his friends and family from badgering him. Realizing the argument wasn't working anymore, he claimed department protocol, but was then reminded that the rule had been changed due to his undercover status. Spastic as usual, Niki jumped to Kevin's other lapse, his belly, or lack thereof, as he hadn't tried to hide his trim physique with padding. This time Jess came to his rescue.

"*My* Santa is hot...just perfect, if you ask me," she championed, reclaiming her seat on Kevin's knee.

"You nut! Come on folks. Santa is late for work. I have a feeling he's got a long night ahead of him, so let's open some presents," Niki shouted. "Come here, David, and help me pass these out."

"Sure, Babe."

Oohs and ahhs chorused the room as everyone tore into their gifts. "I have a little something else for you later," Jess told Kevin.

"I can hardly wait." The floor was strewn with tattered, brightly colored paper and most everyone was admiring what they'd received and watching Kevin and Jess open theirs. "Wow! This is beautiful."

"Son, your grandfather had one of those."

"Yeah, I remember. What ever happened to it, Ma?"

"I don't know, I think maybe Grandma has it put away somewhere."

"Good Lord, Jess! Isn't it enough that he totes a gun?" Niki teased. "Now you got him carrying a blade too!"

"No, this is great. I love it. I used to watch Grandda shave with his, amazed that he did it without cutting himself."

He held it closer to inspect a minute detail, the silversmith's stamp, a dog's head with the numbers 1896 inscribed underneath, which also proclaimed the strait razor's antique status, as Jess continued unwrapping a king-sized box. Inside it was a smaller, wrapped box. She looked up at Kevin who was grinning mischievously.

"Well, keep going."

She tore the paper from the smaller box to find yet another box. She cocked an eyebrow at him and continued. Inside it...another box.

"You're certainly color coordinated, if nothing else. Look at the rainbow of paper," Niki said.

Jess opened the fourth box only to find a fifth. "Did y'all have any idea that Santa was so keen on tormenting people?"

"I can't believe he'd do such a thing, Jess!" Dave said, laughing.

"Humor me. Keep going," Kevin said, grinning.

Yet another box, Jess was becoming impatient. She shot Kevin an exasperated half-smile and ripped the gift-wrap from the box not caring any longer how it tore or where it fell. "Amazing! You mean there's not another one?" Jess parted the layers of tissue paper and let out a squeal. "Oooohh!"

"What is it, Jess?" Niki asked, trying eagerly to see.

"You like him right?"

"Are you kidding? He's awesome! Remember, I had the CD on at the office the other day."

"Yeah, I know. By the way that's a pretty good album...for rock 'n roll. I really like that one song. What was the name of it?"

"*One More Day* or *Forgiveness*?"

"Both."

"What the heck are you two talking about?" Niki asked.

"It's concert tickets and all-access backstage passes."

"For who?"

"Bret Michaels."

"No sh...way! Kevin, how did you score those?" Niki asked.

He only winked at her. "So it's cool? Runt told me about the tour and made me get 'em for you after I told her you loved glam rock," he said, nudging Samantha. "You won't believe how relieved I was when you told me who you were listening to the other day," he said, laughing.

"Well, if Jess changes her mind, I'll be glad to take them off her hands," Niki said as she snatched the tickets from her friend's hand. "Bret Michaels is hot!"

"Hey, what am I, chopped liver?" Dave asked.

"Of course not, Sweetie," Niki cooed. "But I gotta tell you. I've had a crush on Bret Michaels since high school."

"Me too, maybe Kevin'll *distract* her again, Niki, and I can fly back down and go with you," Sam teased.

"There's an idea. Just kidding, here," she said, handing them back. "When's the show?"

"Um, lemme see...February 3 at Ziggy's."

"I am so jealous."

"I have something else for you, Baby," Kevin said to Jess. "And if you don't like it, well...I'll be completely crushed." Kevin got down on his knees in front of her and took her hands, then took a deep breath. "I've been sweating bullets over this one."

The room grew quiet as everyone looked on and wondered what Kevin had up his sleeve. Maggie held onto Dean's arm. Niki stopped picking up crumpled paper when she saw what was coming and sat on the floor between David's legs. George and Betty looked on, holding hands while Terese sat up straighter and looked at Sam with a curious sparkle in her eyes.

"Yes Ma, it's exactly what it looks like," she whispered. "He showed me the ring this afternoon."

"Jess, I am completely, totally, and madly in love with you. I don't know exactly when it happened, but it did. I think deep down I must have known the first day we met. When you yanked open your office door, I was prepared to do battle with some guy, but when you looked up at me, all I could think of was how hot you were. Then there was that wild spark in your eyes, like you dared me to challenge you. I was instantly hooked even though I tried so hard to resist you. You are the most beautiful woman I know, both inside and out. You're smart and witty and I love the way your gorgeous, green eyes get darker when you're..."

Jess' eyes grew wide as she gasped aloud and blushed with sudden embarrassment.

"Oh George, he's going to propose," Betty said breathlessly.

"...ticked off about something," Kevin continued with a devilish chuckle. "Gotcha!" He whispered. His eyes twinkled as he reached into his pocket. "Jess, I love you more than anything or anyone, more than my own life. You've had my heart from day one." Jess knew what was coming. Tears welled up in her eyes. "Jess Mitchell, will you make me the happiest man on the planet? Say you'll marry me."

She sat with her hands over her mouth, speechless for a moment. Joyous tears flowed freely down her cheeks. "Good grief, Jess, snap out of it! Say yes," Niki yelled.

"Oh God, yes! Oh yes, Kevin, I would be honored to be your wife. I love you, so much." She launched herself into his arms, knocking him off balance, then lay across him and kissed him, oblivious to the onlookers.

"Okay, you two," Samantha said. "You got the next fifty or sixty years, at least, for that," she said, laughing.

Jess sat back up on her heels and let Kevin rise from the floor. "Sorry, I guessed I crushed you anyway," she said, smiling.

"I can handle that kind of crushing." He dropped back down to one knee, pulled the ring from its box, and slid it onto the third finger of her left hand. "Look, a perfect fit," he said, raising it for everyone to see.

"Oh, Kevin, it's beautiful." She hugged and kissed him again.

"I love you, Baby. Thank you for making me the happiest man in the world."

"Does this mean I can tell everybody now?" Samantha gushed.

Kevin winked at Jess. "Knock yourself out. The ring's on her finger. She's not getting away now."

"Who said I wanted to get away?"

"Congratulations, Honey," Dean said. "Kevin, I told you it would work out."

"Yes Sir, Dean, you sure did."

"You knew about this?" Jess asked Dean.

"Of course, I had to give him my blessing."

"Of course, you did. Who else?" Right away Niki looked away shamefaced. "You too?" She nodded. "And *you* were able to hold *that* in? Spread out, y'all. Lightning is about to strike. Niki's *never* met a secret she could keep. Amazing!"

Jess spent a short while admiring her new engagement ring and showing it off to all the women. Gradually, the room began to clear as everyone wanted to give the happy couple some time to celebrate privately. Dean left to take Maggie home, with the Shannons right behind him. Niki left David with Kevin and followed Jess into the kitchen for a glass of water.

"Lemme see the rock." Jess held her hand out for inspection. "It's gorgeous. He has great taste."

"Of course, he does. He fell for me. Didn't he?"

"Damn, you're getting as cocky as your fiancé," Niki huffed and giggled with Jess. "But I'm really happy for you. You finally found a winner."

"I did. Didn't I?"

"And terrific in bed too."

"He fucks like a beast, not that I have a lot of beasts to compare him to. But I know now why junkies will do anything for a fix. I think I'm addicted to him. I can't get enough."

"Well, I happen to know for a fact that it's a mutual addiction."

"I never felt this way about Jake or even Billy and I *really* thought I was in love with *him*."

"Ain't love great?"

"Yes, it is, but terrifying though."

"That's part of the fun. Trust me on this one. If you don't mind, I want David sober before we take off. Then you two can celebrate in private."

"Sure, no problem, I don't want you guys in an accident, especially not in a squad car *and* on your way home from the Chief's house. The press would have a field day with that one."

Back in the den...

Jess sat in Kevin's lap. "Whew! Just what I needed," she said, taking a long swallow of the icy-cold water. "My head was starting to spin."

"Starting to? Honey, you were buzzing long before you *ever* hit the rum," Niki giggled.

"I was not!"

"Were too! And now that big-ass rock's throwing your balance off...another mug of rum and Santa would have gotten a lap dance."

"No way!" Jess exclaimed and paused. "Well, not in front of everybody," she added in a saucy tone.

"Hey, what are we waiting for? Beat it you two, while I fix her another drink!" Kevin teased.

"I wouldn't recommend that...not unless you're trying to put me to sleep," Jess purred suggestively, leaning down to kiss him.

"In that case..." He said, looking up to meet her lips. "Mmm." His cock stirred, causing Jess to squirm.

Jess glanced at Niki from the corner of her eye. Niki winked at her. "David, Sweetie, how's your head?"

"I feel great, Babe."

"Good enough to drive yet?"

"Yeah."

"Let's take off and do something fun."

"Sounds like a plan," he said, getting up. "You got any suggestions?"

Niki rose from the couch. "Yeah, I do. Take me back to your place and I'll show you some *real* Christmas cheer."

"Too much information, Nik," Kevin commented in a droll tone.

"Oh please, Santa! Like you're not gonna go stuff somebody's stocking as soon as we leave."

A slow, knowing grin crept across Jess' face as she remembered Kevin using those very words a couple weeks earlier.

"Bye guys, it's been real," Dave said, grinning from ear to ear. "It's been fun, and it's getting ready to be *real* fun."

Kevin bolted the door behind them. "Mmm, now where were we? I believe you had something for me."

"Ah yes, I do. Come with me, Santa," Jess purred, dragging him upstairs. As soon as they entered her old bedroom, Jess gently pushed Kevin down onto the bed. "You wait right there, Santa. I'll be right back." He started to take off his boots. "No, no, don't move."

"Alrighty then."

When she sashayed back into the room a few minutes later, she wore a short, satin robe that revealed none of what she had on underneath. "Good evening, Santa. You ready to open your present?"

"Mmm hmm."

Kevin pulled her onto his lap and kissed her before untying the robe's sash. "Mother of God, Merry Christmas to me," he groaned. "Let me look at you." Kevin stood and took a half-step back and sucked in his breath when Jess let the robe fall to the floor. "Aha, my kinky little elf, that hat was a hint." He traced his fingers along the fur trim at the bust line of the teddy, just barely grazing her skin, raising goose bumps as he went. "Betty was right about this color. God, you look good in red velvet. And I'd wager the leopard skin looks a damn sight better on you than on the leopard, too. It's a shame you won't be wearing it for long." He started to untie the ribbon at the center of her breasts.

"Not so fast, Santa." Jess put her hands on Kevin's shoulders and forced him to sit back down. "I told you I had another present for you."

"You mean this isn't it?"

Jess shook her head and knelt before him, she pulled off his boots and slung them across the room. That accomplished, she unfastened the wide black belt at his waist, and pulled off the fur-trimmed coat.

"Stand up," she commanded.

Raking her nails down his chest, she sank to her knees again and pulled down the matching breeches. Underneath, he wore boxer-briefs. How she loved them on him. She looked up and smiled upon finding his massive, rock-hard erection nigh out of the waistband of his shorts. He offered a sheepish grin when she yanked the red shorts down, freeing it from its confines.

Jess had never really taken a close look at the anatomy of her former lovers, but Kevin was different. She went slow, inspecting every inch of his body. His cock was hard, of course, the skin smooth, like velvet over an iron rod. A nest of trimmed, dark-blond, wiry curls surrounded its base. Even after so many months, she was no less amazed that something so simple in design could bring such incredible pleasure to the both of them. She kissed the tip, causing him to suck in his breath in a long hiss.

Undaunted, she stroked his manhood up and down, basking in his response as the satiny outer skin slid over the inner hardness.

"Does that feel good?"

"God yes, so good." He instinctively moved his hips in time with her strokes, making love to her hand.

Jess continued, gently caressing his balls in her other hand. They were much softer in comparison and sprinkled with downy hairs. Still stroking, she licked his soft testicles, sucking one into her mouth, then the other.

"Good Lord."

She looked up at him and stopped at once upon seeing the pained look on his face. "I'm sorry. Did I hurt you?"

"No, no."

Again, she fondled his sac tentatively while she took his thick cock into her mouth and rotated the tip of her tongue around its satiny head, and licked the veined ridge on the underside before taking his full length into her throat. Looking up at him, Jess sucked softly at first, then harder. After a few minutes, he brushed a few stray bangs from her eyes and held back her long tresses, knocking her hat askew. He moved with her, thrusting in and out of her hot mouth, though not forcing it, until his balls began to tighten. He stopped moving and held his breath for a moment.

"Baby, you can't keep this up. I won't be able to hold back much longer," he said hoarsely.

"I don't want you to," she said, taking his length back between her lips.

"Are you sure?"

"Mmm hmm," she hummed and cupped his bare ass.

He placed his hand on the at the nape of her neck and propelled himself to the back of her throat energetically for a moment until his desire spewed forth in a stream of hot, salty cream.

"Holy Jesus! Oh God," he groaned through clenched teeth.

Jess held his cheeks with one hand and massaged his testicles with the other until he was spent, swallowing every creamy drop. It wasn't bad, somewhat salty, somewhat sweet. So much for Niki's theory, she thought. Kevin stood still, watching her lick clean his still-firm cock before licking her lips and raising her arms up to him. Taking her outstretched hands, he pulled her to her feet.

"Come here, Woman." He leaned down, plunged his tongue between her teeth, and explored her open mouth, seemingly uncaring of what she had just done. "Mmm," he groaned.

Strike two for Niki.

"Merry Christmas, Santa." Jess glanced at his cock, then back up and him, "Oh my, look at that. I got lipstick on you."

"Honey, you can put anything you want on me." He untied the ribbons at the front of the teddy, and then pushed the thin, silken straps from her shoulders, leaving it to hang at her waist. "And you can start with this perfect body," he added in a husky voice.

When Kevin slid the teddy to the floor, Jess stepped out of it and started to slip off the stilettos when he stopped her. The pillows fell onto the floor when he lay back on the bed, pulled her across him, lingering at her lips, then rolled over so that he lay on top of her, and kissed her again; slow, deep, and wet. His tongue darted between her ruby-tinged lips, following the line of her teeth before moving across her cheek and stopping at her sensitive ear.

"You're so beautiful," he whispered.

Warm, ragged breath in her ear sent a jolt of electricity straight to the pit of her stomach as the tip of his tongue snaked a path from her neck to her stiffened nipples. He suckled one, then the other, tracing wet-hot circles around each. Evening stubble made his jaw bristly. That, along with his mustache, prickled the tender flesh of her belly as he moved downward. Her breathing quickened as he inched ever closer to the juncture of her thighs.

Jess arched towards him, anticipating the sensations she knew his mouth would bring, and she wasn't disappointed. He spread her legs open as wide as they would go, exposing her soaking wet sex to the room's cool air, leaving her to moan in expectation. But rather than his mouth, she felt his thumb stroke her throbbing bud while he probed her wetness. She rose to meet his fingers as they moved in and out, her inner heat clenching around them. Finally, he spread her lips and dipped his head for a taste of her nectar, flattening his tongue to lick her from back to front, and with each pass, taking a moment to flick his tongue rapidly across the hardened nub, bringing her off the bed.

"Oh, my God," she moaned. "You're driving me mad."

A wicked laugh passed his lips as his tongue circled her diamond while his fingers probed more urgently. Just when she thought she could take no more, he stopped licking long enough to remove his slippery fingers from her hungry core, and then flattening his tongue, he began licking again in slow, tortuous laps. But this time, he swirled a fingertip around her other tight opening.

"What are you..."

With no warning, he slipped a finger inside the virgin rosebud to the first knuckle. Jess hissed at the unexpected invasion. In seconds, the slight discomfort she'd felt at first gave way to incredible pleasure. Still laving at her, Kevin continued to push deeper, one knuckle at a time, pausing to allow her time to adjust to the new sensations, before finally moving the digit in and out in time with his licks. Adjusted to the incursion, Jess marveled at this delightful, new stimulus. Her climax was imminent.

"Oh, good God," she moaned. "You're driving me crazy, mmm!"

The end was on her, and there was no holding it back. Brought to a fevered pitch, she bucked against his hand and mouth, every orifice tightening, while powerful shudders rocked her entire body. She could hardly endure the intense shock waves surging through her.

"Come on, Beautiful!"

"Oh God, yesss, oh yes, yes, yesss. Oh fuck," she screamed.

Kevin gave light licks to engorged flesh and lapped up her juices as Jess descended slowly from the most vivid experience of her life. Unable to move even if she'd wanted to, Jess lay stiff until her puckered hole relaxed and her body went limp. At long last, he slid his finger out as he had introduced it, one knuckle at a time. Once again, Jess' muscles contracted tighter as she seized through another series of ripples. Then crawling up beside her, Kevin took her into his arms, and brushed damp strands of hair from her face.

Finally, she was able to look into his smoldering orbs. "Merry Christmas, Baby," he whispered. He cupped her chin in his hand and kissed her tenderly as tears welled in her eyes. "What's this? Baby, I'm sorry. I didn't mean to hurt you."

"No, no, you didn't. It was just so...intense. I've never imagined I could feel like this. I'm just so...happy."

"I'm glad, me too."

"Kevin, I love you so much. God, it feels so good to finally say that."

"I love you too, Baby."

Chapter 27

Christmas morning...

When Jess awoke, Kevin was shaving with his new strait razor.

"How do you like it?"

"It's the best, only takes one pass. Thank you again."

"You're very welcome. Hey, I have something else for you."

"I thought you gave me *that* last night," he said and flashed an impish grin. Jess lowered her eyes and blushed furiously at the recollection. "You know what? I have a little something else for you too."

"I have everything I could possibly want." Jess gazed at the new engagement ring. "It's so beautiful."

"It pales in comparison to the lady wearing it." Kevin dried his face and put away the razor. "You really like it?" He walked over and took her into his arms.

"It's perfect."

"It's not too soon is it? I was worried I might scare you off, that it might be too overwhelming."

"I'm completely overwhelmed, but your timing has nothing to do with it." She peered up at him, green eyes glistening. "I love you."

"I love you too, Baby."

He picked her up and cradled her against his chest, as one would a child. Jess wrapped her arms around his neck and looked lovingly into his amber eyes. His soft lips brushed hers in a tender kiss as he walked across the room and stopped by the bed. Jess' long hair fanned out beneath her when he gently set her warm, naked body down and lay beside her. Caressing her face and neck, his eyes roamed over her. This time was different. He took his time and showed a new level of control as he made sweet love to her.

"So beautiful," he whispered.

He traced an invisible path down her cheek and across her lips, inspiring Jess to open her mouth and kissed each fingertip as it hovered above her. He continued down her neck and chest, peppering delicate skin with feathery kisses, while his rigid cock throbbed against her thigh. On impulse, she opened her legs and raised her hips to him as he gently guided himself inside. He moved in an easy rocking motion, pelvis brushing pelvis, while she met every unhurried thrust, squeezing him tighter.

"You feel so good," he said softly.

After what seemed like an eternity, her climax started deep in her belly. Moaning inaudibly and arching, she stiffened as it flowed through in measured waves. For a moment, Kevin's body became inflexible as he came within seconds of her. As his own shudders peaked, he relaxed and rolled to the side, then kissed her while his spent member slipped out.

"I love you, Jess," he said with his eyes fixed on her. "I can't say it enough."

"I love you," she returned, resting her head upon his chest.

"And that's not even what I brought you over here for."

Kevin sat up on the edge of the bed, pulled on his briefs, and grabbed his shaving kit, which he dug through until he found another small box that he placed in Jess' hands. She carefully tore into it and grinned at its contents.

"Is this a hint? Tired of always telling me the time?" She teased.

"No, I just thought it would look pretty on you. Doesn't really matter what time it is anyway, 'cause it's always time for me to love you."

"You're gonna make me cry again."

"Happy tears, I hope. They're the only kind I ever wanna inspire."

"It's beautiful. I love it." Jess removed the watch from its box and handed it to Kevin. "Would you fasten it?"

"Of course." She stretched her arm out to him and he scattered feathery kisses down to her wrist. She giggled when his mustache tickled her arm. "There, look how much prettier it is on your arm than in that box."

"You really are quite the sweet talker." She slipped into her robe, opened the door on the lower half of the nightstand, and rifled through it. She snuck a sideways glance at Kevin, her eyes widening slightly after coming across the vibrator she'd forgotten existed. Jess found what she was looking for, handed the gift to Kevin, and closed the door, again, taking care not to reveal the toy.

"Thank you. You don't have to hide it."

"What?" Wide-eyed, she followed his gaze to the nightstand. Her smile disappeared and her jaw dropped with the realization that he was talking about the vibrator. Jess could feel the blush spreading from her face all the way to her toes. Her pulse pounded in her ears. "Okay, I am officially mortified." She hid her face in her hands and peeked through spread fingers. "How did you..."

"I swear, I wasn't snooping. I thought I was going to stash that," he said, pointing to the watch on her wrist, "And it was just there. It was completely by accident."

"I am *so* embarrassed."

"Why? Lots of women have them, or so I've heard. As long as you don't love it more than me, we'll all get along just fine." He grinned as a devilish gleam appeared in his eyes.

"Actually, I forgot it was in there. It sorta took an early retirement."

"That's too bad." The corners of his eyes crinkled when he smiled.

"What are you trying to say?"

"I think you know exactly what I'm trying to say." Jess studied him for a moment as he gauged her reaction. Satisfied, he ripped at the paper, not caring where the shredded pieces landed.

"Careful," she cautioned. "It's fragile."

Kevin carefully opened the box and unwound the air pillows cushioning the fragile trinket. The globe was nearly perfect with only the slightest ripple marring the hand-blown surface. The base was fashioned from blown glass shaped and colored to resemble a coal pile, and inside the glass ball was the autumn scene of a rail yard, complete with miniature locomotive and rail workers. He listened silently after winding it.

"What's the tune?"

"It's called *The Iron Horse.* There's a card in there detailing it."

"Another antique," he observed.

"I know it's not one of your family heirlooms, but..."

"Are you kidding? This is awesome!"

10:36 AM

"Woman, you're gonna make me fat."

"I'll just have to make sure you get plenty of exercise every day," Jess said playfully.

"I like that idea."

At that moment, Dean walked through the front door, causing the couple to take pause in their conversation. He was whistling a happy melody when he entered the dining room, but stopped mid-note when he saw them. Jess gave him a thorough perusal, trying not to smile at his disheveled hair and somewhat rumpled clothing.

"Morning, Sir."

"Good morning," he said, looking around guiltily.

"Good morning. Would you like to join us for breakfast?"

"No, thank you, Honey, I've already eaten."

"Really? You must have gotten up early. We never heard you leave," Jess said, still trying to suppress a grin.

"I'm...just now...getting home."

"Ah, you stayed at Maggie's place last night."

"Yeah...it looks like I've been caught. I didn't expect to find anyone here this morning."

"Well, I just have one thing to say, young man." Dean regarded his daughter curiously. "I'm glad you two are *playing nice*."

Jess burst into a round of boisterous laughter and glanced at Kevin through the corner of her eye. He was barely suppressing a smile. A few seconds later, Dean began laughing merrily, which was all it took for Kevin to add his rich baritone to their mirth.

"Chief, I mean Dean, how about a cup of coffee?"

"Son, a cup of coffee would be marvelous. Thank you." Kevin poured a fresh cup. "Actually, I'm glad you're both still here. I have something for you. Stay put, I need to fetch it from upstairs."

"Woman, *you* are evil," Kevin charged as soon as Dean left the room.

"Who me? Nonsense, I was only playing with him just like he did us."

"I have to admit though, that was pretty damn funny."

"It was, wasn't it?" Jess said, still giggling when Dean returned.

"You can do what you want with these, but now that you're engaged and officially flying the coop, I thought you might like to have them."

"What is it, Dean?" Jess asked.

He showed them the first of two wedding sets. "Jessie, these belonged to your dear mother. Suzanne gave them to me in the hospital right before she passed and I promised her I'd keep them for you." He paused for a moment when his voice caught in his throat before he showed her the second set of rings. "These belonged to my JoAnna. I think she'd want you to have them."

Tears sprang to Jess' eyes and flowed freely down her cheeks. "Are you sure?"

"Of course, I'm sure."

She stood and squeezed him tight. "You are so wonderful. I can't believe you've kept these for me all these years. Thank you...Dad."

"What?"

"You heard right. John and Suzanne Mitchell brought me into the world, but they left me with you. I think they'd be proud of the job you've done. You've been my Dad and Mom for the last eighteen years. I think it's about time I started calling you by your name," she said, wiping at her eyes.

"Princess, I love you and I can't wait to walk you down that aisle. Take this," he said, handing her his handkerchief. He handed the rings to Kevin. "Son, maybe you can have something fashioned from them for your bride to match the engagement ring."

"Whatever she wants."

New Year's Eve...

David seemed unusually interested in Jess and Kevin's plans for the New Year. He pumped the couple all day for information, but Kevin knew nothing of his fiancé's intensions. She would only allude to champagne, videos, and candles. Dave pestered her until thinking he'd let it go, she finally admitted to having dinner reservations and plans to record the live *KISS* segment of *Dick Clark's Rockin' New Year's Eve* special. After that, she told both he and Bryan a tale of New Year's that she'd heard back in high school.

"Legend says whatever you're doing at the stroke of midnight is what you'll be doing for the rest of the year."

"I think I know where this is going," Kevin said, flashing her a knowing grin.

"What do you wanna do for a whole year, Jess?"

"Don't be obtuse. Use your imagination, David."

"Oh! Ohh okay, I get it now."

"You really doubled up on your blond pills today didn't you?"

"Oh, bite my ass!" He replied as he left her office to the tune of her and Kevin's shared laughter.

CRISORISO

SubMarine: Good afternoon, CJ.
SubDoer: hey Armand, how's it going?
SubMarine: I'm doing ok.
SubDoer: just ok?
SubMarine: It will be. I just received some rather disturbing news, but I'll work it out.
SubDoer: i'll cross my fingers for you
SubMarine: Thank you. Do you have big plans for New Year's Eve?
SubDoer: yes, Reese and I are having a nice dinner, champagne, and who knows what else will happen? ;-)
SubMarine: Good luck with that.
SubDoer: thanks, i need to go, he's waiting for me
SubMarine: Give Reese my regards and have a marvelous evening.
SubDoer: will do, bye
Your status is set to appear offline. All open conversation windows will be closed.

"There's something about that guy."

"Why do you say that?"

"I dunno exactly, can't put my finger on it. It's just a feeling. Besides, what guy in his right mind is gonna let a woman order him around like a lapdog?"

"If I remember correctly, you've let me order *you* around a few times," Jess teased.

"That was playing," he said as he swatted her behind.

"Spousal abuse already, and we're not even married yet," she exclaimed in a playful tone.

"I got your abuse right here," he said, looking at and pointing to his semi-swollen crotch, and grinning.

"Oh my!"

"Seriously, you just be real careful with that guy," Kevin stated seriously.

"Promise, is that coming from Kevin the cop, or from my wonderful, protective fiancé?"

"Both," he growled and pulled her to her feet. Cupping her buttocks in his big hands, he pulled her hips against his middle.

"Ohh Kevin, you're so bad."

"Mmm hmm, so tell me. What *are* we doing tonight?"

"You'll see."

"What are we waiting for?"

"Not so fast, we have to change first."

"Change?" Jess closed her office door and pointed to the garment bags hanging from the coat hook. "Boone's Formal Wear? I gotta wear a suit?"

"Yes."

"And what are *you* wearing?"

"You'll see. I'll change in here, you get the bathroom," she said. "Now scoot. I'll see you in a bit."

Kevin left for the bathroom while Jess closed the blinds and retrieved her dress, then quickly stripped. She slipped into a backless corset of black satin and a matching thong then donned a pair of flesh-toned, thigh-high stockings. Next, she adjusted her breasts, creating just the right amount of cleavage. Made of emerald silk and encrusted with shiny, glass beads, her dress was beautiful. After stepping into it, she pulled the spaghetti straps up onto her shoulders, and reached behind to tug on the zipper until it stopped just above the waistline.

Luckily, the substation was housed in a unit of the Tucker Street public housing complex, so it had all the same amenities as the other apartments, including full-length mirrors in the bedrooms-turned-offices. Jess turned to look at her reflection and smoothed the fabric where necessary. Once satisfied with her appearance, she pulled the plastic clip from her hair and let the thick mane tumble down her back, then pulled a brush through it until it gleamed in the light. Finally, she applied mascara to her lashes, then puckered her lips and coated them with shiny, red gloss. She looked at herself, pinched her cheeks, and then stepped into a pair of four-inch, black stilettos.

CЖФCЖФ

"Dude, aren't you guys leaving?" Gerald O'Reilly asked.

"Eventually, after we get a look at the Sarge and Jess."

"Why, what's wrong with them?"

"They're going out. Sarge took off to the bathroom a little while ago with a bag from Boone's."

"The suit shop?" Dave nodded. "As in tuxedo?"

"I dunno. I guess."

"This oughta be good. Mark's gonna hate he missed this."

Moment's later...

"Holy shit! Who are you and what did you do with the Sarge?" Dave exclaimed when Kevin came into the main room.

Jerry and Brian turned around to look. "Damn, check him out! Is that really you, Sarge?"

"You act like you never seen a guy in a suit before."

"You clean up pretty good for a redneck."

"Yeah, eat me, Jerry."

Gerald's jaw dropped as he looked beyond Kevin. "Whoa!"

"What?" Kevin inquired as David and Brian also became silent and looked over his shoulder. Kevin slowly turned around and looked at his fiancé as she emerged from her office. "Wow!" He closed the distance between them and took her hand. "If there weren't so many witnesses, I'd swear I was dreaming."

"We must be having the same dream. Jess, you look great."

"Thank you, Jerry."

"I was just telling Sarge that he cleans up pretty good, but *damn*. She puts you to shame, Sarge."

"I think you look quite handsome. I should put you in a suit more often."

"Uh, no!" Kevin chuckled. "You, on the other hand, are stunning. But it's cold out, you'll freeze in *that*," Kevin said, staring down into generous cleavage and running his hand up her bare back.

Jess stood on her tiptoes and whispered something unintelligible to the other men. Kevin responded with a quiet chuckle and nodded towards the door. Jess took a moment to retrieve a long, dyed-to-match, hooded cloak of the same base material as her dress, which she threw over her shoulders. Its velveteen lining made it quite warm. Kevin put his arm around her and escorted her out to the car, throwing a quick wink back to his comrades. He leered at the long expanse of leg exposed through the nearly thigh-high slit in Jess' dress when she sat down, before moving to the driver's side.

"I wondered why you were so set on us driving your car this morning. In that dress and those shoes, I don't think you coulda climbed into my truck," he said as he revved the engine.

"Exactly, would you help me with this?" She asked, holding out a strand of pearls that had belonged to her mother.

"Be glad to."

He took the necklace as she turned away, pulled her long hair to the side, and kissed the back of her neck, inhaling deeply of her perfume as he dipped his tongue into the hollow of her shoulder and brushed tiny kisses up to her ear. Finally, he draped the strand of pearls around her neck and fastened them.

"Did I tell you that you look beautiful?"

"Yes, but a girl never gets tired of hearing it."

"You look beautiful," he said smiling.

"You look mighty handsome. We compliment each other rather well, I think. I'll have to fight off all the ladies tonight."

"You think? I'm the one with a fight on my hands...fighting the urge to drive straight home and make love to you right now."

Kevin tried, but failed, to convince his bride to skip dinner in lieu of their bedroom and a private show of fireworks. However, he became intrigued when she revealed her plan to keep him up until at least three AM to cover all three time zones, an idea he liked even more.

The engine roared as they drove off with Kevin rubbing his hand along Jess' thigh between shifting gears. Jess stared at her sparkling engagement ring and smiled, hardly able to believe all that had taken place during the last couple of months. She was engaged to the man of her dreams, literally. His younger sister had become a great friend. Her future mother-in-law loved her even if they *were* living together *and* engaging in premarital sex. Her dad and best friend couldn't sing Kevin's praises loud enough. Jess saw rainbows in every direction she turned.

"What are you thinking about?"

"Just that there is nothing that could make my life more perfect than it is right now."

"I can think of a couple things."

"Do tell."

"A wedding band for one, we need to pick a date."

"Yes, I know. Do you have one in mind?"

"Baby, I'd run off and elope with you tonight, if I thought I could talk you into it."

"Yeah?"

"Hell yeah, but I guess we kinda have to wait for this case to wrap up, eh?"

"Not necessarily, we just may have to postpone the honeymoon. How's April sound?"

"Really?"

"Yeah, assuming you really wanna get married soon."

"As soon as possible."

"You said a couple things...what else?"

"I not sure if you're ready for the other one."

"Try me."

"It's a lot of responsibility." Jess speculated in silence about where he was headed, suspecting that he was about to broach the subject of children. "We still need to get a dog. Remember your American dream with the picket fence and all?"

"Oh yeah," she said with a giggle. "You really do remember every detail."

"It's part of my job description, but I gotta build that fence first, and then we're talking kids. We'll have to have at least four or five," he teased.

"Four or five?! Holy crap!"

"Relax, I'm teasing."

"It's not that. I'd like nothing more than to give you the big family you want. I just never thought I'd ever be having this conversation."

"What conversation?"

"A wedding, a dog, and...babies. We have a lot of plans to make."

"You pick the time and place and I'll be there."

"Oh no, Buddy...you're not getting off the hook that easy. You'll have tuxedo fittings and we have caterers to interview and wedding cakes to sample."

"Oh jeez, women's work!" He teased. "Why don't we just buy this one and be done with it?" He asked, fingering the lapel on his jacket.

"I think not."

"And Stefano can handle all that catering and wedding cake business."

"That's actually a good idea. I hadn't thought of that."

"Speaking of Stefano, we're here." Kevin parked the car, helped Jess out, then kissed her. "Have I told you today how much I love you?"

"I believe so, but you can say it again," she said as she wiped her lip-gloss from his mouth.

"I love you, Jess."

"And I love you."

He put his hand at the small of her back, "After you, my beauty."

Stefano was at the door as usual. "Buon giorno, Signore Slater y Signorina Mitchell, you look splendid this evening."

"Buon giorno, Stefano, gratzie. Right, Baby?"

"Perfetto."

"Is she not the most beautiful woman you've ever laid eyes on?" Kevin asked.

"Sì, soltanto un gioiello raro può confrontare alla bellezza del Signorina Mitchell."

"Gratzie, Stefano," Jess replied, smiling and looking down demurely.

"Prego, Signorina Mitchell."

Kevin wore a curious expression as he studied his bride. "I'll tell you later."

"It won't be Signorina Mitchell for much longer, Stefano," Kevin announced with pride. He held Jess' left hand out to Stefano to show off the ring. "She ran like a wild mustang, but I caught her," he teased.

"Congratulations, I am pleased for you. Per favore, allow me to take your coats and show you to your table."

Kevin handed over his jacket and Jess' cloak, and they followed Stefano to a cozy corner of the restaurant. A stone wall of about five feet in height afforded the couple a measure of privacy and darkened the area to a small degree more than the rest of the room. The table was just big enough for the two of them to sit nestled side by side, and in the center, a small floral arrangement surrounded a lone, lit taper that bathed them in a golden glow.

"What'd Stefano say that had you blushing so pretty back there? I don't need to have a talk with him, do I?"

"Why, jealous?"

"Damn right."

"Don't worry. He said my beauty compares only to a rare jewel."

"He was right on the money." Minutes later, their server, Antonio, came to quote the evening specials, then left them to decide. The man returned moments later with a bottle of chilled champagne and two glasses. "What's this for?" Kevin asked.

"Paolo's celebrates your engagement with a bottle of our finest sparkling wine." Antonio poured a small amount into one of the flutes for Kevin to sample. At his nod of approval, Antonio refilled the glass and poured another for Jess. "Shall I bring antipasto now?"

"Yes, please."

"Very well, Signore." Antonio quietly disappeared.

"Baby, I just thought of something. Where'd you stash your pistol?"

"My Glock is in the car in a lockbox and the snub you gave me is still on my ankle."

11:00 PM

"Hey, that looks good!"

"You want a bite?"

"Yeah." The fork sliced through the layers of tiramisu like soft butter. Kevin raised it to Jess' mouth, then pulled back and watched while she savored the mocha-flavored confection. "Mmm, that was positively heavenly. You better eat that quick or I might want some more."

"Baby, I'll feed you the whole damn thing and order another one if it makes you happy."

"I might not be able to get into this dress again if you do that."

"As good as you look in that dress, I'm more interested in getting you out of it than back into it," he said. His eyes twinkled in impish delight.

"You turkey," she giggled. "Finish up so we can go home."

"You sure you don't want another bite?" Jess shook her head. "A bombshell blonde I know showed me a great work-out. It knocks the calories right off."

"Oh really?" His face took on a devilish look. "You, Sir, are a scoundrel," she said, lowering her gaze, then flashing him a coy smile.

"Nah, I gave up being a scoundrel when I met you." He waved the fork at her. "Last bite."

"Okay, you talked me into it."

11:38 PM

Jess disappeared into the bedchamber for a few minutes and then summoned Kevin, who was tugging at his tie. Champagne was chilling in a bucket on the dresser, and a multitude of candles in varying sizes was lit throughout the room, while *Boney James* played a private concert for two through the stereo. Kevin placed a hand low on her back and took her hand as she leaned closer, resting her cheek on his chest. The short zipper at her waist gave way to an easy tug leaving her dress to hang loose while they swayed to the music. One thin strap dropped from her shoulder. Kevin's hand meandered up her spine, caressing her shoulders, pulling at the other strap until it hung limp.

"You look gorgeous. This dress...the color matches your eyes."

Kevin leaned down, caught her bottom lip in his teeth, and nibbled it. Starving for his kiss, Jess parted her lips in silent invitation as the hand at her shoulders traveled higher. With his fingers entangled in her hair, Kevin pulled her closer still, while exploring her mouth with his tongue. He let go of her hand and pushed the dress down, letting the beaded silk fall into a heap around her ankles.

Without breaking the kiss, he scooped her up, walked to the edge of the bed, and gently placed her on it. Jess sat up and watched him strip away his shirt. She ached for him, throbbed for him. Unawares, she clenched her pubic muscles in anticipation when his fingers moved to the fly of his trousers, releasing the single button, though he made no move towards the zipper.

"Can I help?"

"No."

"Ohh," she groaned in disappointment. "I want you so bad."

"We have all night."

"But only a few minutes until midnight."

"You let *me* worry about that."

Kevin sat on the bed's edge and unfastened the hooks on her stockings. She rose up onto her elbows when he pulled at the thong, drawing the skimpy satin down her hips and legs and throwing it to the floor. Lying across the bed, he eased his hands under her, then pulled her towards his face, and pushed apart her legs. His mustache titillated her sensitive flesh when he leaned down, still looking up into her eyes, and licked her. Jess threw her head back and moaned as fiery sensations shot through her. Swollen flesh pulsed and throbbed. She glanced down at Kevin and quickly turned away when she found him still staring up at her. He paused and raised his head.

"Look at me," he commanded. The silent mastery in his eyes spoke volumes, much louder than his voice.

He went back to his task, lapping harder and faster while she writhed underneath him. Pulling a hand from under her, he spread her labia with his thumb and forefinger, gaining full access to her inner heat. Jess arched almost painfully and clenched the covers in her fists when he drove his hot tongue into her, tasting, drinking in her juices, before laving her button more, and inching a finger inside her. Contractions rocked her body. She stiffened and rose off the bed as his finger slid in and out, drawing a powerful orgasm as first firecrackers thundered outside in the street. He held on, licking, sucking until spasms had drawn her nearly doubled. Jess placed her palms against his shoulders and pushed gently.

"Oh God, oh God...I can't bear anymore. Stop!"

Kevin took pause and looked up, lust darkening his gilded eyes. "Are you sure?"

"Yes, oh yes," she panted. Fireworks boomed outside, proclaiming to all that the New Year had arrived, but paled next to the explosive alchemy inside. "You missed midnight."

"We still have two more time zones to go," Kevin noted, shrugging off her pout.

Chapter 28

January 3...

"What'd you two do after you left the other evening?" Dave asked while Brian looked on.

"We had dinner at Paolo's, and then we went home," Jess said.

"What about midnight? She made such a big deal about it," he directed at Kevin.

"Eastern, central or pacific?" Kevin responded with a chuckle.

"Humor me, all of the above."

"Midnight eastern I had pie for dessert," he said, sneaking a sidelong glance at Jess. "Midnight central I was doing the backstroke, and midnight pacific I cooked up a big sausage for my best girl," he added, shooting her a wicked grin. "She was famished after all the fireworks."

Jess' smile disappeared and her eyes grew wide. "Oh, my God, no you didn't," she exclaimed in shock.

"Right on, Bro! Cherry pie?"

"Best piece I ever tasted," he said with a toothy grin. Jess' face and neck were hot.

"What about you, Jess? How was the sausage?" David looked up as Niki picked that moment to walked in. "Hey Babe! What are you doing here?"

"From the looks of her, I got here just in time to rescue my best friend. What are you guys doing to her?"

Jess was mortified but determined not to let them get the jump on her. She swallowed the lump in her throat and held her chin high, willing away embarrassment, and made the conscious decision to suck it up and let them have it...Niki-style.

"Mmm, oh my God, that sausage was *so* good," she said, almost breathless. "It was so big too, the biggest one I ever had. I'm amazed I was able to eat the whole thing. Oh and juicy...God!" She purred. "I get goose bumps just thinking about it." Kevin's eyebrows shot up in surprised amusement.

"It looks like I walked in on one *real* interesting conversation," Niki said. "Anybody gonna let Niki in on the fun?"

"We were just ribbing her," Dave said. "But Jess just proved that she gives as good as she gets."

"And you guys are just now figuring this out?" Niki asked.

"Yes, they *were*," Jess agreed. "I'm gonna *hurt you* for getting him going," she directed at Kevin with a devilish simper.

"Baby, would you please?" Jess knitted her brow at him and grimaced playfully.

"Hate to run out on you gentlemen, well not really, but Jess and I have a wedding to plan," Niki stated. "Speaking of that, have you set a date yet?"

"April 24."

"Holy shit! You're not wasting any time. That's less than four months." She looked at Kevin. "Are shotguns involved?"

"No! She's not pregnant." Then he looked at Jess. "Are you?" He asked.

"No, I'm not pregnant."

"Good," Niki said.

"That I know of," Jess added. The room became silent as every eye was at once upon her.

"What exactly are you trying to say, Hun?" Kevin asked.

"I'm trying to say it's a good thing Niki dropped in today. We got lots of planning to do, so come on, Nik. April 24 will be here before you know it." Jess stood on her tiptoes and kissed Kevin goodbye. "See ya in a couple hours."

C�ꙴꙴCꙴꙴ

Three weeks later...

"Kev, I have bad news."

"I have a headache. Don't think I can take bad news right now. But what's up?"

"I've been pouring through Lieutenant Daniels' casebook and there's nothing here that will help us get a warrant on Nick Yarboro."

"Are you sure?"

"Yeah, I think it's safe to say it's Mr. Clean's work, but again, he left no trace, no fingerprints, no nothing, and honestly, I don't think there's a judge anywhere who will give us a warrant based on a single fingerprint."

"This fucking sucks! Sorry, Baby," he said and rubbed his temples. "What do we do now?"

"Let me do that." Jess massaged his scalp and continued talking. "All we can do is watch him real close for now. Or we can try to come up with a plan to set him up like we did Headbanger."

"I'm gonna have to think about that. Nick Yarboro is a hell of a lot smarter than Mark Thompson. We won't be able to drop a piece of bait in front of him and get him to bite it that easily."

"True."

"Does he have a new sub yet?"

"I dunno. There are so many women hanging around him at the meetings that I can't tell if he's into a particular lady."

"Yeah, he's a player."

"He's not the only ladies' man there. You draw quite a bit of attention yourself."

"I hadn't noticed. Been too busy making sure all the fruitcakes leave *you* alone. How long before the next meeting?"

"Lemme see, today's the twenty-fourth, next Friday. The topic is...oooh, *Spanking: Approaches and Techniques.*"

"Mmm, I'll have to pay *special* attention to that one. You could use a good spanking every now and then."

"You think so?"

"Yeah, Brat!" Kevin said with a wide grin.

"Are we still going to Elaine's party afterward?"

"Sure, she's a little loopy, but kinda cool in a weird way."

"Should I be jealous?"

"Are you kidding? I'm not into being bullied by girls."

"Mmm hmm."

"Hey, the concert is in a few days too. You ready?"

"Looking forward to it. What about you?"

"Should be interesting. I've only been to a few rock shows, and none of them were at a small club."

"You're kidding."

"Nope."

"Well then we're even. I've never seen a country show at all."

"We'll have to fix that. Some great shows will be in the area this summer."

"Yeah, who?"

"*Alan Jackson, Toby Keith,* and *Brooks & Dunn* to name a few."

☙✻☙✻☙

Valentine's Day...

Kevin brought in Jess' parcels, calling into question if there was anything left in the stores. So many purchases brought out his natural curiosity, he tried to peek, but succeeded only in getting his hand slapped. He poked his lip out and frowned.

"Don't look at me like that. I'm *not* gonna change my mind, Mister."

"What happened to Master?"

"Oh you!"

"Did you get anything I *can* see?"

"Yes."

"Well?"

"Tonight."

"Mmm," he growled and kissed her. Jess dropped her things where they stood and wound her arms around Kevin's neck. "I want you...right here...right now," he ground out between kisses.

"I have a better idea."

"What could possibly be better than me making love to you here and now?"

"You making love to me a little later, *after* I give you your valentine. I have part of it in this bag right here." She held up a single shopping bag.

"*Priscilla's Lingerie and More*, did you get lingerie, or more?"

"You'll see."

"You've sure got my curiosity up."

"Good, let's keep it up. Tell me what smells so good. I thought you didn't cook."

"I do if I catch it."

She cocked a single eyebrow at him. "What are we having?"

"You'll find out when I put it in front of you. You go put your things away and leave the Chef to his work."

"Yes, Sir," she said, giggling.

Jess changed clothes in the spare bedroom, where she was storing everything for the wedding...a bright yellow tank top and a pair of faded, cut-off jeans, then padded barefoot back into the dining room. Kevin turned at the sound of her footsteps. Sparkling, amber eyes roamed lazily down the length of her body.

"Come sit." Kevin pushed her chair in and returned to the kitchen.

"Are you ready to tell me what's on the menu tonight?"

"You mean besides you?" He called from the kitchen. "We'll begin with a salad of fresh, wild greens and radicchio with champagne-tarragon vinaigrette." He went back into the kitchen and returned with a ceramic platter teeming with broiled fish and steamed vegetables.

"Looks like you've been busy. How was your day?"

"Interesting."

"Tell me about it."

"Put it this way. There's a reason why single guys eat out."

"This should be fascinating."

Jess giggled while Kevin relayed his misadventures at the grocery store. He claimed that men were not hardwired for such tasks as cooking and grocery shopping because the more exotic ingredients, as he termed them—leeks, fennel, tarragon, and sea salt—eluded him until another shopper took pity on him and helped him find them.

"She took pity, huh?" Jess asked, still giggling.

"I'd have never found all that stuff on my own. Shopping lists should come with pictures."

"I'm sure it was a tremendous sacrifice helping out such a terribly handsome guy."

"Jealous?"

"Who me?"

"Yeah, you."

"Well, maybe a little, especially now that I know you can cook. As if you don't have enough women, including my best friend, drooling over just your body. I'd have to beat them off with a stick if they knew you came with a flair for cooking too."

"Let's just keep that between us. Did you know that radicchio comes in plain and striped?"

"It's variegated, Love," she corrected him with another laugh.

"And speaking of color...why do they call it red when it's obviously purple?" Jess smiled and shrugged her shoulders at his observation and took a bite of the fish. "Mmm, this is delicious. Are you sure you cooked this?"

"Of course, I cooked it...with a little help." At Jess' quizzical expression he continued. "My Ma, had her on the phone while I was putting this together. She really likes you ya know."

"Wasn't that sweet of her?"

"Guys only get just so complicated," he said, grinning.

Over dinner, they discussed their upcoming wedding. Niki had been a godsend, as nearly all the preparations were finalized. The church was reserved and Paolo's would cater the reception.

"What's left?"

"I have to schedule a check-up with my doctor. My prescription runs out the week before the wedding."

"Prescription?"

"Birth control pills."

"Oh, those." But Kevin had other ideas. "What would you think about skipping that and just letting nature take its course?"

"As in not *trying* to make a baby, but not doing anything to *prevent* it either?"

"Yeah."

"Kevin, you know I love you, and I can't wait to have your babies, but what happens if we get pregnant right away? With the case and all, I mean."

"That never happens, does it?"

"I don't know, but what if it does?"

"To hell with the case. We'll keep you safe behind a desk and I'll get a new *sub* to help smoke this guy out."

"Not."

"Okay, so we'll bust our asses to solve this case before you're pregnant."

"I like that idea much better."

"So is that a yes?"

"Of course it's a yes."

"Wow, that was easier than I thought."

"You thought I'd say no?"

"Not exactly, I just didn't want to push for too much, too soon."

"How did I ever get so lucky?"

"Baby, I'm the lucky one. So...you ready for dessert?"

"There's more?"

"Fresh raspberries with whipped cream."

"Sounds yummy."

CGᏚᎧᏟᎡᏸᎧ

"You have some really neat gadgets in there."

"Girls like their toys too, ya know."

After dessert, they retired to the den where Jess sat in the floor before the fireplace. "Stay there. I have something special for you." Kevin left the room and returned a couple of minutes later. "Close your eyes," he said from behind her.

"They're closed."

"Okay, you can open them now," he said, kneeling before her.

She opened her eyes and looked over at him. "Oh my God, he is so cute. Is it a he?"

"Yeah, you like him?"

"He's adorable!" she exclaimed and rubbed the fuzzy fur coat of the new puppy.

"I hope you don't mind big dogs."

"I love German Shepherds."

"Dean's gonna come over and help me fence in the backyard over the weekend."

"Where's he sleeping now?"

"I've got him set up in one of those big baby corrals out in the garage. What do you wanna call him?"

"I think he looks like a Chief." The puppy only looked at her. "Or maybe a Sarge." This time, he yapped playfully and licked her hand.

"I think he approves. Looks like you're Sarge now, pal," Kevin said to the puppy. They played with their new pet for a while until he collapsed from exhaustion into a fuzzy heap. "Looks like Sarge is ready for bed. I'll take him out. Be right back."

"Meet me in the shower. I'll give you your valentine when we get all the puppy spit washed off."

Later...

Freshly showered, Jess shooed a bare-chested Kevin out of the bathroom so that she could put on the sexy, new outfit she'd picked up at *Priscilla's*. She covered it with a clean pair of cut-offs and a new tank top, and then joined him in the dining room.

"What are these for?" Kevin inquired after Jess placed a brand-new deck of cards on the table before him.

"Happy Valentine's Day, you wanna cut these and join me in a friendly game of poker?" She purred.

"Depends, what am I playing for?"

"Oh, just a few clothes."

"Count me in. Are you sure you want to play me?"

"Why? Are you a hustler?"

"You might be surprised. Not much to do on an Army base, especially in the field. I may have learned a trick or two back in the day."

"That was ages ago. You *must* be all rusty by now."

"You're probably right," he said with a mischievous grin. "What are we playing?"

"*Stud* Poker."

"Really? What's your game? *Cold Hands? Follow the Queen?* Or maybe we'll just *Let It Ride.*"

"I was thinking of maybe a friendly game of *Norwegian Stud,*" Jess teased.

"Can't say I know that one."

"Looks like I'm one up already then, eh? But I gotta feeling we're both gonna win no matter which way the cards fall."

"You could have something there. What's the ante?"

"A kiss, ante up." She leaned over and placed a chaste kiss onto Kevin's lips.

Jess lost her shirt with the first hand. Upon seeing the new red bra, Kevin's eyebrows shot up and his mouth dropped open. He began having trouble concentrating on anything but the pair erect nipples poking through cutouts in the bra cups. A second hand lost, this time earning him Jess' cut-offs. As he reached out to take the shorts from her hand, his eyes dipped to the matching thong. Unbeknownst to him, she had purposely folded two near-perfect hands, which ultimately gave her the advantage.

"Holy Christ!"

The next hand gave Jess his lounge pants. "You shoulda worn more clothes. You know I'm gonna win the next one, don't you?" She teased as Kevin dealt the next hand.

"What makes you so sure about that?"

"Just a feeling."

Pretending to study her cards, she peered at Kevin from the corner of her eye. His eyes were trained on her breasts. Still pretending to study her cards, she reached with her free hand and tweaked a nipple, drawing it to a stiff peak. He sucked in a quick breath and squirmed in his chair. Jess placed her bet, glanced at him, and then licked her lips, puckered up and blew him a kiss.

"Oh, to hell with this! I fold." Kevin flung his cards on the table and stood up, then took Jess' and dropped them on the floor. "Where'd a good girl like you learn to play poker like that?" He growled before sweeping the other cards off the table.

"At the station..." His eyebrows shot up in surprise. "Not much for a girl to do when she's hanging out with a bunch of cops and waiting for her dad to be off-duty," she added with an impish smile.

"Not this kind of poker, I hope."

"Of course not," she said in a dismissive tone. "What kind of girl do you think I am?"

"I think you're a tease."

"Is that good or bad?"

"Oh it's very good as long as you don't forget to please."

"Anything for my Master, I want you."

Kevin picked her up and sat her on the table, then reached around to unhook the bra. Jess let it fall down her arms, then grasped it, draped it around Kevin's neck like a scarf, and used it to pull him forward to stand between her knees. Her eyes dropped to his prick, swollen and trying to escape the confining briefs he'd worn under his skivvies. Jess dropped the bra and reached out to free his stiffened cock, eliciting a groan of both pleasure and pain. Kevin grasped her wrists and with gentle force, laid her flat across the dining room table, then taking the tablecloth in his fists, he dragged it with Jess on it towards him. Catty, she reached between her legs, pushed the thin scrap of material aside, and spread herself, inviting him to drive into her.

"Oh Baby, you've got me," he groaned as he sheathed himself in her velvet heat. "Damn, you feel good," he choked out hoarsely as he watched her squirm beneath him.

Losing the nerve she'd found moments earlier, Jess timidly touched one finger to her clit and stroked in slow circles, to which Kevin nodded his approval. Encouraged by his response, she twiddled her throbbing button, arching more as her muscles contracted around his mighty phallus. Faster, in a side-to-side motion, her touch grew firmer until the first twinges of release began. She threw her head back and closed her eyes, but a split-second later, her inner voice reminded her that Kevin liked seeing her expression when she came, so she quickly opened them again before he could prompt her to do so.

"Oh, God! Yes, please, harder, fuck me," she moaned, squeezing him in a vice-like grip.

"Oh damn," he groaned. "I'm losing it, Baby."

A few strokes later, as she crested, Kevin pulled out and gripped the edge of the table trying to regain his control. Jess wrapped her fingers around his cock and gave it a few quick jerks, pulling another groan from him as he stiffened and spilled his seed across her belly. Having never seen a man's release outside an adult movie, she watched closely. The way his muscles tensed, his facial contortions, the way he held his breath, the whole scene fascinated her. She kept her hand around him until the last droplet was expelled.

"Good God." She finally loosened her hold when he relaxed, exhaling the breath he had been holding, and looked down at her. "I made a mess of you."

"I think I helped a little bit," she said, winking at him.

His eyes widened in surprise. "You're really keeping me on my toes."

"What do you mean?"

"I can't tell anymore if you're gonna be bashful or if you're gonna turn into a wildcat. It crossed my mind a second too late that you might be disgusted by that."

"I heard somewhere that it's really good for the skin," she replied in a saucy tone and rubbed his cum across her tummy like lotion. "I'm not grossed out by anything about you, Kevin. In fact, it was fascinating and might require further study."

"Cosmo again?" He asked with a chuckle.

"Maybe."

Chapter 29

February 16...

"I'm sorry. Professor Yarboro makes his own appointments."

"Is he in class now?"

"No Sir, he's holding office hours at the moment. Would you like me to transfer you?"

"Please."

"Yarboro."

"Professor Nick Yarboro?"

"Yes, who is this?"

"My name is Kevin Slater. I'm a detective with the Burlington Police Department. Professor Yarboro, I'll cut right to the chase. Your name came up in an investigation I'm working on and I'd like to talk with you."

"What do you want to know?"

"I prefer to talk in person. When will you have about an hour?"

"Tomorrow morning, between nine and eleven."

"Good, write me in. I'll be there at nine. Thank you."

"Detective, what is this about?"

"We'll talk tomorrow."

C３ＥＯＣＲＥＯ

The next day...

They knew they were taking a big chance in going to Nick Yarboro's office, so as a precaution, they did nothing to change their appearances, hoping the Professor wouldn't recognize them from KLAASP, or from Elaine's play parties. Nick Yarboro met them at the door. He was tall. Not as tall as Kevin, who still overlooked him by a couple inches, but the man cut an imposing figure, nonetheless. Attractive, he had a dark complexion with coal-black hair and eyes in a matching shade of pitch. Tiny laugh lines at their corners did little to minimize their chill.

"Good morning, Professor Yarboro. I'm Detective Kevin Slater," he said as he flashed his badge. "We spoke on the phone yesterday."

"Yes Detective, I remember. Please, have a seat."

Kevin and Jess took seats across from him. "Professor Yarboro... may I call you Nick?" The darker man nodded. "Do you have any problems with me taping this conversation?"

"Suit yourself."

Kevin switched on a small tape recorder before continuing. "This is Special Agent Jess Mitchell from the State Bureau of Investigation. She's assisting us on a multiple murder case. You may have heard about it in the news. The press is calling the perpetrator Mr. Clean." Nick nodded again.

"Your name appeared in the address book of one of the victims, Sandra Vandenberg," Jess added.

"You look very familiar. Do I know you?"

"No Sir, I don't believe we've ever met," she responded.

"What does this all have to do with me?"

"We're told the two of you were seeing each other socially shortly before Miss Vandenberg was killed," Jess said.

"And?"

"And let me get to the point, Nick," Kevin said. "A woman was murdered around Thanksgiving and you were the last known person to see her alive, which I'm sure you know makes you a suspect."

"Sandy was a terrific lady. I felt terrible when I heard about her passing."

"The depth of your emotion jerks at my heartstrings, Nick," Kevin said. His voice was thick with sarcasm. "Why don't you tell us what happened to her."

"What? You think I had something to do with it?"

"You *were* last to see her alive."

"What makes you think that?"

"Her roommate told us she left for a date on Saturday and thought it may have been with you."

"I don't even know Sandy's roommate. We never met."

"Well she knows you. Apparently, Miss Vandenberg told her all about you, and there was a photograph of the two of you on her nightstand."

"And your point is, Detective?"

"My point is a woman is dead. And those closest to Miss Vandenberg seem to think you were the last one to have any contact with her."

"So."

"Doctor Yarboro, we know the two of you had a, shall we say, very unconventional relationship," Jess added.

"We also know, *Dom*inick, that trouble seems to have a way of following you around. I wonder if one of your, um...sessions...with Miss Vandenberg maybe got outta hand."

Nick's face fell. He took on a worrisome look as he contemplated his next words. "What exactly do you want to know, Detective?"

"Tell us about your involvement with Miss Vandenberg," Jess stated. "How did you meet? What exactly was the context of your relationship?"

"I found Sandy online about a year ago. We met in chat rooms for a couple months and discovered some...common interests, so we agreed to meet in person to see if we clicked."

"What common interests?" Kevin asked.

"You tell me. You seem to already know everything."

"Look, don't get cocky, Nick. I'm here to help you."

"You got a damn funny way of showing it, Detective. Correct me if I'm wrong, but I thought a man was innocent until proven guilty. It sounds like you've already tried and convicted me."

"So change my mind."

"Sandy was into bondage. She'd been interested in the scene for a while, but had never participated in any activities. She wanted to learn, and I was looking for a malleable partner."

"When and where did you meet?"

"We met at the Java Hut, downtown, and we realized then that we were already acquainted."

"How so?"

"DS has a small following in the area, Detective, many of whom share similar interests and activities *outside* the bedroom."

"By DS, you mean dominance and submission."

"That and sadomasochism. Sandy and I had scorching chemistry. We dated a few times a month, took it slow until the end of summer when it became serious."

"Is that when you started playing?"

"No, by serious, I mean in the biblical sense, no playing. I kept the relationship strictly vanilla for the summer. You have to take it slow when molding a new sub, especially one who's new to the scene. The first time we played was in September. We used standard safe words, red and yellow, and it went very well. I was gentle with her. We had a marvelous evening."

"Tell us about it," Jess said.

"She came to my house and served me dinner, and then we retired to my chamber for playtime."

"Which entailed what?"

"We planned the scene for days. As ordered, she wore a black, vinyl corset and a very short, plaid skirt with five-inch stilettos, and nothing else. She was a naughty student, so I put her on the bench and paddled her until her ass and thighs glowed." Nick appeared to drift off into another world. His eyes glazed over as he talked. "She was really into it. *Yes, please, one more, Master*, she'd say after every lick. Her sole duty was to pleasure me. I wasn't disappointed."

"And after that?"

"She drew me a bath. She knew if she performed well, I would allow her to..." Suddenly aware again of what he was saying and to whom, he looked at Kevin and then at Jess, who encouraged him to continue. "We played several times after that, sometimes at parties. If she performed well, I would allow her to come. If she did not perform well or came without my permission, she was punished."

"Punished how?"

"To be effective, punishment must be disagreeable. In Sandy's case, it was anal intercourse."

"So you sodomized her for not being a good slave?"

"Sodomy is such a harsh word, Agent Mitchell. I didn't hurt her. I took care to prep her beforehand with massive amounts of lubricant and a gradual stretch to reduce the chance of injury. The act itself is what Sandy didn't care for, and not because of its potential for physical pain, but for its dehumanizing qualities. It only happened once. She was very well behaved after that."

Jess instantly thought of the autopsy results. Sandy had been violently sodomized before she was killed. She looked at Kevin, trying to gauge his thoughts while keeping her expression ambiguous. His look was intense, relaying nothing, though she was certain he was having similar ideations, given their suspect's admission and what they already knew about Sandra Vandenberg's death.

"You have some of your facts wrong, though."

"Why don't you enlighten us, Nick."

"I couldn't have been the last one to see Sandy alive."

"Why is that?"

"Because the last time I saw Sandy was a couple weeks before she was killed." Nick's revelation was unexpected and caught Kevin and Jess by surprise, rendering them silent for a moment.

"Do you have an alibi to back that up?"

"No, I don't have an alibi. Gee, Detective, if I'd known I'd need one, I'd have planned more carefully," Nick sneered. "My students were giving major presentations the week Sandy died, so I was quite busy and had little time for socializing."

"Can you explain how your fingerprint got on her thumbnail? For all I know, she could've been some sort of nature freak, but given her professional status, common sense dictates that she would've taken several baths between your last date and the day she died."

Nick paused for a moment, realizing he'd been caught in a lie. "We had coffee at the Java Hut on Friday afternoon before she went missing. She must have disappeared shortly after that before she could wash her hands." Kevin and Jess looked at one another before concentrating on the suspect again. "Is there something else?"

"Did you kill her, Nick?" Kevin asked outright.

"Of course not!"

"Then you wouldn't mind if we dropped by your house and had a look around."

"Yes, I mind! Do you have a warrant?"

"I can get a warrant, but if you're innocent, you have nothing to hide and we won't need it. Right?"

"You make a good argument. When do you want to come by?"

"How about right now?"

"You don't mince words or waste time. I have a class to teach."

"Doctor Yarboro, surely a faculty member of your standing and with your high enrollments must have at least one TA who can lead class for you."

"You've done your research, Agent Mitchell."

"Doctor Yarboro, I don't go into anything half-cocked."

"Just a moment." He picked up the phone and dialed his secretary. "Yes Charlene, would you track down Scott and have him take my class today? I have some urgent business to attend to and won't be able to make it." He listened for a moment. "Thank you. Shall we?" Kevin and Jess followed him to the door. "After you," he said, holding the door.

Moments later, in Kevin's truck...

"*Lab, this is Stephanie.*"

"Steph, Slater."

"*What can I do for you, Detective?*"

"Depends on how busy you are."

"*Shoot.*"

"Our number one suspect just agreed to let us search his house. Can you get a team out there, stat?"

"*I'll round up a couple of my boys and meet you there. When?*"

"Now, we're leaving Elon as we speak."

"*What's the addy?*"

"1436 Eric Lane. It's off of Alamance Road, towards Lake Macintosh."

"*I know the area. I'll be there.*"

"Okay, Steph, see ya in a bit." He looked at Jess before pulling into the street. "You were kinda quiet back there."

"I was studying him."

"What's your take on him?"

"I think it's safe to say he's a classic narcissistic personality with sociopathic tendencies, which makes him extremely good at covering his tracks. We're gonna have a hard time making something stick to him."

"I was afraid you'd say something like that."

1436 Eric Lane, Burlington...
11:14 AM

"Just so we're clear, Mr. Yarboro, you've given us your permission to search the premises without a warrant."

"Yes, Detective."

"Then you won't mind signing this waiver."

Nick Yarboro signed the papers handed to him and stepped aside for the evidence team to enter. Jess led the way, stopping just inside each doorway to examine the rooms. The house was very masculine, without a trace of warmth or female habitation. The décor was ultra-modern, white walls and carpet with black, leather-upholstered furnishings and chrome and glass tables.

Throughout the house, there were no photographs or hints of the man's life or personality. Only a large contemporary painting hung behind the sofa, along with a bombastic mirror near the front entryway. Jess continued through the kitchen and dining area. Like the living room, it was cold and devoid of emotion or the slightest trace femininity. Black granite countertops and stainless steel appliances looked as if they had never seen a day of use. She examined every room before concluding that nothing seemed out of the ordinary.

"Are you satisfied?"

"Actually no, Doctor, do you have a dungeon?" She asked.

"A dungeon?"

"Yes, based on our background investigation and your depth of interest in the lifestyle, I presume that you a well-equipped dungeon. This morning, you mentioned your chamber, not your bedroom, which struck me as very archaic for such a contemporary man. And, I've yet to see the aforementioned spanking bench, so I'll ask again. Do you have a dungeon?"

"Miss Mitchell, are you certain that we've never met?"

"Quite, Doctor Yarboro."

"You sound as if you have some experience with D/s." He looked at her, expecting confirmation of his statement.

"I believe in doing my homework. Surely, being an upstanding faculty member at a prestigious university, you can appreciate that."

"This way please," he continued, annoyed when she refused to give him the answer he expected.

He led the team back through the living room, where he stopped in front of the gigantic mirror.

With a pull on the edge, it swung out revealing a set of stairs going down into what must have been the basement at one point. On one wall, various tools of the trade...blindfolds, gags, restraints, and spreader bars among other things...hung in perfect, straight rows, though what caught Jess' attention, was the wide array of floggers. There were about a dozen in varying lengths and materials. Most were plain, but one was more noticeable than the rest. The design was extremely intricate. One might argue that it was more art than toy. Its smooth handle was inlaid with mother-of-pearl, while colorful, glass balls hung from the ends of several tails.

"I've never used that one. It's too fine," Nick said when he noticed Jess examining it.

"It's beautiful, looks as if it could cause serious injury in novice hands," she said as images of tiny bruises from several victims flashed through her memory.

"Another reason I've never used it. While I'm certainly no novice, I prefer my partners unblemished."

"Is that so, Nick?" Kevin asked. "So you wouldn't mind if we took it in for DNA testing?"

"I absolutely would mind. Look Detective, I've put up with you barging into my office and your subsequent interrogation. I've allowed you to walk through my home without a warrant, I might add, but you're going to need one to take anything *out* of my house for any reason."

"You realize that I could have my team bag this stuff up anyway for two reasons."

"And those would be?"

"First, you signed that waiver and allowed us to come in here of your own free will. And next, you're a suspect in a murder investigation, who just happens to have an unusually large collection of items that could be used in a way that would leave exactly the kinds of markings found on our victims and or could be used to kill someone. With your history, you should know that's probable cause in *any* courtroom. In fact, I have cause to arrest you right now, but I'll play it your way. I'll get a warrant," Kevin said as he dialed Mike Shelley.

Not waiting to hear the rest of their heated conversation, Jess continued into another corner of the room. A large, trendy display cabinet held a multitude of dildos, vibrators, and the harnesses and adapters that went with many of them. Every shape, size, and color was accounted for, including glass ones, more of Nick Yarboro's peculiar penchant in art, no doubt. Flanking the cabinet were two large furnishings that no well-equipped dungeon would lack.

"They're almost art in themselves."

Nick joined her, followed by Kevin. "You know these?"

"Sure, this *Saint Andrews Cross* is beautiful," she said, staring at the monstrous wooden X. "Hand-carved?"

"Yes."

"And the spanking bench actually looks quite comfortable. I'm not surprised that Sandy enjoyed it so much."

"Are you sure we haven't met? It's unusual to find someone with your knowledge who claims they're not into D/s, especially a cop."

"I'm positive that we don't know each other, Doctor Yarboro." Jess moved back before the cross. Kevin leaned over and whispered something to her. Taking his cue, she continued her line of questioning. "I've seen only one of these up close, but never in use. How does it work?" She asked.

"With your partner's permission, I'll show you." Kevin nodded his grudging consent, but took the precaution of holding onto Jess' weapons before allowing her on the platform. "I'm disappointed, Miss Mitchell. For a moment, I thought I might find out if you are as glorious nude as you are clothed." Kevin scowled at him and took a step forward. "Relax, Detective. Your wrists go here, and here," Nick said, pointing to the leather cuffs on the upper arms.

"Forward or backwards?"

"Take your pick. It depends on how the scene is to progress," Nick said.

"Since this is a demonstration, I'd prefer to watch." She faced forward, placed her wrists into the cuffs, and allowed the suspect to restrain her while Kevin watched. "What would happen next?"

"Your legs go here, and here," he said, pointing to the base of the cross. He secured her ankles with two additional leather straps. "Of course, you'd be unclothed or in whatever costume we had designated beforehand." Nick studied Jess for a moment. "You are a perfect specimen for flogging, Agent Mitchell. I'll bet you're a sight to behold in all your submissive splendor," he commented as a doorbell rang upstairs.

"Yes, she is, now get her the hell down," Kevin commanded. His voice seethed with a combination of jealousy, fear, and contained rage. The doorbell sounded again. "Let's make it snappy, Yarboro, so you can get that," Kevin snarled.

"Jealousy is an emotion one should never express so vehemently, if at all, before a sub Detective, especially a brat," Nick stated matter-of-factly as he unbound Jess. "It gives them too much power over you."

"Excuse me?"

"You've an incredibly strong dominant force inside of you. Get a grip on your emotions and you'll have quite the harem at your beck and call."

"What the hell makes you think I want a harem?"

"I hope you don't. I rather like having my choice of willing subjects. With the right mentor, you could become a much sought-after Master, too much a rival for my taste."

CRSOGRSO

The evidence team bagged and boxed everything for analysis, much to Nick Yarboro's chagrin. Kevin, Mike, and Jess kept out of the way and watched as the suspect made note of every item removed by the technicians. While they waited, Jess made arrangements for the state crime lab to process the items on a priority status.

"Hey, when will I get my things back?"

"Don't worry, Doc; you'll get it all back once you're cleared," Kevin said with a touch of mirth creeping into his tone.

"And if you don't clear me?"

"Then you won't need to worry about it. Will you? In the meantime..."

"Yeah, yeah, I know the drill. Don't leave town."

"Bingo, you win the prize."

Thirty minutes later...

Back at the substation, Dean was waiting when Kevin and Jess arrived followed by Mike, who had taken the liberty of calling him to the substation for an update. Kevin led the group to Jess' office and poured coffee while Jess called Carl Barnes. She prepared him for the amount and large size of some of the evidence before placing the call on speakerphone.

"*So what about this Yarboro fella?*"

"I was just wondering the same thing," Dean said.

"He's a real creep," Kevin interrupted before Jess could respond.

"Do you care to elaborate on that, Son?" Dean asked.

"It was nothing. He just came onto me...right about the time Mike showed up with the search warrant."

"He came onto you the moment we walked into his office at Elon," Kevin shot back, still fuming from Nick Yarboro's needling.

"Kevin, are you sure you can do this? Do we need to assign a new lead or come up with some other plan to catch this guy?"

"No, Mike!" Jess shouted. "We've all worked way too hard on this to go back to square one now."

"*I agree with Jess, but I also see Mike's point. Slater, your objectivity seems compromised.*"

"That's easy for you to say, Carl," Kevin said. "You don't have nearly as much invested in this."

"Come on now, guys. That's not fair," Jess said.

"*Hold on, Doll. You didn't let me finish. Kevin is concerned for you, but I have no doubt that you'll be fine and everything will work out, especially with him backing you up.*"

"Honey, Kevin is just worried about your safety. And nobody's getting off this case that easily," Dean added.

"Good."

"*So where are we on this? Is Yarboro our man? You're the expert, Jess.*"

"Honestly, I don't know yet, but I can tell you this much. Nick Yarboro is a textbook sociopath." She retrieved a copy of the *Diagnostic and Statistical Manual of Mental Disorders* from a bookshelf, flipped to the section on personality disorders and paraphrased for everyone. "In a nutshell, this is someone who lacks empathy, is callous, cynical, and cares nothing for the feelings, rights, and sufferings of others. He may have an inflated view of himself, and he may display a glib, superficial charm. In other words, he'll be überassertive."

"That's Yarboro, alright," Kevin said. "He was cockier that Rafferty." Everyone laughed for a moment. "He acted like it didn't even bother him a bit that his girlfriend had been murdered. I saw no emotion until he realized we knew about his extracurricular activities."

"This is true."

"Go ahead, Jess."

"Individuals with this disorder have a complete disregard for the law and may be irresponsible or exploitative in sexual relationships. A pattern of impulsivity may lead to sudden changes in jobs, residences, or relationships. They may have never been in a monogamous relationship. They tend to be irritable, aggressive, and may have a history of physical assault. They show little, if any, remorse for their actions and tend to blame victims for their fates, or they may just display complete indifference."

"Couldn't have described him better myself," Kevin said.

"Sounds like a real winner," Mike commented dryly.

"The good news is they tend to grow out of many of these behaviors, particularly the lawlessness, as they age."

"Wonderful, so he'll kill a few more, get bored with it and stop?"

"Actually yeah, that *has* been known to happen. Famous case in point, Gary Ridgeway."

"Ridgeway? Where have I heard that name?" Mike said.

"The Green River killer in Washington state, the only reason they caught him is because he turned himself in."

"This describes Nick Yarboro to a tee. He has a history of assault and displayed blatant disregard for the law in his youth. He's done a lot of job-hopping too. We have his records to back all that up. He's really aggressive, but in a quiet, passive sort of way..."

"Kevin, that was his public persona, the one he knows he has to use for vanillas, or when he's not on his own turf."

"True, he did get pretty irritated when he figured out he couldn't get the jump on us."

"What's a vanilla?"

"Dean, that's a person not into this shit," Kevin answered. "Listen to this."

He set the tape recorder on the desk for all to hear the interview conducted in the professor's office and the subsequent visit to his home. He paused the recording for comments before the dungeon demonstration began.

"*Well I, for one, agree with your entire description so far,*" Carl said.

"Me too."

"What else is on that tape, Kevin?" Mike asked.

"Our trip down to the dungeon." He resumed playing the tape.

Jess continued her assessment when the tape stopped. "In addition to being a sociopath, Nick Yarboro is a sexual sadist. If you didn't get that from the conversation, wait until you see the stuff we carted to the lab for analysis," she told the men.

"*I can see why Kevin is worried for your safety, Jess. That punk seemed taken with you and unconvinced that you weren't acquainted.*"

"I don't think you'd have to worry for long. You heard him. I'm a brat."

"Meaning what exactly, Jess? He'd toss you to the curb before or *after* he beat the hell out of you?" Mike asked.

"Come on, Mike. Give me a little more credit than that. You don't actually think I woulda let him tie me up without Kevin there. Do you?"

"You're right, Jess. I apologize."

"So what's next?" Dean asked.

"We wait," Kevin said.

"For what?"

"*Analysis of the evidence, speaking of which, I'm told just arrived.*"

"And we keep an eye on this guy to make sure he doesn't try to skip town."

"*I'm gonna get outta here and see what I can find out. You folks keep me posted.*"

"Okay, Carl, will do, and you do the same."

Chapter 30

February 22...

"Hey, can we talk for a second?"

"Sure Baby, personal or professional?"

"Personal...it's about the wedding, or rather, the week before. I've been thinking about something a lot for the last few days."

"What's that?"

"It's gonna be tough." Kevin watched, waiting for her to continue. "I want to spend the last week at my dad's house and abstain."

"Abstain from what?" He asked, though he knew the answer. "You're joking, right?"

"No."

"Any particular reason?"

"Two actually, first, I know we've been living and sleeping together for months, but it would be kinda nice to go into marriage fresh, if that makes any sense."

"It does, but doesn't mean I have to like it," he said, scowling. "What's the other reason?"

"Second, and more importantly, my birth control pills run out on Saturday, a week before the wedding, and I refuse to walk down the aisle pregnant, even if it's only a few days. I realize we wouldn't know if it happened, but still..."

"Not to mention the fact that you'd be widowed as soon as my Ma figured it out. This is gonna suck." He looked thoughtful for a moment. "Hey, there's an idea!"

"What?"

"Sucking," he said with an impish grin. "A skill you have perfected over the last few months."

February 24...

"It's been a week, Detective. I want to know when you'll be returning my things."

"Doctor Yarboro, everything we took from your house was sent to the state lab in Raleigh for analysis. I guarantee you'll get every piece back without a scratch as soon as they're done with their tests."

"Does this mean I'm still a suspect?"

"It means the lab has not completed its analysis. I'll contact you as soon as I know something. You have a nice day." Kevin dropped the receiver into the cradle. "Damn! That guy is a nuisance."

February 27...

After careful deliberation, Jess and Kevin opted to skip the February KLAASP meeting. It was too soon after their dealings with Nick Yarboro, and they feared being recognized by him, especially since he seemed so certain of having met Jess.

March 7...

"Hello."

"Good morning, Sweetcakes."

"Carl?"

"Yeah it's me. You know I wouldn't call you at home on a Sunday morning if it wasn't important."

"I know. What's up?"

"Just wanted to comment on the picture and announcement you put in the paper."

"What are you talking about?"

"You're in the society pages, Doll. The wife showed it to me."

"What? Why?"

"*Your engagement announcement.*"

"Carl, we didn't put an announcement in the paper. We intentionally decided *not* to, so we could maintain a low profile."

"*Well Sugar, somebody put you in there because I'm looking at it right now.*"

"Damn!" Jess covered the mouthpiece and yelled for Kevin.

He came bounding in from the back yard with Sarge hot on his heels. "What's wrong, Baby?"

"Carl's on the phone. Somebody put an engagement announcement with our picture in the paper."

"Shit! Who the hell did that?"

"I wish I knew."

"Which paper?"

"I dunno. Carl, what paper are you looking at?"

"*The Raleigh News and Observer.*"

"Is there any way to find out who did it?"

"*I dunno, Sugar, but I'll see what I can do and call you back.*"

"Okay thanks, Carl. It's the *News and Observer*," she told Kevin upon hanging up the phone.

"You want me to go get one?"

"Sure, why not? We may as well have a copy for the scrapbook."

"I guess."

"Maybe we can do some damage control. I'll finish making breakfast while you're out."

"Okay, back in a few. Come on, Sarge." Fifteen minutes later Kevin and Sarge returned. "Honey, we're home and I'm starved."

"Have a seat and I'll bring it right out. I can't believe you're letting Sarge ride in your car."

"I didn't. We took yours," Kevin said, grinning.

"You did what?"

"I'm kidding. We took the truck."

"On your day off?"

"Sure, this article could impact our case, which makes it police business, so it's okay for me to drive the truck."

"Works for me."

"Carl was right. It's us, all right, and it's big, takes up a quarter of the page. Somebody went to a lot of trouble to make sure we got noticed. Have a look."

> Staff Sergeant Kevin Slater and Jessica Mitchell announce their engagement. The groom-to-be, a former Army paratrooper and currently a detective with the Burlington Police Department, hails originally from Minneapolis, Minnesota, but has resided in Burlington for the past five years. The bride-to-be, a special agent with the State Bureau of Investigation, is a native of Burlington. Proud parents of the groom are Terese and the late Charles Slater of Minneapolis. The bride is the daughter and only child of Police Chief Dean Johansen of Burlington, North Carolina. The ceremony is planned for late spring and will be the first marriage for both the bride and groom.

"Boy, that's detailed. It's wrong, but detailed, which tells us one thing," Jess observed.

"What's that?"

"Whoever did this isn't a close friend or relative, or else they'd have gotten their facts straight."

"And they would've run this by us first. By the way, Baby, this is delicious."

"Thank you."

"Tastes almost as good as you did this morning." He waited for a moment, grinning impishly. "There it is."

"There what is?"

"That blush."

"Scoundrel!"

"Brat!"

Catching her off guard, Kevin scooted his chair out and flashed a wicked smile. He leapt to her side and pulled her from her seat, then threw her over his shoulder. Sarge growled and galumphed after them when Jess pounded on Kevin's shoulders and squealed in false terror as he ran with her into the bedroom. He threw her onto the bed and sprang onto it after her, straddling her waist. After pulling her tight tank top up over her head, he wound it around her wrists, restraining her. Then flashing another iniquitous grin, he unfastened her shorts and yanked them down her legs. Sarge growled again, then whimpered and scurried into a corner when the shorts dropped onto his head.

"Damn dog! Get outta here, Sarge," Kevin chastised as Jess giggled. "What are you laughing at?"

"You better watch out, Mister. You're not the only ferocious beast in the house anymore," she teased.

"I got your ferocious beast."

He popped the clasp on her bra, tore it from her body, and flung it across the room, then ripped the satin panties from her hips and added them to the pile of garments on the floor. Finally, he stood up and stripped away his own clothing before flipping Jess facedown and pulling her to her knees. She gasped when he spread her legs wide and speared her from behind. Unable to move, she steadied herself with her shirt-bound hands while he held tight to her hips and pounded her hard, so hard that she had to push back against him to avoid slamming into the headboard. In only moments, he grunted and came. Jess groaned in disappointment when he finished almost as fast as he'd started and turned her onto her back.

"Oh, I'm not done with you yet," he said, grinning.

A stray droplet fell from the shiny head of his shaft when he stood up. He unwound the shirt from her wrists, then walked to the nightstand on his side of the bed and slid out the drawer. Jess' eyes grew wide in surprise when she saw what he pulled from its confines...her forgotten vibrator. He flipped the switch, then listened to it hum and watched the dong as it shimmied in his hand, almost imperceptible to the naked eye.

"Remember this?" She nodded slowly in agreement. "I brought it back with us after Christmas. I've been waiting for just the right time to pull it out." He let out a low, roguish laugh.

"What are you gonna do with it?"

"Nothing, you are."

"What?" It dawned on her what he wanted her to do.

"I'm gonna watch."

"Oh no, Kevin...I can't do that."

"Sure, you can. Just pretend I'm not here."

"I can't."

"How about if I start, and then you take over."

He refused to wait for an answer. He spread her lips, wet with his viscous seed, and pushed the phallus inside her, leaning down to lap at her clit while he fucked her with the rubber dong. Between his tongue and the oscillations from the vibrator, she couldn't withhold a series of moans. Giving in to her own pleasure and his wishes, she took the end of the toy from him and slid it back and forth while he licked her swollen button. Gasping from near sensory overload, Jess worked the vibrator with one hand and pinched a nipple with the other.

"Oh God, I'm gonna come. Oh yesss, God, yes!"

Kevin raised his head to look her in the eye. His tongue fast became unnecessary, as the vibrations flowing from the toy were enough to send a blast of sexual energy exploding throughout her body. She gasped and stiffened, then pushed it in to the hilt. Kevin moved higher on the bed, then wrapped his tongue around a nipple and suckled while the orgasm rolled through her in strong, measured waves. When she could stand no more, Jess pulled the vibrator from her hypersensitive folds, tossed it aside, and tried to regain some composure. Seconds later, Kevin crawled up beside her and rose on his elbow to look down, watching her chest rise and fall sharply as she caught her breath.

"That was impressive." Jess opened her eyes, looked up at him, and frowned. "Don't look at me like that."

"I can't believe I let you do that."

"Sweetheart, you did all the work. All I did was watch." Her body grew hot as she flushed from head to toe. "Wow! A full-body blush." Embarrassed to the core, Jess tried to cover her nakedness with her hands. "Oh no you don't, there's no need to cover up. Baby, I've got everything about you permanently branded into my memory."

"That was deplorable."

"No, that was awe-inspiring."

Kevin reminded her of their recent dining room romp, that this was no different from her own fascination with his bodily functions. He was proud of the part he'd played in bringing her such pleasure. The last thing he wanted was for her to feel ashamed or embarrassed to let go of her inhibitions with him. He growled playfully and rolled atop of her for another round.

March 13...

Jess took the day to go shopping with Niki. With only six weeks left before the wedding, she still needed to select gowns for her attendants and allow time for any necessary alterations. They had browsed through several bridal shops when Niki gushed over a fabulous dress. Taking her friend's cue, Jess insisted that Niki be fitted right away. Niki balked at first, protesting that the bride was supposed to choose the gowns, but Jess would not be swayed. She even decided to use Niki's favorite color, violet, over her own, after a short, but friendly argument that her friend should look terrific, as well, when she stood up for her.

March 16...
10:14 AM

"Anything else on Nick Yarboro?"

"Nope, 'fraid not. How's the profiling coming?"

"Same as before. He's a clear-cut case of psychopathy, but other than his relationship with Sandra Vandenberg and his penchant for bondage, we have no evidence to directly tie him to the murders."

"Well, if it helps, I have complete faith in you."

"That's comforting."

"Mike's told me to stop tailing him so close or he's *really* gonna have a case for harassment, but I'm still keeping a good eye on him."

"Good. Hey, there's Armand."

> *SubDoer: hey how's it going?*
> *SubMarine: Fine.*
> *SubDoer: just thought i'd say hello*
> *SubMarine: Who is this?*

"What does he mean, who is this? He knows damn well who you are," Kevin said. His bewilderment was evident in his tone.

"Uh, yeah."

> *SubDoer: it's me...CJ*
> *SubMarine: CJ who?*
> *SubDoer: CJ from KLAASP...Armand are you okay?*
> *SubMarine: Oh yes, CJ...My apologies. I'm somewhat flurried today.*
> *SubDoer: i see that, are you okay?*

SubMarine: Yes, all is well. I have to go.
SubMarine is offline.

"Baby, that was a little too weird, like talking to a different person."
"You're telling me."
"I don't like that guy."
"So you keep telling me." Jess studied him for a moment. "Okay, now *you've* got the look?"
"What look?"
"The one that says *your* gears are turning at warp speed. What are you thinking?"
"I'll tell you later. I need to toss some ideas around up here first," Kevin said, pointing to his head.
"If you say so."
"Did you talk to Sam yet?"
"Yeah, I did. She's being fitted tomorrow, and Kate and Kinsey are taking Brittany and Kaitlyn to a local shop on Saturday."
"Cool, it's almost time. I can hardly wait. I'm only dreading one thing."
"What's that?"
"That last week, not touching you is surely gonna kill me."
"Oh please, abstinence has never killed anybody."
"There's a first time for everything."
"I'm sure you'll live."

11:02 AM

"Yeah Phil, Kevin Slater here."
"*Kevin, Buddy...hey, I read you were getting hitched.*"
"You weren't supposed to see that, but yes, I am."
"*Congratulations! And you bagged the Chief's daughter? Way to go, Buddy.*"
"Thanks."
"*Jess is a good girl.*"
"I didn't realize you knew each other."
"*Sure, I know Jess. I used to be one of you guys. Remember? She was at the station all the time when she was a kid.*"
"True, I didn't think about that."
"*Yeah, me and some of the guys taught her to play poker. She used to kill us.*" Kevin let out an odd snort. "*What was that?*"
"Nothing."
"*So Kevin, what can I do for you?*"
"I need a favor."
"*Yeah sure, what's up?*"
"I need to find out someone's identity."
"*Kevin, you're a cop. You don't need me for that.*"
"Yeah, but this guy may be involved in one of my cases."
"*Meaning you don't want to get your hands dirty and taint your case.*"
"Exactly."
"*All right, lay it on me. You know I'll do what I can.*"

3:28 PM

"Jess Mitchell."
"*Jess Mitchell, how have you been?*"
"Fine...who is this?"
"*Who is this? You don't remember me? I'm heartbroken. This is Phil Porter.*"

"I'll be. Now there's a voice from the past. I'm doing great. How are you?"

"*I'm good, real good. I'm in the private sector now, got a nice little PI business going.*"

"I heard about that. That's great, Phil."

"*Hey, I heard you were getting married. Slater is a real piece of work, but he's a helluva man. You did good, kid. I couldn't have picked better for you myself.*"

"Thanks, Phil. Now, why do I get the feeling you didn't call here just to tell me that?"

"*That's my girl, still right to the point. Actually, I didn't expect to hear your voice on the other end of the line. I called to talk to Slater.*"

"Sure, he's right here. It's for you." Jess grabbed Sarge's leash from a hook and left with the half-grown pup to give Kevin some privacy.

CB❧O(R8O

"Damn, Phil! How do you get this stuff so fast?"

"*Hey, it's my job.*"

"I'm glad you're one of the good guys. So whatcha got for me?"

Kevin spent the next half-hour taking notes that included some disturbing information about Jess' new admirer, Armand, but was unsure how, or if, it would have any bearing on the case. He pondered his options for a moment, then went out into the main office.

"Where's Jess?"

"She took Sarge for a walk."

"Oh, okay." He picked up a stack of pages from the fax machine and moved to his own office, shutting the door.

March 18...

"Hey Jess, remember the other day when I had that little powwow with Phil Porter?"

"Yeah, what was that all about?"

"I did something that I hope won't upset you." Jess waited for him to continue. "I got him to track down some info on your buddy, Armand."

"You did? How? We don't even know his real name, or is that what Phil called about."

"Yeah."

"Why would that upset me?"

"Well, I didn't think it would, but I wanted to be sure."

"What'd you find out?"

"His name's Joseph, with an f, Armand Bedrich. He's from Texas, a place called New Braunfels, and get this. He's an ex-marine."

"That explains his online alias."

"Yeah, but check this out. He was *booted* on a medical discharge for paranoia and substance abuse."

"Really? He doesn't seem paranoid, but I suppose anything's possible."

"Yeah, well, his COs thought he was a danger to himself and possibly others."

"Looks like you had good reason to be wary of him."

"And I have even more reason to be concerned now that he's your biggest fan."

"And I have even more reason to be extra careful."

"I'll leave this stuff with you so you can look it over. You're the shrink so you'll understand all the medical jargon a helluva lot better than I do, and then you can put it in English for me, 'cause it's all Greek to me."

"Gee, thanks," she said with a grin.

CB❧O(R8O

Jess spent the next several days studying the data Kevin had collected on Armand. She couldn't seem to get his mother's name, Kriszta Olesia Gavrilopoulos, out of her head, but finally dismissed it as just an interesting name. She found Armand's military records vague and conflicting. One commanding officer noted that he was personable and a good soldier, while another stated that he was sullen, quiet, and seemed to seethe with anger at all times. The two descriptions depicted two very different people.

Once again, Jess referred to the *DSM*. Upon researching the possible personality disorders, she concluded that Armand had symptoms of several, including paranoid, schizotypal, and borderline. But not being a trained psychiatrist, she couldn't be sure which one, if any particular diagnosis, fit more than another, so she put in a call to her grad school advisor.

Gavin McGuiness, in addition to being a renowned expert in forensic psychology, was a clinical psychiatrist specializing in abnormal psychological disorders. Delighted to hear from one of his favorite students, he spent a few minutes catching up on her life before agreeing to look at her notes. Taking less than two hours, Dr. McGuiness was of the belief that Armand was a paranoid schizophrenic with borderline traits, but he was unable to elaborate further without studying the patient. Kevin became even more alarmed upon hearing the diagnosis, and warned her, once again, to be cautious in her dealings with Armand.

Carl finally contacted the couple with news of the mysterious wedding announcement. It had been placed anonymously, but more disturbing was the fact that the *Raleigh News and Observer* could find no record of the original ad or the person who had placed it. Every trace of it seemed to have disappeared from their records.

On a more pleasant note, Jess' wedding dress was finished. Niki went with her for the final fitting and luckily, it needed minimal alterations. The in-house seamstress was able to make those on the spot, so Jess took it to back her dad's house that very day and hung it where it would remain wrinkle-free until her wedding day. She also finalized the floral selections for the bouquets, ceremonial and reception arrangements. Everything seemed to be falling into place.

March 23...

"Find anything else in those records Phil sent over?"

"Only that they're not consistent. If I didn't know better, I'd swear the psyche records are for two different people."

"That's interesting. Anything else?"

"Not really, the only other thing that caught my attention was that Armand is positive for thalassemia." At Kevin's dumbfounded expression, she continued. "I had to look it up myself. Nothing terrible, it's a form of anemia common to the Mediterranean region, especially among Greeks and Italians."

"Oh."

"He's got the minor form, so it probably hasn't had an impact on his health. He may not even know he has it."

Chapter 31

March 27...
10:12 PM

"Oh please, God, stop," she begged. "Let me go. I won't tell anybody. I promise."

"Shut up, bitch!"

He backhanded the attractive brunette hard across the face, causing her head to snap to the side before she fell to the floor. Scrambling to her hands and knees, she tried to crawl away, but not before his tanned arm shot out and grabbed the collar around the screaming woman's neck. He pulled back, ignoring her pleas to stop, as she scratched and clawed, trying to pry his hand loose. The more she struggled and tried to escape, the tighter he pulled the collar. Finally, she ceased resistance as she went limp, and fell to the floor when his hold slackened.

March 28...
3:37 AM

"Son-of-a-bitch!" Jess shouted, rousing Kevin from a deep slumber.

"What's wrong, Baby?" He asked, sitting up suddenly when he noticed the phone in her hand. "Oh no, don't tell me, not again." She nodded. "Goddamn it!"

She handed him a pair of shorts after hooking her bra. "This one's at the country club...seventh hole on the golf course."

"Fuck!" They dressed in a hurry and rushed to the golf course. "So much for my goddamn patrols. How the hell are we supposed to catch this sick bastard when he keeps changing on us?"

"He's modified his MO because we're watching the parks."

Kevin immediately radioed a dispatcher with instructions to send a marked unit to Nick Yarboro's house. Knowledge of the professor's whereabouts all evening was crucial, and time was of the essence.

"That was good thinking," Jess said as they turned into the country club parking lot. The pair took careful steps across the green to the seventh hole to avoid disturbing any evidence that may have been left behind.

"Morning, Doctor Mitchell, Slater."

"Bob," Kevin said curtly and sought out the first officer on the scene.

"Morning, Bob," Jess answered, following Kevin.

"Hey Sarge."

"Chris, you're first?"

"Yeah, lucky me, huh?" Christine Parezi commented grimly.

"What's the story?"

"A couple kids found her. They're over there," she said, pointing at two hysterical teenagers a short distance away. "Claimed they meet out here all the time. There's a good make-out spot with a little pond and some trees by the fourteenth hole." Kevin scowled at the woman. "What? You didn't know about that place?

"Uh, no, I try to make out in more comfortable surroundings."

"Yeah, you and me both," she said, laughing.

"Speaking of...how's Steve?"

"He's great. Bet you didn't know you'd be playing Cupid when you picked us for Headbanger."

"You'll find a way to pay me back eventually."

"Count on it. Anyway, they were headed there, but they ran across her and freaked out."

"She looks rough, he wasn't as nice to her as the others," Jess interrupted, as she put on a pair of gloves and checked the woman's garments. "No ID either. We'll have to run her through missing persons." She snapped some photos and made a sketch of the scene, noting the defensive scratches on the victim's throat before raising her right hand to study the nails. "Hey, Kev, she's got dirty nails."

"Maybe we'll catch a break this time."

Jess looked at the woman's other hand. "And he took a trophy this time."

"What?"

"Third finger on her left hand has been severed." Jess waited and watched Bob bag the hands to preserve evidence. "There's nothing else we can do here. Come on. Let's go to the office and add this one to the list. Hey Bob, when can you start on her?"

"I'll get on it in a few hours. For now, I'll go ahead and establish TOD and call you after the sun's up."

"Thanks."

As they were returning to Kevin's truck, Mark Jones radioed from Nick Yarboro's driveway. The man's car was stone cold and his physical condition was of one rudely awakened. They weren't surprised to learn the man had threatened to file harassment charges. Kevin remained deep in thought as they drove through town.

"Rigor was just starting to set in, so she hasn't been dead for long. Would he have had time to ditch a vehicle, get home, and fall asleep that quick? Would he even be able to go to sleep after killing a woman?"

"Anything's possible when you're dealing with a psychopath. Remember, the perp feels no remorse, so it likely wouldn't keep him up. You sound like you're starting to question yourself."

"I am. Dammit, God help me, Jess, but I'm starting to wonder if we've been watching the wrong guy."

"You too, huh?"

"Oh boy, I know I'm in trouble when the behavior expert starts doubting herself. This one is so off from the first six that I wonder if it's another damn copycat."

"It's definitely Mr. Clean. He knows we're onto him. He's losing control and it shows in the scene."

10:14 AM

Jess walked into the main office upon hearing the commotion. "Slater, where the hell do you get off sending someone to beat on my door at four in the fucking morning? What the hell was that stunt all about?"

"Mr. Yarboro...Nick, you're a suspect in an ongoing murder investigation. I or my men will show up at your home, office, or anywhere we want, whenever we want, and there's not a thing you can do about it."

"I can file a harassment suit."

"Go ahead. You'll be wasting your time and money and you'll lose. Now, I'd advise you to leave before I find a reason to arrest you. And believe me; I won't have to be creative to come up with one."

The telephone sent Jess scurrying back to her office, so she missed the remainder of the disagreement. "Yeah Bob, whatcha got for me?"

"Doctor Mitchell, I'm estimating TOD between ten and midnight. COD is ligature asphyxiation. She's got the same markings around her neck, fractured hyoid, multiple contusions, and the like."

"I figured as much. What about evidence?"

"I got nail scrapings, looks like blood and epithelials, and something interesting this time."

"What's that?" Jess listened intently while Bob relayed the rest of his preliminary findings.

"...now get the hell out of here, Nick," she heard Kevin yell as ended the call.

"What was that about?"

"He had a bug up his ass over last night. Who was on the phone?"

"Bob Morton, we have to go if it's a good time. He's put a hold on the rest of the autopsy until we get there." Kevin followed her outside. "She had a golf ball shoved in her mouth," she told him as they got into the truck.

"What?"

"Just repeating what Bob said."

"You mean like a gag?" Jess nodded. "What do you make of that?"

She stifled a yawn. "I dunno. I need to meditate on that one."

11:25 AM

"Hey, Bob."

"Hey, guys. Hold on, lemme wash up. I was just finishing lunch."

"Ewww, how can you eat in here with that stench?" Jess asked.

"You get used to it after a while."

"You can have it. I don't think I would ever get used to the odor of death. It takes a special kind of person to do what you do."

"Yours is no more pleasant, Doctor Mitchell."

"True, but at least I don't have to hang out with the bodies all day."

"Come on. I've got her tabled in here. Oh yeah, I heard you two were getting married. Congratulations."

"Yes, we are, in just under a month. Thanks."

"That soon? Wow! Okay, you guys know the prelim, but there's one more thing that might interest you."

"You mean besides the golf ball?"

"Yeah, Slater, check this out." Bob raised the woman's left hand.

"We already knew about the finger."

"No, not that...look where he separated it from the hand. He didn't quite get it all the way to joint. There's a tan line. She's married."

"He's been going for single ladies. I wonder why he switched." Kevin thought aloud.

"There's something else."

"I'm almost afraid to ask," Kevin said.

"She was a mother too. She has an old episiotomy scar with additional scarring on top of that. I estimate that she's had at least two vaginal births."

"Oh no, that's terrible. How old is she?" Jess asked, clearly upset over the new information.

"Judging from her teeth and overall physical condition, I'd say early-thirties to maybe forty."

"So there's at least two little kids out there without a mom now," Jess said, more to herself than to the men. She didn't say another word until Kevin was ready to leave.

"So we've got a thirty-something, married mother. She's been strangled in the same manner as six previous victims. Any other markings?" Kevin asked as he watched Jess.

"Same pea-sized bruises on her back, sides, and buttocks, and she was whipped," Bob said, rolling over the corpse.

"Raped?" Kevin asked.

"And sodomized."

"God, these poor women," Kevin said, rubbing his temples.

"I know I'm just the medical examiner and you probably can't answer this officially, but are you close to catching someone?"

"Bob, all I can tell you is that we have some good solid leads," Kevin said.

"Good, I sure hope I don't have to do another one of these."

"That goes double for us. Jess, let's go home and get some rest. We've got a lot of work ahead of us." She mumbled something unintelligible and took Kevin's hand.

April 2...
11:28 AM

"Jess, we don't even know yet if it's her."

"Dammit, Mike! Look at this picture. It's her," Jess shouted as she slammed the photograph down on his desk.

"Relax, Jess. You're gonna have a stroke."

"Goddamn it, no, I'm not!" She slumped into a chair, blowing out a long breath. "Mike, we shouldn't have to tell those kids that a sick fucking lunatic murdered their mother."

"Calm down, Baby." Jess closed her eyes, fighting back tears, when Kevin stood behind her, rubbing her shoulders.

"I'm sorry, Jess. I guess this one hits a little too close to home."

"No shit, Sherlock! It took a stroke of genius to come up with that."

"No need to get nasty."

"I'm sorry, Mike."

"Don't sweat it. I'm not taking it personally because I know why it's affecting you like this. Remember, I was there. Jess, are you going to be able to handle this? You don't have to be here."

"I can handle the husband, but I can't stand the thought of having to break the news to those kids."

"I understand how you feel."

"Don't blow smoke up my ass, Mike. You can't possibly understand how I feel about this."

"Then help me understand."

"I knew one day I'd have to tell a kid their mom or dad was dead. And now this, as if their parents impending divorce wasn't hard enough on them. I just feel completely helpless."

"Honey, don't beat yourself up," Kevin said, trying to soothe her. "There's no way you could have prevented it."

"We coulda caught the crazy bastard already."

2:14 PM

"Hi, Mr. Crawford. I'm Kevin Slater. I'm in charge of the investigation. Come on up," he said as he lead the man to Mike's office.

"Detective, I hope you won't be offended when I say the pleasure is not all mine."

"Not at all, and make no mistake. I don't enjoy or look forward to these meetings," Kevin replied as they entered the office. Jess stood when they entered.

Cutting right to the chase, Rick Crawford looked closely at the morgue photos. Everyone in Mike's office knew the man recognized his estranged wife by the tears that welled up in his eyes and rolled down his cheeks. His grief tugged at Jess' heartstrings, forcing her to keep her own ragged emotions in check. Taking several minutes to regain his composure, Rick was slow to remark and spoke to no one, in particular.

"We were getting a divorce. There's been so many times when we didn't get along, but I never wanted anything to happen to her. She was a great mother. What the hell am I supposed to tell my kids now?" He asked as anger set in.

"Mr. Crawford, hold them close and make sure they feel safe and know how much you love them. I know some excellent grief counselors. I really think it would be a good idea for you to have someone there with you when you break this news to your children."

"What the hell kind of advice is that, Agent Mitchell?"

"That's some of the best advice you'll ever get, Mr. Crawford, and from a very caring and intelligent woman," Mike interjected.

"That's easy for you to say. How many times have you had to tell your kids their mother was murdered, Major? Or you, or you?" He added, looking from Kevin to Jess.

"I've never been in your shoes, Mr. Crawford, and God willing, I never will be, so I can't answer that," Mike said.

"How many kids do you have?" Rick asked Kevin.

"None."

"What about you, Miss Mitchell?"

"I don't have any children yet, Mr. Crawford."

"Then how the hell can you stand there and tell me that you understand and so calmly recommend a grief counselor?"

"Mr. Crawford, I've never been in *your* position and I hope to God I never am, but this is tearing me up because I've been exactly where your *kids* are. My mother *and* father were murdered a week before my tenth birthday, but luckily, I had some great people to help me through it. One of those people was a grief counselor."

"I apologize, Miss Mitchell," he said, clearly regretful. "I didn't realize...I didn't..."

"It's okay. Believe me. I understand, probably better than anybody, what you're going through. My counselor was very good. She still practices right here in Burlington, if you're interested."

"That's very kind of you. I should call her...or someone. I'm going to need all the help I can get."

April 5...

"Here Honey, I know this is hard for you," Kevin said as he put his arm around Jess' shoulders and handed her a tissue. "You sure you're up for this?"

"I'll be okay. I just feel so bad for them. I just want to hug them," she said, watching the two bleary-eyed boy and girl drop handfuls of soil onto the casket.

He placed his palm against her chest. "I know you do. Your big heart is one of the many things I love so much about you. Are you ready to go?"

"Not yet, I need to see someone first." Jess pulled away from him and rushed across the cemetery to stop before a mammoth headstone.

JOHN BRANDON MITCHELL and BARBARA SUZANNE EISEN

Husband and Wife
Loving
Father and Mother

September 2, 1952   June 6, 1954

Together for Eternity
July 9, 1989

She stared at it before dropping to her knees. "Hey Daddy, hey Mama. I know it's been a long time and I'm sorry for not visiting sooner. I haven't forgotten about you. I miss you so much and I think about you all the time, especially now." She wiped tears from her eyes. "I'm getting married in a couple weeks. You'd really like him. You've probably heard Dean shouting his praises all the way up there," Jess said, looking skyward and smiling. "And Mama, he's so sweet, but don't tell anybody I told you that. He doesn't show that side to just anybody. I love him so much and he's crazy about me too. I wish you could see us. I'll keep you posted though, and I promise not to stay away so long next time. I love you." When she turned around, Kevin stood several feet behind her.

"You're something else." He looked down at the headstone. Kevin put his arm around Jess and as they turned to walk back to the car, a light rain began falling.

She stopped him from opening an umbrella and looked into the clouds, smiling. "I think they approve."

April 8...
7:30 AM

> *I'd like to teach you all the rules. I'd get to see them set in stone. I like it when you chain me to the bed.*

"Jesus Christ, Jess, turn it down a little! This is a police station, not a friggin' nightclub."

> *I need to feel you. You need to feel me. I can't control you. You're not the one for me, no.*

"Piss off, David! I'm thinking."
"Hey, I like that song too. But how the heck can you think with it so loud?"

I love the way you rape my skin. I feel the hate you place inside. I need to get your voice out of my head. 'Cause I'm the guy you'll never find.

Jess looked up from her computer, hit by an idea, and listened through the next verse.

I love the way you look at me. I love the way you smack my ass. I love the dirty things you do when I have control of you.

"Yes! Hot damn!" She shouted and jumped from her chair, cutting the volume as Kevin, David, and Bryan scrambled into the office.

"What's up, Baby?"

"I just had a major brainstorm! He's not as smart as he thinks he is."

"He who? Enlighten me, please."

"You want the good part first or the bad?"

"What the hell, let's get the bad news out of the way."

"Nick Yarboro is not our killer."

"What?"

"But Mr. Clean knows Nick. I've got him figured out."

"We'd better call the Chief and Mike."

9:14 AM

"Well, if everybody's ready I'll go ahead and start. Carl, ya still there?"

"*Yeah Doll, oh, by the way I got the evidence reports...nothing linking Nick Yarboro to any of the victims.*"

"I'm not surprised."

"So what's the big brainstorm?" Dean asked.

"I'm sticking with the bondage angle, but I got part of the profile wrong, and I could kick myself for it because it's so clear now."

"What is, Jessie?" Dean asked.

"We've been following the wrong guy the whole time. Nick Yarboro is not Mr. Clean, but the real killer wants us to think he is."

"And what brought about this one-eighty?" Mike asked.

"A couple of things...first, the golf ball. It wasn't a gag, at all. It was a clue. Not only is he telling us that this is all just a game, but he's telling us his next move. Kevin, between that, what you said the other day, and *Puddle of Mudd*, I think I have it."

"What'd I say?"

"You wondered why he had switched from single women to the married kind."

"I vaguely remember that. And?"

"He's a switch."

"*What's a switch?*"

"Carl, in the BDSM community, a switch is someone who alternates between dominant and submissive roles. They aren't well-liked, from what I can tell. Die-hard Doms and subs feel much the same way about switches as many from the gay community feel about bisexuals."

"Because they go both ways?" Mike asked.

"Exactly, trust is a major issue in the community, but you can't trust someone who's all over the map. It's like he's got two identities at war with each other."

"Does this mean you have a new profile?" Kevin asked.

"Yes, as a matter of fact, I do."

"*Is he dissociative?*"

"I think so, Carl, with at least two personalities. One's a Dom, and one's a sub."

"What's that?" Kevin asked.

186

"*Psycho babble for multiple personality disorder.*"

"Oh boy! So where does that leave us?"

"Dad, let's assume for a moment that our guy *really does* have a dissociative identity disorder."

"Okay."

"I'm uncertain at this point which personality is in control the majority of the time, though I suspect it's his submissive side. Unfortunately, I think that side is losing ground as the other gets stronger and remains in control for longer and longer periods of time. The Dom, when he's in control, is the killer and he's using KLAASP as a hunting ground. The one thing I'm certain of is the trigger. Something about the KLAASP meetings sets him off."

"...which explains why the murders always occur at the end of the month."

"You got it, Kevin. He just doesn't feel the need to kill each time. Maybe he gets his aggression out in a heavy scene between kills. I haven't figured that part out yet."

"Why hasn't the group figured out his game yet?" Mike asked.

"Because he doesn't want *them* to figure it out. He's playing with *us,* not them, so he doesn't go after established members. It would cause panic in the group if the more active members started turning up dead, thereby cutting off his supply of victims and forcing him to change the way he plays the game. If you'll recall, each of our ladies was new to the scene, or as with Elizabeth Johnson, their attendance was sporadic, at best, so they wouldn't have known he wasn't for real. They also would not have been missed by the others. Sandy Vandenberg was an exception because she was linked to a prominent member, Nick."

"The last one was into that stuff too?"

"Apparently, Mike...in our interview, Rick Crawford described his wife as timid and unassertive, which is just another way of saying submissive, said it drove him nuts when she wouldn't fight back."

"I'm starting to follow now, Jess."

"Well, explain it to me, Kevin."

"She's saying this guy has two personalities, one dominant, and one submissive. The dominant personality wigs out at the end of the month, which sometimes results in a lady being killed. Am I on track, Jess?"

"Perfect."

"Okay, that's as far as I can get for now. Your turn."

"Remember I said *Puddle of Mudd* helped me out too?"

"Yeah, but why's a mud puddle important?"

Jess laughed. "Not a mud puddle, they're a band, but that's not important. It's actually one of their songs, *Control,* that clued me in. I was listening to it when David started griping this morning."

"You were killing us."

"Sorry about that, loud music helps me focus...drowns out all the little distractions."

"Kevin, she's been like that since high school," Dean interjected.

"Great!" Kevin said sardonically. "Something else to look forward to."

"Anyway, the lyrics go like this. *You lock me up inside ya dirty cage when I'm alone inside my mind.* And then later, *I'm hoping some day you will let me go. Release me from my dirty cage.* I bet ya we'll find that CD, by the way, when we catch him."

"And this applies to our case how?"

"It doesn't really. It just made me think about it from a different perspective...that of two conflicting facets of one's personality. Think cartoons, the little angel on one side and the devil on the other, each trying to get their host to do their bidding. Only in this case, it's two completely separate personalities, each fighting for absolute control. Also, if he's typical, the dominant personality will do whatever he feels is necessary to get rid of the other ones, including murdering him or her."

"What?"

"Violent personalities have been documented as trying to kill the lesser ones."

"Doesn't he know that he can't *really* do that?"

"Mike, with a dissociative disorder, they oftentimes don't recognize that they're different parts of a whole. They see themselves as completely different people, although that's not the case every time. Did you ever see *All About Eve*?"

"Yeah."

"That movie was based on a real case. In Eve's case, some of her personalities knew about the others and some of them were oblivious. The good news is the condition is treatable. Psychotherapy, hypnotherapy, and drugs are combined in a number of ways to guide the individual personalities into one in a process known as fusion."

"Is that why he's great at covering his tracks at one crime, but leaves us loads of evidence at another?"

"I think you're on the right track Kevin. Let's say his dominant personality is the bad guy who's out killing people. He was in complete control when he started, but maybe his subordinate figured out what he was doing and is leaving his own marks at the scenes, hoping somebody will put it all together and stop him."

"So what are we supposed to do? Go undercover in leather bars to track *Puddle of Mudd* fans?"

"That would be a complete waste of time, but the Crawford case gave me an idea."

"*Let's hear it, Sugar.*"

"Mr. Clean has pretty much exhausted all the parks, so he's moved on to golf courses. In addition, I don't believe his choice in dumpsites was random this time. She was victim number seven and he left her at the seventh hole."

"You've got that look again, and I have a feeling it's something that we're probably not going to like."

"*Doll, it sounds like you think the guy is setting himself up.*"

"That's exactly what's happening. The sub personality is setting up the dominant one. But he can't stay focused long enough to turn himself in, so he's leaving clues."

"Okay, lemme get this straight, Jess," Mike said. "Mr. Clean has a multiple personality disorder. The bad one is setting up this guy Nick Yarboro for these murders, but his good personality is setting up the bad one?"

"Exactly, they're playing a very complicated game of good versus evil."

"I'm glad you're the one getting paid to figure this out."

When the men had an understanding of the killer, Jess went over her modified profile. She had revised it to include both suspected ids. She only hoped that when caught, the non-violent side was in control.

Mr. Clean, or the dominant side, primarily, would have an over-inflated view of himself and a compulsive need to control his environment. He would be an accomplished liar with exceptional verbal skills, skills that would enable him to anticipate and say with credibility, what people wanted to hear. He would display a near-limitless supply of energy, especially when covering his tracks or pursuing a vindictive vendetta against anyone daring to cross him. Influenced by an abusive childhood and inwardly devastated by separation or loss, he would hide behind a veil of moxie and lash out at perceived wrongs. As a result, Jess predicted this war between personalities resulting in a history of depression and a predisposition towards alcohol or drug abuse as a coping method.

Physically, they were looking for a dark-complected man of Mediterranean decent. Jess estimated him to be a physically fit, and from the handprint he'd left on Sandy Vandenberg's buttocks, he would be large, upwards of six feet tall, and muscular. He would take pride in his desirability, but he would not preen to the point of drawing unwanted attention to himself. Professionally, the unsub's acumen would steer him towards a career that allowed him to flaunt his vast intellect. However, his need for privacy would temper the instinct to show off and give him an air of eccentricity. He would be a self-employed, white-collar professional, likely in communications or a computer-related field.

If in a steady relationship, the perp would have assumed a role opposite his true nature. His partner would have no knowledge of his murderous habits, as he would be adept at hiding his activities. He may even maintain a separate residence, unknown to others, where he feels comfortable being himself. And like most serial criminals, he would drive a nondescript vehicle unlikely to draw attention.

Chapter 32

April 9...
9:30 AM

"Christ, not you two again!"

"Don't worry, Nick. You'll be glad to see us this time," Kevin replied with a smirk.

"Well, make it quick. I don't have a lot of time."

Jess flashed her badge at Nick's secretary before marching uninvited into the man's office. "Doctor Yarboro will be busy for some time. Please get a TA to take his classes today."

"Yes, Ma'am."

"What the hell is wrong with you people? You drag me from my bed at four in the morning and confiscate all of my things. Now you're coming in, taking over my office, and ordering around my secretary. I don't have the time or patience for this. I'm serious about filing harassment charges."

"Make time, Doctor Yarboro. You'll be glad you did."

"Obviously, you two think you own the place, so out with it. What do you want?"

"As far as the two of us are concerned you're no longer a suspect in the Mr. Clean case."

"Well halle-fucking-leujah! So now you can get the hell out of my office and leave me alone."

"You won't get rid of us that easily, Nick."

"Jesus Christ! What now?"

"You're being framed by the real Mr. Clean and we need your help to catch him."

"And if I say no?"

"That's fine too, because *officially* you're still the number one suspect. We'll just let the real killer dig you in deeper. Either way, we'll have someone behind bars and we'll be golden in all the press releases. And with your history, they won't even slam us once we catch the real killer."

"Oh." Nick Yarboro's cocky facade suddenly was replaced with concern. "How can I help?"

"This is what we can tell you. First, you and Mr. Clean know each other. He didn't select you randomly. He knew you'd fit our profile."

"Are you saying this guy knows me personally?"

"Probably not closely, but yes, he's familiar with you and your interests."

"How? What interests?"

"We believe he's an active member of an organization you belong to...KLAASP," Kevin said.

"How do you know about..."

"We're members too," Jess interrupted. "It's quite fascinating, really. I can see how that group and the lifestyle might be attractive to you."

"What are you, a shrink?"

"I'm a forensic psychologist, to be exact. What else would you like to know, Doctor?"

"Wait a minute. I knew I recognized you." He pointed at Kevin. "You had a beard, I think." Kevin nodded. "And you...red hair?" Jess nodded. "You've been coming for about six months, and we've attended some of the same parties."

"Good memory."

"I must say, Doctor. It is Doctor. Right?"

"Yes."

"You look pretty damn hot in fetish wear."

"Look, Pal," Kevin started.

"Did I strike a nerve, Detective? So that's *not* part of the act. You really *are* together."

"We're engaged if you must know, Doctor Yarboro."

"What a shame, a beautiful woman like you tying yourself to one man, but at least he's strong enough to give you what you need."

"And what exactly would that be, Nick?" Kevin asked.

"A secure environment to submit freely and the power control her when she becomes too spirited."

"Listen, I'm not interested in your analysis of my love life, Doctor Yarboro. I'm here to keep you out of jail and make sure the right guy is taken off the street so that you, your lady friends, and everybody else will remain safe," Jess butted in before their rivalry led to an argument.

"How do you propose we do this?"

"You're going to become *Reese's* mentor."

"Right, I remember now, Reese and CJ."

"Exactly, and it would be well worth all our whiles for you to remember that and forget what we do for a living. You'll perform in whatever capacity will be viewed by the others as normal."

"Is there more?"

"Nick, we need you to tell us about the other members, especially those who fit our revised profile."

"This lifestyle isn't one that's widely embraced by the mainstream public. We don't advertise our interests. I could lose my job if this got out."

"Which we already know and we'll try our best to keep certain details about your personal life from becoming public, but it's like this. If you don't cooperate and help us catch the right guy, you're gonna lose more than your job. I'm talking about your freedom and possibly your life."

"My life?"

"It's likely the prosecutor will seek the death penalty against the man doing this. Obviously, you don't realize it, but we have a solid case, and unfortunately for you, the evidence, circumstantial as it may be, points to you, even though *we* know you're not our man." Kevin added.

"Ouch, when do we start?"

"Now."

"Still not wasting any time, I see. Where do we begin?"

"First, I can't emphasize enough how important it is that we maintain confidentiality and believability while also maintaining anonymity. From here on you'll refer to us as Reese and CJ. We'll even stay in disguise from here on in case we're seen together."

"And I need to give you the specifics of what we're looking for," Jess added.

12:14 PM

"Let me get this straight. You think this Mr. Clean is a switch who may also have a multiple personality disorder?"

"Exactly, how many regular members in KLAASP who are known switches?"

"Only a few, but they don't strike me as insane."

"A dissociative disorder is not the same thing as insanity. It's more like having two or more people living in one body. Each is completely rational and won't necessarily advertise his existence apart from the host. In many cases, the separate personalities don't know each other and if they do, they don't know what the others do when they're in control. There have even been cases where separate personalities maintain entirely separate lives, which include differing careers, homes, and personal interests."

"I'm sorry," he said, looking at his watch. "I just realized I'm starving. You two want some lunch? My treat. We can go over to the faculty dining room and continue our conversation there."

Jess looked at Kevin for an answer. "Okay, sure," he said.

"Great! That was perfect, by the way."

"What was perfect?"

"The way you waited for your Master to decide for the two of you. You'll want to play up your relationship like that to keep it real."

"That's good to know."

4:36 PM

"I didn't realize it was so late. I want to apologize for the two of us taking up your entire day, Nick."

"Don't worry about it Reese, CJ. Whatever it takes to get *me* in the clear."

"That's the object."

"I know I was a rotten kid, but I think I've done well at getting beyond all that."

"I believe you and contrary to popular belief, we really do try our best to make sure we have the right people in jail."

"I'm starting to see that. Thanks."

4:45 PM

"Well, that was interesting."

"Yeah, he doesn't seem like such a bad guy now," Kevin said as he helped Jess into the truck. "Except for his constantly coming onto you."

"He does that to needle you."

"You think?" She nodded and smiled. "Well, it's working. It drives me apeshit."

April 14...

> *SubMarine: Good afternoon.*
> *SubDoer: hey, how are you? it seems like forever since we talked*
> *SubMarine: Yes, it does.*
> *SubMarine: It's almost time. Isn't it?*
> *SubDoer: time for what?*
> *SubMarine: Your wedding, it's less than two weeks away.*

"Kevin?"

"Yeah, Babe, what's up?"

"Did you tell Elaine when we were getting married?"

"I haven't even told her we were engaged. Why?"

"Take a look at this."

Kevin read the conversation. "Well, he obviously knows somehow. We need to figure out how *much* he knows."

> *SubDoer: yes, 10 days actually*
> *SubMarine: Big honeymoon plans?*
> *SubDoer: not until later, big project at work caused a delay*
> *SubMarine: That's too bad. Maybe you can take a long weekend.*
> *SubDoer: that's a possibility*
> *SubMarine: Well look, I have to run. When I saw you online, I wanted to wish you well in case I don't see you before the big day.*
> *SubDoer: we should be at the next meeting so i'll see you then if you're there*
> *SubMarine: Wonderful! We'll talk then.*
> *SubMarine is offline.*

"Maybe one of us slipped up or something."

"Kevin, I'm sure I didn't mention it. I even checked my chat logs to make sure I didn't inadvertently spill the beans."

"Should we be concerned?"

"I'm not sure. It just seems weird that he popped in for that when I wasn't even aware he knew."

"Do you think he saw it in the paper?"

"But he only knows us as CJ and Reese, and incognito at that. He doesn't know our last names or anything about us, so even if he saw that, there was nothing there to clue him in that it was us."

"Unless he studied the picture next to one of us in disguise. In any case, you've always known I don't like that guy much."

"Which is why my ears perked up when he mentioned the wedding."

"There's something about him. I wish I could put my finger on it. Just be careful with him."

"Promise."

April 16...

Bright sunlight streaming through the window woke Jess. Kevin had already gotten out up, but the house was silent. She glanced at the alarm clock and scrambled out of bed in sudden panic at seeing the time. 9:42. She quickly wandered through the too quiet house, trying to figure out why Kevin didn't wake her for work when she so obviously missed the alarm.

Kevin sprang through the back door with Sarge hot on his heels just as she walked into the den. "Hey Baby, you're up."

"Uh yeah, and I'm confused. Did I sleep through Friday or something?"

"Nope, it's still Friday. We're taking the day off."

"Why?"

"Because I'm getting ready to be without you for an entire week, so I'm keeping you all to myself for today. Come 'ere and gimme a kiss, Gorgeous."

He dropped Sarge's leash, pulled her into his arms, and skimmed her lips with a quick peck. Groaning and pulling her closer, he planted his full mouth across hers, and deepened the kiss. Jess wrapped her arms around his neck and ran her fingers through the sweat-soaked hair at the nape of his neck. Her touch combined with the cool air in the room generated gooseflesh on his arms. Fed up with no longer being the center of attention, Sarge barked and licked Jess' foot. She jumped and giggled, then broke away when the pup's tongue washed her bare toes.

"Oh! Stop Sarge."

"Damn dog," Kevin added, smiling. "Why'd we get him again?"

"Because he's part of our American dream and he was so sweet and lovable...and you couldn't resist those big brown eyes when you saw them...and you knew how much I'd love him."

"Yeah okay, that's enough, thanks for the reminder."

"So now that you have me for the entire day, what are you gonna do with me?"

"First, I'm gonna go take a shower and then I'm gonna take you back to bed...but not to sleep," he said with a husky laugh and a near-evil glimmer in his eyes. "I got two days to stock up for the next week and I'm gonna take full advantage of them...and you."

"Where'd you get two days? I thought we agreed on a *week* before the wedding."

"*We* didn't *agree* on anything. I'm just going along with it. Besides, if you were staying on your pills, you wouldn't be starting a new week until *Sunday*, so that gives me an extra day."

"You've got this figured out down to the last minute don't you?" Jess asked with a giggle.

"Yes, Ma'am."

"Want me to wash your back?"

"Ohh yeah, I love *your* sponge baths."

April 18...
8:27 AM

"Mmm."

"You like that, Baby?"

"So much...feels so good. Don't stop."

Kevin flicked the tip of his tongue over the stiff peak and suckled it like a hungry babe, continuing down her abdomen, showering every inch of skin with feathery kisses, and following her curves, teasing her sensitive skin with his mustache and newly re-grown goatee. Traveling along a predetermined path, he inched his way towards the straw-colored triangle of curls covering the small, sensitive region where

192

her thighs met. Just as he had done her nipples, he flicked the tip of his tongue in a side-to-side motion across the throbbing morsel until she screamed at the delightful agony his actions left in their wake. Just as she was about to skyrocket to the stars, her eyes flew open and she realized she was dreaming again. However, looking down, she found Kevin was lying between her legs and peering up at her, grinning lasciviously. He dipped his head again, resuming his task.

"It's Sunday. You can't..."

"I can't what?" He hummed and licked some more.

"We can't..."

"What would you say to a little head for the road...to last until Saturday?"

"We shouldn't...but oh God, that feels so good."

"Baby, you won't get pregnant if I don't penetrate." He stabbed his tongue into her throbbing heat, working his lips against her tiny knob, while he tongue-fucked her with a slow, methodical action, sending her to the edge without letting her fall over. "I know you want to."

"Mmm, oh fuckkk, only if you let me do you too."

"I was hoping you'd say that."

He rose from between her thighs, repositioned himself, and instructed her to crawl atop of him sixty-nine style. Jess held herself over his lips while wrapping her own lips around his thick rod. Hard as granite, his beautiful cock was ever ready to be sucked. Once she found a rhythm, she learned that she thoroughly enjoyed the position. Able not only to tantalize his stiffened member, she could play with his sack at the same time, while keeping herself just out of his reach whenever she wanted to postpone her finale. They kept on this way for nearly an hour until neither could endure the teasing a moment more.

Finally, Kevin pulled Jess down by her hips, and pushed two fingers into her yawning hole while he munched. It wasn't long before the familiar tingling she knew so well began deep in her belly, becoming stronger when she ground against his chin. Moaning through her own orgasm, she suckled him harder, feeling his balls draw up. Seconds later, he pulled away from her and groaned, his abdominal muscles stiffening under her as a stream of creamy man juice flooded her mouth. She massaged his bollocks and pulled all the harder on the thick member, swallowing every drop. When his spasms tapered to nil, Jess removed her lips from his spent phallus and rested her cheek against his belly.

"Are you sure you want to do this abstinence thing? There are all kinds of ways we can still play and not make a baby."

"Honey, I can't imagine a more spectacular lover and I will miss you, but I'm still staying at my dad's this week. We'll have the rest of our lives to catch up."

"This is gonna be the hardest damn thing I've ever done in my entire life. I think I'd rather go through basic training again, and that lasted for *six* weeks," he growled under his breath with a grimace.

"You're not supposed to have sex then either, are you?"

"Like a bunch of horny eighteen-year olds are gonna listen to that," he said, chuckling. "Especially with so many ready, willing, and able female troops, and weekend passes...but that's enough about that. I love you, Baby. Come up here and kiss me."

April 22...
7:30 PM

"I can't believe y'all brought me here tonight."

"Why the hell not? Every bride simply *must* have an official bachelorette party, and since you wouldn't let me hire a stripper...Can you think of a better place than the one where you and Kevin had your first date?" Niki asked.

"I guess not."

"Ahh Eric, my favorite barside hunk...Sweetie, what would it take for you to do a strip tease for our bachelorette?" Niki asked.

"Niki!" Jess exclaimed.

"What?"

"That depends on how big and mean the groom is," the waiter answered with a wink and a grin.

"He carries a gun, so I guess that idea is out."

"Yeah, I'd say so. But what can I do the rest of you ladies for?"

Eric made off with the drink order while Niki continued relaying her version of the couple's history to Kevin's sisters. "Did Kevin tell you how she teased him for weeks before she finally gave it up?"

"He'd better not be going around telling stuff like that," Jess huffed.

"Don't worry, Jess. He's been a perfect gentleman," Kate replied, easing her soon-to-be sister-in-law's fears.

"He'd better be. He knows better," Kinsey added. "He'd get his butt kicked."

"Jess was a total prick tease. Hell, she's lucky he didn't do more than kiss her those first couple times. Hmm, things to ponder. Well, did you at least tell them that you dreamed Kevin up out of nowhere?"

"Niki, you're really digging me into a hole."

"What?"

"She dreamed about him before they met."

"Oh really, Jess?" Kinsey asked. "Do I want to know the details?"

"Of course you do Kins," Niki said. "Total smut."

"Ohh, the best kind," Kate added with a laugh.

"Imagine what crossed her mind when she met him in person. I wasn't there but you can bet I heard about it as soon as it happened. By the way, Jess, we're singing tonight."

"No we're not."

"You watch."

"Oh Jess, you have to sing," Sam added. "Kate and Kinsey haven't heard you."

"But we've heard about you," Kinsey said.

"Mom *and* Kev have said many times what a great voice you have."

"Wonderful more pressure," Jess said with a nervous giggle. "Fine, what are we singing, Nik? Do I get any input this time?"

"Sure, I'm thinking something lively and fun, maybe *Lick It Up.*"

"You will *not* get me drunk enough to sing *that* in public," Jess laughed.

"Have it your way. You pick," she said and handed Jess the book. "I'm just glad I don't have to fight you this time."

8:30 PM

"I'll be damned. Look onstage, Bro."

"Hey Sarge, did you know they'd be here tonight?" Jerry asked.

"Nope, Niki and my sisters lit out of the office with Jess...said they were kidnapping her for a bachelorette party."

"Coolness."

"I figured Niki and Sam would drag her off to a strip show or something. Dean?" Kevin asked.

"They didn't mention it to me."

"Don't look at me," Mike added.

"Well, let's just sit back and listen for a few. Mike have you heard them sing?"

"I haven't, Kevin, but I hear they're quite talented."

"That's an understatement, Major," David said. "Lemme buy you guys a beer."

> *This time, this place, misused, mistakes. Too long, too late. Who was I to make you wait? Just one chance, just one breath, just in case there's just one left.*

"Hey, they really *are* good," Mark said.

...I loved you all along. And I miss you. Been far away for far too long. I keep dreaming you'll be with me and you'll never go. Stop breathing if I don't see you anymore.

"They're great, aren't they?" The bartender asked. "Haven't seen them in here in a while. The buzz is that one of them's getting married in a couple days."

On my knees, I'll ask, last chance for one last dance. 'Cause with you I'd withstand all of hell to hold your hand.

"Is that so?" Jerry asked with a grin.
"Yeah..." the bartender confirmed as the men stood and watched for a moment.

But you know, you know, you know...

"Hey, you're the guys they're always with," he said, recognizing Kevin and David. "Which one of you is the groom?"
"That would be me," Kevin volunteered.

...and I need to hear you say that I love you. I loved you all along. And I forgive you for being away for far too long.

"Hey Buddy, congratulations. How about another round on the house?"
"Sure man, 'preciate it."

So keep breathing 'cause I'm not leaving you anymore. Believe it. Hold onto me. Never let me go.

CRSCRSD

"Wow Jess, Ma and Kev weren't playing around. You should be in a band instead of a karaoke club."
"Aren't you sweet, Kate? It's a shame Terese couldn't come tonight."
"She didn't wanna leave grandma by herself in a strange house. This isn't her scene anyway. Damn, that's a loud bunch back at the bar," Sam said. "I can't hear myself think."
"Ladies, this round is courtesy of the group of gentlemen at the end of the bar," Eric offered.
Sam turned to look first. "Oh my God, look who's back there."
The women turned at once to see Kevin and David, and several of their fellow officers leading a round of rowdy whoops and whistles. Holding their beers aloft, the men toasted when they saw the women looking. Jess grinned and bit her bottom lip when she caught Kevin's eye.
"Do you wanna invite them to join us?" Kate asked.
"It would be a sorry excuse of a bachelorette party if we let a bunch of *fully dressed* guys join in," Sam teased.
"Speak for yourself. I'm sure we could find you gals some men that'll take it off," Niki said, laughing. "Me and Jess have two over there who would gladly strip for us. Only problem is *she* cut *her* man off this week."
"Jess, you didn't!" Kinsey shouted and laughed.
"That is hilarious," Kate proclaimed. "Poor Kevin, I almost feel sorry for him now. He's never been a good one for taking orders."
"But this *is* Jess' party, so let's let her decide," Niki added.
"I have an idea," Sam said excitedly before Jess could answer.
"What, Sam?"

"Dude, are you gonna go speak to her?"

"Hell no, I'm not getting blamed for crashing the bachelorette party," Kevin said.

"What if she gets pissed at you for ignoring her?"

"She won't," he returned with a chuckle.

"*Up next we have a big group of big guys. I'm told they're having a bachelor party. Congratulations, or maybe I should offer my condolences. They're doing an oldie tonight. How about a round of applause folks for Kevin, Dave, Dean, Mike, Brian, Mark, and Jerry?*"

"Aw man, this reeks of Samantha," Kevin said.

"And Niki," David added.

"Come on, Son. You're not gonna let them get the best of you," Dean goaded.

"Hell no, they're not. Come on, Sarge," Jerry said, pushing Kevin and Dave towards the stage.

We are young country. We are the pride, the sons and the daughters of American life. Our hair is not orange. We don't wear chains and spikes, but we know how to have fun come Saturday night.

"Take it, Sarge."

We know what's right. We know what's wrong. We know what we like to hear in a song.

Kevin elbowed David to take the next line.

We like some of the old stuff. We like some of the new, but we'll do our own choosing. We pick our own music if you don't mind thank you.

"Woohoo," Niki yelled. "Go guys." Mike and Dean shared the next verse.

We like ole Waylon. Hey, we know Van Halen.

"Who's Van Halen," Dean wondered aloud, drawing laughter from the audience as Mike continued with the next line, trying not to laugh.

We like ZZ Top. We like country and rock. Old Hank would be proud and Elvis would too 'cause we like our country mixed with some big city blues.

"Come on, boys."

We are young country. We are the pride, the sons and the daughters of American life. Old Hank would be proud and Elvis would too 'cause we like our country mixed with some rhythm and blues.

Kevin finished the final verse and swept the group into an exaggerated, goofy bow.

"*All right folks, let's hear it for our bachelor party. Good going guys. By the way, the ladies said you could join them after the song,*" the emcee announced.

Kevin went straight to Jess and swept her off her feet with a searing kiss, not caring who saw, then asked, "What was that all about?"

"I swear, I didn't have a thing to do with it," she said. Her lips pulsed from the crushing kiss.

"I know *you* didn't. That was all Niki and Sam," he said as the two women looked away to hide their guilty smiles.

"What are you talking about, little brother? That was fantastic!" Kinsey squealed.

"It's your own fault, Kev," Sam added.

"Enlighten me," he replied with a grin. "Why's it my fault?"

"Simple...we were here first," she giggled.

"This is a public place."

"You two argue it out. I need to powder my nose," Jess said with a grin.

"I gotta powder my nose too," Kevin stated and followed her.

He caught up with her around the corner from the restrooms. Grabbing her by the elbow, he spun her around and crushed her between the wall and his hard body, and then leaned over, caught her earlobe between his teeth. Passersby were unable to see, but still knew what was going on. His hot breath brought forth chills all over her as he moved down her neck and stopped at her lips where their tongues fought a duel. Finally, he sucked her lips in another bruising kiss.

"Do you have any idea what this week is doing to me?" He asked in a raspy voice when he pulled back.

"God yes, whose idea was this abstinence thing, anyway?"

"Um, yours, my Dear."

"I may have been suffering from a momentary lapse of reason. Why didn't you stop me?"

"I tried! I haven't tucked in my shirt all week...been using it to hide wood for days." Jess suppressed a smile. "You think that's funny, eh?"

"No, of course not, I'm suffering this out the same as you, big boy."

"Suffering...yeah, I'd say that's an adequate description. I thought I was done with wet dreams." She apologized, this time unable to rein a case of giggles. "You go ahead and laugh, but Saturday night, I'm gonna tear this ass up," he said, reaching behind to cup her cheeks and pull her body against his.

"Mmm, growl," she purred. "Let's go back. Our kidnappers will start to wonder if we've escaped."

"Let 'em. I say we make a break for it and get the hell outta here for a while, just the two of us."

"No can do, I'm not sure you'll be able to restrain yourself."

"That's the point. What about a quickie? They don't count, do they?"

"You wish."

"Blowjob? You're *so* good at 'em."

"No!" Jess laughed harder at his pleas.

"I'm trying really hard here," he growled.

"Key word being hard. Just think about what you have to look forward to. No pain, no gain."

"God, don't remind me about the pain."

"You could um, take care of that yourself," Jess said, making masturbatory gestures with her hand.

"That's not *even* the same thing..." A wicked gleam came into his eyes. "...unless it's *your* hand."

"You're good. Keep trying."

"You're really gonna stick to this. Aren't you?"

"Yes, amante il mio, but just think. You've already survived four whole days."

"Four days too many," he grumbled.

"Gosh, whatever will you do when we have those five children you wanted? There's that six-week post-partum thing...each. And you're having major issues with just six *days.*"

"Just don't schedule any dental appointments during those six weeks..." he growled with a low laugh and kissed her again.

April 23...
7:00 PM

"Kevin, you're not gonna pass out tomorrow, are you?"

"Who me? No way, not from the ceremony, anyway."

"What?"

"Think about it, Niki. He's liable to get a head rush at any moment."

"Oh that," she said with a laugh while aiming a cursory glance at Kevin's groin.

"We have to go, Jess. It's already after seven."

"The time got away from me."

"I can't believe you two are cutting out early on the rehearsal dinner for this damn meeting," Niki huffed. "You're getting married tomorrow, for God's sake."

"Nik, we don't have a choice. It's crucial to this case."

"Crucial smucial!"

"We'll see you tomorrow," Jess said as she and Kevin headed to the car.

"You realize I've been cut off for so long that I'm liable to go postal if another man, especially Nick, if he's there, so much as looks at you."

"Oh Lord, don't do that."

"I'm just warning you. A horny guy is dangerous," he said, flashing her a toothy grin.

"Hmm, maybe I should rethink this abstinence thing and um, take care of you before we leave."

"Oh no, I've been cut off this long. I can hang another day," he teased.

"Cut off is kinda harsh, but suit yourself."

"Nobody would ever believe I just did that. Jesus, *I* can't believe I just did that."

"Did what?"

"Turned down a chance to get freaky with you."

8:00 PM

"Good evening, CJ."

"Hey, Armand. How are you?"

"Very good, thanks. Tomorrow's the big day."

"Yes, it is."

"Good luck."

"Thanks."

"Come on Baby, there's Nick," Kevin said, pulling Jess away. "Have I mentioned that I really do not like that guy?"

"Not today," she said, grinning at him.

"Nick, how goes it?" Kevin asked, pulling Jess even closer while reaching to shake Nick Yarboro's hand.

"Pretty good, Reese. CJ, how are you this evening?"

"Lovely."

"Yes, you are." Kevin scowled at him. "Relax Reese, she's too tough for me," Nick said as he studied Jess, then scanned the crowd. "But I'm not the one you need to worry about. CJ has some fans in here."

"Who?"

"Meryl and Natalie, for sure."

"I told you she was hot for you, Babe," Kevin said with a grin as Jess shot him a look of disgust.

"And there's Elaine's slave, I forget his name."

"Armand," Jess supplied.

"Yeah, we know," Kevin said. "I don't like that guy."

"Put him on your list. He's a switch. He's been with her now for two or three years now, I think."

"Really? That's very interesting."

"The guy's a fruitcake, if you ask me."

"Finally, someone agrees with me. Who else in here should we be looking into?" Kevin asked.

"They're starting up. Let's talk after the lecture when we have more privacy."

9:00 PM

"Good evening, Reese. Fetch me a drink, my pet."

Armand averted his gaze, but not before Jess noticed the defiant flash in his eyes. She made a mental note to mention that to Kevin. She stayed a step behind her fiancé, watching as he and Nick talked with Elaine. She tried to keep an eye on Armand, as well, but lost him in the crowded room.

"How are you, Elaine?"

"Marvelous. Nick, you're doing well, I presume?"

"Quite."

"I see you've met some of our newer members."

"Yes, I met Reese and CJ a short while back."

"Nick has agreed to be my mentor."

"Nick's quite popular and an extraordinary teacher. I'm sure you will learn a great deal from him. Armand mentioned your big event. Congratulations, on your upcoming marriage."

"Thank you, Elaine."

"Thank you, my pet," Elaine said when Armand returned. "Very good seeing the three of you again, but we must be going."

"Have a nice evening." Jess, Kevin, and Nick watched Elaine and Armand exit the building. "That woman is either extremely lenient or blind."

"Why do you say that, Nick?"

"Because the look in his eyes when she told him to *fetch* her *a drink* wasn't very nice," Jess interjected.

"Very observant, CJ."

"I try not to miss much."

"Well, I missed the hell out of it."

"He has a disobedient side that I wouldn't put up with, especially from a mere slave."

"Why do you say it like that?"

"There's a huge difference between a collared sub and a slave. Let's go out into the main room where we can talk."

"Do you want some coffee?" Kevin asked as they exited the conference room.

"Sure, thanks."

Jess retrieved a notepad and sat down with Nick while Kevin brought drinks to the table. "A Mountain Dew for you, Milady."

"Thank you. Talk to us, Nick."

A lengthy discussion with Nick Yarboro gave them loads of information. Kevin and Jess learned about seven switches in the group, only three of whom were male, and that narrowed the potential suspect pool considerably, so they happily put the investigation on hold to concentrate on their wedding. On the ride back to Dean's house, Kevin decided to give his powers of persuasion one last test by trying to convince Jess to drop her 'no more premarital sex' clause. Stubborn as ever, she rebuffed his advances, but her playful manner held his manhood intact.

Dean invited his soon-to-be son-in-law to stay for a nightcap, but Niki wouldn't hear of it, especially after Kevin jokingly threatened to throw Jess over his shoulder and take her back home with him. She all but pushed him out the door, but not before he insisted on giving his bride a small token of his love. Jess carefully opened the hinged lid of the small jewel case. Lying on a bed of soft velvet was a row of ten hairpins. At the end of each pin, a single pearl gleamed under a sparkling diamond.

"Oh Kevin, they're beautiful."

"I don't know how you plan to wear your hair, but I thought you might like 'em."

"I'm sure Niki will find a way to use these tomorrow."

"Definitely," Niki said as she looked over her friend's shoulder. "Now, go home!" She ordered.

"Can't I get a good night kiss?"

"Make it snappy, Romeo."

Jess' pulse pounded and her heart did flip-flops when Kevin looked into her green eyes. His gaze was as tangible as a lover's caress as it traveled over her face in a slow, bold assessment. Though she knew he was going to kiss her, the anticipation was nearly unbearable. He seemed to move in slow motion. After what seemed an eternity, he leaned down, cupped her chin and brushed his lips against hers before covering them hungrily. His lips were demanding, but surprisingly gentle, as he nibbled the fullness of her bottom lip.

"Okay, break it up. This is *not* a *Big Red* commercial."

Reluctantly, they separated. Jess' lips were left aching in the aftermath of Kevin's fiery possession. Her body was left with the burning need for his touch, but with a final 'I love you,' he placed another gentle kiss upon her lips and walked out the door.

Chapter 33

April 24...
8:02 AM

"Hey, it's me again," Jess said to the headstone. "Well, this is it. Today's my big day and I wanted to talk to you one last time before I become a married woman. I brought you some flowers too." She set the zinnias down before the marker. "I know you'll be watching from up there, but I still wish you could be here. I miss you and I love you both. I'll visit again real soon." Jess rose from her knees and turned to go back to Dean's Tahoe, but ran headlong into Kevin instead. He held a large bouquet of mixed flowers in the crook of his left arm. "Hey! What are you doing here?"

"Apparently, the same thing as you, but I'll turn around and pretend I didn't see you."

"I won't tell if you won't." Jess wrapped her arms around his neck and kissed him. "Last chance to back out."

"Hell no, Woman! I'll see *you* at the church," he retorted with a wide grin.

5:48 PM

"God Kev, stop moving, or I swear I'm gonna stick you out of spite," Sam said as she pinned the boutonnière to Kevin's lapel. "You're as nervous as a long-tailed cat in a room full of rocking chairs."

"Ya think?" He retorted.

"And I thought Christmas was bad."

"It ain't exactly every day a guy gets married, ya know. I don't see how people do this more than once," he added, laughing.

"There, all done. You look great. Shame you shaved off the goatee. It was hot."

"Thanks, you clean up pretty good yourself for a tomboy," he said, giving her a brotherly shove. "Hey..."

"Yeah?"

"Thanks for being my best woman."

"Anytime, Bro. Isn't it about time?"

Kevin looked at his watch and expelled a heavy sigh. "Ten more minutes."

"Ready for this?"

"Yeah." He took a long drag on his cigarette.

"No cold feet?"

"Hell no, I've been ready. I tried to talk her into eloping months ago."

"Well, I'm glad she didn't listen. You will be too when you see her. Now put that thing out and let's go back inside while I still have time to fumigate you," she said, wrinkling her nose.

"Gimme a break. I'm down to half a pack a day."

5:56 PM

"How do I look?" Jess asked as she smoothed an imaginary wrinkle from the front of her dress.

"You look gorgeous, Jess."

The dress was magnificent. Graceful in design, thin straps held it in place while it hugged every curve, from bust to knees, before flaring into a wide mermaid-style train. Devoid of elaborate ornamentation, the ivory silk had only minimal beading along the bust line and train. In keeping with the unadorned style of her dress, Jess had foregone a veil, wearing only her mother's pearl necklace and earrings for adornment.

"Are you sure I look okay? How's my face?"

"Flawless, now quit messing with it."

"What about my hair?"

"Not a single strand out of place." Jess reached back and touched one of the diamond and pearl-studded hairpins Kevin gave her the previous evening. Niki had arranged Jess' hair in long curls that cascaded down her back, using the pins to hold side locks back from her face. "Stop it. You're gonna screw up my hard work. Come in," Niki called at the knock on the door.

"Wow! Jess, you look..."

"Everybody decent?" Dean called, cutting Kinsey off as he walked in behind her and Kate.

"Sure, come on in."

"My goodness, look at my little girl."

"How'd I do, Dean? Isn't she gorgeous?"

"Breathtaking, Niki, you did a wonderful job. Are you ready?"

Jess took a deep breath. "As ready as I'm going to get." She hooked her arm through his and turned towards the door.

"Wait, you'll need this," Niki said, handing her a bouquet of elegant, white calla lilies and variegated ivy tied with an ivory, satin ribbon. The music changed as the bridal party took their places in the lineup. "There's our cue. Come on, y'all. Au revoir, see ya at the altar."

From the alcove, Dean and Jess watched the bridal party proceed to the front of the chapel. Everyone stood and turned towards them when the bridal hymn began. Dean smiled and hugged his daughter before stepping through the inner doorway that led to the sanctuary. Jess looked up at him, then turned and began the long promenade to the altar, her eyes brimming with unshed tears of joy. Friends and relatives from either side...co-workers, city officials, and other contacts from across the state...were gathered amid a sea of blue-uniformed Burlington city police officers.

Glancing at the front row, she felt bittersweet longing for those not present to celebrate their jubilant union...her mother and father, and though she never knew them, Kevin's father and grandfather. Terese and Kevin's grandmother, Eleanor Slater, sat on one side of the chapel, while the three people who had served as Jess' surrogate family since childhood...Maggie, George, and Betty...sat on the other.

Niki, her best friend and maid of honor, stood straight and tall in a floor-length gown of violet satin. Samantha, serving as best woman, stood just behind Kevin in a gown of the same shade that differed only slightly in style. Kate, Kinsey, and their daughters, Brittany and Kaitlyn, served as attendants and waited for them with the groomsmen behind Niki and Samantha. After what seemed an eternity, Dean and Jess arrived at the altar steps where he hugged her, then moved aside allowing Kevin to proceed with his bride to the end of the nuptial path.

"Wow," Kevin mouthed.

His love radiated from his face as he smiled and raked her body with a salacious, but adoring, gaze. She took his arm and continued the journey with him up the steps to the altar where Reverend Joe Penley waited with a bright smile. Niki stepped forward and took Jess' bouquet when she turned towards Kevin, who grasped her hands as the minister began to speak.

"Dear friends, we are gathered here today before God to celebrate the holy union of this man and this woman, which is entrusted to be honorable among all men, because marriage is one of his most sacred wishes. Marriage is not to be entered into rashly, but reverently, advisedly and solemnly. It is the union of husband and wife in heart, body, and mind. Intended for their mutual joy in times of prosperity as well as in times adversity, it is a means through which a stable and loving environment may be fell upon."

"Through marriage, they pledge together to face their disappointments, embrace their dreams, realize their hopes, and accept each other's failures. Through mutual understanding, openness, and sensitivity to each other, Kevin and Jess will promise one another to aspire to these ideals throughout their lives. This occasion marks the celebration of love and dedication with which they begin their life together. Through me, God joins you together in one of the holiest of bonds." He looked from the couple to the congregation. "Who gives this woman in marriage to this man?"

Dean stepped forward, "I do."

"Today is a new beginning and a continuation of their growth as individuals. With mutual care, respect, responsibility and knowledge comes the affirmation of each one's own life happiness, growth and freedom. With respect for individual boundaries comes the freedom to love unconditionally. With care and responsibility towards self and one another comes the potential for full and happy lives."

"By gathering together all the wishes of happiness and fondest hopes from all present here, we assure Kevin and Jess that our hearts are in tune with theirs. These moments are so meaningful to all of us, for what greater thing is there for two human souls, than to feel that they are joined together, to strengthen each other in all labor, to minister to each other in all sorrow, to share with each other in all gladness..."

Jess glanced at Kevin. He was standing straight and tall, concentrating on every word Reverend Penley uttered.

"...stands for love, loyalty, honesty and trust, but most of all for friendship. Before they knew love, they were friends, and it was from this seed of friendship that their destiny bloomed. We mustn't think that we can change the path of fate, for fate, if it finds us worthy, shall direct us."

"Marriage is more than simply a legal contract. It is a spiritual commitment, an act of faith, as well as a physical union between two people. It is a moral commitment that requires daily attention. It is the best and most important relationship that can exist. Marriage is a life long consecration of the ideal of loving kindness, backed by the will to make it last..."

Jess grew more impatient with each passing second as Reverend Penley's voice seemed to drone on and on.

"...in Genesis, *therefore shall a man leave his father and mother and cleave unto his wife*, and in Proverbs, *whoso findeth a wife findeth a good thing.* Love each other as you love yourselves for as we read in Ephesians, *no one ever hates his own body, but nourishes and tenderly cares for it, just as Christ does the church.* Kevin and Jess have some special words they wish to share with each other today. Kevin?"

Jess looked up at Kevin and smiled. Amber eyes twinkled as he grinned down at her and held her hands.

"What have I to give you, Jess? The promise to take you as my only love from this day forward, the promise to be the shoulder you lean on, the rock on which you rest, your companion for life. Time will pass. Fortune will smile upon us. Trials may fall on us. But no matter what lies ahead, I vow here that your love will be my only love. Baby, som jeg elsker De. Jeg lever ikke uten De mer enn jeg lever uten pust. De betyr alt til meg."

Jess was unsure of what he said, but judging from his mother and sisters' sudden weeping, she knew it must have been a Norwegian endearment.

"You stole my heart the day we met and as freely as God has given me life, I join myself to you for the rest of our lives. I take you as my wife and will give myself to no other."

"Jess?"

"Today Kevin, our lives become one. I join you not merely as your wife, but as your friend, your lover, and your confidant. I promise to support you, to listen when you speak, to console you in times of sorrow, to laugh when you laugh. Wherever you go, I will follow. Whatever hardships you face, we'll face together. You're my destiny and together we'll walk the path set before us. With a free and unconstrained soul, I give you all that I am and all that I am to become. And hereto, I pledge my faithfulness only unto you."

CB∞CB∞

"Excuse me, Sir. May I help you?"

"Oh, no Ma'am, I arrived a bit late and didn't want to disturb the ceremony. I'll just watch from here."

"Bride or groom?"

"Beg your pardon?"

"Are you a friend of the bride or groom?"

"Oh yes, I've known them both equally as long. We belong to the same club."

"They make such a lovely couple."

"CJ is simply ravishing."

"CJ?"

"I mean Jess. Everyone calls her CJ."

಍ఞಂ಍ఞ

"Kevin, do you, here in the presence of these witnesses, declare your commitment to Jess and choose her as the one with whom you wish to spend the rest of your earthly life? Do you pledge to endure all of the difficulties which life may offer even as you look forward to sharing the joys to be experienced together?"

"I do."

"Jess, do you, here in the presence of these witnesses, declare your commitment to Kevin and choose him as the one with whom you wish to spend the rest of your earthly life? Do you pledge to endure all of the difficulties which life may offer even as you look forward to sharing the joys to be experienced together?"

"I do."

"What tokens of your commitment do you offer?" Niki and Samantha stepped forward with the rings. "Would you place the rings in my hand?" Reverend Penley held the rings up high for all to see. "May these rings be blessed as the symbol of this affectionate unity. Let us pray. Oh Father, these two lives are now joined in one unbroken circle. Wherever they go, may they always return to one another. May they find in each other the love for which all men and women yearn. May they grow in understanding and in compassion. May the home, which they establish together, be such a place that many will find there a friend, and may these rings on their fingers symbolize the touch of the spirit of love in their hearts. In the name of the Father, the Son, and the Holy Spirit, we pray. Amen."

He turned to Kevin, "Kevin, in placing this ring on Jess' finger you are now consecrated as man and wife from this day forward. What vow have you for her?"

"Take this ring and with it my promise of faith, patience, and love for the rest of my life. I have chosen you to be my wife to have and to hold, from this day forward. For better, for worse, for richer, for poorer, in sickness and in health, to have and to cherish, as long as we both shall live."

Reverend Penley had Jess recite a similar vow before closing the ceremony.

"Jesus said from the beginning of creation, God made them male and female. For this reason, a man shall leave his father and mother and be joined to his wife, and the two shall become one. So they are no longer two, but one flesh. Therefore, what God hath joined together, let no one separate. And so by the power vested in me by almighty God and the state of North Carolina, I now pronounce you man and wife. Kevin, you may kiss your bride."

Kevin folded Jess in his arms and pulled her close. Her face became hot when he drove his tongue between her teeth and sucked her bottom lip in a far-from-chaste kiss, leaving her heart pounding when he pulled away and winked at her.

"I love you, Baby."

"Oh Kevin, I love you too."

The minister continued, "Now you will feel no pain, for each of you will be shelter to the other. Now you will feel no cold, for each of you will be warmth to the other. Now there is no loneliness, for you for each of you will be companion to the other. Now you are two persons, but there is one life before you. Go now to your dwelling place to enter into the days of your togetherness. And may your days be good and long upon this earth. Ladies and gentlemen, may I present to you, Mr. and Mrs. Kevin Slater."

಍ఞಂ಍ఞ

"I'm going to just slip out so I won't disturb the recessional. It was a lovely ceremony and a pleasure meeting you."

"And you too...Mr.?"

"Lavache."
"Have a good day, Mr. Lavache."

☙❧☙❧

"This is unusual. You guys don't usually do police escorts for weddings, do you?" Jess asked.

"It ain't every day the Chief's daughter gets married either," Kevin replied with a chuckle. "Come over here, Mrs. Slater."

"Mrs. Slater, I love the sound of that."

"It does have a nice ring to it. Come here, Baby. I got a present for you."

Kevin pulled his wife onto his lap, his granite cock straining against the fabric of his breeches, as he drove his tongue between her lips, tracing the ridge of her teeth. He pulled her closer, crushing her breasts against his massive chest, and brushed her long curls aside to caress her bare back, then groaned and pulled away.

"God, I've missed you."

"You've seen me every day."

"Seeing you and making love to you are two entirely different things. Sarge is okay company, but he's just a dog."

"You've had your Ma and sisters there fussing over you for days."

"Let's not even go there. You have no idea what it's been like for me to have to take you to Dean's every night this week, and then go home and sleep without you."

"Yes, I do. Every night it's taken me hours to fall asleep without your arms around me."

"Damn! I knew I shoulda figured out a way around those damn rose bushes," he replied with a chuckle as they recalled their first night together. His erection pushed harder against her bottom. "You feel that? I've been like this all week."

"Calm down, Tiger. We still have a reception to get through and a cake to cut."

Kevin groaned in disappointment. "Maybe we can get the driver to take a long detour around town. The week's over and we're married now, so how about a quickie, Mrs. Slater?"

Jess put a finger to her lips and gave him a thoughtful expression. "Hmmm, tell you what, there's no way I'll get out of and back into this dress in time for a quickie, but..." She trailed off as she pushed the intercom button to buzz the driver. "Hey, Vincent?"

"Yes, Madam."

"Lose the escort and take your time getting to Paulo's, and when we get there, stand outside and don't open the door until we signal you."

"Yes, Madam."

"Thanks. I hope he doesn't hit any potholes."

Jess pulled her dress above her knees so she could kneel before her new husband, then unzipped his black trousers. Pulling his shorts down just enough for his massive cock to spring free, she took him fully into her mouth and bobbed up and down, sucking fiercely, twirling her tongue around the purplish head. Drawing his length further down her throat, she hummed and looked up at him through a fringe of bangs. His eyes glowed with both love and lust as he put his hand to the back of her head, guiding her actions.

Jess took only vague notice when Vincent exited the limo after coming to a stop in front of Paulo's, and continued giving lip service to her handsome, but very aroused, husband. After a week of abstinence, they both knew he wouldn't last long, so Jess didn't try to prolong his orgasm as she normally would. Instead, she suckled harder and faster when his scrotum tightened. He threw his head back and groaned as he came, ejecting a forceful stream of warm custard. So powerful was his climax that his hips rose from the seat. He stroked Jess' hair as she lapped a stray drop of his creamy juice.

"Good God, Woman, we gotta take limo rides more often." Jess held her hand out and he pulled her to a seated position next to him, then helped rearrange her dress.

"Ya think?"

"Nah, thinking gets me in trouble. Ready?"

205

"Wait! How do I look?"

"Ravishing, I can hardly wait for the ride home." She licked her lips, gnawing on the bottom one. "You know I can't resist an invitation like that."

He pulled her against him and kissed her, delving into the dark cavern of her mouth with his tongue, tasting the residual saltiness left behind, while tugging at the door handle, which he left slightly ajar. On cue, Vincent opened the door fully and stepped aside for Kevin to exit the car. He reached inside and took Jess' hand to help her out, and they swept through the restaurant doors being held open for them.

8:30 PM

The room became quiet at the sound of a fork tapping on a champagne flute as all eyes became fixed on Samantha.

"Good evening, everyone. It means so much for me to be here tonight to celebrate my brother's wedding. On one hand, I didn't think he'd ever take the plunge, and yet, it's hard to believe it happened so quickly. As you know, the first toast is supposed to be reserved for the best man, but since Kevin sidestepped tradition, it's fallen into my lap, so here goes...I'm sure you're all wondering why Kevin picked *me* to stand up for him rather than one of the boys. I asked myself that same question. Then it dawned on me. He's *finally* realized that women really *are* the superior sex. Took you long enough, Kev." Laughter filled the room. "No seriously..."

"Not to mention the only one who could put up with such a brat..." Kevin interrupted.

"As I was saying, Kevin's not just my brother. He's been my best friend for as long as I can remember, and I'm truly honored to be here tonight, but let's get straight to the dirt...you know the embarrassing secrets, since I know that's what you all *really* came here for."

"Here, here!" David shouted.

"Looking at him tonight in all his finery, the words that immediately come to mind are respectable, honorable, and reliable. But ladies and gentlemen, I'm here to tell you that impressions can be deceptive. Kevin doesn't have a few skeletons in his closet. He has a whole graveyard," she said, shooting a smirk at her brother.

"Oh boy, here we go," Kevin mumbled. "Time for the roast."

"The fact is, folks, this man who proposes to be the father of Jess' children, has a past...a past full of wine, women, and song...and *not* always in that order." Kevin glared at her in silent castigation. "My brother and I have shared some amazing life experiences together though, especially when we were roommates. The number of times I had to drive him home blind drunk..." She trailed off.

"Sam, I think you have that backwards."

"This is my story and I'm sticking to it. You'll get your chance later," she proclaimed over the guests' laughter. "Anyway, normally it would be my duty to point out that from this day on, Bro, your sex life will never be the same. But since you had to go the non-traditional route and have a best *woman*, I'm warning your new bride instead. You see, I know things. Jess, if he pulls out the handcuffs and there's no suspect nearby, take off, because from what I hear, he turns into a real animal."

"Just what did you tell her and Niki?" He whispered.

"Nothing." Jess felt her face go red when Kevin grinned at her. "Well not about *that*!"

"Speaking of ex-girlfriends, being best woman *and* his sister, I suppose it's my responsibility to ride the groom about some of them. I've known quite a few of them, and I can personally say that a hundred forty-six is, indeed, your lucky number. Good one, Bro."

"A hundred and forty-six? Where'd you come up with that one?"

"Well let's see, there was Cynthia and Nicole, Lisa, Danielle...Cheyenne, Allison...need I go on?"

"I don't think that's necessary," Kevin said in a wry tone while everyone laughed.

"In all seriousness though, you always know when the right person comes along. Personally, I knew Jess was the one for Kevin when I spent Thanksgiving with them. Sure, I had talked to her on the phone a few times, but I was still undecided about her until I actually met her. Then, I understood immediately why Kev loved her so much. She's a great lady and I'm glad she said yes."

"Aww..." Jess fought back tears.

"Of course, that left me wondering about her sanity, hanging out with *him* and all. But before things get too weepy, I just want to thank the bride and groom for allowing me the pleasure of being your best *wo*man, your confidant, and your friend. It's been a real honor watching your love and devotion grow with each passing day. I only hope to find the same someday. And if I can pass on any advice, it's simply this."

She raised her glass in one hand, sniffled, and pretended to wipe at a tear with the other. "Come on. What is it?" Someone called from the back of the room.

"Make sure you have someone handy to check on the goose in case you get distracted."

"Oh my God, no she didn't," Jess gasped quietly.

"Sam!" Kevin said sharply, drawing ribald laughter from the crowd.

"On behalf of everyone here tonight, let me be the first to say, here's to many happy and healthy years together. And when you leave here tonight to begin your journey together in life, I have just three final words for you both."

"Oh God, here she goes again," as more dread crept into his voice.

"I love you."

"Aww..."

"Here, here!" Niki called and held up her glass. "Great speech, Sam," she added as the wait staff began setting dinner plates before the guests.

Later...

Their song, *You Shouldn't Kiss Me Like This*, boomed from the speakers as Kevin pulled Jess close and leaned down to whisper in her ear, "I love you, Baby."

At the end of their first dance as husband and wife, the guests applauded and many more couples joined them for a few more before the couple was pulled from the dance floor. The time had come to unveil the wedding cake. They talked quietly while they waited for Stefano.

"Samantha has a fan."

"Who?" Kevin asked.

Jess pointed to the dance floor. "They've been inseparable most of the evening."

"Who is that guy?"

"His name is Josh Kelly."

"The name rings a bell, but I can't place him."

"Remember the Warren case?" He nodded. "He was the prosecutor."

"Is he a good guy?"

"She could certainly do a lot worse. He's quite a gentleman, very charming and intelligent."

"Did you and he ever..."

"He asked me out right as the trial was starting, but I turned him down." She knew his next question before he uttered the first word. "I was already hung up on you."

"Really?"

"It was about the time you first invaded my dreams," she answered. "By then, I was ruined for anyone else. Nobody could measure up to the man in my fantasies," she added, prompting her sexy, new husband to flash her a wide, toothy grin just as the Stefano rolled out his magnificent creation.

"Man, look at that!" Kevin exclaimed.

The towering confection consisted of five square layer-cakes that had been hollowed out and filled with their favorite dessert, Paulo's delicious tiramisu. Tiers of fresh ladyfingers were interspersed between layers of mascarpone cream and topped with fresh, edible flowers. The uppermost, and the one they were supposed to save for their first anniversary, was a mocha infused cheesecake crowned with porcelain bride and groom figurines hand painted to resemble the couple.

"Stefano, it's too beautiful to eat."

"And let it go to waste? Nonsense," Dean scoffed. "You two get up there and cut it. I'm ready for a taste."

10:25 PM

The pair made one last round to thank their guests, finally arriving at Carl, who was talking with Dean. "Hey Doll, before you go run off, Dean and me have a little wedding present for the two of yous," he said.

"I'm almost scared of that, Carl."

"Oh, come on Sugar, you'll love it. We hooked you up with a couple days off at a nice, little place down in Beaufort, the Jackson House Inn."

"You did?"

"Yeah." He shook Kevin's hand and gave him an envelope.

"Thank you." Surprised, Jess hugged both men at the same time.

"Yeah thanks, that was very thoughtful of you both," Kevin added.

"You're quite welcome, Son," Dean replied.

"Hey, wait a minute. What's the catch? This doesn't mean that you're reneging on that vacation deal, does it?" Jess asked.

"Absolutely not, Sugar. The Missus..." He looked around the room. "She's around here somewhere. Anyway, the Missus laid a guilt trip on me for keeping you so busy you couldn't take any time off, and now you're getting married and can't go on a real honeymoon because of this case."

"She's so sweet. I'll have to thank her when I see her."

"Besides, if anything goes down while you're gone, we know how to find you. We'll just drag your butts right back home," he teased.

"Carl, you'd better hope that nothing happens because as much as I like you, I can just about guarantee you that you won't get anything but voicemail once we leave this building, so you may just regret that," she said, laughing.

"Good, that's what we wanted to hear," Dean piped in. "Don't concern yourselves with this case. It'll still be here when you get back. Oh, and before you go, the cleaning lady at the church mentioned a guest who stood at the back and watched. He left just before the ceremony ended."

"Who was it?"

"Don't know. The name was...Lavahshay."

"Who is that?" Jess asked Kevin.

"I haven't a clue."

"What did he look like?"

"She said he was about yay-high, dark hair and eyes, a good-looking guy."

"Hmm, I wonder who he was."

"Well, don't worry about it. We'll figure it out. Now go on. Get out of here."

"You don't have to tell us twice," Jess said, grabbing Kevin's hand. "You ready?"

"Baby, I've been ready," he said, practically dragging her to the door.

The guests lined up on either side of the couple and peppered them with birdseed as they left the restaurant. Kevin helped his wife into the limo when Vincent opened the door. Crawling onto his lap, she wrapped her arms around his neck when he sat down. He twisted his hands through her hair and pulled her close, and then his full lips covered hers in a searing kiss, his mustache tickling her nose as he explored her mouth with his tongue. The ride was a short one, so within minutes, they were home and surprised to find a uniformed officer standing guard outside.

"Larry, what are you doing here?" Kevin asked.

"Chief Johansen thought it would be a good idea to have someone looking out 'cause of you two being so high-profile right now. Oh and Rafferty's cute redhead dropped off a bunch of wedding gifts and got your fireplace going so it'd be all cozy when you came home. Then she took off to the Chief's house with your dog."

"Great, thanks Larry, you can take off now."

"Anytime Sarge, and congratulations. One more thing, some guy left this for you." He handed Kevin a wrapped box.

"Did you get a name?"

"Lava-something."

"Lavache?"

"That's it."

"What'd he look like?"

"Oh 'bout my height, black hair and dark eyes, tan, and nice suit. Said he couldn't make it to the reception but wanted to make sure you got this."

"Ethnic?"

"Not Latino, maybe Italian or something like that."

"Okay, thanks again."

"No problem, Sarge. See ya." They watched him drive away while Kevin fished his keys from his pocket.

"That's really odd," Kevin said as he shook the box. "It's not ticking, but I think we'll leave it out here for now, just in case."

He put the package down on the step, turned the knob and swept Jess up into his arms, then kicked the door open and leaned down to kiss his wife again as he carried her over the threshold. The tears of joy she'd held back for so long finally streamed from her eyes when he pulled back and smiled.

"Welcome home, Mrs. Slater. Now, come with me. I've waited a week to make love to you, and now that I've got you all to myself, I'm not waiting another minute."

He kissed her as he guided her towards the bedroom. Shadows danced as gilded light from a number of candles flickered throughout the house. Several steps later, Jess' legs brushed the edge of the bed. She stopped short of sitting down and reversed their positions, gently pushing him down to sitting, and turned her back on him.

"Unzip me."

"Gladly," he said in a husky tone. His fingers left a trail of goose bumps in their wake as he slid the zipper down to her waist.

"I'll be back."

"Don't be too long or I'll be forced to come and get you."

"Yes, Sir."

Jess went into the spare bedroom where her wedding night ensemble had been laid out by Niki and shimmied out of her dress, hanging it in the closet, before donning a corset that perfectly matched the thong and stockings she had worn under her wedding dress. It, too, was fashioned from ivory silk and hugged her curves like a second skin and pushed her full breasts higher, making them appear even larger. Tiny pearl buttons concealed the clasps that held it closed. Using a full-length mirror to guide her, Jess reached behind to adjust the satin ribbon crisscrossing her back. As a final touch, she removed her jeweled hairpins and pulled a brush through her tresses before stepping back into the ivory slippers and promenading back to Kevin.

His jacket, shoes, and socks lay in a crumpled heap in a chair, forcing her breath to catch when she looked at him, so handsome. The cravat hung untied around his neck and the first few buttons of his shirt were open, adding to the raw masculinity oozing from his every pore. Her pulse quickened and a throb started in her loins as she watched him undress. Looking down and concentrating on the task, he didn't see her when she first stopped in the doorway. He shrugged out of his shirt and flung it on top of his coat before he caught her voyeuristic vigil. His eyes widened and his breath caught in his throat.

"Sweet Jesus!"

"Can I help with that?" She purred.

Closing the space between them, she slid her fingers into the waistband of his trousers, slowly unfastening them, then moving to his zipper, she pulled it down and ran her palms along tight, abdominal muscles, raking her nails up his chest, and finally resting her fingers on his shoulders. He pulled her closer, then picked her up again and cradled her against his chest. Turning around, he leaned over the bed and laid her in the center, then straightened to remove his trousers, and leaving them where they fell, he crawled across her and stroked her cheek with the back of his hand. Then wiping a stray tear from her eye, he rained butterfly kisses all over her face, on her lips, across her nose and cheeks, even her eyelids.

"You look so beautiful. I love you," he said in a hushed tone.

"I love you too. Make love to me."

One by one, he separated the tiny hooks down the front of the corset and planted a feather-light kiss upon every inch of skin he revealed. Having been apart for most of a week, Jess was eager for his brand of lovemaking. She considered rushing him, but realized they had the rest of their lives. She arched, allowing him to remove the corset completely, then watched as he stood and tossed it atop the pile of clothes in the chair, but before rejoining her, he stripped away his shorts, revealing his rigid phallus.

Moving back over her, Kevin caught her nipples and rolled them between his fingertips and rained kisses across her abdomen, his tongue snaking a hot path all the way to the edge of her thong. Catching the hem of the fabric between his teeth, he tugged gently, pulling the material down her hips and thighs to expose the throbbing flesh where her thighs met. Inching the ivory fabric down further, he stopped short of her shoes, which he cast off before removing the slip of silk and speedily tossing it to the floor before moving back up her legs and gently rolling her delicate, silk stockings down without snagging them.

Having removed all of their clothing, Kevin lay beside his wife and caressed her sides and belly in a fluid manner, every touch drawing a new moan from her, then rising over her, he took a semi-firm nipple into his mouth and suckled it, pulling it to a firm peak. His tongue flickering over the stiff nub elicited a gasp from her as he kneaded the other breast in his hand while his cock pulsated against her belly, prompting her to spread her legs and squirm towards it.

"Patience, my love."

"Easy for you to say after your quickie."

"Hey, that celibacy thing was *your* idea," he teased. "So soft, so sweet...God, you turn me on," he whispered into her ear.

His tongue darted inside as he suckled the lobe, bringing forth a round of aroused shivering, after which he slowly kissed his way down her neck, back to her breasts where he licked a fiery path across her upper ribs, along the underside of each soft globe before moving down her stomach towards her aching sex. Easily parting the trimmed golden curls, he touched the tip of his tongue to her swollen mound and licked slowly around it, then flitted rapidly over the hidden bud.

"Oh God," Jess moaned, arching against him.

She was consumed with an urgent need as he pushed her down and hooked his arms around her knees, holding her in place and licking her from back to front, and back again. Still able to reach her cleft, he parted her lips with his fingers and stabbed his tongue between them while caressing her nub with his thumb. Moaning, Jess pushed her pelvis closer as he lapped up her sweet nectar. After a moment, he let go of her knees only to replace his tongue with a thick finger, sliding it in and out, while he went back to circling that tiny button of flesh with his tongue, bringing her just to the brink of orgasm, before drawing back.

"Oh God, don't stop!" She begged.

"All in due time, Love."

Kevin stood on his knees and nipped the inside of her thigh as he moved down her leg, trailing kisses along her inner thigh, pausing to lick the back of her knee. He continued down her calf, hugging it in the crook of his neck and shoulder, massaging smooth skin all the way to her ankle, finally arriving at her foot. Jess straightened her leg and rested the sole against his pilous chest, the fine hairs titillated the sensitive pad, inducing her to curl her toes and emit a low giggle.

"Does that tickle?"

"Yes, a little."

"What about this?" He asked. Still holding her knee in the crook of his elbow, he ran a fingertip along her hip and up the side of her ribcage.

Jess sucked in a long breath, "Mmm hmm."

"And this?" He dragged his mustache halfway up her inner thigh, leaving a trail of goose bumps.

"Oh yes."

Finally letting go of her leg, he rested between her legs, gripped her buttocks in his hands, and drew closer to her core. His hot tongue snaked out to draw circles around her tiny protuberance as he sucked it gently between his lips and slid a finger back inside her silken heat. Her breath came in short pants as her climax loomed, once again. Adding a second finger, Kevin flicked the tip of his tongue across the hypersensitive nub, sending his new wife over the edge. She gasped, arched towards him, and locked her thighs against his temples as her body quaked with seismic waves.

"Oh God, oh God, oh God...yesss...ungyeah yesss."

Not waiting for her to come down, he crawled over her and plunged into her satin folds. Still shaking from the orgasm, Jess rose to meet him, tightening further around his thick shaft while hard, driving thrusts brought her to the brink, yet again, in just minutes. Realizing she was so close, Kevin slowed his movements to prolong her pleasure. At a snail's pace, he slid his full length in and out of her wetness, grinding his pelvis against hers, his balls slapping her bottom with every stroke.

After a short while, the effort to retain control set his body to quivering from head to toe, but rather than help him, Jess urged him along, cupping his cheeks and pulling him deeper. Stiffening, she locked around his member, pulling forth a second tiny death. Kevin groaned and drove into her fiercely, and in three quick thrusts, his love gushed forth. Jess' nerves were so finely tuned, she felt his seed as it coursed out of him and beat against her inner heat. Spent, he collapsed on top of her, rolling aside to avoid crushing her with his greater weight. Warm and damp from lovemaking with their hunger sated at last, they slept snug in each other's arms, and bathed in the warm glow of golden light cast from the all-but-forgotten candles.

Chapter 34

April 25...

"Mr. and Mrs. Slater, welcome to Beaufort."

"Thank you, very much."

"I am Beatrice Jackson. Come, I'll show you to your room."

The newlyweds followed the elderly woman upstairs and down the long hallway of the gigantic Victorian-style mansion, stopping inside a large, ornate bedchamber. The room was dominated by a mammoth poster bed draped in yards of decadent, hand-crocheted lace that hung from the post heads and pooled in the floor at each clawed foot. The bed itself, bedecked with an overstuffed comforter of burgundy moiré, was adjacent to a Victorian-style sofa, which sat on a cream-colored, shag rug and faced a small fireplace. Fresh flowers filled a pair of antique, crystal vases displayed atop a matching dresser and sofa table.

"Beautiful," Jess observed and breathed in the fresh, salt air flowing inside through an open window.

"Please ring if you need anything at all. Fresh fruit, coffee, and tea are available all day. Breakfast is from eight each morning until ten, and dinner is served each evening at seven o'clock, though being newlyweds, I'll understand if you wish to dine privately." She turned to leave the room.

"I'm sure the dining room will be perfect. Thank you, Mrs. Jackson."

"I'm sorry, there's one more thing. We're a smoke-free establishment. I hope that won't be a problem."

"No, but I'll need a lot more of this," Kevin said as he unwrapped a fresh stick of gum. "And maybe a quick trip or two outside. Come here, you," Kevin said and pulled Jess against him, leaning down to kiss her.

"Mmm, what did I do to earn that, Mr. Slater?"

"You're breathing, aren't you?"

"You're quite the charmer today, Sir."

"Only telling the truth. Baby, I love you."

He sat on the edge of the bed and pulled her onto his lap while she twisted around to return his kiss. Her hand traveled up the nape of his neck into his hair as he tugged her camisole-style shirt from her jeans. Sliding his hands underneath to unhook her bra, he pulled her ever closer and thrust his tongue between her lips. Spicy and sweet, the potent tone of cinnamon flavored his kiss while the taste and aroma of tobacco, usually lingering about him, had grown much fainter over the past weeks.

Lying back on the bed, Kevin pulled Jess across him, and still caressing the soft skin of her back, he inched her top up and off, then easily pulled off her bra. Her nipples hardened the instant the soft, cotton fabric of his t-shirt rubbed against them. Lying atop him, Jess explored his mouth...kissing him, nibbling his lips, wrestling his tongue with her own. Finally, he rolled her over and stood up, stripping away his shirt, and pulling off his wife's jeans and panties before removing the rest of his clothing.

Though no stranger to his body, Jess was still amazed by the sight of him. With his sun-bleached hair and the sandy hairs sprinkled across his chest and down his arms and legs, along with his naturally-tanned skin, he could have passed for a local. He was perfect, god-like. Big, strong arms extended from his wide shoulders. Tight pectoral muscles led to a rippled abdomen. The corded muscles of his thighs and calves flexed with every movement he made, and topping the package was his massive cock. Before Kevin, a man of his stature, let alone his endowment, would have frightened her, but having experienced both his tender and his aggressive sides, Jess knew she was in for a lifetime of incredible lovemaking.

She scooted back to lounge against the fluffy pillows, beckoning with a single finger, an invitation he couldn't help but accept. But rather than join her on the bed, he remained standing, grabbed her ankles and pulled her to the edge. With a low, guttural growl, he hooked his elbows under her knees and sank into her ready depths, giving her time to adjust to him, as the position allowed for greater penetration and had the potential to bring pain had he not been so gentle. He began rocking to and fro when she tightened around his shaft and spurred him on with a throaty moan. It was just enough to stimulate her tiny button, making her want more, so she reached between her legs and twiddled herself, encouraging him to quicken his motion.

"Oh Kevin, you feel so good," she moaned.

"You like that, Baby?"

"Mmm yesss," she moaned in a breathless whisper. "Oh God, please..."

"Please what?"

"Fuck me. Fuck me harder," she gasped as waves of exquisite pleasure rippled from her core in a floodtide.

He pounded harder, stiffening. A pained expression came across his face as he came with a muffled groan. Jess took great delight in the knowledge that even in her inexperience...especially in her inexperience...she could bring him the same euphoria she knew from his skilled touch. He took a moment to regain the strength in his legs before disentangling himself to lie down and draw her into his arms.

"Le petit mort," Jess whispered.

"What?"

"That's what the French call an orgasm...the small death."

"I didn't know you spoke French, too."

"I don't. I learned that from Niki."

"Aha, of course Niki would teach you all the naughty words, but I don't know if small is accurate." Jess glanced at his cock, flaccid but still impressive, and smiled at him. "I quite agree."

"Crazy woman, I wasn't talking about the size of my dick," he returned with a chuckle. "But I'm glad it makes you happy."

"Very much, just remember, I married *you*, not your body. *That's* a fringe benefit. Ti amo così tanto. I love you, so much."

"Som jeg elsker De også." Her look was full of curiosity. "I love you too."

"That reminds me. You did some ad-libbing yesterday. Are you gonna translate for me?"

"I said 'I love you and couldn't live without you any easier than I could live without breathing because you mean everything to me.'"

Her eyes filled with tears. "No wonder your mother and sisters got all weepy."

"Sweetheart, I only spoke the truth. I don't know how I made it all these years without you because I can't imagine my life without you in it." He wiped away her tears with the pads of his thumbs. "It's early yet. What do ya say we get dressed and I take my beautiful bride to the waterfront for some lunch?"

"That sounds wonderful."

"And since you're so fond of antiques, myself included, maybe we'll take a stroll through the historic district."

"Oh please, you're far from being an antique. Besides, like fine Chianti and Harleys, I know you'll get better with age."

"I just hope I don't spring a bunch of leaks like an old Harley," he said with a chuckle.

"And you think *I'm* crazy," she replied, laughing merrily.

2:56 PM

"*Goldfish?*"

"Don't ask me why. I just gotta have them."

"Honey, we just had lunch a couple hours ago."

"I don't care. I want 'em."

"Hey, you can have whatever you want," Kevin said as he peeled off a crisp new dollar bill to pay for the snack. "Maybe I'll grab another bag in case that's not enough," he teased.

"I don't think that will be necessary."

They continued strolling down the waterfront, ducking into the various shops and admiring the many old homes along the way before finding their way back to the inn shortly after five, just in time for a hot shower to wash away the day's sweat and grime. Dressed in fresh, clean clothes, they wandered outside to the wide back porch where a lazy swing overlooked the wharf. Kevin sat on the wide bench, stretching a leg across the length of it while Jess scooted between his legs and rested against his chest with his arms wrapped around her and his chin perched on the crown of her head.

6:48 PM

Jess raised her head and looked around. Kevin's mustache tickled the back of her neck when he nuzzled closer. "Have a nice nap?"

"Yeah, I guess I did. I didn't even realize I was tired."

"Well, good evening, it appears your sleepy bride is awake again." The old woman smiled at them from the open door.

"Hello, Mrs. Jackson," Jess managed through a yawn.

"She just woke up."

"Then my timing is perfect. I'll have supper ready in the dining room in ten minutes."

"Thank you," Kevin said. "Do you mind?" He asked as he reached for the pack of cigarettes he'd left on the rail.

"Go right ahead. You've been doing so good with your smoking. You should be proud of yourself."

"I was just telling Sam yesterday that I'm down to half a pack a day."

"Mmm, that smells good."

"Honey, have you completely lost it? I've been smoking for more years than I care to count and I *still* think they stink."

"Not the cigarette, the lighter fluid. It smells really good, and I think *you* smell delicious. You've got your own unique man smell that I love."

"Thank you, but *Zippo* fluid? The salt air must be getting to you," he razzed. "Must not be enough pollution here for you." Through her laughter, Jess let him know, in no uncertain terms, that he was crazy.

7:43 PM

Two other couples were staying at the inn, one of them newlyweds, like Kevin and Jess, and the other was celebrating their twenty-fifth anniversary. The other newlywed couple, not surprisingly, was dining in their room.

"Kevin, right?"

"Yes Sir," Kevin replied to the older man.

"Michael Malone, and this is my wife, Miriam."

"Pleasure to meet you, this is my...wife, Jess," Kevin returned with a grin.

"Takes a little getting used to, eh... calling someone wife over girlfriend?" Michael asked with a chuckle.

"Actually it hasn't been that difficult."

"I love newlyweds," Miriam added.

"So what brings you two to Mrs. Jackson's place? Not many folks know about it."

"Neither did we. It was a wedding gift from Jess' dad and boss."

"Really? How nice," Miriam said.

"Honey, you've barely touched dinner. You feel okay?"

"I feel fine, just don't have much of an appetite."

"As long as you're not getting sick."

Mrs. Jackson bustled into the dining room to check on everyone. "Mrs. Slater, would you prefer something else?" She asked, glancing at Jess' nearly untouched plate.

"No, Mrs. Jackson, it's delicious. I just don't have a big appetite tonight."

"Honey, I've never seen you turn down a shrimp. Are you sure you're okay?"

"No really, you two, I'm just not very hungry."

"If you're certain," Mrs. Jackson added before returning to the kitchen.

"I'm sure I'll be starved later. I guess the wedding and this mini-vacation has just got my system all outta whack."

"You're probably right."

"What exactly do you two do?" Miriam asked.

"I'm a forensic psychologist with the SBI."

"And I'm a detective."

"Really? That's fascinating. I read something a while back where a forensic psychologist was brought in...happened in...where was it, Dear? Greensboro?"

"Close to it, I think." Kevin and Jess exchanged knowing smiles. "Miriam and I are high school teachers from Raleigh. Where are you from?"

"Burlington."

"That's it, Miriam...Burlington. Wait! You're the two who caught that guy, aren't you? I thought you looked familiar. You're in the paper again today."

"We are?" Jess asked uneasily.

"Yes, let me get it and I'll show you. It's a good-size article, tells how you met on that case and progresses to your marriage. Yesterday, right?"

"Yes, Sir."

"Hold on, I'll be right back." Mr. Malone returned a few minutes later with the society section of the *Raleigh News and Observer*.

> *Whoever said one couldn't find love in the workplace, never worked at the Burlington Police Department. Yesterday, Doctor Jessica Mitchell, a forensic psychologist with the State Bureau of Investigation, exchanged vows with Detective Kevin Slater, a Staff-Sergeant with the Burlington Police Department. The couple met last summer while working together on the headline-grabbing murder investigation that nabbed serial killer, Mark Thompson, also known as Headbanger. The black-tie ceremony was held yesterday evening in Burlington at the United Methodist Church, and was officiated by Reverend Joseph Penley.*

"Boy, they sure got a lot of details."

"It gets better, Mrs. Slater."

> *From all across the state, anyone who was anyone, was in attendance. VIPs included everyone from Dean Johansen, Chief of the Burlington Police Department, and incidentally, father of the bride, his right-hand man, Major Mike Shelley, and an ocean of uniformed police officers, to state government officials, including Governor Patrick Randall and SBI Director, Jonathon Rickert.*

"How in the world did they get our guest list?"

"That's not all."

"I'm afraid to ask."

"They have your vows and a photograph too."

"You're kidding."

"May I see that, Mr. Malone?" Kevin asked. Kevin scanned the article and photo. "He's right, Baby, but they left out the Norwegian part; guess they couldn't figure out how to spell it. It says *the couple was not available for comment due to their joint involvement in yet another high-profile investigation.*" He skimmed further down the article. "Hey, guess what?"

"I hope it's good news."

"Could be, guess who wrote the article."

"I haven't a clue, but they had to have some really good inside sources."

"Jacques Lavache."

"Really? We have to call my dad and Carl. This sucks. Work is *not* supposed to be intruding on our long weekend."

"So we'll call your dad and let *him* deal with Carl. They can figure out what happened and how to fix it. I apologize for us running out so suddenly, Mr. and Mrs. Malone. Maybe we'll see you a bit later."

"Thank you for showing us the article."

"You're welcome. I hope I didn't spoil the honeymoon by mentioning it. Hey, take that with you. I don't need it."

"No, but you may have helped save someone's life. Thanks again." Kevin said. "We may have missed it if you hadn't pointed it out." Kevin took the stairs two at a time and waited for Jess at the top.

"I'm not in *that* big of a hurry to get back to work," she said with a grin.

"Neither am I, but I figure the faster we get this over with, the sooner I get you back, all to myself," he said, pulling her into a quick kiss as she reached the landing.

When they reached their room, Jess wasted no time in dialing her father, Dean, who was happy to learn they were having such a good time, but became alarmed upon hearing of the latest intrusion into their lives. Being in law enforcement for more than thirty years had taught him to take nothing for granted, especially where dangerous criminals were involved. To Dean, nothing was more valuable than his daughter's safety, so he promised to contact Carl Barnes immediately and have a look into Jacques Lavache's background.

April 26...
8:30 AM

"Whoa, holy cow! Baby, do that again. That is one thing that I will *never* get tired of."

"What's that?"

"Those cat stretches you do every morning...I'm talking instant wood."

"Is that what causes that? I thought men just woke up that way."

"Oh we do, but that's a different kind of wood, goes away after the morning whiz. *This* is the kind that sticks with you for a while," he commented, gesturing towards his crotch.

"Is that so? We'll just have to do something about that. Won't we?" He nodded in agreement. "But first, I simply *must* have food. I'm starving."

"I'm not surprised. You didn't eat a bite last night."

"I beg to differ. I got a little protein."

He looked away, shaking his head in amusement. "Yep, it's confirmed. I have married a monster." Jess' stomach lurched with a long, painful growl. "What was that?"

"My stomach, I told you I was starving."

"Good grief! Let's get dressed and feed you."

9:46 AM

"It appears you've regained your appetite, Mrs. Slater."

"Yes, I think so. I don't know what was wrong with me last night."

"Would you like something else, my Dear?"

"I think I'm finally full, but I would love some water."

"Of course, and Mr. Slater?"

"No, thank you, Mrs. Jackson, I've had quite enough."

"I'll be back shortly."

"You're a bottomless pit this morning. You sure you're full?" Kevin teased.

"Yes."

"You're a complete one-eighty from the woman I met last summer."

"How so?"

"The Jess I met last August barely ate breakfast at all, but this new version can't get enough."

"I have to keep my energy up. My handsome new husband gives me quite the daily work-out."

216

"You're something else. What do you want to do today?"

"I dunno. It's been so long since I've had a vacation, I'm not sure what to do."

Mrs. Jackson returned and placed a pitcher of crystal-clear ice water on the table as she bustled about clearing the breakfast dishes. Overhearing their discussion, she recommended one of the harbor tours just starting up for the season. The idea was exciting to Jess, who couldn't wait to get to the dock. But knowing it would be windy on the water, the couple left with time to spare because Kevin wanted to pick up a windbreaker for Jess to keep her from catching a chill. He even teased her with the promise of more *Goldfish* if she behaved on the tour.

3:02 PM

"Kevin, look!" Jess squealed with childlike delight, pointing seaward at a family of dolphins.

"You're really getting into this."

"This is great. I'm so glad we came here."

"Me too, Baby." He stood behind her with his arms around her waist and his chin on her shoulder. "It's a damn shame we have to go home tomorrow."

"*Ladies and gentlemen, Harbor Tours hopes you've enjoyed the dolphin show this afternoon. Luck was smiling on us today...lots more dolphins than usual, must have been our newlyweds. We hope you'll join us again soon.*"

"How'd he know there were newlyweds on board?" Jess asked.

"What? You mean we don't look like newlyweds? No seriously, I asked the Captain if he'd take our picture before we got off the boat." He put his arm around her waist as they stood on the bow with the harbor as their backdrop. "Smile."

"I wondered why you went back for the camera."

"Congratulations, folks. Come back again."

"Thank you, Captain."

Kevin lifted Jess down from the gangplank as if she weighed no more than a feather, and back on solid ground, talked her into lunch at a restaurant not far from where they had gone on the harbor tour. They strolled a short ways down the boardwalk before coming upon the *Sanitary Seafood Market* where they were seated at a table overlooking the water. Taking a moment to peruse the menu, Kevin decided on a surf and turf style lunch...skewers of steak, grilled scallops, and prawns...a real man's food he called it, while Jess hid a yawn ordered a grilled chicken Caesar salad.

Taking note of her exhaustion and her sudden distaste for shrimp, which had been her favorite, Kevin, again, expressed concern for her health, to which she insisted was her body's rebellion against so much rest and relaxation. But to waylay his worry, she agreed to let Kevin pamper her with a full-body rubdown with lotion to counteract the sun she'd received during their time away.

Chapter 35

The next morning...

"Good morning, Sleeping Beauty. I thought I was gonna have to come wake you up."

"Why, what time is it?"

"It's eleven o'clock."

"You're not serious," Jess said as she jumped out of bed, but quickly sat back down when the room did a quick spin.

"Yes, I am. You okay?"

"Head rush...stood up too fast."

"Maybe we oughta get you checked out when we get back home to make sure you're not coming down with a bug."

"Honey, I just had a physical. I'll be fine, probably had too much sun."

"If you're sure, but if this keeps up..."

"You're gonna make me go see my doctor."

"You got it. I've got us all packed and ready to go, so there's no need to rush."

"God, I can't believe I slept so long."

"We have been up kinda late these last few nights," Kevin said with a wink. Heat flooded Jess' cheeks. "You must have needed it, so relax. It's not like we're gonna have the luxury of sleeping in after today, not until we catch Mr. Clean, that is."

"True."

"We'll be ready to hit the road after your shower. I'll come wash your back if you want."

"I'd love that."

4:23 PM

Kevin woke his wife as they came up on Raleigh, thinking she might want to stop by her office since they were so close. Knowing he wasn't familiar with the streets, Jess shook herself awake, surprised she'd fallen asleep on him again, and gave him directions. Ten minutes later, Jess made small talk with James, the security guard, while he underwent the motions of checking Kevin's gun and assigning a visitor's pass. Before they headed upstairs, James handed Jess a card and laughed at himself when he mistakenly called her Agent Mitchell.

Jess scaled the stairs a bit slower than normal. "I'm outta practice," she said, laughing at the top with Kevin hot on her heels.

"Hey, Sweetheart," Carl called from the end of the hallway. "Maybe I shouldn't call you that anymore now that you're an old, married woman," he said as he looked from Jess to Kevin.

"Carl, Buddy if it were anyone but you, I might take exception," Kevin chuckled and shook the man's hand.

"Glad to hear it. It's a hard habit to break after what, five years. Any other broad woulda clocked me by now, but Jess just cuts her eyes and curses me. I'm not sure which is worse. How'd you like the beach? Looks like the sun took a shine to you."

"So I keep hearing. I never realized I was so pale, but it was great. Mrs. Jackson was such a sweet lady and the inn was beautiful."

"I thought you'd like it. I take the wife a couple times a year."

"Really? I had no idea you were the romantic type Carl."

"Well, you know, I try not to let that get out."

"God, you men are all alike...scared to death someone might think you're nice."

"Doll, you know what they say about nice guys."

"Yeah, they always get the girl."

"That's not exactly what I was going to say, but it works better. Wouldn't you agree, Kevin?"

"Guess that means we're two of the good guys, Carl, but I still think we should keep it under our hats," he teased.

"Okay, have it your way. I won't tell a soul that you're two of the biggest teddy bears I know."

"So what brings you by?"

Jess put her hand to her heart in feigned shock. "Oh my God! Who are you and what have you done with my boss? He woulda never asked me that. No, he woulda been harping on me for going four days without checking in."

Kevin joined Carl in hearty laughter before Carl answered. "Toots, you got no idea what the wife woulda done to me if I'd made you check in during the last few days."

"Sounds like a good woman to me. You should listen to her more often. So how'd we handle the newspaper fiasco?"

Carl had the editors at the *Raleigh News & Observer* eating from the palm of his hand. First amendment or no, they became nervous at the suggestion of injunctions, lawsuits, and arrests for police interference, not-to-mention the likely plummet in sales if readers thought them responsible for another injury or death at Mr. Clean's hands due to their revealing critical information. Carl didn't have such luck with Jacques Lavache. The reporter was freelance, so the paper had little information on him, which forced Carl to call in dozens of favors. He started by running the man's name through every database available, but so far, nothing had turned up.

"Great," Jess huffed. "Now I know how movie stars feel when the paparazzi stalks them."

"Dean told me this guy left something at your house."

"Yeah, I wanna know who he is. Anyway, we have to get home."

"Bye, Doll. I'll let you know if anything comes up. Good seeing you again, Slater. Take care of my Jess."

"Will do, Carl."

CB&CR&

"*Hello, Porter.*"

"Phil, Kevin Slater here."

"*Kevin, what's up, Buddy?*"

"Hey, remember a few weeks back you did a background for me."

"*Yeah, yeah, what was his name? Bedrich, right?*"

"Yeah, that's the one. I got another job for you."

"*Same guy?*"

"Nah, a guy by the name of Jacques Lavache."

"*Slater, you and your goddamn foreign names, so what are we looking for?*"

"Anything. For all I know, it's an alias. Apparently, he's a freelance reporter. He slipped into our wedding and then showed up at my house while the reception was in full swing. Then while Jess and I were in Beaufort, he ran a huge article in the *Raleigh News and Observer* covering our wedding, had the vows, guest list, a photo...all kinds of shit, and with this Mr. Clean thing going hot and heavy, I don't know that I like this guy being so damn interested in us. He's not making it easy for us to fly under the radar, if you know what I mean."

"*I do. You got it, Buddy. So all you got is a name?*"

"Unfortunately yes. We've run the name through every database available, but nothing. However, Chief Johansen had an officer posted at my house that day who saw and talked to him, gave us a description if that helps...about six feet tall, medium build and dark complexion. Larry said maybe Italian or something like that, but not Latino."

"*Well, it's not much, but at least we have something to work with. I'll see what I can dig up for you.*"

"Thanks, Phil. I wish I had more to get you going. I'll fax you the details."

"*Sure thing, Slater. I'll be in touch.*"

One week later...

"Now who's tired?" Jess purred.

"Me! I think you're trying to kill me. Not that I'm complaining about all this loving you've been giving the last couple days."

"I dunno what's come over me. Guess I just can't get enough of you, Honey."

"Keep it up. I love it. We have gotta change that ring tone...damn thing gets on my nerves," Kevin said to the shrill ringing of the telephone. "Hello...yeah, hold on Dean, she's right here," he said and handed Jess the telephone.

"Hello."

"*Good morning, Princess.*"

"Hey, Dad. What's up?"

"*I wanted to touch base regarding the lab report on that wedding gift.*"

Jacques Lavache was as thorough as Mr. Clean. Stephanie collected no additional trace from the packing materials. But odder than the lack of evidence were the contents. The reporter had bestowed the couple with some atypical stemware, three crystal champagne flutes from the opulent Mille Nuits line by Baccarat. Stephanie located them at dozens of online retailers for no less than $130 apiece, but the trail went cold there, as she was unable to find them at a local shop. Jess and Kevin were baffled by the reporter's epicurean gift, but Kevin's suspicious nature convinced Jess of a connection to the investigation, so they had the glasses stored in lock-up with the minimal evidence they'd collected, thus far.

May 13...

Phil Porter hit one brick wall after another, but he still managed to come up with more information on the mysterious Jacques Lavache than the State Bureau of Investigation. In addition to his recent society piece in the *Raleigh News & Observer*, the freelance journalist had written articles for dozens of small publications, mostly newspapers, in Virginia, Texas, and Georgia. But as luck would have it, he received paychecks at post office boxes where he left no forwarding addresses, and he cashed them outright rather than making bank deposits, causing his trail to vanish.

May 19...
1:01 PM

"I got a delivery for Jessica Slater."

"She's out to lunch. Can I sign for it?" Brian asked.

"Doesn't say *she* has to, so I guess so. Right here, please. Thanks, man," the courier called on his way out.

1:28 PM

"Man, I'm tired. I'm going to your office to sack out on the couch," Kevin said.

"Mmm hmm...are you *sure* you're okay, Honey?" Jess asked sweetly. "You've been so tired lately. Do we need to go get you checked out?"

"Oh yeah, sure, real funny. I was just telling a couple guys the other day I thought you were trying to kill me with sex."

"You did not!"

"Sure I did, but they told me to enjoy it while it lasted because it was just a matter of time before you cut me off. No, I haven't been discussing our sex life with anybody," he added with a chuckle at his wife's shocked expression. "But come on, we're newlyweds. Everyone's bound to know we do it more than average couples."

1:46 PM

"Welcome back. Hey Jess, a package came while you were out."

"Thanks, Brian."

"Hey, Kevin, you wanna come in here, and bring print dust."

"Sure, Babe. What's up?"

"I got another present...from Jacques Lavache."

"Maybe we'll get the matching goblets this time," Kevin joked.

Jess put on a pair of latex gloves and carefully opened the courier wrapper, revealing the box inside. Again, it was wrapped in decorative wedding paper. Kevin returned with another pair of gloves and a lift kit, which he used to collect fifteen fingerprints from the outer wrapping while Brian, David, and Jess watched.

"That's a lot of prints. The last one didn't have any."

Jess opened the wrapping paper, taking great care not to damage it in case they needed it later, and found inside another nondescript, cardboard box sealed with clear, packing tape.

"Either of you guys got a knife?"

"Sure, here Jess." David fished a small pocketknife from his uniform. "Why don't you just rip it open?"

"There could be prints, or fibers, or something on the sticky side that would be compromised or destroyed by steaming the tape off."

"That makes sense. Did you used to be a CSI or something?"

"No, but I've spent my share of time in the crime lab. You pick up a few things."

Jess cut a slit down the middle of the packing tape, and then folded back the flaps of the outer carton. Mounds of tightly wadded tissue paper surrounded a styrofoam carton, also sealed with the same clear tape. Oddly enough, the carton was cool to the touch. She handed it to Kevin for dusting, which resulted in several more prints. At last, she cut through the tape and swallowed the bile that rose in her throat when she opened it.

"Holy shit!" She gasped, wide eyed.

"What the fuck?" Kevin said in sync. The fourth Baccarat champagne flute was inside the carton. "Brian, get hold of that courier ASAP. I'll get Steph. What's the name on the package, Jess?"

"What is it? What's wrong?" David asked.

"It's someone's goddamn finger in dry ice," Kevin shouted.

"No shit?"

"Triple A Delivery Service from Durham," Jess said as Kevin dialed the lab. "Yeah, Steph, this is Kevin Slater. You need to get over here with a quickness, and bring preservation gear."

"*Why, what's up?*"

"Remember the wedding gift you processed for Jess?"

"*Yeah, Chief Johansen says you want me to keep it in lock-up.*"

"Absolutely, Jess got another delivery here today containing what I assume is the missing flute."

"*And?*"

"And a frozen finger."

3:48 PM

"Yeah, Slater."

"*Afternoon Sarge, Stephanie here.*"

"Whatcha got for us, Steph?"

"*The prints on the package belong to whoever used to be attached to that finger.*"

"Madeline Crawford?"

"*That's my guess. I sent it on to the state lab for DNA analysis.*"

"He really plans in advance. Thanks, Steph."

"Kevin! I've got him on IM."

"Hold up, Steph. What's that, Jess?"

"Jacques Lavache, he just IMed me. Look!"

> *JacquesLavache: Good Afternoon, Agent Slater.*
> *SubDoer: hello*
> *JacquesLavache: You received my wedding present, I presume?*
> *SubDoer: yes, the flutes were quite lovely, thank you*

"Steph, I'm gonna put you on speaker. We may need your help on this. Can we trace him?"

"*Can you get his IP address?*"

"How do we do that?" Kevin asked.

"*What chat software are you on, Jess?*"

"My Space."

"*Damn, they don't play well with law enforcement. I doubt we'll get anywhere without a subpoena, but it's worth a shot. What's his handle and I'll get to work on it.*"

"That's easy enough. It's JacquesLavache, all one word, first letters capitalized."

"*I'll get right on it.*"

"Thanks, Steph. I'll keep him talking for as long as I can. I wonder if Niki can crack the program."

> *SubDoer: i read your article on my wedding, it was a lovely piece*
> *JacquesLavache: Thank you, I'm glad you enjoyed it.*
> *SubDoer: i'm curious; how'd you get the details*
> *JacquesLavache: I was there. It was a beautiful ceremony, though I regret missing the reception.*
> *SubDoer: that's quite all right; jacques, not to be rude, but have we met? i'm afraid i don't remember you*
> *JacquesLavache: Not officially. Would you like to?*
> *SubDoer: yes, i'd like that very much, i'd love to thank you in person for the gift and wonderful article*

"No, Jess, absolutely not!"

"Why not, Kevin?"

"Because you're my wife and I love you."

"Kevin, Jacques Lavache is our man. Damn, why didn't I think of it! He fits the profile perfectly. Can you think of a better way to catch him?"

"I haven't yet, but I'm working on it."

"You'll be there to protect me."

> *SubDoer: time and place?*
> *JacquesLavache: I need to get back to you on that.*
> *SubDoer: i'll be waiting*
> *JacquesLavache is offline.*

"I don't like this at all, Jess. If he's Mr. Clean...I don't even want to think about it. Baby, no, it's too dangerous."

"Danger is part of our job, Kevin. We're here to protect everyone else."

"I know, but dammit, I just found the love of my life only to learn that her biggest groupie is a goddamn psychopath. The Chief and Mike, and probably even your boss, ain't gonna go for it either."

"Let's at least wait until he contacts me again. There's no reason getting everyone's hackles up when he may not even come through. Jeez, I'm popular today."

SubMarine: Good afternoon, CJ.
SubDoer: hey Armand
SubMarine: How was the wedding?
SubDoer: beautiful
SubMarine: And the honeymoon? Beautiful also?
SubDoer: oh yes
SubMarine: The mistress allowed me to buy you a wedding present.
SubDoer: really? how very thoughtful
SubMarine: I'd love to give it to you before the next KLAASP meeting. Will you be around town in the coming days?
SubDoer: i'm sure i will between grocery shopping and errands, we can meet at the Java Hut
SubMarine: Splendid. How about Friday afternoon?
SubDoer: let me check my calendar

"What do you think, Kevin?"
"I want to know why all these damn fruitcakes are so interested in my wife. I don't like the guy, but the Java Hut's a public place, so it's probably harmless...as long as you don't mind being tailed."
"By all means, if it makes you feel better."
"Who knows, maybe we'll make some headway on this case."

SubDoer: Friday afternoon looks good, what time?
SubMarine: I have some errands to do for the mistress, so it'll be late afternoon before I can get there. How's 4:00 sound?
SubDoer: that works for me, i'll see you then
SubMarine: great, it's a date, i have to go now, bye
SubMarine is offline.
SubDoer: cya

"Dang, he's fast!"
"I still don't like it. I have a bad feeling about that guy, something about him ain't jiving."
"I'll be extra careful. Let's go home."
"That's the best idea I've heard all day. I'll set up the tail in the morning."

Later that evening...

"Dad, we weren't going to get into this until a date and time was set, but since you insist on talking about it, yes, Jacques Lavache contacted me today. He wants to meet."
"No, it's too dangerous. Kevin, I hope you were able to talk some sense into her."
"I tried. He's off the deep end and I don't want her anywhere near him."
"Guys, come on. Wire me, tail me, do whatever it takes to get more comfortable with the idea, because Jacques Lavache is a cold-blooded killer and we have a responsibility to take him out."
"Jessie, I just don't like this idea. It's harebrained."
"Oh, so now I'm dumb?"
"Princess, you know that's not what I meant."
"Baby, your dad is worried about you just like me. Are you forgetting this guy has killed seven women and had one of 'em's severed finger delivered to you today?"
"Hell no, I haven't forgotten. I also haven't forgotten the looks on those children's faces when they dropped dirt on their mother's casket. You two need to remember that *you* asked for *my* help on this. Dad, Kevin and me finding each other was an unplanned byproduct of this case, the only good thing that's come from it, if you ask me. And Kevin, I love you dearly, more than anybody on Earth, but you

can't let personal feelings keep us from taking this guy out. Hells bells, if anything, I'd like to thank the man because we wouldn't be together if not for him."

"Let's not get all worked up again," Dean placated. "We need to look at this rationally. Jessie, this fella seems to know an awful lot about you, though we know next to nothing about him. We can't track him because he seems to have materialized out of thin air. He has no personal history or identifying information to speak of. All we know is that he has a dark complexion and he's about the same size as Larry Dixon. That could be half the men in the city."

"True, but it's something, and Steph's trying to track his movements online."

"And I've got Phil Porter chasing anything that might lead us to him."

"Well, if anybody can find him, it's Phil. Let's just see what they turn up before we take it further."

"Okay fine, lemme get that. It might be one of them," Jess said, jumping up to grab the ringing telephone.

Stephanie Andrews got nowhere with My Space. As expected, the corporation refused to cooperate without a subpoena, but upon hearing about the problem, Dean assured Jess that he would have a talk with Judge Hastings on his way home. Kevin was clearing the table when she returned to the dining room and put her arms around his waist, then laid her cheek against his broad, muscular back. He paused in his task and put his hands over hers.

"I love you, Honey."

"Jess...Baby, I love you too."

"Let's finish this later."

He turned and caught her lips in a heated kiss. Breaking away, Jess smiled up at him before pulling him towards the bedroom, leaving a trail of cast-off clothing all the way to the bed. He pulled away just long enough to help as she tore at his shirt. Tossing it aside, he kissed a hot path down her neck and into the valley between her breasts. All the while, Jess tugged Kevin's fly in a hurried attempt to remove his jeans while he cupped her heavy breasts in his hands and squeezed as he licked the hollow at her collarbone. She moaned, half from pain, half from the exquisite pleasure brought forth by the pressure of his hands on her bosom.

"Did I hurt you?" He whispered.

"They're a little tender, but don't stop."

He swung her up, laid her in the center of the bed, and shucked his jeans and shorts before crawling over her to catch a hardened nipple in his mouth. Jess' breath whistled through her teeth when she inhaled sharply and drew up as he suckled the ultra sensitive peak. He rose onto his elbows and looked for her response, seeking consent to go on. She smiled and glanced at her other breast. Permission granted, he twirled his tongue around the twin, pebble-hard summit.

She arched against his mouth and moaned while he pushed her legs apart with a knee, reaching down to massage her pubic mound, testing her readiness. Hot and wet, she was eager for his possession, but rather, he probed her channel with two fingers for several minutes, then rose to turn her onto her belly. Reaching under and pulling her to her knees, Kevin rammed his rock-hard cock into her, pushing deep inside. A split-second later, he grabbed her hips and began moving in and out. Faster then slower, harder then easier, he varied the pace until she could scarcely stand anymore.

Jess reached between her legs and alternated stroking herself and then him. The tightness of his sack told her he was fighting to maintain control. She rubbed harder and faster, prompting Kevin to let go of one hip and lean back to stroke the crease between her buttocks, lingering at her puckered back door. Her quick intake of breath proclaimed her anticipation louder than words ever could. Jess pushed against Kevin's finger while he pounded her minge. Quick as lightening, seismic waves flew through her unexpectedly and with such ferocity, she stiffened and screamed, begging him to fuck her harder.

"Jesus Christ, ease up, Baby. I can't hold it with you squeezing so tight."

"Oh God, fuck me. Don't hold back. Give it to me."

The removal of his finger spawned another powerful aftershock from deep within her core. Grabbing both hips again, he pulled her towards him and ground into her. Little time passed before he stiffened and groaned, turning loose his steaming seed. He relaxed and leaned over her, pushing her onto her belly, then turned so they lay with her backside spooned against his pelvis, his arms wrapped around her. Some time later, having done its duty, his member softened and slipped out. Jess couldn't remember falling asleep, nor did she have any idea how long she'd slept, but she awoke to Kevin brushing her long hair aside and kissing the side of her neck.

"Feels nice," she purred. "Is it time to get up yet?"

"Baby, I'm always up for you."

She rolled over to face him. "Not that kind of up."

"I'm teasing. It's only midnight. Are you tired?"

"Not really."

"Good, maybe whatever's been sapping your energy is gone."

Kevin pulled her closer, kissed her, giving a gentle push with his tongue until she parted her lips, allowing him entrance. He explored her mouth, sucking her lips, wrestling her tongue, skimming her teeth. After a time, he pulled back, intertwined his legs with hers, and held her against his broad, naked chest.

"Good night, Baby. I love you."

"I love you too, Kevin. Good night."

They slept in each other's arms until dawn when the first rays of the sun awakened them.

Chapter 36

Thursday morning...
5:15 AM

Jess awoke with a smile. To Kevin's amusement, she blushed crimson when he inquired if she'd had another of *those dreams*. But to his surprise and delight, she'd been dreaming of something wholly different. She was pregnant with their child, almost due, though unable to remember most of the details, except that he'd been rubbing her stomach, just as he'd been doing in real life.

"I'm not nearly as lucid in my sleep as you, my beauty. I never remember my dreams, but I'm sure they're all about you," he answered with a chuckle. His deep voice reverberated in her ear. "Let's take a shower, then we can finish clearing off the table from last night and work on some breakfast." Kevin got out of bed and went around to his wife's side just in time to catch her when she wavered in a moment of dizziness as everything turned black. "Whoa, slow down. Where's the fire?"

"I guess I got up a little too fast."

"Woman, you just took ten years off my life. I thought you were getting better. Looks like I was wrong. Jess, are you sure you're okay?"

"Just a little dizzy, like I've got a hangover."

"Honey, we haven't had anything alcoholic since the champagne at our wedding reception."

"I know." Jess discounted the swoon to early morning hypoglycemia and pulled him towards the bathroom.

10:45 AM

While Jess was engrossed in toxicology reports, Kevin went, unnoticed, to his office and made a quiet call to Dean. His goal was to learn Jess' family health history, if there were illnesses he needed to be concerned about. However, he knew of nothing, leaving Kevin with more questions than answers.

Later that afternoon...

Carl called with the lab results on the severed finger. As expected, it belonged to Madeline Crosby. He also took the opportunity to voice his thoughts on his favorite agent's plan to meet with Jacques Lavache. Prepared for another argument, Jess was shocked to learn that her boss did not share the opinion of her father and husband. In fact, he made arrangements for a team of agents to help cover her when she met with the suspect.

Late Friday morning...

"Slater, it's Phil."

"I hope you got something for me."

"Maybe, you know my daughter works with me."

"Yeah."

"She started *Googling* different spellings of that name you gave me, and came up with an apartment in Danville. Five minutes is all it took her, and get this. The place is leased to someone named Jean-Michele de la Vache. She tells me that Jean is French for John, and Jacques is..."

"Jack, a nickname for John! Phil, this is awesome news."

"Listen, I'll fax my report over to ya. What the hell is *Googling*, anyway?"

"Search engine."

"Oh, you're a big help."

Kevin chuckled, "Hey, Jess and her friend, Niki, are big into that internet crap too. I just leave 'em alone. Thanks for your help, Buddy. I've got a good feeling about this."

Later...

"Have you heard anything else from Lavache?"

"Not a word."

"I talked to Phil this morning. He faxed me a shitload of information, but we don't know yet if this is our guy.

"Hmm, Jean-Michele de la Vache, the similarity is uncanny for such an unusual name, especially around here."

"Well, I think it's for the best that he hasn't contacted you again. You're still meeting Armand at four, right?"

"Mmm hmm."

"I have the tail set up. I'll be in the SRT van and Larry Dixon will be in an unmarked unit in the parking lot across the street."

"Okay, speaking of Armand..."

> *SubMarine is available.*
> *SubDoer: hi there, are we still on for today?*
> *SubMarine: Yes definitely, 4:00.*
> *SubDoer: great, just wanted to confirm*
> *SubMarine: I wouldn't miss it. BTW, I heard some stirrings about Sandy's murder.*
> *The mistress had another party. Some people were talking. I wonder if I should go*
> *to the police.*
> *SubDoer: wow, really? what'd you hear?*
> *SubMarine: I'll tell you later.*
> *SubDoer: okay, but even if it doesn't seem important, you should go to the police*
> *and let them decide; they can use all the help they can get to get this creep off the*
> *street*
> *SubMarine: I know, but let's talk later. I'll decide what to do after we talk.*
> *SubDoer: okay that's cool, i need to get back to work, just wanted to say hello*
> *SubDoer you are appearing offline. All conversation windows will be closed.*

"That's the most interesting thing that guy's ever said. Maybe this meeting wasn't such a bad idea after all."

"I agree. He's really got my curiosity piqued."

"Me too, maybe we should fit you with a wire."

"Do we have time?"

"We should, but I'll have to check."

3:00 PM

"Jess, you know how this works. Right?"

"Yeah Reid, and we have the court order? I'd hate for anything we get to be inadmissible."

"Right here," Kevin said, waving a piece of paper.

"I don't think you'll have a problem with range or interference but we're gonna give you a good, thorough testing, anyway."

Kevin and Jess followed Reid through various parts of the building, including the holding area and weapons vault, and finding no problems with the body wire, went back to the man's office long enough for him to log Jess' GPS-equipped cell phone into the system. That accomplished, the men got her on the road, then joined two more officers. They would monitor her meeting with Armand from the SRT van parked a block from the Java Hut.

3:55 PM

Jess parked her motorcycle and paused to make a mental note of Larry's location across the street before going inside. The coffee house wasn't in full swing yet due to the early hour. That would keep the noise level to a minimum. Looking around, she didn't find Armand, so she bought a Mountain Dew and sat near the back of the room to wait for him. He was running late, finally arriving at ten minutes past four.

CB&)CR&)

"*Dixon to Slater, come in.*"
"Yeah, Larry, what's up?"
"*I got a heads up for you.*"
"Heads up on what?"
"*I know he's not the guy I'm supposed to be looking out for, but that reporter just went inside the coffee house.*"
"Lavache?"
"*Yeah, same guy that crashed your wedding.*"
"Thanks Larry, we'll let Jess know. Call me if you see either of them leave. I don't want to take him in a crowd where he might hurt someone."
"*No problem, Sarge. Over and out.*"
"Reid, you got that?"
"Working on it right now. Hey, Jess, got some recco for you." No response. "Jess? Jess? Are you reading me?"
"Is there a problem?" Kevin asked.
"She's not responding. I can't tell if she's receiving, but I'm getting hers loud and clear."
"Go ahead and tell her about Lavache. Maybe Armand is there and she can't let on that she's hearing you without blowing her cover."
Kevin reread the transcripts from the chats with both Armand and Jacques while Chuck transmitted the new information. He couldn't shake the suspicion that something was not quite right.

CB&)CR&)

"Hey, Armand," Jess said as he joined her.
"CJ, how are you?"
"I'm terrific. It's a beautiful day out."
"Can we sit in the back room? I'm not comfortable talking out here where everyone might hear."
"Sure, okay."
Armand motioned Jess ahead to the deserted back room normally reserved for KLAASP meetings or other special functions, then pulled the door closed. Jess had no time to react when he shoved her against a wall, shushed her with his free hand warning her to remain quiet. A moment later, he ripped off her auburn wig, tore open her shirt, and yanked the wire from her chest before throwing it to the floor and crushing the transmitter underfoot.
"What the fuck is that about? What's with the goddamn wire, bitch?"
"I'm sorry, Armand. When you said you had information about Sandy's murder, I went to the police. I didn't think you'd go."
"Jessica! Don't fuck with me. I'm well-aware that you *are* the police, you *and* your new husband, Staff-Sergeant Kevin Slater. But at least you weren't stupid enough to come armed. It would have been terribly sad if I had to kill you with your own gun. Let's go."
He grabbed her left arm in a vice-like grip and dragged her from the room behind him. As they passed the men's restroom, the door opened enough for Jess to see Nick Yarboro. She looked at him in a silent plea for help, though she was uncertain if he noticed.

"Slater, I lost her!"

"What?"

"The wire, it's not transmitting."

"Shit! Get down there, now." Kevin's cell phone rang. "What!"

"*Slater, this is Nick Yarboro.*"

"Look, Nick, this isn't a good time. Can I call you back?"

"*Make it a good time. I just saw that loser, Armand, dragging your wife towards the back door of the Java Hut. Didn't look like she was going on her own.*"

"Dammit! Thanks, Buddy, I owe you one." He put away the phone and pulled out his radio. "Slater to Dixon, come in."

"*Dixon.*"

"Larry, I just heard that Jess left through the back door. Go check it out."

"*Copy that, I'm on my way, Sarge. Over and out.*"

"Get that goddamn GPS up!"

CRITICAL

"You couldn't leave it alone," Armand growled as he forced Jess into a small, black pick-up truck. "You had to keep fucking with me. Now it's your turn."

"My turn? For what?" She searched frantically for the door handle.

"A waste of time, there's no handle. You didn't think I'd let you escape, did you?" He asked with an evil laugh. "Does the number eight mean anything to you, my dear?" He asked. His eyes were wild and his smile, deranged.

"Number eight?" Jess tried to remain calm on the outside while she panicked on the inside.

"It's a shame too, because I really liked you."

"Armand, what is wrong with you?"

"Armand!" He spat in a malicious tone.

At that moment, everything fell into place when she realized that Armand and Jacques Lavache were one and the same. "You're not Armand."

Stealthily, she pressed the dial button on her cell phone, knowing it would automatically redial the last number she'd called, which happened to be her father's office. She only hoped he would understand and know what to do. Then she prayed the volume was low enough that Jacques wouldn't overhear the call.

"How'd you guess? Am I so transparent?"

"No, Jacques, you're quite skilled. I'm impressed."

"Before I kill you, I'd like to know when you figured it all out. It might help with my plans for the future."

She thought for a moment, hoping for an idea that might stall him and buy her some time. "I'm a forensic psychologist, Jacques. I solve puzzles for a living, but you knew that. And you're wrong about me having *you* figured out." She made mental note of every turn. He was driving in a northwesterly direction. After a quick mental calculation, she guessed that he was driving to the country club. If her latest theory was correct, they would stop at the eighth hole on the green.

"I don't think so. You knew it was me."

"Not until you sent me Madeline Crawford's finger. But even then, I didn't know you were hiding in Armand's body."

"This is not Armand's body! I'm in control. He lives here only when I let him."

"You're exactly right, Jacques. Where is Armand now?"

"Armand is dead."

"Just like the women you killed."

"Yes."

"You're gonna kill me anyway, so tell me why you did it, Jacques."

"They failed to please me, and now with Armand finally gone, I'm free."

CR&CR&O

"Yeah, Slater."

"*Kevin, I'm listening to a bizarre phone call from Jess. I don't believe she knows she dialed me.*"

"Slater, I got her GPS. She's moving northwest."

"Northwest? What the hell is northwest?"

"*What's going on, Son?*"

"Jess has been kidnapped."

"*By who?*"

"The guy she was meeting with today...Armand."

"*Can't be. I'm sure she just called him Jack.*"

"Jack? You mean Jacques?" Kevin didn't listen for a confirmation, but looked around, wild-eyed, before the light of realization came into his eyes. "Holy shit! Get a move on it. She's in a hell of a lot more danger than we thought."

"*Talk to me, Son.*"

"Chief, I got word that she was dragged out of the Java Hut by Armand, but you're telling me she's talking to Jacques. That can only mean one thing, that her split-personality theory was dead-on. Armand and Jacques are the same guy."

"*Good Lord!*"

"Damn, that's why the chats seemed off. He was talking as Jacque half the time, only we didn't know it because he was using Armand's screen name. Dammit! Why didn't I see that?"

"*Kevin, she said he'd move on to the golf courses. Is it possible they're headed back to the country club?*"

"You're exactly right Chief. Reid, country club," Kevin yelled to the front of the van, then radioed dispatch. "Officer abducted. Send backup to the eighth hole, Burlington Country Club. Remain hidden as long as she's unharmed; he may kill her if he sees us. Suspect should be considered armed and extremely dangerous."

"*Roger that, Slater.*"

"Step on it. Reid, can you route Chief Johansen's line into the van? Jess somehow dialed him on her cell phone."

"This van's not equipped for that."

"Damn! Chief, keep that call online."

"*Okay Kevin, I'll put it on speaker so you can listen in.*"

CR&CR&O

Jess sat quietly for several minutes, trying to collect her thoughts and formulate a plan. Unfortunately, she was failing miserably, so she started over from the beginning, mentally reviewing the facts. Seven victims, and seemingly, Jess was to be number eight. Ligature asphyxia was the cause of death. The killer is Mongoloid? It didn't fit. Josef Armand Bedrich was from Texas and certainly not Asian. She pondered it a moment longer.

Jess tried to remember every conversation she'd had with Kevin regarding Armand, but drew blanks. *It's all Greek to me.* Something he'd said kept echoing in her mind. *It's all Greek to me.* A second later, it hit her. Jess couldn't believe she'd missed it after years of watching the Cooper family on *Guiding Light.* Mom's name, Kriszta Olesia Gavrilopoulos, is Greek. Greece borders Turkey, probably a lot of mixed blood between both populations. Yes! Of course, but that only confirmed the evidence that Mr. Clean was Mongoloid, probably of Middle Eastern ancestry.

All this time, she'd had the perp right under her nose and didn't realize it. She needed to buy herself more time. Armand was a nice guy, but had also been described as an angry man. His dissociative

230

disorder was so obvious to her now. Jacques Lavache must have been present for some time, though maybe not as big an influence on Armand in earlier years. She tried to remember some other small detail from Armand's military records that might get her out of her quandary. Drawing another blank, she decided to keep him talking, hoping it would keep her alive until someone figured out what was going on.

"Where are we going?"

"You tell me."

"The country club?"

"Getting warmer, I know you have this part."

"The golf course."

"Come, fair Jessica, I think you're stalling. You're so much smarter than you want me to believe. Armand left you an excellent clue. Regrettably, I didn't realize it until it was too late to retrieve it, so I've had to step up my plan. It appears we may go down together. Now where?"

"Eighth hole."

"Brilliant, I knew you were much brighter than you were letting on." Jacques drove through a little-used service entrance and continued through the woods, stopping a short distance from the green. "Put this on," he shouted as he threw a studded leather collar at her.

"No."

"I said put it on."

"Is that what you want? You want me to be your slave?"

"It's what I've wanted from the moment we met."

"Jacques, if you want me to wear your collar, you're gonna have to put it on me yourself."

"You're absolutely correct. A slave can't collar herself." He glanced at his prisoner, his crazed leer raking her body. "Magnificent, you were created to be whipped into submission."

"Like you whipped Sandy and Madeline?"

"Yes!" He shouted with a visible shudder. He got out of the truck, went to Jess' side and yanked open the door, and then pulled her out to her feet by the hair. "Such beautiful hair," he said as he inhaled its scent. "You should never have covered it with that awful red wig. Go!" Jess stumbled when he shoved her forward.

"Chill the fuck out! I'm going."

"Such ugly words from such a beautiful mouth." The eighth hole loomed a hundred yards ahead. Jess dug in her heels defiantly. "I told you to go!" He shouted.

Out of the blue, she remembered Kevin's backup revolver. She'd become so used to wearing it that she'd all but forgotten that it was strapped to her ankle. Turning to face him, she refused to take another step. "No! You don't think I'm just gonna let you kill me without a fight do you?"

"Oh, I hope not. I love it when you fight. It makes the game so much more enjoyable." He drew back and backhanded her hard across the face, spinning her around, and knocking her to the ground. "Get up, bitch!"

Shaking off a moment of blindness, she inched her fingers towards her right ankle, intent on pulling the revolver when she heard a shout from the nearby wooded area.

"Hold it right there, fella!" It was Christine Parezi.

He spun around in surprise. "Excellent, two beautiful women for the price of one. One more move, Officer, and she's dead," he called as he reached into his jacket.

"Don't do it, Jacques!" Jess yelled as she leaned into position, drew Kevin's revolver, and took aim.

He whirled around and she fired. One, two, three shots from five feet away, all hitting him in the chest. He stiffened and a look of wide-eyed surprise came across his face as he looked down and touched the bloodstain spreading across his shirt.

CRLL

"Three shots fired, Slater!"

"Shit! Hurry up! Fuck the green! Drive across it. They can fix it later. We don't know who, if anybody, just got hit."

"Was that gunshots, Kevin?"

"Yeah, Chief, at least three of 'em, but we're almost there."

⋘⋙

Jess crept closer to lean over Armand's motionless body. He opened his eyes and looked up at her when she checked for a pulse. "CJ, I'm so glad you're here. You changed your hair. It's beautiful."

"Armand?"

"Yes, thank you."

"Thank you for what?"

"For killing Jacques. I tried to make him go away, but he just wouldn't leave me alone," he whimpered.

"I'm so sorry, Armand," Jess wept as Kevin ran to her and dropped to the ground.

"Baby, are you okay?" She nodded. Kevin eyed the bruise left where Jacques had struck her, then grabbed Armand by the shirt, yanking him off the ground. "You son-of-a-bitch, you'd better pray you die, because if you don't, I'll kill you for hurting my wife."

"You're too late, Reese. CJ already did," Armand responded before lapsing into unconsciousness.

Officer Parezi abandoned her cover, her weapon still trained on Armand, and dropped down beside Kevin. "Sarge, put him down. You're gonna kill him," she shouted.

"Good, I hope the hell so."

"No, you don't, then *you're* the one looking at jail time. Let him go, Sarge. I won't let you kill him and put yourself in a bind. Consider this repayment. Go see about your wife. She needs you. I'll take care of this one." Kevin dropped Armand, unconcerned if it caused the man further injuries, and took Jess in his arms while Christine radioed for help. "Parezi to base, suspect is down, one officer with injuries, requesting medical assistance, stat!"

The remainder of the SRT team finally caught up with Kevin, followed by Larry Dixon and two additional officers who had been making their way through the woods. The green was, at once, flooded with uniforms. Jess barely registered the paramedics telling her to move away from Armand's body. Kevin wasted no time swinging his wife up into his arms and carrying her to a nearby ambulance when she was unable to stand on her own.

"Put her up here, Detective," the medic said, pointing to a gurney. The EMT draped a blanket around Jess' shoulders and turned her head to clean and dress her swollen cheek. Jess jerked away at his touch to the painful bruise. "She's in shock, but she doesn't appear to have any serious injuries. We should still take her in for evaluation to be sure."

"Absolutely."

"Hop on in. Do you have a hospital preference?"

"Duke Medical Center, Doctor Frances Elliott."

"Roll on, Terry. We're going to Duke. Call ahead and have them page Doctor Frances Elliott."

"Oh, I don't feel so good," Jess said just in time for the medic to hold out an emesis basin.

Chapter 37

"Mr. Slater, your wife is fine, but she was in shock when she came in. Luckily, I don't think she'll remember all that happened today, at least not right away. However, it would be a good idea for us to hold her overnight, just to keep an eye on her."

"Thank you, Doctor. Please, call me Kevin. Since she's sleeping and can't hear us, I'd like to talk to you about something."

"What's on your mind?"

"Can you give her a good check-up?"

"Jess just had a thorough physical a few weeks ago."

"I realize that, but she's been having some odd symptoms."

"Tell me more."

"She started out tired all the time, slept a lot. Then her appetite started swinging back and forth."

"Anything else?"

"Twice now she's gotten out of bed and nearly passed out."

"When did that happen last?"

"Yesterday morning, she would have hit the floor if I hadn't caught her. She said it was low blood sugar."

"Any headaches or visual impairments?"

"None that I know of."

"Changes in sexual habits?"

"What's that got to do with it?" Kevin asked, suddenly embarrassed.

"Maybe nothing, but many illnesses aren't noticed by a partner until they cause changes in the patient's sexual patterns."

Still rattled, Kevin elaborated. "Well...she's been very um...enthusiastic...for the last three or four weeks. I keep asking her if she's trying to kill me," he said with a chuckle.

Doctor Elliott smiled and shook her head, then ran down the remainder of her mental checklist and assured Kevin that she would have an answer for him, soon. She turned and left the hospital room before Kevin caught sight of the knowing gleam in her eye.

The next morning...

"Good morning. How's my patient?"

"Ravenous."

"That's a good sign. Kevin, would you mind stepping outside for a moment? I need to examine my patient."

"Sure, okay." He walked into the hallway where Dean waited.

CB&ි◌ℭ&ℭ

"How's she doing, Son?"

"Seems great, she slept all night and woke up cheery...and starving."

"I'm glad to hear that. I'm told that Jacques Lavache, Armand, or whatever his real name is, made it through surgery and is hanging on, but he's in critical condition."

"I don't know if that's good or bad. Dean, I'm not gonna lie to you. Yesterday is about as close to murder as I've ever been. If Parezi hadn't been there to stop me, I woulda killed him, and with the state Jess was in, she'd have never known it. I coulda probably gotten away with it too. The ME woulda declared the shooting as the cause. The DA woulda called it a clear-cut case of self-defense. Jess wouldn't have been charged with anything, and nobody woulda been the wiser."

"I know and understand perfectly well your temptation to hurt the man, and in your position, I would have done the same thing. Good morning, Niki."

"How's Jess?"

"She's gonna be fine. She was in shock yesterday and she's got one hell of a bruise from where that bastard hit her, but she's doing great otherwise."

"Good, I nearly had a heart attack when David called me. I brought some clothes."

"Thanks, Nik. I didn't even think about it."

CB&SOCR&SO

"Jess, your husband is very worried about you. He expressed some concerns over some apparent symptoms you've been experiencing, so at his request, I ran a few tests."

"He's been threatening to bring me in kicking and screaming. So what's the prognosis? Is it bad?"

"I don't think so. I'm betting you'll be quite happy about it."

"So tell me."

"First, I want you to know that I have not discussed the results with your husband. I like to leave that to my patients in cases like this."

"Doctor Elliott, you're killing me. What is it?"

"Jess, you're pregnant."

"Oh my God," Jess said, not trying to hide her excitement.

"Good news, right?"

"Oh yes, it's wonderful news! I didn't think it would happen so fast, but oh, it's the best news you could've brought me today."

CB&SOCR&SO

"What's the word on that apartment?"

"We had no trouble obtaining a search warrant after finding that Armand's black truck was registered in Virginia to Jean-Michele de la Vache. I contacted Carl Barnes, and he sent a team with Mike and some of our folks to execute the search and collection."

"Great, so everything is admissible."

"Yes, and the best part...they found several items linking Mr. Bedrich to our murders."

"Such as?"

"News clippings, of course, but also Sandra Vandenberg's identification, an unidentified key ring that may also be hers, and a wedding ring believed to belong to Madeline Crawford. The state lab is trying to get DNA from them."

"Awesome!"

"And there was one you couldn't officially link to that group, I believe."

"Yeah, that was Elizabeth Johnson."

"Right, he had her membership card."

"This is excellent. So we've got the right guy and plenty to back us up."

CB&SOCR&SO

"Shall I call your husband back in now?"

"Oh yes, please do."

Doctor Elliott stepped into the hallway to get Kevin. "Good morning, Baby," he said after he kissed her. "You have some visitors."

"Visitors? I thought you were springing me from this joint."

"I am, as soon as Doctor Elliott gives me your clean bill of health. Dean, you and Niki come on in."

"Good morning, you must be the father and best friend. I've heard a lot about you in the years I've had Jess as my patient."

"Yes Ma'am, and thank you. So tell us, how's my girl?"

"Yes, how is she?" Niki mimicked.

234

"Jess is as fit as a fiddle. Yesterday was a bit of a shock to her system, but her recovery will be quick and mostly painless."

"Mostly?" Niki asked.

"She has a pretty nasty bruise that will probably look and feel much worse before it gets better."

"And our discussion from last night?" Kevin asked.

"She's anemic, so when I release her, you're to go buy her some vitamins with iron. Can you handle that?" Kevin nodded. "*Centrum* or *One-A-Day* should work, but if there's no improvement in her follow-up blood work, I'll prescribe a supplement, though I'd prefer not to do so because sometimes iron supplements come with some unpleasant side effects."

"Such as?"

"Nausea or even vomiting until the body becomes accustomed to the changes, but don't become alarmed if this happens. We'll go with a lower-dose or children's formula. As long as it doesn't progress to hyperemesis gravidarium, there's no harm."

"What's hyperemesis gravidarium?" Niki asked.

"Severe and persistent nausea and vomiting that leads to weight loss, dehydration, and vitamin deficiency."

"All those symptoms were from anemia?" Kevin asked.

Doctor Elliott shot a conspiratorial look at Jess and winked. She went on to explain how the symptoms led from one to the next at an insidious pace, and what else Kevin should do to speed his wife's recovery. She then promised to have Jess' discharge papers ready soon.

"Now, one of you, tell me how Armand is."

"Jess...Honey, your doctor just told you to take it easy."

"Dad, I'll be more stressed if you *don't* tell me something."

"Dean, you know she'll stay worked up until you tell her how the bastard's doing," Niki added.

"Niki, that's not nice."

"Yeah, well, I'm not feeling very charitable towards the son-of-a-bitch."

"Okay, you two. Princess, he made it through surgery, but he's in critical condition, so it could still go either way. You hit a lung, which collapsed, and may still require further surgery."

"I'm just glad I didn't kill him."

"Baby, it sure wasn't for lack of trying," Kevin added. "I checked on him last night, *after* I knew you were going to be fine. Another inch woulda been a major artery. I hope I don't ever piss you off," he added with a chuckle. "We got back some of the lab reports on the Crawford case. You won't believe what's in one of them."

"What?"

"The fingernail scrapings contained epithelials that weren't hers, so they ran a whole slew of tests on it. The donor was a thalassemia carrier."

"You're kidding." Kevin shook his head. "It sure would have been nice to know that a week ago."

"No shit, woulda saved me the ten years I lost yesterday."

C3∞C3∞

As expected, Jess was relegated to administrative leave, pending the investigation into the shooting of Josef Armand Bedrich. Kevin left his wife in bed asleep most mornings when he worked dayshift, but Jess gathered up Sarge and went to the substation anyway to avoid the boredom of sitting at home alone.

Friday afternoon one week later...

At around lunchtime, a fowl odor permeated Jess' former office. She sat for a moment, trying to ignore it, but had little success. Kevin glanced at her just as a strong wave of nausea hit and sent her on a beeline to the bathroom, certain she'd lose it at any second. A moment later, Kevin tapped on the door.

"Are you alright?"

"I'll be out in a minute." Jess sat on the floor with her face against the cold, porcelain bowl, waiting

SLOAN CHRISTOPHER

for the queasiness to pass before attempting the return trip back to her office. "God, what the hell are you eating, David?"

"It's Chinese...same thing we order every week. You want some?"

"Hell no! It smells revolting," she grumbled before slamming the door, leaving Kevin in the outer office.

ଓଷ୍ଠୋଓଷ୍ଠୋ

David looked at Brian and Kevin, then shrugged his shoulders. "I thought she liked Chinese."

Kevin cocked an eyebrow before replying, "Yeah, me too."

"Sarge, is she sick? She's been a little off since she took out Mr. Clean."

"Her doc says she's fine, but put her on some strong vitamins because she was anemic. She said they might give her the queasies."

"Anemia is blood-related, right?"

"Low iron...causes fatigue, low appetite, and fainting spells, among other things. And in people who aren't used to it, the extra iron can make them sick to their stomach until their levels get back to normal."

"That explains why she's been so mean lately."

"Hmmm, maybe. I'm gonna go check on her."

ଓଷ୍ଠୋଓଷ୍ଠୋ

Kevin found his wife lying on the sofa. Sarge was on the floor in front of her with his cold nose pressed to her cheek. "Baby, are you feeling better?"

"I'm okay."

"You been a little green around the gills for a few days. Maybe we ought to try the other vitamins."

"That's probably a good idea."

"I have to run an errand. I'll pick up some on my way back."

"Thank you, you're so good to me."

"Anything for my Baby. Do you want me to get you something for lunch too?"

"Sure, that might be a good thing."

"Anything in particular? *Goldfish* maybe?" She giggled. "That's what I was looking for, that beautiful smile."

"Surprise me, but nothing too spicy or with strong odors. I don't think I could handle it today."

"Okay, I'll be back soon." He leaned over and kissed her forehead.

ଓଷ୍ଠୋଓଷ୍ଠୋ

"It's been two weeks. How have you been feeling?"

"Absolutely awful, you weren't kidding about odors and some foods. I have to close the door or even leave the building sometimes to keep from gagging, especially when the guys order Chinese, and my Mountain Dew is history. Too sweet, makes me nauseous. But suddenly, I love the smell of Kevin's coffee. This morning, I almost asked him for a cup."

"Anything else?"

"I'm almost embarrassed to say," Jess said, feeling her face grow warm.

"What is it?"

"Sex, I can't get enough. Kevin swears I'm trying to kill him."

"He mentioned that, but don't worry. It's perfectly normal. And it gets worse too, by the way," Doctor Elliott said with a smile. "Has your husband figured it out yet?"

"Not yet, but there's been a couple times when I thought I might have to explain myself, thanks to their Chinese food. However, it's been bad enough that he bought me children's vitamins."

"Did that help?"

"I think so, but since I've never been pregnant, I have nothing to compare it to."

236

"True, every pregnancy is different. You may not have any morning sickness with the next one, or it could be much worse. But it's only another week, we'll see if we can hold him off. I do want to make sure the new vitamins are sufficient though. But first, lay back and let's measure your uterus." Doctor Elliott stretched a tape from Jess' pubic bone up her tummy. "Jess, are you positive on the dates of your last period?"

"Absolutely, it was when I saw you for my physical. Why, is something wrong?"

"No, but by the numbers, you should be no more than seven weeks along. However, you're measuring slightly larger. We'll monitor it and if the accelerated growth rate continues, I'll schedule an ultrasound when you come in for your next appointment rather than waiting until the normal sixteen weeks."

"I can hardly wait. Kevin will be with me for that one."

"Let's get you to the lab now to check that iron level. I want you back in here again in four weeks."

Later that day...

"*Hey, Girlfriend, I called your office and Kevin said I should give you a couple hours then ring you at home. He said you went to the doctor. Are you okay?*"

"Yeah, just a follow-up from two weeks ago."

"*Still on admin leave?*"

"Probably for a couple more weeks. You know how long it takes to wade through government red tape. But if the internal wraps up soon, I may just take some sick leave."

"*Why?*"

"For the hell of it. I've never taken a vacation, and Carl owes me big time. Besides, Doctor Elliott wanted me to have several *weeks* of recovery time after the shooting."

"*Why so long?*"

"I dunno, I guess to make sure I'm completely in the clear with this anemia thing."

"*I guess that makes sense, and the rest will be good for you. Let's get together. I haven't seen you since you tried to get yourself killed.*"

"Sure, when?"

"*How about right now? Kevin's working late. Isn't he?*"

"Yeah, he's finishing paperwork from the case, and he's been in and out of meetings with the DA. I'm supposed to meet with him too, but Kevin's been using my doc's orders for R&R to stall him."

"*Well, you have to eat. Let's have an early supper, my treat.*"

"I don't have much of an appetite today."

"*I'm sure I heard your doctor tell you to eat right too.*"

"Yeah, but I feel like shit."

"*I'm coming over, so you will eat, and if you turn me down, I'm calling your husband.*"

"Fine, I'll try. I'll see you in a little while."

Three hours later...

"It's open, come in," Jess called from the couch. Sarge ran to the door, wagging his tail.

Niki reached down and scratched him behind the ears. "How's my favorite puppy wuppy? Hey, you!"

"Hey," Jess croaked in a weak voice and sat up on the sofa. Sarge ran over, laid his head in her lap, and whimpered. "Hey, Sweetie."

"The bruise is almost gone, but damn, you still look like hell," Niki observed aloud.

"Thanks, lovely to see you too," she snapped. "Ewww, what the hell is that smell?"

"Um...dinner? I saw your buddy from Paolo's, and told him you'd been under the weather, so he hooked me up with some of your favorites and said to feel better soon."

"It smells vile."

"Did you bump your head?"

"I told ya I didn't feel well when you called."

"Maybe you got a bug or something."

"Yeah, maybe."

Another wave of nausea hit Jess like a truck and sent her flying into the bathroom where she heaved until there was nothing left. Niki was right behind her, pulling her hair back, and when the sickness abated, she stood up and soaked a washcloth with cold water, then wiped her friend's face and neck.

"Girl! What is up with that?"

"I'm sorry, Nik."

"Hell, what are friends for? It's not like you haven't held my head out of the toilet plenty of times. Of course, I was plastered, but still. How long has this been going on?"

"I've been queasy off and on for a couple weeks, but this just started today."

"I remember now. Doc said the vitamins might make you sick. Did you mention this to her today?"

"Didn't start 'til I got home."

"Don't you think we should let Kevin know how sick you are?"

"No!"

"Why the hell not?"

"Because I don't want him to worry over nothing."

"Nothing? Jess, *you* don't puke! First time I think I've ever seen that in all the years I've known you, actually."

"I expected this was coming."

Confusion flooded Niki's features. "Okay, you wanna back up and start over? I missed that left turn at Albuquerque."

"You're a smart woman, Nik. It won't take much for you to figure it out."

She stood there for a moment looking dumbfounded before her eyes lit up with sudden clarity. "Oh my God, you're pregnant!"

"About seven weeks."

"Damn!" She counted on her fingers. "A honeymoon baby! Aww, well Honey, come over here, and lay down. Let Aunt Niki take care of you and her little niece or nephew. Are you hungry, or thirsty, or anything?"

"I'm starving, but everything I've swallowed for the last two hours has come right back."

"Does Kevin know yet?"

"No, I wanted to surprise him...for Father's Day."

"That's still another week off."

"I know."

"Honey, I hate to break it to you, but he's not gonna sit back and let you puke for a week without an explanation. You'll be in the emergency room so fast it'll make your head spin."

"I know. I'm praying it eases off before he gets home. I've been managing until today."

"Where's your laptop?"

"Over there on the desk. Why?"

"I'm going surfin'." Moments later, "Okay look, I found a whole list of stuff that is supposed to relieve morning sickness."

"It's not morning," Jess interrupted in a laconic reply.

"Ha-fucking-ha, humor me and listen...salty foods, like plain potato chips or saltine crackers, ginger snaps, ginger tea, ginger ale, Coca-Cola, dry toast, mashed potatoes, rice, lemons. You got any of that stuff around here?"

"Probably. What's with all the ginger?"

"Ancient Chinese secret."

"Nik, I feel like hell warmed over, not a good time for jokes."

"I'm not joking. The Chinese have been using ginger for centuries to ease morning sickness and other stomach ailments. What off this list do you have around here?"

"Bread, a couple cans of Pepsi, um...hell, I dunno. Go fucking look."

"Okay, I will, grouch! You know, you're not a very good patient."

While Niki was in the pantry, Jess became hungry again, so she ventured a look inside the take-out bag and found a loaf of Paolo's crusty bread. "Mmm, this smells good." Her stomach lurched in a hungry growl, so she tore off a thick chunk and nibbled it until she thought it might stay down. When Niki returned to the living room, Jess had consumed half the loaf.

"Oh well, it looks like you've found something on your own, so I won't make you anything else, but here's a Pepsi."

Jess gulped most of it at once, then sat up straighter on the couch. "Oh man, that was good."

"You're not feeling sick?"

"Not at the moment, but this is how I've been, spewing and then starving a few minutes later."

"Well, let's see if this stays down."

Soon after, Jess was sitting up, having a real conversation, and more animated than she'd been all afternoon. Her color had improved and she was energetic.

"You look much better. How do you feel?"

"Super."

"Great! Maybe that bread did the trick. You could be in for a few weeks of bland eating."

"Oh yay, that sounds good. Not!"

"One of my coworkers was pregnant last year, and I swear all she ate for six months was potato chips and Dr. Pepper. She swore it was the only thing that didn't make her sick."

"Oh joy, guess I'm stuck with bread and Pepsi."

"Hey, Baby!" Kevin announced cheerfully as he walked through the door, surprising the two women. Sarge was up, at once, to greet him. Niki quickly shoved her printouts under a cushion.

"Hey, Handsome. I didn't expect you until late."

"I just said to hell with it and left. Hey, Nik, glad you're keeping Jess company. She won't admit it, but I know she's been bored sitting around."

"Glad to help, Kevin. Hey, you're just in time for dinner. I brought food over for Jess, but she only wanted the bread, so you can help me eat the pasta."

"Baby, what is going on with you? What did Doctor Elliott say?"

"She said I'm doing great. My iron count is up, but I need to stay on the vitamins a while longer."

"Dammit!"

"What? Isn't that good news?"

"Jess, something is wrong with you and it's not anemia. In fact, the damn vitamins seem to be making it worse. I'm gonna call her."

"No, don't!"

"You give me one good reason not to."

"That's my cue to leave. Ciao, y'all," Niki called on her way out the door.

"I can't, not yet, anyway. Oh God, I'll be back."

Kevin jogged behind his wife to the bathroom and jammed his toe in the door when she tried to shut him out. Assuming the position Niki had held earlier, he pulled back her hair while she heaved, then dabbed her face and neck with the cool cloth. After giving her a sip of water to rinse her mouth, he picked her up, cradling her to his chest. He slowly ambled back into the living room and sat on the couch, and held her in his arms. She laid her head against his broad chest and sighed when he started rocking slightly to soothe her.

"Baby, I know you're keeping something from me. Please tell me what's wrong."

"It's supposed to be a surprise." Jess sniffled and became teary-eyed.

"What surprise?"

She broke down crying. "Just one more week...why couldn't I hang on for one more week?"

"Hang on? Jess, you're scaring me. What's wrong? What's in a week?"

She pulled his right hand around and laid it against her belly. "Father's Day."

"Father's Day?" Kevin realized, as soon as he looked into his wife's eyes, what she'd been keeping secret. "Honey, are we? Are you..."

"Pregnant? Yes, Kevin, we're having a baby," she said in a weak voice, still managing a big smile.

"Oh my God!" He leaned down and kissed her. "How long have you known?"

"I found out when I was in the hospital, after the shooting. That's why Doctor Elliott sent you out that morning, so she could tell me privately, in case it wasn't a joyous occasion."

"Wow!" He paused for a moment to let the news sink in. "Wait, it is a joyous occasion. Isn't it?"

"Absolutely."

"We're having a baby." He looked thoughtful for a moment. "That means you were pregnant when that son-of-a-bitch..."

"A few weeks, yes."

"I'll kill him if I ever get my hands on him."

"Kevin, don't talk like that."

"I'm serious, Jess. I coulda lost you and it scared the hell out of me. Still scares the hell out of me just thinking about it."

"It's over now, and he can't hurt any of us again."

"What about all that stress? Did it hurt the baby? And what about you?"

"Doctor Elliott has been monitoring us very closely. My uterus is measuring a little bigger than it should, but everything is going well, otherwise."

"When?"

"When what?"

"When's he due?"

"What makes you so sure it's a he?"

"Of course, it's a he. Slater men always make boys," he boasted.

"Which explains why you have three sisters," Jess giggled.

"Bah, they don't count. So when's he coming?"

"Mid-February, I'm about six or seven weeks."

"We've only been married seven weeks. Damn that was fast!"

"Uh huh, and who said it would take a while."

"God, this explains everything...especially the seafood cravings..."

"Seafood cravings? That's the *last* thing I've wanted. You noticed that weeks ago."

"Oh no, no, I'm not talking about all the shrimp you've been passing up. I'm talking about all the damn *Goldfish* you've been slaughtering lately..."

"You turkey...I thought I'd finally lived the *Goldfish* down."

He laughed and continued. "Then there are all the other symptoms. This explains everything."

"Mmm hmm."

"Must be why she asked me about our sex life."

"Kevin, what are you talking about?"

"When we were going over your symptoms, Doctor Elliott asked me if your sexual habits had changed. Is this pregnancy the reason you've been so horny too, or is that just me? I mean, you jumping my bones four times a day is great, but um..."

"Are you kidding? That's definitely all you. How could any girl resist having such a sexy guy in her bed all the time?"

"Good answer. You're not upset that it happened so fast, are you?"

"No way, I'm so happy about it, I'd jump up and shout it from the roof if moving didn't make me so queasy," Jess replied, managing a small half-laugh. "I wanted you to be the first to know, but Niki, she figured it out as soon as she had to hold my hair out of the toilet. I'm sorry."

"It's okay, Baby. I'm not upset," he said in a soothing tone while he stroked her hair and back. "I just hate I wasn't here to do that for you. But that's changing, starting right now."

"You're gonna spoil me."

"That's the plan."

"I love you, Kevin."

"Oh, Baby, I love too...so much."

Epilogue

7 months later...

Jess opened her eyes and looked around the room for Kevin. He was stretched out, sleeping soundly on the hard sofa. Lying across his chest, facing each other, were their identical twin sons, born just hours earlier. The room was dark and the hallway lights were still dimmed, telling her that morning had not yet arrived. Still groggy from the medications she'd received during the eighteen-hour labor, Jess smiled and drifted back to sleep. When she next awoke, she squinted against the bright sunlight streaming through the partially opened blinds. Kevin was sitting up, holding the babies in his lap, and murmuring softly to them. He looked up at his wife when she stretched.

"Good morning, Beautiful. Mmm, do that again. Hey boys, Mommy's awake."

"Good morning. How are my guys?"

"We're doing great." He scooped the babies up, then came and sat down on the edge of Jess' bed. "How's *my Baby* doing this morning?"

"Your Baby's still tired, but feeling great." Then Jess noticed his bandaged left hand. "What happened?"

"What this? It's nothing."

"*Nothing* doesn't require a bandage."

"I cracked a little bone in the back of my hand. It's nothing."

Jess scowled at his hand again, then back at his face. "Did you hit something?"

"No." Deep furrows of concern etched her forehead. "Don't do that. Smile, it'll be healed in no time," he said, grinning. "Just remind me to stay on your good side."

"What?" Sudden clarity dawned on her. "Oh, God! Did I do that?"

"I plead the fifth."

"Tell me."

"Hell no! You'll tell Niki, and she'll tell Dave, and oh hell. He'll tell the whole damn department. I can't let this get out!"

"Let what get out?" Jess scrunched her eyes. "You better tell me or I'll break the other one," she threatened playfully.

"Uh huh, now who's guilty of spousal abuse?" He teased. "That's a powerful crunch you have, you brute. Funny thing is, you don't look so tough."

"Oh yeah? That's not what you tell everybody when Bob Morton is the topic."

"That's different. You're not gonna tell anybody about this. Are you?"

"I wouldn't dream of ruining you tough-guy image! But I don't remember doing that. I musta been *seriously* stoned."

"During the pushing phase. Remember, you were squeezing my hands? But it's fine. I swear. I didn't even feel it, not until much later, when you were asleep. Doc Elliott x-rayed it and fixed me right up after she gave you a clean bill of health. Don't stress over it."

"But..."

"Ah ah, shhh...stress isn't good for milk production, which will make this guy very unhappy." Right on cue, the older of the twins began sucking his fist and cooing. "Looks like somebody's hungry," he said as he handed her their mewling son.

Jess opened her dressing gown and put the babe to her breast, where he latched onto the swollen nipple hungrily, evoking a wince of discomfort from his mother. After a few minutes, he fell asleep, just in time for his brother's round of famished cries. Kevin exchanged babies, then watched and smiled as Jess nursed their second son.

"Honey, I'm sorry about your hand."

"Hey, I told you, it's nothing. At least it wasn't my shooting hand." Jess looked her husband as teardrops streamed down her face. His own eyes were glistening brighter than normal. "What's this?" He asked, wiping at her tears.

"Oh, Kevin, I'm so happy. I didn't realize what I was missing before I met you and now we have these guys." Jess looked down at her sons. "Having you and our boys has been so..."

Before she could complete the thought, her doctor entered. "Knock knock, how are we today?"

"Very well, thanks, Doctor Elliott."

"Great, and how's Dad?"

"A little stiff from the lumpy couch, but otherwise, never better," Kevin said with a chuckle.

"And how's that hand?"

"A little sore, but not too bad."

"Good, I'll give you a scrip for some Percoset if you want."

"What kind of wimp would I be if I had to have Percs for *this* after watching *her* give birth...twice?"

"I had massive amounts of drugs," Jess observed aloud.

"Drugs, shmugs! I don't need no stinkin' Percs," he added in a bad Mafioso impression. Kevin then looked from his hand to the twins, and then at his wife's thighs and raised his eyebrows, comparing sizes. "Have you noticed how big they are and how little..." He glanced at Jess and grinned. "Hey Doc, that's gonna snap back, right? I mean they were kinda big for such a small exit door."

"Oh Kevin, for God's sake," Jess wailed as her cheeks pinkened while Dr. Elliott smiled.

"Of course, Jess' body will be back to normal before you know it. *But* she needs at least six weeks with *no* sex."

A painful groan escaped Kevin. "Hey Baby, you don't have any dental appointments scheduled in the next couple months, do you?" He asked, causing Jess to gasp and blush a deep crimson.

Not one to add to her patient's embarrassment, Dr. Elliott continued. "In the meantime, I need to check Mom out, and then you have some excited visitors, if it's not too early."

"Bring 'em on," Jess said while Kevin resumed his seat on the sofa with his eldest.

"How's the breastfeeding going?"

"It's a bit uncomfortable when they first latch on, but not bad, once I get them positioned right."

"That's great."

"They're gluttons."

"Wait until the real milk comes in, or worse, when they're teenagers."

Doctor Elliott conducted the physical part of her examination and gave the couple a thumbs up, then opened the door fully and stepped aside. In walked Kevin's mother, Terese, followed by his older sisters, Kate and Kinsey. On their heels was Sam, leading their frail-looking grandmother. Kevin put the sleeping babe in Jess' free arm and went to the door.

"Grandma?" He leaned down and kissed her cheek, then took the older woman's arm and led her across the hospital room. "I didn't know you were coming. What a surprise!" He kissed her cheek again and hugged her tightly against him.

"Not so hard, boy, I'm not as spry as I used to be."

"Sorry, Grandma. Jess, you remember my grandmother, Eleanor," Kevin said as he made the old woman comfortable on the sofa. Terese sat beside her.

"I certainly do. How have you been, Grandma Slater?"

"Very well, Dear. Now, young man, bring me my great-grandsons."

"Yes, Ma'am." Kevin took the babies, one at a time, and laid them both in his grandmother's lap before taking a seat beside his wife.

"Well...fine, strapping boys you are, handsome and sweet, and no mistaking your Slater bloodline." She looked skyward. "You see, Bradley, I told you he'd settle down and make us proud one day," she said as Dean, Maggie and Niki entered the room.

"Hey, y'all! Dad, come in here and meet your grandsons."

Dean reached out to shake Kevin's hand, but drew back when he saw the bandage. "Good heavens, Son, what happened?"

"Ask that savage you raised," he teased, then smiled and winked at Jess. "She, uh...squeezed a little too hard during the delivery and cracked a bone."

"Okay, tough guy, I thought you weren't gonna tell anybody."

"I changed my mind. It's too damn funny *not* to tell it," he said as he glanced at her. "She said she wanted me to feel her pain," he told everyone else. Merry laughter filled the room. "I think she even growled at me once. Scared the hell out of me, I half-expected her head to start spinning."

Jess gasped. "You're making that up!"

"No I'm not, but I won't hold it against you," he added, smiling.

"You'll look back and laugh about it after they're all grown up," Maggie said.

"I think it's pretty damn funny right now, Maggie," Kevin said, laughing, until he received a sharp poke to his ribs. "Jesus, Ma!" To which she poked him again. "Ow!"

"Me too," Sam said, giggling.

"Runt, nobody said you were allowed to laugh."

"Shut up, Kevin!" Sam exclaimed, wrinkling her nose at him.

"Jess, have you named them, yet?" Eleanor asked.

"Yes, Grandma, that's Brandon Reese, after my father and all the Slater men, on your right," Jess said.

"Oh, how wonderful, you carried on the family tradition!" Terese exclaimed.

"And on your left, is Zakkary Richard, after Jess's grandpa and Dean," Kevin added. "We're gonna call them Brandon and Zakk."

"Sweetheart, you shouldn't have," Dean said.

"Nonsense, Dad. Kevin and I named our sons for *all* the special men who have meant so much to us," Jess said.

The End